SECRETS OF THE PAST

After growing up in an orphanage, Lizzie Bartholomew goes into service. As a maid in a select academy for young ladies, she meets the wilful Sarah Chamberlain. When Sarah leaves in disgrace, Lizzie does not expect to hear from her again—until she receives a letter asking her to be Sarah's personal maid. Life is much better in the great house at Hyde Park Square. Both Lizzie's parents were in service in the same area but when she asks if anyone remembers them, she gets more than she bargained for.

SECRETS OF THE PAST

SECRETS OF THE PAST

by

Rose Boucheron

Magna Large Print Books
Long Preston, North Yorkshire,
England.

British Library Cataloguing in Publication Data.

Boucheron, Rose
   Secrets of the past.

A catalogue record for this book is
available from the British Library

ISBN 0-7505-0875-2

First published in Great Britain by Judy Piatkus Publishers
Ltd., 1994

Published in Large Print February, 1996 by arrangement
with Piatkus Books Ltd.

Magna Large Print is an imprint of
Library Magna Books Ltd.
Printed and bound in Great Britain by
T.J. Press (Padstow) Ltd., Cornwall, PL28 8RW.

For My Husband

CHAPTER 1

They stood facing each other, the steam from the wash boilers all around them, the laundry teacher and the girl. Hatred in the girl's eyes, malevolence in the teacher's. The laundry room was impregnated with the stench of past boilings of dirty clothes and bed linen, even now bubbling away in strong soda water. The steam rose up to the green painted iron rafters, rusty and blistered from continual damp.

'You!'

The teacher had no need to point, for her steely eye was fixed on the girl whose gaze didn't falter under the terrifying stare from those tiny bead-like eyes. The other girls, fourteen of them, stood frozen to the spot, like statues in a play, eyes wide, waiting. They had seen it many times before, this battle of wills between Miss Baldwin and their champion, Lizzie Bartholomew.

Miss Baldwin also waited, waited for Lizzie's admission that she had spoken, even though silence as she well knew was the order of the day.

'I did.'

'I did what?' the woman shouted at her,

brawny arms folded over her ample bosom. You could almost hear the crackle of the starched voluminous laundry coat.

'I did, Miss Baldwin,' Lizzie said, lower lip stuck out, green eyes flashing, though her voice was low and clear.

'Oh, you did—and what was it you said, Bartholomew?'

Lizzie took a deep breath. 'I said Nancy shouldn't stand ironing because her foot hurts.'

They daren't turn and look at Nancy, who they knew would be as red as a beetroot. Poor Nancy, who was lame and often paid a price for having Lizzie champion her.

'You will stay after school and do two hours' ironing,' Miss Baldwin said. 'Perhaps that will teach you to obey orders.'

'Yes, Miss Baldwin,' said Lizzie. Ugly old bitch, was what she thought.

Miss Baldwin walked heavily away, hiding the satisfaction she felt at scoring once again over the objectionable Bartholomew. Although they all wore white caps to cover their heads, it was with no little satisfaction that she had seen the shorn hair beneath Lizzie Bartholomew's. It had been at her insistence to the matron of the orphanage that Lizzie had her curly luxuriant black locks cut short.

10

'Unhygienic,' she had said, 'an orphanage is no place for long unruly hair,' aware that Lizzie would never forgive her, not if she lived to be a hundred. Anyway, it was time the girl left—she had been at the home since she was nine years old and had been more trouble than any of them.

Alone after the others had left, Lizzie tackled the pile of clothes, the heavy flat iron being put back on the black stove to re-heat each time. She put a damp finger to its base to test the heat, while Miss Baldwin, who had to stay behind with her, watched her from time to time as the pile of ironing mounted. Behind her cool exterior, Lizzie was seething. She hated the laundry class, even though it only came once a fortnight, like housewifery and cookery. The housewifery class was her favourite because it was taught by Miss Erica Rowena Shawcross, and if there was anyone she loved more in this world than Miss Shawcross, Lizzie had yet to meet her. As for cookery, the quicker she got through that the better.

Besides, she loved going to the little house which stood at the far end of the playground in Sussex Street School. It had an outside fire escape, which you walked up, then through a front door, with its highly polished brass knocker and letter box to polish, all part of your training.

11

Inside there was a bedroom, and a kitchen with a yellow sink and a kitchen range which had to be blackleaded every day, and saucepans to clean, and linoleum floors to wash. Since girls came from council schools over a wide area, the tiny house was kept spotless. After you were eleven, you could go to the baby class where you were taught how to bathe babies and dress them. She liked that bit, although she never minded what Miss Rowena Shawcross told her to do; Lizzie would have done anything for her. She was so pretty, and so gentle, and never raised her voice. Working for her was a real pleasure, even doing rotten jobs like floor washing and polishing brass.

Lizzie broke into a little run on the way back, taking in the fresh salt air, thinking that now she was fifteen she would be leaving, going home. Only four more weeks to Easter and her birthday. If it had come before the end of last term she could have left then. She was the only girl in the home who had a parent, but had been there for five years because there was no one to care for her, her mother being sick and unable to work. She was always too ill to come to see Lizzie, and at holiday times there was so much to do at home that she returned to the orphanage almost with a sense of relief.

Once back at Strawn House, she took off her school hat, revealing the cropped hair which the other girls were as sorry about as Lizzie herself. They all adored her, even those who had begun by being frightened of her, especially Nancy who was lame with a deformed foot which pained her sometimes. Nancy had been put in the orphanage soon after she was born, and had never known relatives of any kind. Now she was thirteen and her one dread was the day that Lizzie left, for what would she do then?

'Don't you worry—I'll look after you,' Lizzie always said.

Adoration shone out of Nancy's eyes. She thought Lizzie was the most beautiful and the bravest person she had ever known. She wished she was like Lizzie, but the trouble was she had no guts to stand up for herself, whereas Lizzie knew no fear of any kind. Oh, to be like her! She had wept when they had cut off Lizzie's hair, but it hadn't seemed to make her less beautiful. The green eyes looked even greener, the long black lashes swept her creamy cheeks, the small nose looked pert in an oval face. Even the school bully, Violet Rawlinson, had in her turn succumbed to Lizzie's charms.

'Here she is!' they cried as she came into the dormitory. 'Miss Hawkes wants to see

13

you—she said as soon as you came in.'

Lizzie frowned, and hung up her hat and coat.

'Now what've I done?' she said, making for the door.

She tapped on Matron's door, and at her bidding, entered. It wasn't the first time Lizzie had been here, not by a long chalk, and it was as depressing now as it ever had been. White-painted brick walls, high ceilings, wooden flooring, tall narrow windows almost up to the ceiling, while the long pole stood alongside with which to open them. At her table sat Miss Hawkes, writing, as formidable a lady as you would wish to meet in her woollen jumper, hair scragged back into a mean little bun, scrubbed face falling into folds and down into her double chin. She kept Lizzie waiting for some time before she looked up.

'Come in, Bartholomew. Sit down.'

Lizzie sat bolt upright on the wooden chair facing her.

Miss Hawkes blotted her book, closed it, and laid her hands on the table in front of her, looking straight at Lizzie who faced her unflinchingly.

Miss Hawkes tried to soften her face into what she supposed was an expression of kindliness, but it was more of a grimace.

'I have a message from a neighbour

14

that your mother is seriously ill,' she said, and saw the faint tremor that crossed the girl's face.

'It is for that reason that I have been asked by the board of governors to allow you to leave immediately in order to take care of your mother. This anticipates your leaving the home by a few weeks, but I am sure that time will be usefully employed looking after your ailing parent.'

Lizzie bit her lip. 'Yes, Matron.'

'You must pack your things and be ready to leave immediately as I understand that there is some urgency.' And she saw Lizzie's eyes open wide in trepidation.

'She's not going to—'

'I am afraid so. Or so I have been given to understand.'

Lizzie swallowed hard. Having a sick mother had been so long a part of her life that she had never thought about her actually dying.

'Just take what you need and come back for the other things later. When you return I shall want to have a word with you about what to do in the event of—'

'Her dying,' Lizzie said slowly.

'Yes. You remain in our care until Easter,' Miss Hawkes said, 'so you must keep in touch with us in order that we may place you in a suitable position.'

'Yes, Matron.'

'You may go.'

'Thank you, Matron.'

Something in the green eyes prompted Miss Hawkes to speak.

'And Bartholomew—'

Lizzie turned.

'Good luck.'

She flushed with embarrassment. It was the first kind word the matron had ever spoken to her.

'Thank you, Matron.'

Somehow Miss Hawkes' last words lightened Lizzie's step as she hurried back to the dormitory where her friends waited for her anxiously.

'Wha'd she say? What's up?'

Lizzie opened her locker.

'I've got to go home. My mother is very ill.'

'Crikey!'

'You mean—to stay home?'

'Yes. I don't suppose I'll be back—only to see you.' And she saw their faces, the long sad faces, and hated the fact that after all this time she was going to leave them. Nancy was crying quietly, and Lizzie hurried over to her.

'Nancy, it'll be all right—honest. I'll be back to see you and I'll visit.'

'Oh, Lizzie!' And Nancy threw her arms around her neck and sobbed, while Lizzie, seeing the other girls and their looks of

16

sympathy and despair, knew how much she was going to miss them, despite the times that she had prayed for leaving day to come round.

It was Violet Rawlinson who saved the day. She clapped her hands and they all jumped.

'Come on, you lot. Pack it in! Can't you see how bloody awful it is for Lizzie? Don't make it worse for her.'

Lizzie threw her a grateful look and grabbed her few personal possessions and threw them into a bag, then taking the small black doll from her locker, her most prized possession, she gave it to Nancy.

'Here, you can have her. And take care of her.' The doll had cost a shilling and been given to her when she started at Strawn House by Mrs Ransome who lived in the downstairs flat of the house where she and her mother had lived.

'Oh, Lizzie!' And Nancy hugged the doll to her, the tears spilling down her face, while Lizzie looked in her purse and saw that she had one shilling and sevenpence ha'penny. Well, that would do—the fare home to Kemp Town was only twopence.

She put on her coat, and rammed her school hat on her head, then took it off and hurled it to the other side of the room. Lizzie's hat was a special shape where she had battered it to make it wearable.

'You can have that!' she cried as they all rushed to pick it up where it had fallen.

Poor little devils, she thought. I won't need that where I'm going.

She knocked with the iron knocker on the front door of number fourteen Rodney Street. Above the door, the glass transom bore the fading paint of the name Fairview, although what was fair about the view was questionable, since they were terraced houses exactly like those on this side of the street, each as ugly as the other.

The door was opened by Mrs Ransome whose strong but tired face lit up at the sight of Lizzie.

'Ah, there you are, duck! Oh, your mum will be glad to see you! She's very poorly,' she whispered, as though her voice could be heard upstairs.

The familiar smell of polish and washing and old varnish greeted Lizzie's nostrils, and the overriding presence of illness and decay which was always present, at least upstairs, and seemed to permeate throughout the house.

'Matron said I was to come home at once... Is she very bad, Mrs Ransome?'

'Doctor's just been, dear. I'm afraid she is. I don't think it can be long—poor thing.' She looked sympathetically at Lizzie. Mrs

18

Ransome was a tall woman, well-built and not unattractive.

'I'd better go on up,' said the girl, dreading what she might find.

In the small front room, her mother lay in the double bed, the bed in which Lizzie had been born, her once pretty face ravaged by the curse of tuberculosis, her thin blue-veined hands picking at the coverlet, her great eyes watching the door for the first sight of her daughter.

Lizzie, shocked at her appearance, for she was so much worse than she had been at Christmas, fell at the bedside and took her mother's hand, smoothing the hair which had been black like her own but was now almost white. She wanted to cry, to scream at the unfairness of it all. Her once beautiful mother, only now thirty-three years old, what kind of a life had she had? But that wouldn't help, would it? She had to get on with it, and try and ease her mother out of this world and into the next—where perhaps she would find peace, for she was going to die, there was no doubt about that.

'Elizabeth,' the dying woman whispered, for she had never called her anything else. 'Your hair—what have they done to you?'

The gentle Irish accent was unmistakable, and it was all Lizzie could do not to cry, but she bit back the tears, and went over to

19

the washbasin and damped a cloth which she applied gently to her mother's forehead and flushed cheeks.

'It'll soon grow,' she said.

'Are ye goin' to stay, Elizabeth?'

'Of course I am! You won't get me going back to that old place,' she said with a jauntiness she was far from feeling.

She went over to the mantelpiece and looked at the various bottles and their instructions. 'Have you had this one?' she said.

'Yes, Mrs Ransome gave it to me. Elizabeth, tell her I don't want anything to eat. She gives me groats and I don't want—'

'You have to keep your strength up,' Lizzie said firmly, and tucked the blankets in, and plumped the pillows round her.

'Now I'm home you're going to get well,' she said bossily, and saw the weak smile playing round her mother's pale lips.

'I'll just see to a few things and be back again in a jiffy. Don't go away.' And she saw her mother's lovely eyes give the merest sparkle. 'I'm just going down to see Mrs Ransome.'

Downstairs, she tapped on the kitchen door. 'Can I come in?'

It was different down there, with the plush tablecloth, the canary in its cage, the mantelpiece full of brightly coloured ornaments and vases, the range beneath glowing with its front down, and a saucepan of porridge keeping warm on the hotplate.

Catching Mrs Ransome's eye, Lizzie bit her lip, and her neighbour put an arm round her shoulders.

'Never mind, my dear,' she said. 'She can't last much longer—she's going to a better place. It couldn't be worse than this one, that's for sure. I've got a cup of tea here, I'm sure you'll be glad of it, and I've put a bottle in that bed of yours. It's not been slept in since you was home at Christmas.'

She busied herself pouring the tea.

'She said she didn't want anything to eat.'

'No, I daresay, but she must eat something.'

'I should have come before,' Lizzie said fiercely. 'Not now, just when—'

'You couldn't have done nothing,' Mrs Ransome said. 'Don't punish yourself. I waited until I thought she couldn't go on. You couldn't have done nothing—the doctor told me at Christmas that she couldn't last long.'

'You should have sent for me—' Lizzie began.

'And have you sit with her, getting more

21

and more miserable at the sight of her? No, my dear, she wouldn't have wanted that, and neither would I. You're here now, best make the most of the time she's got.'

And then Lizzie cried, and Mrs Ransome took her in her arms.

'There, there, get it off your chest. You're a brave little girl.'

After that, Lizzie sniffed a bit, and knew that whatever happened now, she had done with crying. From now on, she had to be strong for everybody's sake.

The days passed slowly, one going into another, with her mother growing weaker, until one day, she seemed almost to have gained strength. It was the week of Good Friday and Lizzie had bought her daffodils which shone like the sun. Her mother couldn't take her eyes off them.

'Do you remember when you were little?'

'Yes, lots of things.'

'You were born in this house.'

'Yes, I know.'

'When I came here from London, Mrs Ransome was so kind. I was carrying you, and I used to go for walks along the front—I thought Brighton was the most beautiful place in the world. The air was so lovely.'

'It still is,' said Lizzie.

22

'I used to push you in your pram, you were such a lovely baby, so pretty. I used to think I was nearer your father—just across the water, fighting in France.'

She was silent for a long time, so that Lizzie looked at her swiftly but saw that she was still breathing with her eyes closed.

Suddenly her eyes opened wide. 'It's your birthday on Monday,' she said, her eyes filling with tears. 'You will be fifteen.' And then she was quiet for some time. 'Oh, your father was a lovely man,' she said, 'and he never saw you.' And Lizzie saw that her eyes were wet and went over and held her hands.

'Don't talk, Mum.'

'He was a gentleman,' she said, 'a real gentleman.' And Lizzie was amazed to see the look of pride on her face.

Lizzie smiled. 'Of course he was.'

That night when she went to bed she lay awake for a long time, and when she finally slept dreamt of herself as a small girl holding her mother's hand tightly as they walked on Black Rock.

She woke early with a premonition of something wrong. Hurrying into her mother's room, she found as she had almost expected that she had died sometime during the night.

Bending over, Lizzie kissed her face

which was as cold as marble but looked so peaceful. Almost in a dream Lizzie went to find Mrs Ransome, who came upstairs at once.

'We'll have to get the doctor straight away,' she said. 'We shall need the death certificate. I'll lay her out, I'm used to it. I used to be a nurse once upon a time.'

The funeral took place on a lovely day in April, with daffodils dancing on tombstones and the green sward, beneath cherry and almond trees in full bloom. Mrs Ransome and two neighbours and Lizzie were the only mourners, and as they lowered the coffin into the grave, Lizzie was dry-eyed.

I'll never live like my mother did, she vowed. There's got to be more than the life she had.

Back in Rodney Street, Mrs Ransome made tea and served home made cake and biscuits and a glass of sherry to the two neighbours. Afterwards, when the visitors had gone, she patted Lizzie's hand.

'Well,' she said kindly, 'we shall have to work out what you're going to do, and sort out upstairs.'

Lizzie had been dreading it.

'I'll give you a hand, it's not a very nice job, and your mother didn't have much, poor soul.'

She had already folded the bed linen and

blankets which were stacked on the bed. 'I expect they'll be fumigated and given to charity. About the furniture—the chest of drawers and chairs, the kitchen table?'

Lizzie shook her head.

'I have to report back to the orphanage, and they'll find me a job where I shall be living in. There's not much else I can do,' she said.

'Well, my dear, you couldn't stay here anyway. Although you're always sure of a bed downstairs if you're stuck, don't you forget that. I'll sell the bits and pieces to the ragman.'

'Do whatever you want, Mrs Ransome,' Lizzie said. 'You have been very kind. I'm very grateful, and I know my mother was.'

'The least I could do,' she said. 'Now, what about her personal things?'

'I'll go through those but there's not much,' Lizzie said, eyeing the bottom drawer of the chest.

'I'll leave you to it, then,' Mrs Ransome said, and closed the door behind her.

Left to herself, Lizzie pulled out the drawer, and couldn't escape the feeling that she was prying. There was an embroidered tablecloth, and in a pillowcase, a handkerchief sachet. Lizzie thought she had never seen anything so pretty in all her life. It was made of pink silk, embroidered with roses and lilies and edged with white silk cord, and had a white silk lining. There were four things inside. Her mother's wedding certificate, Lizzie's own birth certificate, a small black box and an envelope containing a photograph. She opened the stiff, starchy paper of the marriage lines. The wedding had taken place at St Mary's, Marylebone, in the County of Middlesex, on 18 November 1914. Lizzie sat back on her heels. She had been born on 21 April 1915, and now she opened her birth certificate. It gave her date of birth and place of birth as 14, Rodney Street, Kemp Town, Brighton, and she allowed herself a smile. Well, at least she was legitimate. Her mother was Mary Grace Daly, Maidservant, of Hyde Park Square, and her father George Alfred Bartholomew, Manservant, of Seymour Street, Paddington, London.

She replaced the certificate, and opened the small black box. Inside was a silver locket, ornately chased, on a heavy chain and she recalled that when she was little her mother had often worn it. After trying for some time she managed to open it, and saw inside the photograph of a young man, a fair-haired young man, handsome, with a small moustache, smiling into the camera, in army uniform. Her father! It was the only photograph of him she had—and how handsome he was! She would treasure it forever. She kissed him, and put the chain over her head, and jumped up to look at herself in the mirror. It was beautiful. She tucked it inside the neck of her blouse, and opened the envelope. Inside, the photograph might have been of herself—but it couldn't be! This young woman was about seventeen, but they were so alike that a tear escaped unbidden from Lizzie's eye. Her mother as a young girl. She stared hard into the mirror. The likeness was extraordinary, and then her eyes clouded over. She wasn't going to end up like her poor mother. Not if she knew it.

When she had finished, she made her way downstairs, taking the photograph with her.

'Oh!' Mrs Ransome cried when she saw it. 'Your mother, bless her! That's just how she was when she first come to me! As pretty as a picture—you are the spitting image of her! Well, I never!' and she stared at it, and sniffed once or twice before she handed it back.

'She always wore nice white blouses, and tailored skirts—oh, she was a neat little thing. 'Course, she was pregnant when she came. They'd just got married, I mean—'

'Oh, I know, I saw the marriage

27

certificates,' Lizzie said.

Mrs Ransome sat down heavily. 'I only saw your dad the once. When they took the flat. He was a soldier boy, so young, he couldn't have been no more than twenty, and off to France, it did seem cruel. But then the war was. He never come back,' she said sadly. 'Never saw you.'

'I know my mother was in service, but I wonder what my dad did? It says manservant on the marriage lines.'

'He was a footman, in a grand house in London, and he and your ma used to go walking in the park on their off days—your ma told me. 'Course that was before he was called up.' She sat staring in front of her.

Lizzie delved down her blouse and brought up the silver locket. 'Look, I found this,' she said proudly, and opened it and held it out 'My Father—isn't he handsome?'

Mrs Ransome stared. 'Yes, he certainly is,' she said at length. 'A very good-looking man.'

No point in telling the child that that wasn't her father. Her father had been a handsome chap, too, but he was dark, very dark, with black hair and moustache—nothing in the least like the man in the photograph.

Who could that have been, then?

CHAPTER 2

'Now, Bartholomew, you must be on your way,' Miss Hawkes said, handing Lizzie the letter of introduction for her new job. 'Get off the bus at Brampton Corner, and walk along until you come to very tall iron gates. It's quite a walk up the drive, but eventually you will come to Casson Manor—and you will go to the house adjoining the Manor, where the housekeeper lives, Mrs Dawson. Give her the letter and tell her I sent you, and give her my regards.'

'Yes, Miss Hawkes,' Lizzie said, already in a fair state of excitement at the prospect.

'Always remember: do as you are told, mind your manners—and don't forget how lucky you are to have found such a good position. I wouldn't send every girl of mine to the Manor, but if you work hard, you might end up with a very good job, I shouldn't wonder. It's up to you.'

She eyed Lizzie's coat and hat.

'That's new, isn't it?' she asked, her small light eyes peering at Lizzie's coat.

'Yes, Miss. Mrs Ransome the landlady

29

took me to buy it, with the money from the furniture.'

'I see.' She cast a doubtful look at the blue coat. 'Plain navy would have been better.'

Lizzie couldn't wait to get away, terrified that somehow the new blue coat would be taken from her.

'Yes, Miss Hawkes.'

'You may go, Bartholomew.'

The smile she gave was more frightening than her stern face, Lizzie thought, as she walked slowly to the door, then, hampered by her case which held all her belongings, hurried the rest of the way until the orphanage was out of sight. She sat on a seat to get her breath at the bus stop and waited, looking down at her new coat with sheer pleasure.

It was blue tweed, with flecks of white in it, but the important thing was that it had the new collar which was all the rage that year. She and Mrs Ransome had noticed it when they shopped in Brighton. The collar had been elongated into two scarves, so that you could leave them untied, or throw one casually over your shoulder—the coat was quite the most exciting article of clothing Lizzie had ever possessed.

She thought of those she had left behind, Nancy particularly, because of her foot, but their time to leave would come, she reassured herself. Well, Lizzie would go to see her whenever she could, it would depend what sort of time she got off. Anyway, if she didn't like this job, she would leave, there was no doubt about that.

When the bus came along, she got on, putting her case on the conductor's platform, and took her seat just inside. Opening her handbag, she asked for a ticket to Casson Manor, feeling quite grown up.

The Manor was about half an hour away from the centre of Brighton and she contented herself with looking out of the window at the lovely views. Green fields with grazing cows, church spires, fruit trees in blossom—it was a lovely time of year. Not only that, but she felt free for the first time in her life.

When the conductor called out her stop, she stood up and he held her arm and handed down her case. She thanked him with a ravishing smile which he remembered long after he came off duty. Then flinging the scarf nonchalantly over her shoulder, she made her way along the road until she came to a pair of ornate iron gates. Each held a centre design of the intertwined initials C and M, and a highly polished brass plate on the brick plinth announced that this was the home of the Casson Manor School for Young Ladies. Quite overcome by the splendour of it all, Lizzie made her way up the long drive to the house.

She hadn't realised how warm it was, but was determined to wear her coat and that was better than having to carry it in the case.

A quarter of a mile later the house came into view, its tall Elizabethan chimneys standing out against the blue sky. Lizzie held her breath. So this was it? Why, it was beautiful—she hadn't known such places existed. She rested the case for a moment, and stood looking around her. Miss Hawkes had told her that it was a finishing school for young ladies, whatever that meant, the daughters of rich families or girls whose parents were abroad. There were about twenty of them, and they were aged between sixteen and eighteen.

She picked up the case. Rather them than me, she thought. At least I'm free and out in the world with a job of my own.

The house was even more impressive as she drew near to it, beautiful brickwork and mullioned windows, and the gardens surrounding it full of flowers, like the flower beds on Brighton front, she thought. Gardeners were busy working, and away to the right she could see a tennis court on which two girls were playing.

The front doors were enormous, and she made her way to the side of the house which she could see would be the home of the matron or housekeeper, and a white notice on the gate told her she was right.

She rang the bell, and a young woman came to the gate to unlock it and allow her in.

'Hello, I'm Lizzie Bartholomew,' she said to the maid in the blue working apron and mob cap.

'I'm Nellie Freeman—I work here,' she said shyly.

Lizzie smiled. She was determined to make herself pleasant and to enjoy the job, whatever it was. Stillroom maid, Miss Hawkes had said.

'Would you come this way?' the girl called Nellie asked, and Lizzie followed her into a large kitchen which unlike the room in the orphanage was almost luxurious with scrubbed tables and masses of copper utensils lining the walls. It was scrupulously clean, but in a different way. It didn't have the strong disinfectant smell of carbolic soap for one thing. 'Mrs Dawson will be right down.'

Lizzie dropped her case on the floor and stood waiting. Almost at once, a kindly-looking woman came in and smiled at her.

'Lizzie Bartholomew?' she said. 'Sit you

33

down then. All right, Nellie, you may go.'

She sat down at the table opposite and Lizzie handed her the letter, which she opened and read and then put aside.

'I understand your mother has recently died,' she said kindly. 'I am sorry to hear that and I hope you will find yourself happy here. The work is not too hard. Not as hard, I imagine, as you have been used to.'

She smiled, looking up into Lizzie's green eyes.

'Your duties will consist of looking after four dormitories on the first floor, with two girls in each dormitory. That means looking after their laundry, the ironing, the bed linen for the eight beds, keeping the dormitories clean and polished, and generally seeing to their immediate needs. The washing is done by the laundry women, but it will be your job to collect it when done and see to the ironing and place the clean linen and clothes in the linen cupboards. Do you think you can do that? You will be on a month's trial.'

And so will you, Lizzie thought as she listened to every word. Just my luck, she thought. Laundry! Still, it can't be anything like old Baldy's...

'I understand you have had quite a bit of experience in this sort of thing? I have always been pleased before with the girls Matron has sent.'

'Yes, Mrs Dawson.'

'You will have a room at the top of the house next to Alice. She is the still room maid for the second floor. You will receive a weekly wage of fifteen shillings, and of course your board and lodging. Nellie will explain it all to you when she takes you round.'

She rang the bell on her desk.

When Nellie appeared, she gave her instructions to show Lizzie to her room at the top of the house where she would put her things and afterwards report for duty on the ground floor.

The top floor consisted of several small attic rooms, and Nellie showed Lizzie into one. It was tiny, with a single iron bed and table, a corner cupboard and shelf, and a washstand with a bowl and pitcher of water. Lizzie ignored the furnishings and ran to the window to see the view.

'So high up!' she cried, opening the window. The room smelled of all its past residents, but she would soon put a stop to that, she thought. In her luggage reposed a special bar of Yardley's oatmeal soap which she couldn't wait to unpack.

Nellie stood at the door watching, eyeing the lovely face of the new dormitory maid. Without her hat, her shiny black hair fell into curls, obviously growing out from a close hair cut, and her green eyes shone with excitement. Nellie, who had no claim to prettiness except a lovely shy expression, watched Lizzie enviously. Not only did she have that beautiful hair but she had wonderful green eyes and a face as pretty as any she had ever seen.

'You can put your clothes in the cupboard,' she said, 'and there are two drawers at the bottom.'

Lizzie threw open the cupboard door. 'Plenty of room!' she cried. She was so excited she would have put up with anything.

'And your photographs and things go on the shelf,' Nellie said, as if it needed explanation.

'Photographs? Oh, yes, that's good,' Lizzie said, anxious for Nellie to go so that she could make herself at home.

'The staff bathroom is at the end of the corridor, and you have to put down when you want to use it.'

Luxury upon luxury.

'Well, then, I'll leave you. As soon as you're ready, you'd best come along to the linen room and I'll explain.'

'Lovely,' Lizzie said, sitting on the bed and feeling its iron hard surface, but she was used to that.

She swung herself round with excitement

when Nellie had gone. Her very own room! What did it matter how tiny it was? You could only be in so much space at one time.

She unpacked her things, and washed with the soap and emptied the dirty water in the enamel pail below. Oh, it wouldn't take long for her to settle down here!

Her tasks, she thought eventually, were easy. In each of the two dormitories, as they were called, were two beds, dressing tables and wardrobes. In the drawers were the girls' underwear and nightclothes, while in the wardrobes hung their uniforms and other clothes. They even had cooking aprons and working overalls, but what Lizzie liked most was to see the things on each dressing table, each denoting the personality of the owner. How she loved to dust and polish the cut glass scent bottles and powder bowls! She got to know all the girls after a time, but she had her favourites. She liked Miss Tessa Melville for she was short and plump and jolly, and gave Lizzie little things like unused powder or lipstick, and when Lizzie took her evening gown for the Summer Ball, all freshly ironed and laid out on her bed, Tessa gave her a pound note which was a fortune.

And Lizzie liked sorting out the freshly ironed sheets and pillow cases, not in the

37

least like those in the home. These were fine linen and embroidered, unlike the calico sheets she was used to, and she enjoyed nothing more than to sort out the linen chests and see the piles of freshly laundered linen.

The young man who delivered the groceries twice a week was quick to see the charms of the new maid, and winked at her, and pressed her hand when she took the grocery boxes from him. Until the day when he attempted to put an arm around her waist, when she sharply trod on his foot. At his pained expression, she opened her green eyes wide and smiled sweetly. 'Sorry, Norman.'

As for the life that was going on around her, she was completely enthralled by it. All these young women, not much older than herself, being taught to cook, to iron, to keep house, to do accounts, to play tennis, golf, arrange flowers—so many things—and most of them, she suspected, would never use any of them. She learned too, from the staff gossip, who was about to leave and marry. Most of the prospective husbands' names meant nothing to her. But she learned, and she learned fast.

She disliked intensely, for instance, Maybelle Dyson. Some May Belle, thought Lizzie. Hook-nosed and forbidding in demeanour, she frequently berated Lizzie for tasks left undone, even though she knew perfectly well that Lizzie had done everything she was expected to.

Best of all Lizzie liked Sarah Chamberlain. Sarah, who was tall and beautiful. It seemed ridiculous but they had something in common, Lizzie thought. The laughter and humour in Sarah's eyes always made Lizzie want to smile, and there was nothing she liked more than doing something for Sarah.

One evening in late summer, long after lights out, she was disturbed by a noise below her. It sounded like a window being opened. Hurriedly putting on her dressing gown, she crept downstairs just in time to meet Sarah Chamberlain climbing backwards through the small window, obviously startled when her feet reached the floor to see Lizzie there, stifling her laughter.

'Oh' she cried, hand to heart, 'you made me jump!' Then she smiled at Lizzie with relief, looking down ruefully at her torn skirt. 'Did I make an awful noise?'

Lizzie shook her head. 'I was awake and I heard something.' She looked down at the rent in the navy skirt. 'Don't worry, Miss, I'll mend it for you.'

'Oh, you are a dear.' And without more ado, Sarah unhooked the skirt and dropped it round her feet. 'Here you are.' And she hurried back along the corridor to her room clad in her pink satin slip. 'Night,' she waved.

Lizzie looked after her. Where had she been? To meet some boy, she'd guess, knowing that most of the girls' conversations were concerned with the opposite sex.

She picked up the skirt and took it back to her room. Tomorrow she would repair it. She was quite good at sewing, having been taught assiduously at the orphanage by nuns who came in every week to take a sewing class. Not that she liked it mind. Still, anything to help out a friend, and she found she was quite fascinated by clothes, always looking to see what the students wore, what sort of things they chose to wear in their off moments, how some had style and some had no idea at all as to what suited them.

When she returned the mended skirt to Sarah by replacing it in her wardrobe, she found a tiny bottle of French perfume on the dressing table with a label on it addressed to her. 'Thanks, Lizzie.'

Oh, it was fun to be working here, but when she had heard Sarah come in twice running and making a noise with the window which was immediately below her room, Lizzie waylaid her and suggested that she would see that the window was left open after lights out, just a little way, to enable Sarah to slide it up more easily.

'Oh, you are a poppet!' Sarah cried, her blue eyes radiant with the fun of intrigue.

It all added a bit of interest to Lizzie's life at the school. It became apparent to her after a time that the girls spoke differently from anyone else she had met. Sometimes she practised the accent, which came fairly easily to her, and she took to getting books out of the local library to read. After all, she told herself, education is what matters. But money certainly made a difference. One day she would have enough money of her own to enable her to study and take lessons—in deportment, table manners, meeting people. There was no end to the things you had to learn. Sometimes, surreptitiously, she read the notes the girls left lying about and was amazed at what she read. For instance, she thought you put cut flowers in a vase, but there seemed to be no end to the things you could do with them. Flower arranging, they called it. Laying tables...you would have thought anyone would know about that. Still, it was a bit difficult with all those glasses and knowing which ones were for what. The housework course was a riot, for it was obvious that none of them would be doing any. It mostly consisted of how to treat one's servants—and Lizzie laughed out loud at that. 'One's servants'—it sounded quite royal. There was apparently an art to employing staff, and consequently lessons on how to be a good mistress.

I could tell them about that, Lizzie thought darkly.

She made friends with Nellie Freeman, and the two of them went for walks together on their half days, or into Brighton. Nellie thought Lizzie was the cat's whiskers because she made her see the funny side of things, and apparently feared no one. God nor man. Once they met two young men on the front and went to the pictures with them. It would have been fun if Nellie hadn't been so nervous.

'What are you afraid of?' asked Lizzie. 'They won't get up to any hanky panky with me around, I can tell you!'

Nellie looked at her adoringly.

She was very religious, very gentle and sweet, and somehow Lizzie was drawn to her. Alice, the maid in the room next door, held no appeal for Lizzie at all. A great fat lump of a girl, with the face and manners of a pig.

Shocked at Lizzie's language, nevertheless Nellie had to laugh for Alice did have the appearance of a fat porker, 'She can't help what she looks like, Lizzie,' Nellie reproved gently.

'Course she can!' Lizzie jeered. 'She could stop eating so much. And wash!' She looked darkly at Nellie. 'She smells,' she said at length.

'Oh, Lizzie!' Nellie said, and blushed.

On one of her half days in August, Lizzie went back to the orphanage to see her old friends. She took with her a bag of assorted sweets, knowing which ones they all liked best.

As she walked up the path and into the home, she shivered. Although the day was warm, and the sun was shining, she felt cold, cold at the memory of the long years she had spent here. It didn't seem possible now. Who could have guessed that there was another world going on outside the home? Poor little devils, she thought.

'Well, Bartholomew,' Miss Hawkes said, waylaying her, 'I have had a good report from Mrs Dawson. She says you work well, and are popular with the staff.'

'Thank you, ma'am.'

Miss Hawkes glanced at her watch. 'It is four o'clock so the girls will be finished with class for today. I expect they will be pleased to see you.'

'Thank you, ma'am.' And Lizzie couldn't get away fast enough.

They fell on her, hugging her, grabbing

the sweets, and talking nineteen to the dozen.

'What's it like?'

'Smashing,' Lizzie said, and told them about the girls and what they did, and what she did in her working hours, while twelve pairs of eyes eagerly surveyed her. The girls roared with laughter at her stories; they thought they had never heard anything so funny. Nancy sat close to her, her gammy leg stuck out in front of her, her huge round eyes fixed on Lizzie's face.

'I do miss you,' she said, almost in tears.

''Course you do!' Lizzie said stoutly. 'I miss you—all of you—too.'

I'm a fifty-one AR she told herself, that being the way they used the word 'liar'. I do miss Nancy—well, a bit—but its a funny thing, once you're away from them, you forget them for most of the time. Still, I do think about Nancy. The others not so much.

'I'm leaving in December,' Violet said proudly. 'Going to live with my brother in Camberwell. It's lovely up there in London.'

Lizzie considered this for a moment. 'Yes, my parents came from London,' she said. 'I might go there one day.'

She kissed Nancy goodbye and hugged the others and made her way back to the bus stop. Oh, but she was glad to be going

44

back home. Strange how it seemed like home to her. But it was, with her own little room and the books she had bought to read, and Nellie and Miss Sarah—even Mrs Dawson was nice—and her soap, and perfume—and the box of hankies Miss Devereux had given her because she didn't like coloured ones. Oh, it was all lovely. Even Dora, the fat lady who did the washing, always had a cheery word for Lizzie.

When she got back she suddenly remembered the landlady, Mrs Ransome. Perhaps she should have gone to see her? Then decided, no, perhaps, not. That side of her life was finished. And she wouldn't even go to see her mother's grave. Not yet. It was too soon. One day perhaps.

CHAPTER 3

One afternoon in late-September Lizzie walked up the stairs, her arms full of ironed clothes and linen. She put the bed linen in the cupboards and made her way to the first dormitory, but when she tried to open it she found it was locked. There were no keys to the doors, but she guessed someone had bolted it from the inside.

She tapped gently at first, then louder, and whispered. 'It's me—Lizzie.' Presently the door was opened by Sarah, hankie to her eyes, which were red with crying. Wordlessly she turned and made her way back to the bed, flinging herself face down on it and erupting into more sobs.

'Oh, I thought it was you, miss,' Lizzie said drily, going about her business of putting things in drawers and on hangers. She waited until she had finished, then folded her arms and stood by the bed. 'What's up?'

There was no point, she thought, in beating around the bush. When a girl cried like that, rich or poor, the reasons were usually the same, give or take.

Sarah shook her head violently.

Lizzie sat down on the bed and waited. Sarah was bound to say something sooner or later.

Presently Lizzie said, 'Are you crying because you haven't anything to wear to the ball?' and saw Sarah's shoulders shake with silent laughter.

This coming Friday night was a special evening, the annual Harvest Ball.

Sarah sat up, drying her eyes and blowing her nose.

'Oh, Lizzie, you don't know how lucky you are!' she wailed, wrapping her arms around her knees. 'It's all right for you,

you're free as a bird, while I have to do as I'm told.'

'Well, you can't have everything,' Lizzie said.

'I had a letter this morning from my mother and as far as I can make out, once I leave here—and of course after I'm presented—my engagement will be announced to Lord Devenoke's son, the ghastly Joshua. Apparently he's already spoken to my father. Oh, I can't bear it!' And she flung herself down again on the pillows.

Lizzie was at once impressed and horrified.

'They can't make you marry him, can they?' she asked in disbelief.

'Oh yes they can!' Sarah cried, sitting up again. 'Well, I mean, I could run away—'

'Where would you go?' Lizzie asked practically.

'Oh, I don't know. I haven't thought about it. I only know that it's all being arranged behind my back, as if I was a parcel or something. Anyone would think I was an Indian girl.'

'Do they do that?' Lizzie asked. She was really interested.

'Yes,' Sarah said irritably. 'The parents arrange the marriages, and if that's not just what my parents are doing, then I don't know what is. I wouldn't mind, but he's such a weed!' And she cried again.

Lizzie got up. 'Well, I don't know, I'm sure,' she said, sounding like a thirty-year-old parent.

'Anyway, apart from that,' and Sarah sniffed, 'it means I shall have to give up seeing Archie.'

'Who's he?' Lizzie asked. This got more and more interesting.

'Archie Toogood, the man I've been meeting after lights out,' Sarah said, and already a twinkle had come back in her blue eyes as she tossed back her mane of fair hair.

If Mrs Dawson only knew! thought Lizzie.

'Who is this Archie?' she asked. She felt since she had connived at Sarah's nocturnal jaunts it might be better if she knew what they were all about. Perhaps he was an undesirable person? Lizzie began to feel a little guilty.

'Oh, someone I met on Brighton front. He's a wonderful dancer—he's appearing at the Hippodrome there.'

Golly! Lizzie thought. A *most* undesirable person, even she knew that. It wouldn't do at all if Sarah's parents or Mrs Dawson found out about this.

'He don't sound much good to me,' she

said carefully. 'I mean, a dancer. He can't be a gentleman.'

'What's that got to do with it?' Sarah asked, hugging her knees again, except that this time there was quite a wicked gleam in her eye, and Lizzie began to wonder if, well, perhaps they had—well, you never knew!

'Seems to me it'll be a good thing when your time comes to leave, miss,' she said.

'Oh, what shall I do?' Sarah cried, somewhat theatrically it had to be said.

Lizzie turned on her sharply. 'You're not—you haven't been—'

'Mind your own business!'

Lizzie sat down on a chair, thinking. She was very fond of Miss Sarah, although they were poles apart.

She put on a stern face. 'You might have a baby,' she said grimly, and saw the fear come briefly into Sarah's eyes.

'Don't be so ridiculous!' she said, getting up and hitching her belt tightly round her waist. 'I think you forget who you are talking to!' And her nostrils flared as her head went back.

'No skin off my nose,' Lizzie said, getting up and going to the door.

'Wait!' Sarah called her back, and now she was her usual friendly self.

'I'm sorry, Lizzie, I didn't mean that,' she said. 'You've been a little brick to

49

me—you're only a kid yourself. How old are you?'

She often thought Lizzie should be working somewhere where her good looks and deportment would be better appreciated. Her lovely black hair and green eyes, the character that showed in her face, were all wasted working as a stillroom maid.

'Going on sixteen,' Lizzie said, jumping a few months. 'I left the orphanage when I was fifteen.'

'Orphanage?' Sarah shrieked, genuinely shocked.

'Yes,' Lizzie said brightly. 'I'm an orphan.' And she pulled a sad face, which made Sarah laugh for a moment.

'I think that's terribly sad,' she said. 'I mean, I know my parents are a nuisance, organizing my life and all that, but I can't imagine what I'd do without them—'

'Well, you'd have to, miss, there's no two way about that,' Lizzie said. ' 'Course, I can do as I like, not having a family, see. I'm as free as a bird, miss, but I'm going to do something with my life. I'm not staying here forever. I got to make plans.'

'I see,' Sarah said slowly, her mind taken off herself for a while.

'You've got to look after number one in this world,' Lizzie said firmly. ' 'Specially when you're on your own.'

Her problems forgotten, Sarah sat thinking. Fifteen, and alone in the world! She couldn't envisage what it must be like.

'Well, I'll have to go,' Lizzie said, looking down at her seriously. 'I've a good mind not to leave that window undone. You ought to have more sense, miss.'

'Yes, I know,' Sarah said, picking up the letter that lay by her side on the bed. 'Still—Joshua! Ugh, what a prospect.'

Laughing to herself, Lizzie went out to collect more linen from the laundry room.

They didn't know they were born, these young ladies, she thought.

A few days later, Sarah asked her advice about the dress she was wearing to the ball. All her clothes were spread over the dormitory since the girl she shared with had gone home for a spell.

'What do you think, Lizzie?'

Lizzie glanced at the blue dress lying on the bed.

'Old hat,' she said briefly. She fingered the material. 'Feels like silk,' she said, 'but it's old fashioned. Can't you buy a new one?'

Sarah shook her head vigorously. 'No, I don't want to ask my mother just now—I'm not talking to her,' she said sulkily.

'Right, then.' Lizzie was nothing if not practical.

'Could you do something with it? You're good at sewing.'

'I don't know about that,' Lizzie said. 'But I can see where it could be brought more up to date. You want straps, not little sleeves, and straight skirts are all the rage. Not much good for dancing. Still, if that's the fashion...'

'Oh, that doesn't matter,' Sarah said.

'Well, it would mean cutting it up and starting again.'

'Could you?' Sarah's eyes were sparkling.

'S'pose I spoil it?'

'You won't...anyway, I would have to buy another one then. Why don't we have a go?'

'I'm game if you are.'

'Done,' Sarah said. 'I never liked it anyway. It was Mummy's idea of my first evening gown.'

'And very pretty,' Lizzie said. 'Mind, I can't start on it yet. I might get an hour or two this evening.'

'But you haven't a machine!' Sarah cried.

'I wouldn't know how to use it if I had.' Lizzie grinned. 'Besides, you should always sew pure silk by hand, miss.'

'Oh. I didn't know. Well, I'm happy for you to play with it.'

'Right you are, miss. I'll take it with me and start unpicking. When are you free tomorrow?'

Sarah consulted her timetable. 'Only in the morning. I suppose I could skip tennis in the afternoon...'

'No, I've no time then. Look, leave it to me—I might get Nellie to give me a hand.'

Sarah frowned. 'Oh, I don't think—'

'Just as you say, miss. Leave it with me.'

By the time Cynthia Hughes-Burroughs returned to school on Friday in time for the dance, the dormitory had been cleared and Sarah's dress lay spread out on her bed, finished and ready to wear.

She had tried it on, and it fitted like a glove. With the sleeves taken out and the neckline cut deeper and wider, it was now a dress with straps, while Lizzie had reshaped the skirt and cut it fairly straight, with a long slit at the back.

Sarah lifted her name of fair hair on top of her head and eyed herself in the mirror.

'It's gorgeous,' she said. 'No one would ever guess what it had been.'

'Them buttons at the back took ages,' Lizzie said.

'Those,' Sarah said automatically.

'What? Oh, those buttons,' Lizzie said.

53

Sarah often corrected her, something for which she was grateful.

'I'm delighted,' Sarah said. 'And I'm going to pay you, Lizzie.'

Lizzie blushed. 'No, really, I enjoyed doing it.'

'I am glad you did. But here's five pounds. No, take it, I mean it. I'm delighted.'

Five pounds! The crisp white note was just asking to be accepted.

'Thank you, Miss Sarah.' But the girl had turned away and was looking at herself in the mirror, smoothing the front of the dress, flicking her head from side to side, eyeing her young bosom and trim waist, and liking what she saw.

Lizzie thrust the note down into her overall pocket. Her turn would come. One day.

By the end of November Lizzie had decided to better herself. Excited at the thought of going up to London to try for a job, she was perhaps not as observant of her young ladies as she usually was. Going about her duties in weather that was dull and dismal, days when the sea mist covered the downs for much of the time, she carried out her duties automatically.

Thus is was that she failed to notice, on the odd occasions she saw her, that Miss

Sarah was not her usual self. She answered irritably when Lizzie spoke to her, not unusual with many of the students but rare with her. It took a few days before Lizzie realized that Miss Sarah, with dark circles under her eyes, pale face and withdrawn manner, was not at all her usual self.

'Can I ask you something?' she began one day, anxious for her friend, for so she liked to think of her.

'Yes? What is it?' Sarah sounded irritable.

'I just wondered if you was—were all right, Miss. If there was anything I could do.' She stood helplessly by while Sarah fidgeted with a hankie, then a hairbrush, then changed her shoes.

At length she spoke. 'I'm perfectly all right, thank you,' she added. 'Just—busy.'

'If there was anything I could do—' Lizzie said, concerned now, for she was sure something was wrong.

'No. Nothing. Thank you.'

'Very well, miss.' And Lizzie made for the door.

'Lizzie—'

She stopped, her fingers on the handle, and turned expectantly. 'Yes, miss?'

'Oh—nothing. Nothing. You may go.'

Two days later, Sarah left. Lizzie had been told to strip her bed, wash and dust the personal dressing table, clean out the wardrobe and polish it ready for a newcomer. It was the usual procedure—as cold and impersonal as if someone had never been.

Lizzie was surprised at her own sense of loss. She had felt somehow related to Miss Sarah, been fond of her, and the new girl who duly arrived in no way replaced her. A jolly hockey stick, Lizzie thought mutinously—none of the others held one-tenth of the appeal of Miss Sarah.

Oh, well, she sighed, and felt upset that she might never know what had happened to her.

On the day she decided to make a Christmas visit to the orphanage, a letter arrived with a London postmark, the only letter she had received since she had been at Casson Manor.

She tore open the thick white envelope in a fever of curiosity to see a black-printed London address at the top, and at the bottom, the signature 'Florence Chamberlain.'

It must be from Miss Sarah's mother.

My dear Miss Bartholomew
I understand from my daughter Sarah that you wish to leave Casson Manor where you are employed as a stillroom maid.
My daughter is soon to be married and will require a lady's maid, and is of the impression

that you would be suitable for the position.

I enclose a stamped addressed envelope for your reply so that you may let me know if you are already suited or interested in applying for the position, when perhaps we may arrange an interview.

Yours faithfully,
Florence Chamberlain.

Well! Lizzie sat back and re-read it three times.

So Miss Sarah was to be married after all—and her not yet eighteen—and to that lord's son that she didn't like. Oh, why hadn't she run away?

But more to the point was the offer of a position. Chester Square, London. It sounded jolly interesting but was that what she wanted to do? A lady's maid? Well, it might be a step to bigger and better things. For Lizzie had no intention of being a servant girl all her life.

She would think about it. How she longed to know about Sarah, though. In the meantime, she must prepare for her Christmas visit to the orphanage.

They all greeted her with mad enthusiasm, even the two new girls who had only heard about her up to now. Nancy clung to her as if she would never let her go, and Lizzie was surprised to find how much Nancy had grown. She was tall, and had filled out a little, although she still walked with a limp.

Violet had already left, and they all sat talking and asked Lizzie what she was going to do, but apart from telling them she would probably go to London, she said nothing about the offer of employment. When she said goodbye to them, she realised it might be for the last time, although she would keep in touch with Nancy.

Leaving the orphanage, she walked down to the front at Brighton, the cold wind slapping her face. The air was so fresh, it really did seem to blow the cobwebs away. In the side streets it was warmer and still, and she made her way to a cafe where she bought herself a cup of tea.

She was quite sure now that she was going to take up the offer of a job with Sarah's family—that way she would get to London, where her new life would begin. It didn't need much thinking about—she certainly had no wish to stay at the Manor, it was a dead end job—and once in London, the whole world would open up to her. She began to get excited at the prospect.

Christmas came and went before she answered the letter. Then she sat down and began to write carefully on notepaper she had bought when she first went to Casson Manor. Up to now there had been no one to write to. 'Dear Mrs Chamberlain' she began, in her very best writing. When the letter was finished, she sat back to await events.

CHAPTER 4

The answer came promptly from Mrs Chamberlain requesting an interview, for which she enclosed a postal order for the return fare to Brighton.

In a fair state of excitement, Lizzie set off, wearing her blue tweed coat, the scarf tied high beneath her neck to keep out the cold, a navy dress which she had made herself, and a rather nice pull on felt hat with a turn back brim which suited her and showed her lovely face.

Her gloves were kid, old ones of her mother's—for if there was one thing she had been told it was that a lady always wore gloves and kid ones at that. Never cotton or wool.

She was fascinated by the journey, seeing the countryside rolling past her, the trees black and bare against the sky, the rows and rows of cottages with their lines of washing and back garden sheds. The views became more and more dark and depressing as they reached the city, and when she got out of the train at Waterloo, the difference in the air from Brighton was quite noticeable, with the smoke from the steam train filling the station platforms.

But it was exciting, and having asked her way to Chester Square, she found herself outside the station with the noise of a city all around her, red buses and taxicabs, people moving along like armies on the march, and she felt at once an accord with London that she was never to lose. Imagine, this was where her parents came from—it was at once overwhelming, busy and full of promise.

Two buses took her to her destination, and she sat on her seat, engrossed. There was so much to see all around her, she didn't know which side to look at first. Past St Paul's and Charing Cross, places which up to now had been only names in a book, the Mall where the buildings were so white and so beautiful. The Houses of Parliament and Big Ben...it gave her a lump in her throat that she should be here, riding right alongside.

It was with a feeling of anti-climax that she reached Chester Square and looked up at the dark brick buildings, for she had had no idea what to expect, and had half thought to find a large white stone house set in a glorious garden, but five minutes in London had told her that she couldn't have been more wrong. The first feeling of disappointment swiftly disappeared to be overtaken by the knowledge that this indeed was a very expensive area. The very buildings looked luxurious as though run by armies of servants, the windowsills filled with flowers, the curtains hanging heavily in windows which were so highly polished that they showed reflections in them—and this in a place where passing traffic must dirty them every day.

Lizzie was very impressed.

She stood for some moments before walking to the top of the area steps, then taking a deep breath, boldly made her way down the steps and knocked at the black-painted door.

It was opened by a short young man with a friendly shiny face, his hair greased back smoothly, who almost whistled when he saw her.

'Yes, miss?'

'I'm Miss Bartholomew—I have an appointment with Mrs Williams, the house-keeper.'

'Right, miss. Come in, miss. This way.'

She followed him into a gloomy passage which was white-washed to make it lighter, and waited as he asked her to when he re-entered what was obviously the kitchen.

'Someone to see you, Mrs Williams. Name of Miss Bartholomew,' the boy said.

'Show her in then,' came the reply, and Lizzie followed him into an enormous basement kitchen where the dressers were filled with crockery up to the ceiling, and the shelves above the fireplace were hung with copper saucepans and huge steamers. All in all, it was the most beautiful kitchen Lizzie had ever seen.

'Good morning,' she said.

Mrs Williams appraised her before saying anything. Then she nodded.

'What's your name?'

'Lizzie—Lizzie Bartholomew.'

Mrs Williams glanced up at the clock. 'You're on time then. Well, give her a chair,' she said to the lad. 'He's Percy. And you wait there 'til I say.'

'Yes, Mrs Williams.'

'Oh, you know my name then?' She folded her arms and looked pleased.

Lizzie took the letter out of her handbag, the precious letter which she would always keep, being the first real letter she had ever received.

'Yes, I was told to ask for Mrs Williams.'

The housekeeper nodded. 'Sit down until I tell you,' she said, and disappeared.

Lizzie sat looking round her under Percy's admiring gaze until one glance from those green eyes made him turn his away and get on with stoking up the range.

Presently Mrs Williams returned, slightly out of breath and asked Lizzie to follow her.

They walked up the narrow stairs until they came to a door, which when opened led into a sumptuous hall. Lizzie almost gasped at the rich furnishings for she had never seen anything like it in her life. A huge chandelier hung from the ceiling, and the walls were crimson and lined with portraits. So this was where Miss Sarah lived—she could hardly believe it. And Miss Sarah had slept in that little dormitory at Casson Manor without turning a hair.

'This way,' Mrs Williams said, leading her up the thickly carpeted stairs, and past even more portraits on the crimson walls. On the landing, her stout form was obviously overcome by the climb and she stood for a moment before going on. On this landing, which was like a room, there were carpets and another chandelier and various highly polished doors leading off. The housekeeper led the way to the far door and knocked.

'Come in,' a voice called, and Mrs Williams opened the door to allow Lizzie in. 'Miss Bartholomew, madam.' And Lizzie walked inside to find herself in a large room overlooking the square. Seated at an elegant desk was a small plump lady wearing a cream silk blouse, with her abundant dark hair taken back into a chignon.

So this must be Miss Sarah's mother, Lizzie decided, although they bore no resemblance to one another at all.

Having been brought up not to speak unless spoken to, she kept silent, until Mrs Chamberlain, wearing a slight frown, took her eyes off Lizzie's face.

'So, you are Miss Bartholomew. You're very young.' She sounded almost reproachful.

'I'll be sixteen in April.'

'Mmmmm,' Mrs Chamberlain said doubtfully.

'I've had a lot of experience looking after people and clothes and that,' Lizzie offered. If they didn't want her, she was sure someone else would. Still, she would like to see Miss Sarah again.

'My daughter tells me you are an orphan. Have you no ties at all? No family?'

'No, madam.'

'That can be an advantage,' Mrs Chamberlain said drily.

'Yes, madam.' Lizzie tried hard not to stare at Mrs Chamberlain's hands, which were white and soft with many beautiful rings which flashed in the sunlight that filtered into the room.

'My daughter seems to have become quite attached to you when she was at Casson Manor, and as you are aware, she is shortly to be married—in March, as it happens—and since she will be leading quite a busy social life, she will need a personal lady's maid. This will entail travelling—how do you feel about that?'

Lizzie could not have felt more excited at the prospect. 'Oh, all right, madam.'

'My daughter is not used to fending for herself—my own maid who has always been on hand is leaving at the end of the month, otherwise I would have transferred her to Miss Sarah, but since I have to train a new maid myself, it might be a good idea for you to come on a month's trial. What do you think of the idea?'

Lizzie's green eyes were shining. Mrs Chamberlain thought she had never seen such green eyes, such beautiful eyes.

'Oh, yes, madam.'

'My daughter will have a house in London, not far from here, and your duties will be to wait on her at all times—and solely her. So, you see, it is a very important position and if you make the best of it, very pleasant. It is a pity you have had no training with a senior lady's maid. Still, it cannot be helped. My daughter is very keen that you be given a chance.'

'Thank you, madam.'

'You will be going to Scotland after the wedding, and from there travelling to London. Since you have no family, I don't suppose that will matter. Your wages will be thirty shillings a week and I leave it to my daughter to tell you what the hours will be.'

She stood up and came round to where Lizzie sat. Lizzie stood up automatically. 'Now, show me your hands.'

Lizzie held them out for inspection, nails well trimmed and clean. Then Mrs Chamberlain asked her to take off her coat and hat.

She did so, and the dark curls having escaped the confines of the hat leapt into a life of their own. Lizzie's clean fresh skin glowed, and Mrs Chamberlain felt a sudden wave of envy of the girl's youth and beauty.

Without the coat, she stood there, slim and neat in her navy dress. Mrs Chamberlain leaned forward and felt the skirt.

'Did you make this? It is very nice material.'

'Yes, madam. I bought it in the market at Brighton.'

'I see. Turn around.' She looked down at Lizzie's heels and saw that the seams of her stockings were straight then went back to her chair, glancing at the kid gloves and the small leather handbag, which had she known it had been given to Lizzie by one of the students at the school.

'Put on your clothes,' she said. 'I am quite satisfied. You keep your things very nicely, well ironed and pressed. Now sit down and we will talk about the arrangements for your starting here.'

Still wearing her slight frown, which Lizzie decided must be a permanent part of her expression, she folded her hands together on the desk and looked at Lizzie.

'Being a lady's maid is a very good position, and of course as yet you will be in training, but I have to stress that the most important things are confidentiality—and loyalty. I am sure you have had good training in these things, but you are about to take up a very important and trusted position—not like the servants in the kitchen, this is quite different, and everything you hear must be treated with the utmost confidence. Do I make myself clear?'

'Yes, Mrs Chamberlain.'

'After she is married, you will call Miss Sarah "My Lady".' And she could not help showing her feelings as her nostrils dilated with pride. So Sarah is marrying that awful son Joshua, thought Lizzie.

'Since she is to be married in March, I suggest you start here some time in February, before the wedding, so that you will be on hand to see her through the wedding and the honeymoon.'

Golly, thought Lizzie.

'It is not possible for you to see Miss Sarah today—she is in the country for a few days—but when she returns, I will tell her that I have arranged for you to start working with us as a personal maid on a month's trial.'

She consulted her diary.

'Would the eighteenth of February suit you? It is a Sunday and that will give you time to settle in before starting your duties on the Monday.'

'Yes, madam.'

She had hoped it would be before.

'Very well. We expect to see you on Sunday the eighteenth then. Report to Mrs Williams as you did today.' Mrs Chamberlain rang a bell on her desk, and presently a young maid answered. Her dark eyes looked at Lizzie and right through her.

'Will you take Miss Bartholomew downstairs now, Mary?'

'Yes, madam.'

Lizzie followed her down the stairs,

unable to prevent a grin from appearing. It must be galling for this twenty-year-old maid to be escorting a youngster like herself down the stairs. Still, she'd make the best of what life had to offer in this house. Indeed she would.

'Thank you,' she said politely, and when she was let out, took off her hat and almost threw it over the railings with glee.

London! She was here at last. Blowed if she wouldn't go and buy herself a cup of tea somewhere, just to make the day perfect. She almost danced along the streets, not stopping until she came to a cafe, where she bought a pot of tea and a cake and sat watching everyone going past until the waitresses thought she would never go.

Pity she didn't see Miss Sarah. Still, that didn't matter. Just two weeks, two weeks before she said good-bye forever to Casson Manor.

Though she had to admit she had enjoyed it. Every minute of it.

It was a freezing cold day in February when she arrived at Chester Square with her bag and baggage. Percy let her in, and she was shown by the back staircase to an attic room on the top floor, not unlike the one at the Manor except that it was bigger and held a nice washstand, jug and basin, a large wardrobe, and on trying it, a more comfortable bed of double size.

'This is all yours, miss,' Percy said. 'We don't all get one to ourselves.'

'Thank you, Percy,' she said, feeling very superior. 'I will come down when I am ready.'

There was a hush everywhere in the house as though everyone was sleeping on this winter Sunday afternoon, and glancing at her watch, Lizzie saw that it was just two-thirty. She unpacked and washed which took no time at all, and decided to go down to the kitchen at tea time. In the meantime, she would read the book she had brought with her. If anyone wanted her, Percy would tell them where she was.

It took time to get used to the different sounds: of doors closing softly, of a church bell, and the noise of traffic along the road. There was a hum behind everything, the sounds of a city, its heart throbbing—unlike her last home, where you could have heard a pin drop on a Sunday except for the sound of tennis balls being whacked and the shrieks of the girls' voices.

But she couldn't relax, and at three-thirty went downstairs to the kitchen.

The maid, Mary, was in the kitchen, sitting at the table reading a book. She looked up as Lizzie came in.

'Oh, it's you,' she said. 'Miss Sarah would like you to go up to her room about four o'clock, she'll be ready then.' She looked Lizzie up and down. 'What's yer name?'

'Lizzie—Lizzie Bartholomew.'

'I'm Mary,' she said. 'The parlourmaid —or one of them. You look a bit young to be a lady's maid. Have you done it before?'

'Sort of,' Lizzie said. 'In a finishing school.'

'What's that?'

And Lizzie explained.

'That's not a proper school, and not a lady's maid to one lady. That's different.'

'Yes, I expect so.'

'You've got a uniform—I don't expect it will fit you. It's navy blue. Miss Sarah chose it.'

'Sounds nice,' Lizzie said.

'I like black meself,' Mary said. 'There's a pot of tea here, do you want some?'

When Lizzie nodded, she said, 'Get yourself a cup—over there. 'Course, you won't be doing any of the dirty work, not like we have to do.'

Lizzie busied herself pouring milk into the cup and then tea. She sipped it slowly. This girl could easily become an enemy, she had met many of them in the home.

71

But Lizzie reckoned she knew the answer to most things.

'You've got lovely hands,' she said. 'I don't blame you not wanting to do dirty work. Lovely smooth white hands.'

'Really?' The girl blushed, pleased with the compliment, causing her to say to the others when they came down: 'Lizzie's very nice—friendly. 'Course, she's only a kid.'

At four o'clock promptly, Lizzie was shown into Miss Sarah's dressing room. Through the open door she could see an enormous four poster bed with dark silk curtains, and by the window Sarah who was buffing her nails.

'Just coming!' she called out, and at the sight of Lizzie ran into the room.

'Oh, you can't know how glad I am to see you!'

For one moment Lizzie had thought Sarah was going to throw her arms around her.

'Me too, Miss,' she said fervently. They looked at each other, and it was Lizzie who saw the greatest change. In just three months Sarah looked a different girl. Older, quieter, pale, her large blue eyes a little wary.

'You look wonderful!' Sarah said.

'So do you,' Lizzie lied. She took a deep breath. 'Well, Miss Sarah, here I am.'

'You found your room all right?'

'Yes, I unpacked, and I'm all ready to start work.' Lizzie automatically picked up a stray garment from a chair and folded it.

'Hey, don't start yet. It's your day off. Besides you haven't got your uniform yet.'

Lizzie looked down at her navy dress. 'So I haven't.'

'Sit down for a minute—there's no one about.'

Lizzie did so, and Sarah sat on the velvet chaise.

'Mother told you I am being married in March?' And she made a face.

'Yes, that's why I am here, isn't it?'

'Right.'

Lizzie couldn't get over the change in her. She wasn't happy, that was evident. Why was she going to marry this man of her parents' choosing?

'I thought it was going to be later, when you had been presented?'

'Well, it was—but things turned out differently. You see, Lizzie, my parents are anxious for me to make a good marriage—I'm their only daughter. They have oodles of money. I expect that's become fairly obvious to you?'

'Well...'

'Soap. That's where it was made—the money. In soap.'

She lit a cigarette as Lizzie watched. She didn't remember her smoking in the old days.

'Well, Josh—he's the man I'm going to marry—comes of a good line. Good family,' she stressed with a faint sneer. 'Broke, mind you. Not a bean, and we're buying our way into the aristocracy, isn't that fun? His family needs the money, and mine wants the prestige. Yes, it's still done, in this day and age. It's still done. So there it is.'

'But you don't have to, do you?' Lizzie cried. 'What would happen if you refused?'

'I couldn't. I love my parents, it is their dearest wish, and anyway. I'm not averse to the idea—just averse to Josh.' And Sarah laughed grimly.

'But why couldn't you wait a while? Until you are really sure?'

'Because I'm damaged goods,' Sarah said with an attempt at a grin, stubbing her cigarette out on a Chinese plate which stood on a nearby table. Lizzie got up and threw it in the fire grate, clearing the mess away automatically.

She couldn't answer for she didn't know what to say.

'Aren't you going to ask me what I mean?' Sarah suddenly turned her back on Lizzie.

'Yes, miss.'

'When you came for the interview I was resting in the country after having had...' And Lizzie's colour paled as she realised what Sarah was about to say.

'A miscarriage?' she whispered.

Sarah nodded. 'It's called an abortion—and you were right. I was pregnant and couldn't hide it. I was so sick everyone knew there was something wrong, so there seemed to be no alternative but—but to have it done, and hurry the marriage along as soon as possible. Before I did anything else foolish,' she said, and her laugh bordered on the hysterical.

'Oh, Miss Sarah,' Lizzie said sadly.

'Mind you, I did insist on one thing. If I had to marry Josh, I said I must have Lizzie. There—aren't you pleased?'

'Yes, miss. Thank you, miss.'

'It's best to start with a clean slate. My mother would be horrified if she knew I had told you, but now you know, and it's all hands on deck towards the marriage—let's get it over and done with, I say!' She twirled round, her short dress showing captivating legs. 'I shall be free at last! Free from the parents, bless them. And Josh, bless his little cotton socks, will be delighted—he adores me. Everyone will be as pleased as punch. Except me, of course.' And she flung herself down on a chair as if she was exhausted.

'Seems downright cruel to me, miss,' Lizzie said. 'I mean, you don't love him, seems to me you don't even like him—and I don't know how you can think of marrying him, knowing that. You ought to be sure. It's your whole life you might be throwing away.'

'Of course I'm sure, silly.' Sarah sat up straight and blew her nose. 'Oh, I'm a clot. You must think I'm a poor weak thing. But I'm not really. I just thought everything was going to be such fun—and it isn't.'

'It'll all come right,' Lizzie comforted. 'You'll see—'

'How do you know?' Sarah asked.

'Because I'm clever!'

CHAPTER 5

Lizzie stood looking down at the portmanteaux and boxes which were ready to be taken to King's Cross for the overnight journey to Scotland.

There were clothes the like of which she had never seen before folded in reams of tissue paper: evening gowns, day dresses, tweeds to be worn on the moors, shoes and soft leather boots of every description, to say nothing of the exquisite undies. Of pure silk, made and embroidered by convent nuns and purchased at a small exclusive salon in Bond Street, it had been a joy to handle them, to feel the soft fabric slip through her fingers and examine the fine, beautiful workmanship of the embroidery and appliqué work. Cami-knickers so delicate, trimmed with hand-made lace; slips she could crumple in one hand; transparent nightgowns of filmy ninon silk; and crepe-de-chine negligees such as she had never seen before, even in the most exclusive shops, and almost all purchased in Paris, where she had gone earlier that month on a shopping expedition with Miss Sarah and her mother.

And what an eye opener that had been!

The wide streets of Paris were like nothing Lizzie had imagined: the lights of an evening, the hotels, the taxis, the scent of French perfume, the general air of gaiety and good living. And the fashions! She had thought London was the epitome of all her dreams but just as she settled down to make her home there, she had been whisked off to this fairy tale city. People said it was a feminine city, and she could quite understand why.

The shops! Accompanying Miss Sarah and her mother, waiting quietly in the background to do their bidding, Lizzie walked closely behind them as they chatted and discussed and then purchased. In the shops and salons there was a deferential attitude, as though they were the most important people in the world—as indeed they were, thought Lizzie grimly, with all that money to spend.

The elegant boxes were delivered to the hotel and soon were being packed up and sent on their way to England, while even more shopping was done. Miss Sarah would return from the great couture houses like Worth and Molyneux and Jacques Fath with excited descriptions of the gowns she had ordered. And it was a strange thing, Lizzie thought, that during all these wonderful four days in Paris, Joshua, Lord Devenoke's name was never mentioned.

Well, she was learning all the time.

Then the big day arrived and Sarah stood before her, a vision in white. Her fair hair was carefully dressed in a long page boy style, curling under and towards her cheeks; her gown of silver and white brocade clung to her slim figure. The deep neckline suited her. Her hair acted as a frame for her lovely face, and she wore the pearls that her husband-to-be had given her for a wedding present. They seemed to come to life against her skin, and she wore pearl stud earrings, a gift from her father.

The dress had long narrow sleeves, was tight-waisted and billowed out from the knees down while on her hair, secured by a wreath of orange blossom, she wore Lord Devenoke's family veil of Brussels lace.

Sarah was a vision of loveliness. Only Lizzie knew of the tears the night before, the avowals that she couldn't go through with it. Then after a tempestuous storm of weeping, she had dried her eyes and made herself a promise from which, she said, she would never look back.

Lizzie thought she had never seen anyone look more lovely on her wedding day, and as she followed Sarah down the winding staircase, carrying her train to where the bouquet of roses awaited her, saw Sarah's father, an immaculate short figure in morning dress, hold out his arm for her to take. He looked as proud as a peacock, Lizzie thought, and swallowed hard. It really was an emotional moment. Well, that was something that would never happen to her, for she had never known a father.

Then Sarah had gone, following her eight bridesmaids, and Lizzie was left to clear up and fold away and prepare the room ready for the going away outfit. There was so much to do that in no time at all, it seemed, the wedding was over, and Lady Sarah was back downstairs greeting her guests. Looking over the banisters, Lizzie saw the young couple, Lord Devenoke looking no more than a boy himself, with his black shining hair and dark good looks. He was the same height as Sarah, and there was no doubt of his feelings for her as he stood near her, his eyes never leaving her face. Soon, Lizzie thought, she will be coming upstairs to change.

Sarah came back into the room, closing the door softly and standing with her back pressed against it, her blue eyes unnaturally bright, her lips quivering with excitement.

'It's over, Lizzie,' she said, and took a deep breath. 'I am Lady Devenoke—and I tell you, it's not a bad feeling. I thought Father was going to burst into tears when Josh put the ring on my finger. I saw his shoulders heave beside me. You know, he's quite a sentimental old thing.'

'Congratulations, milady,' Lizzie said, and Sarah smiled.

'It all went rather well, don't you think?' she asked, sinking into a chair and examining a neat foot from which she had kicked off a white satin shoe, then stretching out her hand to look at the rings on her fingers, her blue eyes sparkling like sapphires.

'Oh, milady, it was wonderful!' Lizzie

cried, her face slightly flushed beneath the small white cap which sat atop her black curls.

'Yes, thanks to Mama,' said Sarah, getting up and going over to the mirror where she stood regarding herself for a few moments.

Presently as Lizzie watched her face darkened, and she tugged at the pins holding her wreath of orange blossom.

'Milady!' Lizzie cried. 'Here, let me. Sit down here.' And when Sarah flopped into the white damask-covered chair in front of the dressing table, she began to unpin the veil and headdress.

Lizzie kept her eyes on what she was doing, knowing that Sarah was looking crossly at herself in the mirror—probably miles away in her thoughts.

'It was a beautiful wedding, Milady,' she said, a kirbygrip in her mouth. 'His lordship looked so manly standing there beside you. So handsome.'

'Do you think so? Do you think he is handsome?' Sarah asked, as if Lizzie's opinion mattered to her.

'Oh, yes, milady.' What matter if it wasn't really true? He was a good-looking man but with a trace of weakness in his face. It was hard to put a finger on it, but it was evident to the extent that there was no doubt that Sarah would be able to wind him round her little finger—and probably would.

'There.' The veil safely rescued, Lizzie placed it carefully over a chair, to be rolled against creases and stored away ready for the next Devenoke bride.

Free of the veil, Sarah shook her hair and idly began to comb it, while Lizzie undid all the tiny buttons on the back of the dress. She stood up as Lizzie carefully allowed her to stand out of it where it assumed almost a life of its own on the floor.

Lizzie shook her head. 'This is the most beautiful dress I've ever seen.'

While she busied herself with the veil, Sarah stood looking at herself in the mirror: at the pale blue satin camiknickers, the lacy suspenders, the smooth white bosom which protruded slightly above her brassiere. She smoothed the silk against her body and hips, moving slightly as though captivated by what she saw.

She was lovely, Lizzie thought. It was just such a pity that she wasn't happy.

Then, amidst final packing of the honeymoon garments, and seeing Sarah changed into a going away outfit—a suit of navy and dusty pink tweed with a pleated skirt and jacket, navy shoes and a smart little Tyrolean hat pulled down over one eye with a feather springing out of the band—Sarah said goodbye to her parents who stood on the steps with the wedding crowd behind them, and went down the steps to be showered with rose petals and confetti, Lord Devenoke at her side, Lizzie bringing up the rear holding the hat box carefully.

They were on their way to King's Cross to catch the night sleeper to Scotland.

As the train roared its way through the night, Lizzie slept, and wakened at dawn to glorious views of the highlands, where sheep grazed on incredibly green grass and there was not a sign of habitation or a building as far as the eye could see.

They had breakfast on the train, after which Lizzie helped Sarah to dress for her arrival at Devenoke Castle, and glancing at his Lordship saw that his eyes still held the look of anticipation and concealed excitement that she had seen there the day before.

So, she thought, he hadn't demanded his rights as yet. His pleasure was still to come.

Then they arrived at the station where several cars were waiting to receive them, and as if in a dream Lizzie found herself in one of them with a manservant who spoke with such a strong Scots accent that she could hardly understand him.

He was a footman, she gathered, in Devenoke Castle, the family seat of the Devenoke family, and when the castle finally appeared in the distance, Lizzie's heart leapt at the sight of such beauty.

It was like something out of a fairy tale, built of stone with turrets and long narrow windows, and the drive up to it was so long, she imagined she was still on the road.

A retinue of servants waited to greet them, and holding back, Lizzie watched as they curtsied and greeted Lord Devenoke's new bride.

And him, she thought, not much more than twenty-one himself.

Then it was into the great cool flagged hall where the heads of deer looked down from dark walls and a huge fire burned in an enormous fireplace, and she was so overwhelmed that it was almost with a feeling of gratitude that she met Mrs Groom the housekeeper who took her upstairs still carrying the hat box and Lady Sarah's precious jewel case.

The stairs were wide and stretched endlessly, past portraits lining the walls and sconces with their dimmed lights. At the top Lizzie found herself on a great landing where red patterned carpets lay on the floor and several suits of armour stood around. When Mrs Groom turned round,

Lizzie smiled at her, and received a dour nod of the head in return. The housekeeper led her towards a brass-embossed door where she inserted a key from the chain round her waist and opened it.

'This is the mistress's bedroom,' she said in her soft highland accent, gesturing to Lizzie to follow her into the room. A fire burned in the grate for it was a cold day—much colder than in London, Lizzie decided—and in the centre of the room was a high four poster bed hung with crimson drapes and a counterpane. Out of the mullioned windows Lizzie could make out grass as far as the eye could see, and in the distance a faint line of shining blue. It must be the sea, she decided, and turned to thank Mrs Groom.

'If ye've not all ye want, let me know,' she said. 'Ye'll find the bathroom through here.' And she opened a door to reveal the largest bathroom Lizzie had ever seen. High-ceilinged like the bedroom it held a white enamel bath on legs, and a large square wash basin standing in a brass surround. Towel rails were hung with soft white towels and there were bowls of soap and a vase of white scented lilies.

'I think ye'll find everything here, miss,' Mrs Groom continued. 'Your own room is straight above this one, on the second floor. Ye'll be wanting something to eat,

I daresay, so if ye'd like to come doon to the kitchen when ye're ready—'

'Thank you, Mrs Groom. That will be fine,' Lizzie said, noticing that the luggage and boxes had already arrived. In the dressing room an ironing board had been put up and an iron stood waiting to be used.

Couldn't be easier, Lizzie thought. In a moment I'll wake up and find I'm dreaming.

She unpacked and ironed the clothes, putting things away in the vast wardrobes which stood around the dressing room. She eyed the great bed quizzically and wondered what it would be like to make love in that as Miss Sarah would. She must remember to call her 'Milady'.

When Sarah arrived upstairs, she flung her handbag and furs on to the bed and collapsed into a chair. 'God, I'm exhausted!' she cried, without even looking round to see what the room was like. Lizzie marvelled.

Sarah glanced at her minute watch, encrusted with fine diamonds. 'I wonder what his lordship has planned for today?' she said, going to the dressing table where she dabbed at her delicate nose with a swansdown powder puff.

'Here, help me get out of this,' she said to Lizzie, who by now knew most

86

of Sarah's moods, and recognized this one which could mean trouble. Sarah glanced around the rooms then went over to the window.

'God, how boring!' she said. 'These Scottish castles give me the creeps—so dark and old fashioned. Oh, Lizzie, what will we do with ourselves while we are up here? I shall go mad, stuck out here in the middle of nowhere!'

'Now, Miss Sarah—milady—I'm sure there are lots of lovely things planned for you to do. Tomorrow for instance, Mrs Groom says you'll be taking a picnic out on to the moors.'

Sarah gave a little scream. 'I can't bear it,' she cried, stuffing her hankie into her mouth. 'Oh, Lizzie, give me some of your courage—'

Lizzie studied her. Did she really feel that desperate or was she acting? Sarah tended to sometimes when things weren't quite to her liking. She was melodramatic, that was the word. Lizzie was very pleased with herself for knowing it. She had read and absorbed so many new things since she had worked for the Chamberlains. Knowing she was going to have lots of spare time, she had armed herself with books with which to while away the time. The staff in London had told her she would find it very dull in Scotland. And if she found it dull, what on earth must Miss Sarah be thinking—and her with a new husband?

'Now, milady,' Lizzie said bracingly. 'You are very lucky. I wish I was in your place! A wonderful wedding, a honeymoon in a Scottish castle...'

'Oh, what do you know about it?' Sarah stormed, sending a pillow across the room.

'And that, milady,' Lizzie said calmly, 'is the quickest way I know to get my notice.'

'Oh, Lizzie!' But she had gone into the dressing room where the sound of drawers being opened and closed was enough to tell Sarah that she was extremely busy and not to be disturbed.

That evening Sarah had recovered her usual bright spirits. She appeared for dinner in a long black velvet gown which showed off her shapely figure, her white skin like ivory, pearls and long diamond earrings glowing. Lizzie had done her hair in an Edwardian upswept style which suited her, and on her breast she wore a pheasant brooch made of rubies, emeralds and sapphires. The young couple sat at either end of a long table, candles throwing a soft light over the old oak, a fire burning in the great stone fireplace, while Robby the footman stood at one end of the table, and

Margaret the serving maid at the other.

Conversation was stilted for both the newlyweds were apprehensive of the prospect of the night before them—but for different reasons.

When Sarah came up to bed, Lizzie had her nightgown ready, the negligee thrown carelessly on the bed. It was of finest satin, pale pink, trimmed with lace. Sarah stepped into it and Lizzie handed her the scent spray. Then waited as she made her way to the turned down bed where snow white pillow slips, edged with ruffled lace, shone in the half light.

'Good night, milady,' said Lizzie, closing the door behind her, and waited in the dressing room until she heard his lordship leave his own room.

Her heart was pounding as though it was she herself who was going to be deflowered. She grinned to herself.

Well, not exactly deflowered, she thought. Still—I know what I mean.

Joshua Devenoke took off his dressing gown and climbed in beside his new bride. It was the most wonderful thing that had ever happened to him. To have and to hold this beautiful young creature to worship her, to have her for his wife. He put his arms round her and gathered her to him.

He kissed her gently, then again, and held her close, her head upon his breast, as he murmured, 'Sarah, Sarah!' It might have been afterwards instead of before, she thought. Her head was spinning—after all, how well did she know him?

'Josh,' she whispered, taking his hand and putting it on her breast, her other hand moving over his body. She leaned over and kissed him as only she knew how, and when he began to fondle her, guided him as, unbidden, memories of other nights flooded her brain. Archie's handsome face looking down into hers... It can only get better, she thought. After an abysmal few minutes, when she thought she must be dreaming, so bitter was her disappointment, Josh rolled off her and lay at her side where he soon slept like a baby.

She wept, soundlessly, far into the night.

CHAPTER 6

The next morning Sarah was subdued, and it was obvious by her eyes that she had been weeping. Feeling desperately sorry for her, Lizzie went about her duties without asking any questions. As the days passed, she saw Sarah gradually grow more cheerful, her good humour restored, but she was not her old self. That's what marriage does for you, I expect, Lizzie pondered, not knowing exactly what to expect when you slept with a man, but having a fairly good idea. A lord might be different, she supposed.

She liked Josh though, on the odd occasions she saw him. She had less contact with him than any of the other servants, being Sarah's personal maid. She passed him on the landings when he would nod to her, his dark eyes serious, hands behind his back like an elderly gentleman. But after a week or two she saw a change in him, he seemed more relaxed. He and Sarah were both out most of the time, and Lizzie was busy preparing her ladyship for one thing or another. A country house party, days on the moors, shooting parties—which Sarah loathed—sightseeing trips, picnics, and visiting friends and relatives.

Lizzie had a lot of free time, which when not spent mending and keeping Sarah's wardrobe up to scratch, she passed in reading or walking. She had made friends with one or two members of the staff, mainly Jamie, a young footman, who thought she was the prettiest girl he had ever seen. But at eighteen he had his way to make in the world for he had ambitions to become a butler to the royal family.

The prospect of this filled most of his young life.

One Sunday when Sarah had gone to an exalted house party Jamie took Lizzie to Fort William for the day. The town was quiet but they found somewhere to eat and afterwards walked by the sea, then out of the town where they sat on a grassy knoll to admire the view.

'That's my village over there,' said Jamie, pointing to a cluster of cottages in the dip between two hills.

'Golly,' Lizzie said. 'It must be so quiet, cut off from anywhere.'

'Aye, it was—it is,' he said. 'I canna imagine being born anywhere else—I'd not been anywhere else 'til I came to Devenoke.'

'How old are you, Jamie?' Lizzie asked.

'Eighteen,' he said. 'That's older than ye, isn't it?'

'Yes, I'm not sixteen yet. Soon will be though, in three weeks,' she said.

'Do you want to stay with her ladyship when they return to London?'

'Yes, of course,' Lizzie answered, although in fact she was not quite sure.

'I'm certain glad they didn't ask me to go. I couldna bear to go to London.'

'Really?' Lizzie asked incredulously, turning her brilliant green eyes on him.

He really wanted to kiss her, but was

not sure what she'd say. He'd never seen anyone with such milky white skin and black shiny hair, which today she wore tumbling about her shoulders. He thought it should have been the other way about, Lizzie as Lady Devenoke, being waited upon by Sarah, and played with the idea for a few moments.

'I expect you'll be married by the time you're my age,' he said.

'I won't,' Lizzie retorted firmly. 'I got things to do with my life.'

'Such as?' he asked. What could she have to do beside getting married?

'Things,' Lizzie said. 'I'm not spending the rest of my life waiting on other people, that's for sure.'

London people were strange, he thought. Even though she had lived in Brighton for a long time, she was still south of the border. They were a strange lot, what he'd seen of them.

'Come on,' he said, getting up and pulling her to her feet. And then seeing her standing there, half captive, kissed her swiftly on the mouth.

'Oh!' Lizzie put a hand to her lips. It was the first kiss she had ever had. His lips had been soft, and not at all as she had imagined. When she said nothing further, he took her in his arms and kissed her again.

'Oh, Lizzie, you're so pretty,' he said. 'I couldna help it.'

Her green eyes shone as she smiled back at him. 'Don't apologise. I quite liked it.' But when he went to take her in his arms again, she gave him a gentle push.

'No, Jamie. Let's run.' And feeling exhilarated at receiving her first kiss, her heart light as a feather, she ran down the hill, hair flying, with Jamie in hot pursuit.

He soon caught her and breathless they stood facing each other, laughing with the sheer exuberance of youth. Then hand in hand they walked back to the bus stop for the long journey home.

She sat with her arm through his on the bus, and every now and again they would look at each other and smile, until they reached the gates of Devenoke Castle, when they walked decorously up the drive side by side.

Lady Sarah was in a good mood when Lizzie returned on Sunday evening. She flung her tweed coat on a chair and began to unpeel her leather gauntlets, blue eyes sparkling. She had been quite reserved with Lizzie of late but now she was her old self, treating her more as a confidante than a lady's maid.

Lizzie stood by taking the things as Sarah took them off, waiting to hear more.

'You'll never guess who was there!' Sarah said, her blue eyes shining.

Lizzie shook her head.

'The Prince of Wales!' And Lizzie gasped in disbelief and wonder. 'And, Lizzie, his lady friend—Mrs Simpson.'

Lizzie frowned. 'Who's she?' she asked, never having heard of her.

'Oh, well, no one important.' Sarah decided not to elaborate on this. 'Just his lady friend of the moment—you know how he is. First one, then the other. After all, if a prince of the realm can't please himself, who can?'

But her blue eyes were staring unseeing in front of her, and Lizzie knew she harboured some secret thoughts. Something had happened to give her that look, she knew Sarah of old. The Prince of Wales—well!

Lizzie was dying to ask if he had spoken to her mistress, but dare not. She hadn't long to wait to find out, though.

Sarah inserted a cigarette in an amber holder and blew out a long stream of smoke as Lizzie wrinkled her nose.

'We danced,' she said dreamily. 'One fox trot—apparently he likes fox trots—and really I felt shivers going down my spine when he held me.'

In for a penny, Lizzie thought, unable to curb her curiosity further.

'What's he like, milady?' She laid Sarah's gloves on the table and busied herself with hangers for the clothes.

'Not awfully tall—not as tall as I am,' Sarah said, dreamily. 'But he has the most amazing blue eyes, light blue eyes, and when he looks at you...mmmmm!' and she shivered deliciously.

She suddenly seemed to remember where she was and came down to earth.

'Do be careful when you unpack my cream crêpe dinner gown—there's a slight rent in the hem where I caught my foot in it.'

'Of course, milady.'

'And you can run my bath now. The journey was hot and tiresome—'

'Yes, milady.'

It was enjoyable enough, this job, Lizzie thought, kneeling over the bath and watching the water pour in. You didn't need soap with this highland water, it was so soft. She added bath salts and a splash of Sarah's Bal de Versailles perfume to the water, then almond oil, and made sure everything was to hand: the sponge, the loofah, the soft towels hot on the towel rail. Then she returned to the dressing room to deal with the rest of the weekend's unpacking.

That evening she sent yet another card to Nancy who was still at the orphanage.

She knew her friend would like the lovely views on the picture postcards—they looked almost unreal. When they arrived back in London, Lizzie would go to see her on her first free day.

They had been in residence for six weeks at Devenoke Castle when Lizzie was told that they would be returning to London at the week end.

'We shall be living in his lordship's town house in Hyde Park Square, quite near my old home.' And Sarah saw Lizzie's look of astonishment.

'What is it? What's the matter?'

Lizzie was quite overcome by the coincidence of it all.

'That's where my mother was in service!'

'Really?' Even Sarah was surprised. 'Perhaps she was with my husband's family?'

'I don't know, milady. Of course, it was a long time ago, before I was born.'

'Oh.' Sarah had lost interest.

Lizzie could hardly contain her excitement. Just imagine—in the same square! She had forgotten the number but knew without a doubt it was Hyde Park Square. She couldn't wait to get back to London.

There was a great deal of packing to do, even more than they had brought for her ladyship had purchased lengths of Scottish tweed to be made up in London, and the softest of cashmere sweaters and skirts. It took almost all day for Lizzie to see to everything, and she was glad when the car arrived to take her and the hatboxes and the jewel case to the station where she would catch the overnight train.

She had no feeling of regret at leaving the highlands. Much as she had liked them, she had a feeling of insecurity within such wide open spaces, and longed for the narrow confines of the city. She smiled as she remembered Jamie's goodbye kiss—they had promised to write to each other, but now she was on her way home, she doubted if they would.

The Hyde Park Square house turned out to be very similar to the one lived in by the Chamberlains—tall and narrow, on five floors from basement to attic. Perhaps smaller than Sarah's old home, it was quietly elegant, with none of the Chamberlain grandeur. Lizzie recognised this, pleased with herself that already she could tell the difference between old money, as she had heard the servants call it, and new. Her room was on the top floor, small with a sash window which she was able to push up and down. She was able to look out over the roofs of London, and see into the tiny back gardens which had a surprising number of leafy trees, already gold and amber and brown with the onset of autumn.

There was much to do on their return. The house had been taken over by the new bride and there were many changes to please her, although Sarah's husband had lived there quite happily before his marriage. Sarah had had the bedroom re-decorated, which meant everything had been cleared out while they were away, and it was Lizzie's job to settle in and line the cupboards and drawers and set out the new mistress's bedroom and dressing room to her liking and satisfaction.

Sarah was a different person these days. Mature, cool, a little distant—only natural, Lizzie thought. After all, she was Lady Devenoke now, and someone of importance. She had assumed many responsibilities as Lord Devenoke's wife, various hostessing and charitable tasks being passed on to her by his mother, Laura, Lady Devenoke.

Lizzie often wondered how the newly married couple got on, for apart from dining together and going out into the social whirl, they had little time together. Sarah never mentioned Josh to Lizzie. But then, Lizzie reasoned, why should she? She was Sarah's personal maid, and that was the end of it. They made a handsome couple, and sometimes she saw their pictures in the *Tatler* or the *Sketch*, with Lady Sarah looking absolutely stunning. Lizzie was quite proud that she had dressed her. Sometimes she suggested alterations, a last-minute tweak here and there, an adjustment to a hat. 'What would I do without you?' Sarah sometimes cried, but Lizzie knew it was a momentary thing. The old camaraderie and youthful humour that had been between them had gone. And no wonder, she thought. That's only right.

Christmas came nearer, and Sarah gave her some money and a tweed suit which was almost new. With a few tucks here and there, Lizzie was delighted with it.

She had been kept so busy with Sarah's new social life that she had been run off her feet, but just before Christmas Sarah unexpectedly offered her the day off. Lizzie was surprised, but by now recognised that Sarah was liable to do impulsive things.

'Oh, thank you, milady!' she cried, for she knew at once what she would do with it. She would call at the house two doors along and go to see the housekeeper. She had already ascertained that this was the house where her mother had worked. After all, it was not beyond the bounds of possibility that the housekeeper might remember her.

But this was not to be because the

day before her birthday Lizzie received a letter with a Camberwell postmark from Violet Rawlinson, telling her that Nancy had died. She wept as she read it, guilt flooding through her as she faced the fact that she hadn't been to see Nancy since she got back from Scotland—but there had been no time. Even tomorrow, she had planned to do something else. She finished the letter, in which Violet said the funeral was on Thursday, and wondered if Lizzie could possibly get there for two o'clock.

'After all, Lizzie,' she finished up, 'she's got no family. There'll be only you and me.'

She would go of course. Take a train down to Brighton. Oh, why had Nancy died? She was so young. And then she remembered that Nancy had a weak heart. Poor girl—she never really had a chance.

On the train, armed with flowers, Lizzie thought back over the years. Nancy had adored her, and she had made so many promises. Yet Violet, tough-hearted Violet, the bully of the orphanage, had been the one to keep in touch.

How strange it was to see Brighton from the train. Already Lizzie could smell the fresh sea air, and feeling a bit choked, made her way into the town where she had a sandwich and a cup of tea before making her way to the orphanage. She was early, it was only one o'clock, but if she went there first, she would be bound to see someone she knew.

She rang the bell, and one of the girls answered and told her to take a seat inside. She sat on the bench and placed her flowers alongside, and presently was joined by another girl, also carrying flowers. For a moment Lizzie didn't recognise her. Then, trying to hide her surprise, she jumped up, and they embraced, both in tears.

'Oh, Vi!'

'Lizzie!'

They broke away and stared at each other, but it was Lizzie who had the bigger shock. For Violet Rawlinson was quite the young woman, looking old beyond her years. She was in a black suit, very tight fitting, and her hair was a mass of golden curls where originally she had been dark haired. Her eyebrows were plucked to a thin arched line, and she wore heavy make up and glossy scarlet lipstick.

She seemed taller than ever in her six-inch heels, and it flashed through Lizzie's mind that her mother would have said that Violet looked common. But all she could think of was how kind it had been of Vi to come at all.

They smiled at each other broadly, delighted to meet again, and then Miss Hawkes appeared and greeted them.

'Come into my office, girls,' she said, leading the way.

'It is very nice of you to come down for the funeral—a very sad affair,' she said. 'Poor Nancy, she was never really well. She caught a chill, pneumonia set in, and it was all over very quickly.'

Lizzie bit her lip, on the verge of tears.

Miss Hawkes eyed them, two very different girls, each about to make her own way in the world. She had always had a soft spot for Lizzie Bartholomew, but it never did to show favouritism. Besides there was never time for it.

'She had no relatives other than an uncle who I believe is in Australia so I am particularly pleased that you are here. It will be a small private service at St Paul's, and I shall be coming with you. If you would wait here.'

Just the three of them and the vicar stood by the graveside on a bitterly cold day as Nancy's small coffin was lowered into the grave. Violet wept, the mascara running down her cheeks, but Lizzie felt only anger—anger that someone like Nancy had never had a chance. Poor little devil!

They left the flowers at the graveside and made their way back to London, their usual high spirits dampened by what they had just experienced. But by the time the train reached Victoria, they had recovered enough to talk over old times.

'So what're you doing?' Vi asked, looking at this quietly dressed girl. If it hadn't been for her pretty face, you wouldn't have looked twice at her, the way she was dressed.

'I'm a lady's maid.'

'Cor!' Violet exclaimed. 'She give you time orf to come, did she?'

'I had the day off for Christmas shopping.'

'Crikey!' Violet laughed as the train stopped. 'Come on, let's go to Lyons—I'll buy you a cream bun! Let's hop on this bus.'

They walked into the Corner House and sat down at a table where a Nippy served them with a delicious chocolate-covered cream bun.

'Oh, that's good!' Lizzie cried. 'A real treat.' She looked across at Violet, aware that people were looking at her, particularly men.

'You haven't told me what you're doing?' she said presently, drinking her second cup of tea.

'Me? Oh, well—this and that. I started off in Peak Frean's, the biscuit factory, you know, on London Bridge. But after a while I thought, Sod this, so I left. I'm not quite sure what I'm going to do next...'

Lizzie thought she knew what the answer was. She wasn't born yesterday. And if that was what Violet wanted to do, good luck to her. She had guts, and had grown into a really handsome-looking girl.

'Well, I'd best be getting back,' she said, and dived into her handbag. But Violet put out a hand.

'No, my treat,' she said. 'Honest.' And looked straight at Lizzie, who realised she had never known what nice eyes Vi had. Huge lavender-coloured eyes with little specks in them.

'Thanks, Vi,' she said. 'See you then. Happy Christmas.'

'You too, all the best,' Violet said, watching her go. Then she got up and went to the Ladies' Room.

When she emerged, she had repaired her make up. Her eyes were sparkling and scarlet lipstick shone on her wide mouth. The seams of her stockings were dead straight above the very high heels, and the low neck of her blouse showed off her artificial pearls to perfection.

'Taxi,' she called, on her way to the West End.

Lizzie, though, was still upset and angry. It had been like a bad dream, the whole thing. Brighton, the orphanage, even Vi—to say nothing of the funeral and that small coffin.

105

It was another world. How lucky she was to be out of it. She'd put it behind her, which was the best thing.

There was one thing she knew now, though. She was more determined than ever to get on in this world—and not by Violet's means either. When the time, or the chance, came she would leave her position and make her own way. She didn't intend to wait on other people all her life. Let them wait on her for a change!

CHAPTER 7

In the first-floor drawing room in Hyde Park Square, Isabel Lister sat waiting for her father to appear. These days it took so much longer for him to dress, and he insisted that she accompany him to his club, even though it usually meant she had to turn right round and come home again. But what else did life consist of for her but taking care of this very difficult old man?

How different things had been when her mother had been alive, but that was all so long ago. No good dwelling in the past. Isabel had been brought up at a time when filial duties took precedence over everything else. First her mother's long illness, and now her father, who was becoming more and more irascible with his increasing loss of memory and the physical pain of arthritis. Poor Father, he didn't deserve this, and it was her own fault if she hadn't gone out and made a life for herself after the war, that terrible war which saw the death of her beloved Rudi, and Edmund, her only brother. She had had ample time since then, but neither the opportunity nor the inclination. She was her own worst enemy.

A small slim woman of forty-two, she had given up all thought of marrying now. Who would she meet, at this age? So many men had been killed in the war, and at a time when she might have married, the demands made on her by her parents had precluded romance. Voluntary work when possible, and the ongoing care of her father, were what took up her time nowadays.

She heard him call from the hall downstairs.

'I'm coming, Father!'

'Where were you?' he asked irritably. Just the sight of her sometimes was enough to put him in a temper. There had been occasions in the past when he had wanted to shake her. 'Do something, my girl! Do something with your life!' But he had never spoken to her like that and could hardly do so now, for what would he do without her?

Watching her stand there, putting on her gloves, he thought she was nothing like her pretty mother had been at that age. Dun-coloured. Dull. With her heather tweed suit and pull on felt hat, she belonged in the country rather than town.

Isabel looked through the lace curtains. 'The car is here, Father.'

'Then come along.'

His gold-topped cane rapped on the tiled floor of the hall. She opened the front door and guided him through it, then helped him down the steps. Before they reached the bottom, however, she stood rooted to the spot. Standing at the entrance to the area steps was a girl she recognised—or thought she did. Her father had stopped too, momentarily, but went on regardless while Isabel was left to watch the girl descend the steps. What tricks the imagination played! For a moment she thought she was looking at Mary, the young Irish maidservant they had employed during the war. This girl was the living image of her: those same dark curls, the lovely face and magnetic eyes. She had met them briefly before the girl turned away. Of course it wasn't Mary—how could it be? It was years ago, and Isabel made an effort to calculate. Seventeen, eighteen years ago. This girl was about the age Mary was then.

'Come along, what are you waiting for?' Her father's irritation was obvious, and she hurried to him, taking his arm.

Once inside the car, she tucked the plaid blanket over his knees and they both sat looking out of the window, Isabel busy with her own thoughts until the car stopped in St James.

The chauffeur opened the door and helped her father alight. She took his arm and helped him to the door of his club where the commissionaire took over.

'Four o'clock,' her father said to her without preamble.

'Yes, Father.' And getting back in the car, Isabel waited for the chauffeur to take her back home, her thoughts still in the past.

She took off her gloves and laid them on the hall table, putting her hat alongside. Looking at herself in the mirror, she saw a woman in her early-forties, perhaps looking older, neatly dressed, her hair once very golden now faded to an ash blonde, softly waving. Tired blue eyes reflecting her feelings.

That girl...the sight of her had really disturbed Isabel and set all sorts of thoughts racing through her head. What had she wanted downstairs in the servants' quarters? Was she still there? And she went upstairs to the drawing room, going over to the window where she could see if and when the girl left.

She sat down by the table in the window, her mind in a whirl. The war years—and before the war, that wonderful summer of 1914 when she had been young and oblivious of anything that might be going on in the world outside. Children in families like hers saw little of the world. It was easy to say afterwards, well, you knew it was coming—that war was inevitable—but Isabel had not.

In June 1914 she had gone to stay with a cousin of her mother's who had married an Austrian count. He had large estates along the River Danube in Austria, close to the Czech border, and an extensive family, including Rudi, a little older than herself. Nineteen to her eighteen. Inevitably, they had fallen in love.

He was so fair, a golden boy, his skin the colour of a ripe peach. That summer they worked side by side in the vineyards, watering the young vines that grew from the schloss high up on the hill almost down to the water's edge. The sun had shone down on them, hot and life giving; the skies remained blue. They knew nothing of any rumours of war. Isabel's only wish was that she could stay on, if not forever, then at least until the harvest later in the year, but it was not to be. At the end of June Archduke Ferdinand of Austria was assassinated at Sarajevo by a Bosnian student, and the whole world was turned upside down. Three days later her father summoned her home. 'At once', had been his message, and she had no choice but to do his bidding.

She and Rudi had lain in the long grass, bodies touching, lips meeting, his vows of eternal love setting her young body on fire. She relived the memory now and her face softened.

That night, when she felt her heart was breaking, Rudi's father was unusually serious. Not only was she to go home, but his two eldest sons, Rudi and Johann, were to be called up into the German army as conscripts.

Never as long as she lived would Isabel forget the journey home, nor the news that was about to break on the world, that by 4 August England was at war with Germany.

Not only had she been parted from her young lover, but soon her beloved brother Edmund had been called up into the army, and for two long years fought in France.

Isabel looked out of the window from behind the white lace curtain. There had been no sign of the girl coming back up the area steps. Perhaps she had already left. It was incredible, the likeness. Was it possible there was a connection?

Mary Daly had been with the family two years, fresh from Ireland, as pretty a girl as you could wish to meet and a favourite maid of Isabel's mother. As for her brother Edmund, when he was around those lovely green eyes of Mary's would look down shyly. Surely Isabel wasn't the only one to see it? But perhaps it was because she was so much in love herself, although had she but known it her beloved was already dead. Isabel was relieved in a way when Edmund left for France with his regiment. In September, with a slight leg wound, he had come home on leave, and then she had been sure. Had she been the only one who heard him tiptoe up the stairs to the attic rooms long after everyone was asleep?

Who could blame him? Fighting in France, perhaps about to die, seeking solace from a pretty young servant girl at home.

Then he had gone back to the front.

By November Mary was going about her duties in a very lack-lustre way, her green eyes dull, dark shadows beneath them, her face pale. Then came the day when Isabel's mother told her that Mary was leaving. To be married, she said. She had a nice young man apparently, a soldier who had enlisted, and before he left for France he would marry her.

Isabel had been astonished. How could Mary marry some other man when she was in love with Edmund? Only someone as young as herself could imagine that any good would come of Mary's friendship with her brother. But being young and romantic, Isabel saw no reason why Mary and her brother should not marry—what did it matter that she was a servant girl?

It was not until long after, when she had grown up a bit and recognised the fact that Mary had probably been pregnant, that her curiosity was aroused. If she was pregnant, whose baby had she been carrying? Isabel had kept this doubt at the back of her mind all these years—but really she had nothing to go on. Perhaps Edmund had never crept up those stairs as she imagined. Perhaps Mary had been in love with her soldier boy. Isabel would never know.

But now she had come face to face with a young girl who was the exact image of Mary Daly as she had been in those far off war days.

She started as she saw the girl come up the area steps, pause for a moment to look up at the house, then walk on. Isabel watched her walk a little way, head held high, tall and proud in her bearing—just like Mary—when she suddenly disappeared down the area steps of the house next-door but one.

Isabel dropped the lace curtain. Perhaps she was calling from one house to another selling things. And yet—

Oh, the tragedy of war! Rudi killed on the battlefield, their promises to each other never to be realised. She had never got over it, never tried to find anyone else. What was the point? Her one true love was dead, and over in France men were being killed in the trenches in hundreds of thousands. The newspapers printed long lists of dead and wounded daily.

Isabel had got used to the idea that she would be left on the shelf. Had almost wanted it. To look after her mother, who had been ill for a long time, and when she died to take care of her father. How often she had been tempted to say: 'Mother, do you remember Mary, our parlourmaid? When she left was she pregnant?' But she daren't. In those days such things were never mentioned between mother and daughter. Mother would have been horrified.

She sighed and glanced at her watch. Just gone three. She would have time to ask Mrs Baines, the housekeeper, about her caller. In the most casual way of course. Before she went to get her father.

She rang the bell on the side table, and smiled when Mrs Baines entered the room in answer to her call.

'Ah, Mrs Baines. This afternoon I saw a young woman going down the area steps as we were going out—do you know what she wanted?'

'Yes, miss. Bartholomew—that was her name. She came to see if anyone remembered her mother who used to work here, oh, ever such a long time ago—long before my time.'

But the colour had receded from Isabel's cheeks.

'Bartholomew, you say?'

'Yes, miss. Pretty girl, she was. Works at Lord Devenoke's house as a lady's maid.'

'I see.' Isabel's heart was beating fast. 'Did she say what her mother's name was? I might remember her, although I was young at the time,' she added vaguely.

'Yes, Mary—Mary Daly, miss.' And Isabel thought her heart would stop beating.

'Yes. I seem to recall the name. I thought she looked a little familiar.'

She smiled across at Mrs Baines. 'Thank you, you may go. I am just off to collect Father—we shall be in to tea.'

'Yes, miss.'

When the door closed behind her, Isabel

115

sagged back in the chair. After all this time.

For a few days she watched at the window, but there was no further sighting of the girl. Only Lady Devenoke coming and going, sometimes on her own, sometimes with her husband. Isabel imagined being a lady's maid to the new Lady Devenoke would be a full-time job.

She was rewarded on Thursday afternoon, when soon after lunch she saw the girl leaving the house by the area steps, wearing a fashionable dress with matching jacket, and a perky little hat perched on her black curls. Isabel watched her make her way down Hyde Park Street towards the park.

Since Isabel herself frequently took a walk in the park, she decided that she might do just that, and right away. It took a matter of moments to put on her hat and gloves and leave the house, knowing she had an hour before picking up her father from his club.

She strolled to where she could see the girl in the distance walking towards the Round Pond. Presently she saw her sit down, and as Isabel drew nearer, the girl took a book from her pocket but left it unopened, staring into the distance, a smile playing round her pretty mouth.

As Isabel came nearer her courage deserted her and her intention of sitting beside the girl was abandoned. However, she nodded to her pleasantly. 'Good afternoon,' she said, and the girl answered her. And Isabel walked on.

Well, she had broken the ice, she thought, as with hurried steps she walked home.

Lizzie watched her go, looking after her. Such a nice little woman. She had seen her before, and had an idea she lived in the square. It was nice when people acknowledged you—a friendly gesture.

She had half a mind to walk down to Selfridges to look again at the hand sewing machine she was saving up for. Of late she'd had a lot of time to herself, and had spent it making clothes. She had made the dress and jacket she had on—but, oh, the time it took, all done by hand! That was the best way, she knew, but it would make life so much easier if she had a sewing machine to help out with the seams. Now she found she got quite excited at the idea of designing a dress and making it. She liked to be unusual. The things in the shops that everyone bought were not for her. She liked to be distinctive.

'You know, you have style, Lizzie,' Sarah had said more than once.

Sarah... That was another thing. In the last month things had not been going too well in the house. Lizzie had an idea that things were going from bad to worse in the Devenoke marriage—and them only wed five minutes! She felt so sorry for his lordship. Sarah could be difficult, as Lizzie well knew, while he was always so nice to everyone. The trouble was that Sarah wanted everything her own way, and if she had fallen for that Archie chap, then ten to one his lordship wouldn't appeal to her. He was much too nice. A different kettle of fish altogether. Boring, Sarah said. Well, it depended on the sort of things you liked, and his lordship liked fishing and shooting, or going for walks in the park. Lizzie knew because she had seen him there. You'd think Sarah would try to please him just a little bit.

Well, it was her half day and she wouldn't dwell on their affairs any more. What she was most disappointed in was her visit to the house next-door but one. She couldn't have explained what it was, but she had felt immediately at home there. She thought it was perhaps because she could imagine her mother there as a girl, carrying out her duties as a young parlourmaid. Mary had been there in that house, looking just as she did in the photograph.

Of course, Mrs Baines the housekeeper had only been there ten years, and the manservant, who was a young chap, had been only recently employed, since the old butler had passed on. There was a parlourmaid, whom Lizzie hadn't seen, but she was new too. She sighed. Never mind, she had enjoyed going inside. Although the houses in the square were outwardly identical, inside they were very different.

She watched a small terrier playing with a ball being thrown by its owner, a middle-aged man, who presently came and sat down beside her, the dog on a lead.

He smiled at her, and she thought what nice teeth he had.

The dog tried to jump up on Lizzie's lap, but his owner pulled him away. 'Down, boy!' he said, and Lizzie smiled. There was always so much to see in the park. Now a nursemaid was coming along with her charges, two little girls, so fair and pretty, in pink dresses and white bonnets, the underside lined in pink silk.

A pair of lovers passed her, arms entwined, and Lizzie felt a pang of envy. There really wasn't much opportunity for meeting boys—perhaps it was time that she joined something or took up a hobby. She doubted very much if she would be staying in this job much longer, she was getting very impatient with Miss Sarah and her ways. On the other hand, where would she go, and what would she do? Mind, she was lucky to have such a job, most people would call it easy. But at this moment, she thought, what I would like most would be to get up and run all the way across the park until I was out of breath. The thought brought a smile to her face.

The man eyed her, seeing the lovely green eyes beneath black-fringed lashes, but she didn't look the sort of girl who would be easily picked up. A ladylike girl, he thought.

Lizzie put her book back in its bag and stood up, deciding after all to walk down to Selfridges. There was always lots to see there, even if you couldn't afford to buy anything.

That evening, she laid out Sarah's evening gown with its matching evening bag and furs. She was usually back home around six after going out for the afternoon.

Today she was not back by seven, and when there was a tap on the door, Lizzie was astonished on answering it to find herself facing Lord Devenoke.

It was the first time she had seen him really close to, and she felt herself blushing. He was really nice-looking. He had a kind face, she thought.

'Lizzie?' And she nodded. 'Has her Ladyship returned from her afternoon walk?'

Afternoon walk? That was news to Lizzie.

'No, my lord,' she said.

'Do you know where she went?' he asked, looking very apologetic.

'No, my lord. But I think she was going to have lunch with a friend who was coming up from the country.'

'I see,' he said. Then gave her a brief smile. 'Thank you.'

She closed the door after him. What was all that about? Should she have told him about the friend coming up from the country, for that's where Sarah had said she was going... Oh, fiddlesticks! She couldn't worry about that now. And Lizzie set to work on a fine tear in a lacy slip.

That evening when at last Sarah came in, she changed to go out again in a great hurry. It seemed that her mother had been taken ill and his lordship had been unable to contact her. That night she stayed in her parents' home.

The next day she returned in a state of high dudgeon. When Lizzie asked how her mother was, Sarah turned on her.

'There was nothing wrong with her—she just wanted to make me toe the line and go home! Oh, I'm sick of it all.' And she flung down her gloves and sat at the dressing table in a fury, drumming her fingers on the table top before getting out her cigarettes and lighting one.

'His lordship did seem concerned, and

asked me where you were. I said I thought you had gone to lunch with a friend.'

'Oh, did you? Well, I hadn't, and he had no right—'

'I'm sorry,' Lizzie began, but Sarah stubbed out her cigarette and began to weep.

'It's not your fault,' she said. 'Oh, Lizzie, I'm so miserable.' And Lizzie wondered where she had heard that before. Surely she wasn't pregnant again?

'I can't go on like this,' Sarah said, facing Lizzie. 'You must see that?'

Lizzie shook her head.

'But you haven't been married long, milady.'

'Long enough,' Sarah said grimly. 'Long enough to know that it was all a mistake from start to finish. Oh, I'm not blaming Josh—I feel sorry for him—but I can't be expected to share my life with a man I don't love.'

'You knew that before you married him,' Lizzie said with some asperity, and marched off to the bathroom to rinse through the soft kid gloves.

When she came back, Sarah was rocking herself backwards and forwards on the bed.

'What am I going to do?' she asked, and for the first time, Lizzie felt a sharp stab of impatience. Lively and prepossessing as

122

Sarah was, and much as she liked her, there was a limit. Lizzie didn't intend to wait on her hand and foot for much longer—there had to be more to life than this.

'You must be a right old worry to your mother,' she said, folding her arms and looking hard at her mistress.

'She shouldn't have encouraged me to marry him,' Sarah sulked.

'You could have refused. You just liked the idea of being Lady Devenoke,' Lizzie said daringly, only by now she didn't care, and was surprised when Sarah didn't turn on her in a fury, but nodded in agreement.

'Yes, it was partly that. Still...' And now she brightened. 'Yesterday, I saw Archie Toogood again—he's in a revue at the Haymarket Theatre.'

Lizzie looked at her in disbelief.

'Oh, Miss Sarah!' She quite forgot the new title.

'Well, why not?' Sarah said, pouting. 'Oh, Lizzie, he's wonderful, and he still feels the same about me.' And she hugged herself, lovely blue eyes sparkling now.

'But you're a married woman!' Lizzie said, shocked, and surprised herself by feeling so.

'Oh, my dear Lizzie, when did that ever matter? Look, be a darling and find my new blue dress—the one with the buttons. I shall dine with His Nibs this evening, that'll please him, and before you know it, everything will be all right again. That should shut Mummy up!'

Lizzie stared after her. What an eye opener working for the rich could be. You couldn't tell her Miss Sarah wasn't over the moon to be Lady Devenoke. The trouble with her was, she wanted it all.

CHAPTER 8

Having carried the little sewing machine all the way from Selfridges in Oxford Street, Lizzie made her way up the back stairs and once in her room, dumped the package on the bed. With impatient fingers she untied the string and opened the thick cardboard box wherein sat the coveted machine. It was a Singer hand model, and as bright as a new pin. Lifting it out, she placed it on the washstand and began to read the instructions.

What a difference this was going to make. She had used a machine now and again in the orphanage, but it had been a heavy treadle model. This one was different. There was no end to the things she was going to make.

Of late things had been a little better. Miss Sarah was in a better temper, though Lizzie was quite sure that what was keeping her so were her meetings with Archie. Lizzie had looked up the advertisement and sure enough, he was the male lead in a new revue. There had been a picture of him in the *Evening Standard,* and Lizzie made a face as she read it. Spanish-looking, with glossy black hair and a small moustache. He looks like a dago to me! thought Lizzie. Still, there was no accounting for taste.

Not for me, Lizzie thought firmly. She often wondered what sort of man she would marry—that's if she ever did marry. If Miss Sarah and his lordship's partnership was anything to go by, she'd stay single. There were some nice young men about, only she never got to meet them. Opportunity would be a fine thing.

Tomorrow, after she had had her walk in the park, she was going to Berwick Street market to find some material after seeing a pattern in a magazine for the latest in afternoon dresses.

Of soft crêpe, the dress was cut on the bias, so that it clung to the figure and then fell with a slight flare at the hem. It might be difficult to cut on the cross, but she liked a challenge. Also it would take more material. Still, she had some of Miss Sarah's birthday money over after she had paid for the machine, and material was always cheaper in the market.

She always enjoyed her walk in the park, in the fresh air, with the lovely trees all around and the flower beds stocked with spring bulbs. She looked forward to meeting Miss Lister, the lady from two doors down, who nowadays often came and sat on the seat for a chat. She was so nice, and obviously lonely with nothing to do but look after her father all the time. Forty or so years old. Her life almost over. She had told Lizzie that her fiance was killed in the war. Imagine never having another boy friend. She must have loved him. And they had something in common, for Miss Lister remembered Lizzie's mother. She was very sorry when she heard she had died, tears had come into her eyes—it showed what a kind person she was.

'Oh, my dear!' she had said, so sympathetically that Lizzie herself almost felt like shedding a tear.

'Well,' she'd said, 'she wasn't very strong. She'd been ill a long time.'

'You were so young! What did you do then?'

'Well, I got a job in a young ladies finishing school where I met Miss Sarah—

she's now Lady Devenoke,' Lizzie continued proudly, 'and she suggested I work for her as a lady's maid. So I,' she was just about to say 'come' but remembered in time, 'I came up for the interview with Mrs Chamberlain, that's Miss Sarah's mother, and got the job.'

'And do you like it?'

'Oh, yes, miss.'

'Does it keep you busy?'

'Most of the time, but sometimes I get time to myself—and that's why I saved up and bought a sewing machine.'

Isabel looked quite puzzled.

'Just a small hand machine. I do a bit of dressmaking—I quite like it.'

'Really?' Isabel said faintly. This girl, a mere child, was already working to keep herself as there was apparently no one in the world to look after her.

All Isabel's frustrated motherly instincts came to the fore. Oh, if only... But she knew that wanting to find out about the girl and her background had become an obsession. What if she truly was the child of Mary Daly and the man called Bartholomew? She would have no meaning to Isabel then at all. But suppose—just suppose—she was Edmund's daughter. What then?

Sometimes, when they sat on the seat, Isabel searched the girl's face for some semblance to her brother, but there was none. She was fair skinned but her eyes were Mary's, and her hair too. There was a finesse about her, a ladylike air—but then Mary Daly had had that, too.

'Your father was killed in the war then?' she said, although Lizzie had already told her two or three times.

'Yes, before I was born—he was a soldier. I don't think he was always one, he was in service it says on my mother's marriage certificate. A manservant.'

Isabel's heart sank. So she was barking up the wrong tree. What more logical than that Mary would have had a boy friend, a manservant from one of the neighbouring houses, had fallen in love with him, and they planned to marry. Perhaps Edmund didn't enter into it all?

She felt quite downhearted.

'Well.' She got up and smiled at Lizzie. 'It has been so nice talking to you. I have to go now and collect my father from his club—he's not too well.'

'Oh, I hope he gets better soon,' Lizzie said. She had often seen the elderly gentleman being helped down the steps into a waiting car.

'Thank you, my dear,' said Isabel. He could be your grandfather, she thought, but knew she was off again into the realm of make believe. Her mother had always said she had her head in the clouds.

I don't know which is worse: to be rich and lonely like Miss Lister or rich and naughty like Miss Sarah, Lizzie thought, half smiling as she opted for being rich and naughty. Still, she didn't ought to. She shouldn't treat his lordship the way she does. It's not his fault he's—well, gentle, quiet. But Lizzie supposed it would get on your nerves after a time, especially if you knew young and exciting men like Archie Toogood. Oh, well, time she got back.

'Look, Lizzie,' Sarah said that evening before going out. 'I don't think I want this tweed—the colouring is all wrong for me. It would suit you, match your eyes.'

Lizzie glowed with delight.

'You can have it,' Sarah said nonchalantly. 'You'll be able to make something on your little machine.'

'Thank you, milady.' She had always admired the length of tweed that Sarah had brought back from Scotland.

Sarah had just reached the door, her silver fox cape slung around her shoulders, a small black bag and silver headdress pinned to her fair hair. She looked dazzling.

'Yes, milady?'

'Er—if his lordship asks where I am, you

can say I've gone to see my cousin Rose who is in town.'

Lizzie looked at her. 'You didn't have to bribe me, milady. I'd have done as you asked.'

'Oh, Lizzie, you're a dear. Bye.'

Still, thought Lizzie, I did like that tweed. And humming to herself, she put her ladyship's afternoon clothes away, tidied the bedroom and bathroom, and went upstairs to her room to work on her dress.

Once she'd mastered the machine, she got on like a house on fire. With the pattern pieces laid out on the floor, she would cut out the material, tack the pieces together, machine away at the seams and finish off with hand sewing. One day, when she wore her new dress in the park, Isabel told her how smart she looked, and was very complimentary.

'It seems to me, my dear,' she said, 'that you could do something in that line—I'm sure you could get a job in one of the fashion houses or the big stores. I have often thought that you are wasted as a lady's maid—although I am sure you do it very well,' she apologised hastily.

Lizzie sat thoughtfully. Perhaps that was the answer? Perhaps she could enquire as to what positions were going in the dressmaking world?

'You certainly have a flair for fashion,' Isabel continued. 'You can always tell by the way a girl puts on her hat, or wears a scarf.'

Lizzie thought that was very observant of Miss Lister, while Isabel was thinking she shouldn't encourage her to leave Lady Devenoke since she had no wish to lose sight of this girl. The more she talked to Lizzie and got to know her, the closer she felt to her. She had almost convinced herself now that Lizzie was her brother's child. There was an emptiness in Isabel's heart which she longed to fill.

March came, and with it a bout of very severe weather, when icy cold winds blew round the square, and flurries of snow set people scampering indoors to make up the coal fires and shut out the draughts. The early daffodils in the park were flattened by sudden snowfalls and cruel winds, while only the most hardy took their daily walks in Hyde Park.

When the snow cleared to give way to cold but bright weather, Lizzie took her weekly trip to the park and was disappointed when Miss Lister was not there. During her long sojourn indoors owing to the weather, she had made two more dresses, one of which Miss Sarah had bought, she had thought it so stylish.

'You could go into business making

frocks,' she said, and had hurriedly tried to bite back her words. 'I hope you won't. I don't know what I would do without you, Lizzie.'

How you would manage to have your little outings without his lordship knowing. She was always overcome with a feeling of guilt when she saw him and had to make excuses.

'Oh, I'm not going to do that yet,' Lizzie teased. It wouldn't hurt to keep Miss Sarah in suspense. She relied on her too much. She did, however, often think about changing her job, especially when her ladyship went a bit too far, which happened quite often these days.

Lizzie's birthday came and went, and as the weeks passed she was more and more inclined to ask Miss Lister about her father whom she hadn't seen of late. Was it perhaps a bit presumptuous between a lady and a servant girl? Their friendship was odd to say the least, yet they seemed to have so much in common. Lizzie had become fond of Isabel. Perhaps she could call on the housekeeper and ask after the old gentleman?

Had Lizzie but known it, Isabel was nursing a very sick old man. He had taken to his bed, his chest so weak that the doctor advised him not to go out, and when the bad weather came and bronchitis set in, Isabel began to wonder if he would get better. He seemed to have no strength and no will to live, and frequently talked about her mother, who had been dead for six years, but mostly about her brother Edmund, who had been the light of his life.

Isabel was not surprised when the doctor informed her that he wouldn't be able to go on for long, weak as he was. One morning the nurse who had been engaged to look after him went to his room and found that he had passed away in his sleep. He looked at peace, and while Mrs Baines shed a tear, Isabel was dry-eyed. She wished she could have got closer to him in these past few weeks, but despite many efforts to talk to him, he wanted only to discuss his son or his wife. He never asked Isabel about herself—what she would do with her life when he had gone—or told her what provision had been made for her. She had, however, often read aloud to him from his favourite books which seemed to please him.

Only after the funeral did she break down and weep, realising now for the first time that she was really alone in the world, apart from distant cousins, most of them in the Far East, for the Listers had always been men who went to farflung places to work for King and

Empire. 'Empire builders is what we are,' her father often said proudly. 'My father, and his father before him.'

Isabel was impressed with this, remembering as a child those hot, steamy vacations spent with her parents in Malaya and relatives in Assam, the long boat journeys with Edmund from their schools in England in charge of some responsible person.

When her father's will was read, she realised she had been left comfortably off. Now was the time to do something. She must be strong and determined if she was to get through the rest of her life and make something of it. When a little note arrived through the door from Lizzie, sending her deepest sympathy, Isabel was pleased and that more than anything strengthened her resolve for her future.

Whatever she did, she hoped Lizzie would be part of it. But how to go about it?

Lizzie first heard the news of the old man's death from the housekeeper downstairs. She announced it on the very morning he died—which showed, Lizzie thought, that news in the square travelled like wildfire. Poor Miss Lister would miss him for she had no one else, and Lizzie knew how that felt. Perhaps after a while she would begin to take her walks in the park again? She hoped so.

In August, Sarah informed her that she would not be accompanying his lordship to Scotland for the shooting season. 'Not right away, that is. I shall follow on at the end of the month. My engagement book is full—I can't think how I can fit everything in.'

'You'll manage, milady.' Lizzie had heard all this before.

'Anyway,' Sarah said irritably, 'I just hate shooting parties—that sort of thing. Ghastly. And boring too.'

'Yes, milady.'

'I shall be going to the Somervilles at Aston Park for the weekend—should be interesting. Lady Somerville always invites the most marvellous people.'

'Yes, milady. This weekend?'

'Yes, Lizzie. It's in Surrey so I shall need my tweeds and cashmeres in case it's cold. Oh, and a couple of dinner gowns. You know the sort of thing—country house party—'

'Leave it to me, milady.'

Sarah sighed gratefully. 'Thanks awfully, Lizzie. We shall arrive on Friday evening for dinner and leave late on Sunday afternoon.'

'Yes, milady.'

'You'll have plenty of time to get ready for Scotland.'

'Yes, milady.'

Aston Park sat in the middle of beautiful scenery, undulating hills and woodlands. There was a long drive up to the house which looked as if it had grown out of the land with its weatherbeaten plum-coloured bricks and creeper-covered facade. Lizzie's spirits rose. She always enjoyed these trips to other peoples homes, although sometimes they were a disappointment, especially if they had no heating and inadequate bathrooms which always put Miss Sarah in a bad mood.

This one, though, was a delight. Warm and comfortable, a huge log fire burned in the halls even though it was August, and Miss Sarah's suite was on the first floor, with its own bathroom filled with soft towels, while the bedroom was furnished almost exactly as it had been in the fifteenth century, with a four poster bed, overhanging beams and thick tapestry curtains.

Lizzie hung the clothes and filled the drawers and inspected the bathroom, making sure everything would be to Miss Sarah's liking. Looking over the minstrel's gallery down into the hall below, she couldn't help wishing that she could be part of the scene which would follow later. She wouldn't see the dining hall but could bet it would be laid out with silver and exquisite china and candles—oh, she could imagine it all! After that she might take a peek into the drawing room, and would suggest to Miss Sarah that tonight she wore her black velvet dinner gown, which was strapless and showed off her beautiful fair skin. With those long diamond and sapphire earrings his lordship had given her, and a black velvet band around her throat—no, perhaps the small black velvet hair ornament with the diamond pin.

When everything was laid out and Miss Sarah was resting, Lizzie went down into the kitchen where at least six of the staff were busy, preparing for the pre-dinner drinks, polishing the glasses until they sparkled, and two more sat at the long table preparing vegetables.

'Hallo,' she said. 'I'm Lizzie Bartholomew —Lady Sarah's maid.'

'Sit you down, miss,' said Mrs Sidney the housekeeper, a fat jolly-looking woman with a cottage loaf figure and a neat bun on top of her head. 'When would you like to eat, m'dear! Would you like something now before we really get busy, or wait until later?'

'Now, please,' Lizzie said. 'I'm starving.' Her mouth watered at the scrumptious smell of cooking.

'I've some nice soup, and some cold beef

and salad—or if you can wait until after when there'll be plenty left over—salmon, and the first grouse, I daresay, though not everyone likes game.'

'I'll have the salad,' Lizzie said. 'Oh, and some of that delicious soup I can smell.'

Mrs Sidney ladled out the soup into a bowl and passed it to her as a man came in with a basket of fresh vegetables and tomatoes.

'Right, Sidney,' the housekeeper said, establishing the fact that they were husband and wife. 'Can you find me some lemons?'

'Yes, I'm just on my way to the conservatory,' he said, giving a swift look at Lizzie, whose green eyes sparkled up at him. He touched his cap. 'Evening, miss.'

'Evening,' Lizzie smiled.

'Don't hang about then,' Mrs Sidney ordered.

Lizzie enjoyed it all: the atmosphere, the humour and the fun that existed between them all. It was a happy household—not, she thought, in the least like the kitchen below stairs at Hyde Park Square.

'Quite a few guests this evening,' Mrs Sidney said, sitting down opposite her and taking a bowl of soup for herself. 'A dozen or more. The Moorhouses and the Bensons, and Sir Geoffrey Dunoon.'

There was a little squeal from one of the maids.

'That'll do,' Mrs Sidney said sternly.

'Well, he's smashing,' one of the others said.

'Yes, I grant you that,' Mrs Sidney agreed, looking at Lizzie. 'And your lady is a bit of all right, isn't she? I saw her picture the other day—she's a real beauty.'

'Yes,' Lizzie said proudly, 'she is.'

Afterwards, she made her way up the back stairs to Miss Sarah's room, where the chaise being empty, she calculated her mistress had gone to bathe. Lizzie had left the warm towels ready, and presently Sarah emerged glowing from her bath, scented, skin gleaming like silk, wearing a cornflower blue satin peignoir which exactly matched her eyes. Lizzie thought she had never seen her look so lovely.

'How are you going to have your hair tonight?' Lizzie asked.

'Upswept or down?'

Sarah contemplated herself in the mirror, a small smile playing around her luscious mouth. 'Do you know, I think down,' she said softly.

Her thick hair fell like a curtain of gold, softly framing her face.

She was smoothing cream into her hands which were beautifully shaped, the fingers round and tapering, the filbert nails pointed. She stretched out her hand. 'What shall we have? Scarlet or raspberry?'

'Soft pink,' Lizzie said. 'You don't want to look like a Jezebel.' She always thought Sarah wore her nails too long, and with scarlet polish they looked like talons.

'Oh, Lizzie, you are funny!' Sarah laughed. She was in a very good mood, Lizzie thought, giving a final pat to her hair.

An hour later Sarah was ready, and looked a dream in the long dress cut on the bias, which moulded her figure to perfection, the black velvet band round her creamy throat, the earrings which matched the sparkle in her eyes. Her shoes were black satin with diamante buckles, which shone just below the hem of her dress.

Lizzie felt a pang of envy, which disappeared as fast as it came. She really wouldn't wish to change places with her mistress just to have some of the lovely things which Sarah took for granted.

'There we are then,' said Lizzie, holding out a hand mirror.

Sarah peered at the back of her head. 'Super,' she said, and glanced at her tiny diamond watch.

'I'll ring for you in the morning. I expect it will be late.'

'Yes, milady.'

Lizzie sat at the open window sewing until it got dark. Below her, she could see people on the lawns, smoking or walking round the garden arm-in-arm. It was a beautiful evening, and the strains of music reached up to Lizzie who thought she had never experienced such a magical night. When it was too dark to see, she pulled the curtains to and switched on the light, vowing to finish the dress she was making. Then she would have three finished dresses hanging in her wardrobe—but when would she wear them? One day, she told herself. Let's hope they don't go out of fashion.

She had been given a room on the other side of the bathroom from Miss Sarah's, a small room but comfortable. It was late when she went to bed for she knew she had no need to wake early. Miss Sarah would sleep on, Lizzie knew of old.

She was awakened by a sound and sat up at once, not knowing what it was. It was always difficult to pinpoint noises in a strange house, but presently it came again. It sounded as if someone was making a noisy exit from a bedroom or had fallen against a door.

She smiled to herself as she thought she heard giggling and wondered who else slept on this floor. Unable to get back to sleep, she lay half listening and presently heard the sound of low talking and laughter.

She'd bet some fun and games went on at these house parties, and thought of Lord Devenoke with his honest brown eyes, and almost soulful expression. He'd probably bagged his birds, or whatever it was called, and was sleeping it off as happy as Larry. Then the whispering came again, and low laughter, and Lizzie sat up in bed with a sudden thought. Wasn't that coming from Miss Sarah's room? Then the sound of footsteps. She leapt out of bed silently and tiptoed over to the door. Opening it slightly, she saw Sarah's bedroom door closing behind a man whose face she caught in the gleam from the moon's bright light—a handsome, dark-haired man who carried his shoes in his hand. As he passed her door, unaware that she was there, she closed it softly and stood for a moment, her heart beating fast, the fury mounting.

What a bitch she was! Pretty, lovely Sarah, who looked as if butter wouldn't melt in her mouth and who didn't think twice about cheating that nice husband of hers. So he was dull and boring—that was no excuse.

I'm not going to stay with her, Lizzie thought furiously. I am only helping her to deceive her husband. She might say it's

142

none of my business, I'm paid to do a job, but it is. She will have to manage without me. I've got other things to do with my life. See if I haven't!

She lay awake for a long time but by the morning had cooled down, making a sober decision to leave Miss Sarah's employ.

When her mistress's bell rang at ten-thirty, Lizzie went in to find her still in bed.

'Shall I draw the curtains, milady?' she asked coldly.

'What sort of day is it?' Sarah yawned.

'A beautiful day,' Lizzie answered. And a fat lot she knew about it!

'Then pull them.'

Lizzie did so while Sarah shielded her eyes against the light. She had nothing on, was as naked as a baby, and when she saw Lizzie glance down at the heap of clothes on the floor, the black velvet in a crumpled heap, the cream silk French knickers, the silk stockings, pulled the clothes around her to hide her nakedness.

She sighed loudly. 'I was exhausted when I came to bed—I danced the night away.' She yawned. 'And it was so hot in the night.'

Lizzie picked up the dress and shook it gently, put it over her arm and picked up the underwear, then turned to look at Sarah, who looked back at her with a mixed expression of bravado and apology.

As well you might, milady, Lizzie thought grimly.

'Shall I run your bath?' she asked politely.

Sarah let out her breath, relieved.

'Oh, please, Lizzie.'

She stretched her arms above her head, like a cat, a smile hovering about her mouth, while Lizzie went into the bathroom and ran the bath. Then she went back into her own room where she flung herself down on the narrow bed feeling hot and cold by turns. What was the matter with her? Where was her sense of humour?

Her face was flushed, yet she felt cold, angry and disillusioned. She didn't know if she felt envy of Sarah's experiences, or pity for his lordship, or anger with Sarah—she also felt like an idiot. She thought of her mother. Hadn't she vowed she would make more of her life than that?

She would, she vowed, and presently felt better.

There was no one more relieved than Sarah when Lizzie presented her usual pleasant face later in the day. You could almost see her sigh of relief. It didn't mean, though, that it put paid to her weekend's pleasures for that night Lizzie was awakened by the same low noises. She turned over and went back to sleep.

She was awake at her usual early hour, and thought out her plans carefully. It might be better to apply to one of the big London stores for a job as an assistant in the gowns department. She could live in the hostel attached to the store—that way she would have no rent to find and be free. It was only until she made her way, which she had now decided was to be in the world of fashion, and she needed the experience. She seemed to have a flair for it, so why not use it? Being a lady's maid to Lady Sarah held no future for her at all. She would be better taking the bull by the horns than waiting until it was too late. It was easy to swan along with every week very much like another. You could edge yourself into a rut that way.

She waited for a few days after the return to London, then just before Sarah was about to announce her decision as to when they would be going to Scotland, dropped her own bombshell.

'I think I ought to tell you, milady, that I am looking around for another position.'

Sarah swung round to face her, mouth open.

'What?'

'I am giving your ladyship notice that I am looking for another position,' Lizzie repeated.

'I don't believe you!' Sarah cried. 'Why on earth would you do that?'

'Because I think it's time I moved on,' Lizzie said reasonably.

'Have you found another post?' Sarah asked suspiciously.

'No, but I shall be looking for one.'

'Then if you think you are going to do that in my time, you are very much mistaken!' Sarah's breath was coming fast.

'Very well, milady.'

'Where will you go?' Curiosity overcame Sarah's anger.

'I'm not sure, milady,' Lizzie said. 'I'm going to look around.'

'Are you indeed?' Sarah's fine nostrils quivered, and Lizzie felt a moment's sympathy for her. It must have been a shock. She just couldn't imagine Lizzie wanting a life of her own.

'I thought I'd better tell you so you could find another lady's maid before you leave for Scotland,' Lizzie said reasonably.

'You aren't giving me much time to find a replacement.'

'Oh, I am sure you will have no difficulty, milady.'

Sarah shook her head, trying another

tactic. 'Well, Lizzie, I'm really surprised,' she said sorrowfully. 'I thought we were friends?'

'I hope we are, milady.'

'You're not behaving as if that's the case.'

'Well, milady, I've got to look after myself and get on with my life—I can't stay a lady's maid forever.'

'I thought you were happy here?'

'I have been,' Lizzie said. 'Now it's time for a change. Will that be all, milady?'

'Yes, you may go,' Sarah said haughtily, and Lizzie closed the door behind her, thankful to have got that over. The first thing she would do would be to get in touch with Marshall and Snelgrove, where she had heard they were looking for staff. A whole new world might be waiting for her there.

The next morning when Sarah emerged from her bath and Lizzie stood waiting beside her with her bathrobe, she wrapped herself in it without a word. Then imperiously she walked through to the bedroom where she sat down by the mirror, waiting for Lizzie to do her hair.

'You can take a week's notice,' she said without a tremor.

'Thank you, milady,' Lizzie said.

Now she really had burned her boats!

CHAPTER 9

Isabel Lister had been making plans too, exciting plans which involved the future of Elizabeth Bartholomew, and she had come up with a few ideas. Dwelling on the girl's talent for designing clothes and sewing, why not try to get her something in that line—and who better to help out than Tatiana Tetbury? Tatiana with whom she had gone to school, the youngest daughter of an earl, who had shocked everyone when she announced her intention of opening a dress shop in Brook Street, Mayfair.

Isabel's own mother had been horrified, but all the girls who left that year, having been presented and thrown on to the marriage market, had envied her, and wished they could do something similar. At first Isabel had patronised Tatiana's small but elegant salon, but somehow after the war more important things took over, and she had gradually drifted away. She knew that Tatiana had had some difficulty in keeping going in those post-war years, but she was a survivor, and now her exclusive salon was patronised by women who liked to be in the latest fashion without trekking over to Paris to see what was what.

Suppose Tatiana would agree to take on Elizabeth as an assistant in some capacity or other? She could but ask. They had been such friends in the old days. The question was, should she try to do something about it now? Suppose she asked Tatiana and she was willing—would Lizzie trust her enough to accept her suggestion? Perhaps she had no desire to leave her present situation. And yet, in the last few weeks, Isabel had thought the girl was becoming restless, anxious to do more with her life. What better time to suggest a change of situation? It surely would be tempting. Also at the back of her mind was the idea of giving Elizabeth a home. The house was far too large for one person, and Isabel had no desire to move. It was her home, she had been born there. Why not have Elizabeth to live with her? There was even space for a workroom for the girl, and Isabel's heart quickened with excitement at the prospect. It seemed such a logical thing to do. Always she ended such discussions with herself by maintaining that as Edmund's daughter, Elizabeth was entitled, and the more she saw of her, the more confident Isabel was that they were related.

She thought about it overnight, and by morning decided that she would go to see Tatiana that very day.

Dressed in her best costume, she made her way to Brook Street. There the shop was, although she hadn't been here for some years, the name above in pale blue and gold: Tatiana. Isabel paused in front of the window where a chestnut brown velvet dress was displayed, pearls thrown carelessly over the skirt; in the corner a cream cashmere sweater and a crocodile handbag.

Her heart quickened.

A young vendeuse smiled as she entered, and Isabel took a deep breath. 'Is Madame Tatiana here today?' she asked, and was rewarded by the sight of her old friend coming through the silk curtain from the inner sanctum. They stared at each other for a moment, and Tatiana spoke first.

'Isabel—Isabel Lister, isn't it?'

'Tatty—you haven't changed a bit!'

They embraced, laughing, then Tatiana put an arm round Isabel and led her through to the private sanctum.

'What on earth are you doing here?'

'I suppose you could say I want something from you, a favour if that's the word—and I think I may need some new clothes.'

'My dear Isabel, you've come to the right place. And not before time, if you don't mind my saying so!'

Isabel laughed. She could never be

offended at anything Tatiana said.

Her friend hadn't changed a bit—or seemed not to have. She was as slim as a reed, and wore a figure-hugging dress of blue morocain. Her hair was fairer than Isabel remembered and fell to her shoulders, making her look absurdly young. Her make-up was faultless, her eyes as blue as cornflowers on a summer's day, her lashes darkened and her eyebrows plucked to a thin arch.

'Well, what have you been doing with yourself all this time?' She sat down and beckoned Isabel into a chair. 'It must be all of five years? By the way, I was sorry to hear about your father. He was such an old sweetie, wasn't he?'

'Yes,' said Isabel. 'Thank you. But now, as you may imagine, free from parental duties, I want to be up and doing. I seem to have wasted so much time.'

'You have indeed,' Tatiana said, crossing one elegant leg over the other.

Isabel regarded her. 'And how are you? I heard you got married again.'

'My dear, I sent him off with a flea in his ear. But there, Daddy did warn me,' Tatiana said happily. 'I don't know, Iz, I don't seem to have much luck with men. I always pick the wrong ones.'

'Perhaps that's preferable to not having one at all,' Isabel said drily.

151

'Now come on, you could have married,' Tatiana said. 'You just didn't bother. After the war you buried yourself!'

'Yes, that's true. Anyway, what I am here for is to ask if you could possibly help me to place a young friend of mine? She's a very pretty girl of seventeen and wants a job in this business. She's most awfully gifted at designing and that sort of thing...' She saw a frown slowly cross Tatiana's face.

'Oh, darling, things aren't that good, you know.'

'I do understand. But put it like this. The child has nothing—no money, no family.'

'Then why—'

'Let's say I want to do something to help. She has a post as a lady's maid but she is far too intelligent for that.'

'Hmm,' said Tatiana.

'I suppose you charge a fee for an apprenticeship?'

'I used to—not now. They just get pin money, enough to buy themselves stockings, that sort of thing.'

'Suppose I pay for her tuition? She need not know. Indeed, I would not want her to know.'

'You're a strange bird.' Tatiana smiled. 'Still, that would help. Why don't you send her around for me to look at? I warn you, I'm awfully choosy. She'd have to be suitable, and I couldn't guarantee anything.'

'Of course not,' Isabel said hurriedly. 'Would you really, Tat? I would be so grateful.'

More here than meets the eye, thought Tatiana, but what the heck did it matter? The girl might be good.

'She can do with a bit of luck—she hasn't had it very easy, being brought up in an orphanage.'

Tatiana consulted her diary. 'How about this Friday?'

'I'd have to let you know. You see, she's still employed by Lady Devenoke.'

Tatiana whistled. 'No! Really? She's one of my clients, and I don't imagine her ladyship would suffer fools gladly, for all she is so young.'

'Maybe,' Isabel smiled. 'Well, I'll see what I can do, and be in touch.'

'What's her name?' Tatiana asked, pencil poised.

'Elizabeth—Elizabeth Bartholomew.' How she wished she could say 'Elizabeth Lister'.

She reached the door and turned. 'Thanks awfully, Tatiana.'

'Hope to see you,' Tatiana said, and watched her go from behind the lace curtains. What on earth was dear, staid Isabel up to?

153

Meanwhile, Lizzie had got herself an appointment at Marshall and Snelgrove in Oxford Street, where if she got the job she would be able to live in at the girls' hostel. The pay was not much, but at least she would be free to keep herself—something she had never done yet. The interview was for three-thirty on Thursday afternoon, and on Sunday evening she walked through the park, hoping to find Miss Lister on the seat they usually occupied. But there was no one there. In fact she had not seen Miss Lister since her father had died.

Lizzie was almost home when she saw her hurrying through the square on her way to church. Seeing Lizzie, she stopped. 'My dear, I am so glad to see you. Do you think you could come round to see me when you can—sometime this week before Friday?'

Lizzie was quite taken aback.

'Yes. Yes, of course, Miss Lister. When would be suitable?'

'Any time for me, my dear, but I expect you would have to fit it in with your duties.'

'Thursday afternoon is my free afternoon —would that suit you?'

Isabel thought. 'Well, if you can't do before...'

'No, I'm sorry.'

'Then I will see you then. Goodbye, my

dear,' And beaming like a Cheshire cat, Isabel hurried on her way.

What could she be up to? Lizzie thought. And what did she want with her?

Just after two on Thursday afternoon, Lizzie walked along the square. She rang the bell and the door was opened by Mrs Baines who seemed a little mystified to find Lizzie standing there.

'I have come to see Miss Lister,' Lizzie explained.

'She's expecting you. Come in—I'll take your coat.'

Lizzie found herself upstairs in the drawing room where a bright coal fire lit up the room.

'Oh, it is nice to see you,' Isabel said. 'I have so few visitors.'

Lizzie looked around. Such a pleasant room overlooking the square, with its pretty carpet, and Chinese furniture, the beautiful pieces of oriental china and splendid table lamps.

'Sit down, my dear,' Isabel said, noting how nice the girl looked with her navy fitted dress and jacket, the smart little felt hat worn at an attractive angle over one eye.

'Would you like some tea?'

'No, thank you, Miss Lister? I can't stay long, I have an appointment at three-thirty.'

155

'Oh.' And Miss Lister's face fell.

'At Marshall and Snelgrove,' Lizzie said, her green eyes dancing at the prospect.

'Really? What for?' Isabel asked.

'I am leaving Lady Devenoke's employ.'

And Isabel's heart leapt.

'Oh,' she said. 'Then—'

'Yes, it's time I moved on.'

'I see.' Isabel bit her lip. 'What will you do at Marshall and Snelgrove?'

'I hope to be a salesgirl in the gown department if they'll have me with no experience.'

Isabel took a deep breath and glanced at her watch.

'I wonder, my dear, whether you would consider an idea I have had?'

Lizzie's eyes were wide. What could Miss Lister have in mind?

'I have a friend who runs a small exclusive dress salon in Mayfair. You may have heard of it? Tatiana of Brook Street?'

'Oh, yes! Lady Devenoke goes there.'

'Well, I mentioned you to her, not knowing of course that you were about to leave Lady Devenoke's employ, and asked her if she would be interested in taking you into the shop as an assistant. I am not sure in what capacity, I don't know enough about the gown trade. I hope you don't think I was too presumptuous?'

'No, but—'

'Of course, if you don't like the idea, I quite understand.'

'Oh, no, Miss Lister! It's just such a surprise, that's all.'

'Well, I thought you deserved more than working as a lady's maid, estimable though that may be, and I had the feeling you might feel it was time for a change.' She could almost see the questions going through Lizzie's mind. 'I thought if you went to see Mrs Tetbury and she was prepared to take you...'

Lizzie's eyes were shining with excitement. 'It sounds too good to be true.'

'Well, it's up to you. I had intended to ask you anyway, but now you say you are leaving Lady Devenoke's employ—'

'I told her that I would be looking around for something else and I'm afraid she gave me my notice.'

Everything was going her way, Isabel thought happily.

'I see. Then you will need somewhere to live in the meantime.'

'I had booked into the YWCA for next week.'

'I'm sure that won't be necessary. You could stay here.'

'Oh, I couldn't!'

'It was just another idea I had. I have been doing a lot of thinking since my father died, and realise that I have wasted a great deal of time and would like to make up for it. I have no family, no ties, and I am lonely. It seemed to me that if you were prepared to come and live here it might suit both of us.'

Did she have any idea, Lizzie thought, what a shopgirl earned? How could she possibly afford to live here?

'I know what you're thinking—but it would be company for me. If it makes you feel better, you could give me a hand sometimes, or accompany me when I go anywhere, I loathe going to the theatre alone. You would be a sort of companion, except that you would have your own job too.'

The idea had enormous advantages, Lizzie thought, but what were the dis-advantages? She would be no more free than if she was still working for Lady Sarah and she had no wish to be beholden to anyone—but the idea of working in an exclusive salon was more than she could have hoped for. At least she would have her evenings free. Or would she? It seemed to her that the one proposition went with the other. But first she must get the job with Mrs Tetbury. She glanced at her watch. 'Goodness, it's almost three! What about my appointment at Marshall and Snelgrove?'

158

'I think it might be a good idea if you kept that, see how it goes, then you won't feel under any obligation to me. You might decide to take it—and that's only fair. Run along now.'

Lizzie picked up her handbag. Really, Miss Lister was awfully kind.

'Thank you,' she said. 'I'll let you know how I get on.'

Isabel watched her go from behind the curtains. It seemed so right for her to live here. She might well be entitled to anyway, if you looked at it in one way. How she prayed that Elizabeth would not be so impressed with the shop job that she wanted to take it! She crossed her fingers. What was to be, would be, she thought philosophically.

Lizzie sat in the Staff Manager's office, facing a tall dark man, his jet black hair so shiny you could almost see your face in it from across the desk. He had rosy cheeks and wore a dark little moustache that looked as though it was painted on. But surely not? thought Lizzie. His hands were beautifully kept, and as he spoke he often looked down at them, as though admiring them.

'So you want to work in the gown department?' he said, eyeing her, not unaware that this was where she belonged, with those looks and that figure. Smart, too. Quite an air about her. But rules were rules.

He placed his fingertips together and eyed her with small dark eyes.

'While it is true to say we require staff, nevertheless new members have to work their way up through the departments. Female staff automatically start in haberdashery and progress through handbags and hosiery, then lingerie and into the gowns—always supposing that they are suitable, of course. There is no short cut, Miss Bartholomew, do you understand?'

'Yes, Mr Chapman.'

'Very well. What experience have you had?'

Lizzie recited the story of her working life up to now, and he made notes.

'Lady's maid,' he wrote. 'Well, that's a promising start. I imagine you have to toe the line in that job, eh?'

Lizzie smiled sweetly.

'Now—you live, I see, at Hyde Park Square. That, I take it, is your place of employment?'

'Yes, Mr Chapman.'

'Where is your home?'

'I have no home now.'

'Ah. You can supply references, Miss Bartholomew?'

'Oh, yes, Mr Chapman.'

'And you would want to live in the staff hostel provided?'

'Yes, sir.'

'At your age, your starting wage would be twenty-five shillings a week, less...' But Lizzie wasn't listening. Her mind was on the small exclusive salon in Brook Street. Oh, if only she could work there! There was no comparison between the two jobs. But suppose she didn't get the job with Miss Lister's friend, and had refused this one? Oh, what a predicament! But a girl had to look after herself...

'Well, I think that's all. Is there anything else you wish to ask me?'

She shook her head. 'No, thank you.'

'Well, I think we may say that we are prepared to take you on, starting on Monday week. That will be the—' He saw her blush furiously.

'Is there something worrying you?'

'No, well, if I could have until Friday to think it over—it's quite a big step from being a lady's maid.'

He frowned and looked annoyed.

'I understood that you were keen to start here?'

'Yes, I was—I mean, am—if I could let you know on Friday afternoon.'

'Very well, Miss Bartholomew. It is a highly unusual procedure, but perhaps I can understand your concern.'

161

'Oh, thank you, Mr Chapman.' She was genuinely grateful.

'Very well, Miss Bartholomew. We shall hold the position open for you until tomorrow afternoon.'

He'd never done such a thing in his life before. If it hadn't been for the way she looked, with those green eyes, that lovely face...

'Good day, Miss Bartholomew.'

'Good day, Mr Chapman. Thank you.'

She positively danced on the way back to Hyde Park Square, wondering if she was on her head or her heels.

'So how did you get on?' Isabel asked, having difficulty in hiding her anxiety.

'Well, I've got the job if I want it, starting a week on Monday.'

'Did you accept it?'

'No. I asked him if I could let him know tomorrow afternoon.'

'And what did he say?'

'He agreed! Isn't that wonderful?'

'Couldn't be better!' cried Isabel, and she meant it. 'Now come in and sit down for a moment. You don't have to get back, do you?'

'Not until six o'clock,' Lizzie said, following Isabel up the stairs into the drawing room of a house that already felt like home to her.

Isabel poured tea.

'Now, you will think about what I said—about living here with me?' she asked. 'You promise to come here just as soon as you leave Lady Devenoke's? I don't like to think of your going to the YWCA.'

'It's very nice there,' Lizzie protested.

'You've had enough of living in places like that—you need a proper home.'

But Lizzie still looked doubtful. 'I feel a bit like Cinderella.'

'And what's wrong with that?' Isabel asked.

Lizzie didn't say that in her world treats like this didn't grow on trees, and she had discovered in her young life that nobody gave anything away for nothing. But cheer up, she told herself. Grab the chance with both hands, and begin to enjoy yourself. Miss Lister seems to think you are doing her a favour, so look at it like that.

By the time she was ready to leave at the end of the afternoon, she didn't know if she was on her head or her heels.

'What is your real name?' Isabel asked as she saw her to the door. 'I suspect it is Elizabeth, isn't it?'

'Yes, Miss Lister.'

'Then that's what I shall call you. You don't look like a Lizzie,' she smiled. 'Do

163

you mind being called Elizabeth?'

'No, not at all—only my mother ever called me that.' And Lizzie bit her lip.

The excitement was proving too much for her, Isabel thought, and spoke briskly.

'Now, I will telephone Mrs Tetbury and tell her that you will be there on Friday at two-thirty.'

Lizzie thought hastily. Miss Sarah—how difficult was she going to be?

'Yes,' she said suddenly. 'That's fine. I'll be there.'

The atmosphere between her and Sarah was somewhat strained this last week, and Lizzie felt she would be glad when it was time to leave. Apparently Sarah had interviewed someone else whom she announced was highly suitable. Experienced in a lady's ways, she emphasised, to which Lizzie replied, 'Then that's all right, milady,' leaving Sarah to walk off in a huff.

Not until Friday morning did she ask where Lizzie was going, and then in a very off hand way.

Having thought about it for a time, Lizzie had decided to tell the truth. There could be nothing wrong with that.

'Going where?' Sarah almost shouted.

'I am going to stay with Miss Lister for a while until I get settled. As a sort of companion, although I have another job, milady.'

'I don't believe you,' Sarah said at first.

'Very well, milady,' Lizzie said and walked out of the room. But Sarah returned to it again an hour later. As Lizzie brushed her hair, she looked through the mirror at her accusingly.

'What have you been up to?' she asked suspiciously. 'How do you know Miss Lister?'

'I met her in the park, and she said since her father died, she finds the house too large and suggested that I take a room there.'

Said like that, it sounded highly unlikely. She didn't blame Sarah for doubting her.

Sarah frowned. 'A likely story.'

'Very well, milady.'

'You are being very cagey, miss,' Sarah said icily.

'Not at all, milady. I'm telling you the truth.'

'We shall see.'

With this somewhat ominous remark, Sarah left the room, to return a few minutes later to say she would be going out in the afternoon, and would not return until evening.

Lizzie heaved a sigh of relief. Now there would be no need to ask for time off to go for the interview. She would have time to prepare and dress herself suitably for what she hoped would be the most important interview she had yet had.

CHAPTER 10

Tatiana's was just the sort of shop that Lizzie most admired—smart and exclusive. She opened the door to find herself deep in pale beige carpet, while a tall, slinky girl in black satin-backed marocain smiled a little superciliously at her. But Lizzie refused to be put off. She had Miss Lister behind her.

'I am Elizabeth Bartholomew and I have an appointment with Mrs Tetbury.'

'Miss Bartholomew. Just a moment.' And she disappeared into the back room. Lizzie looked about her. How she would love to work here—in any capacity.

'Would you come this way?' the girl said, and Lizzie followed her.

The elegant and beautifully dressed Tatiana looked exactly as Lizzie had hoped she would, and she prayed that she had chosen the right clothes to wear, for she knew first impressions were important.

Tatiana saw a girl who without a doubt

would be an asset to any business like hers. The girl had dress sense, she was beautiful with that black hair and those green eyes, she carried herself well, and unless Tatiana was mistaken, had made the dress she had on, which was cleverly cut with exactly the right sleeves and cuff length. The slim legs were in silk stockings and high heels, and the hat perky as today's fashions were—she couldn't have been more impressed.

She waved a hand towards a chair. 'Elizabeth, please sit down.'

The voice though—how would that be? It was a give away in her business.

'Thank you, Mrs Tetbury.' And Tatiana sighed with relief. Not upper class for sure, but not Cockney either, low-pitched, with the very slightest burr to it—that would soon be ironed out, she thought. Six months with Tatiana and her clients in whatever capacity and she would soon learn.

'So what experience have you had?'

And Lizzie told her. Not about the orphanage, but about the finishing school and working for Lady Devenoke.

'Did you make the dress you have on?'

'Yes, Mrs Tetbury.'

'Come here and show me.'

Lizzie got up and went over to her. Tatiana examined the seams and the set of the sleeves, noted the fine hem stitching.

She got up and brought out a length of emerald green taffeta.

'What would you do with that?' she asked. 'Draw something for me. How would you use it?'

This was something Lizzie loved to do, draw and design clothes, and with a clean white sheet of paper and pencil, she sketched quickly, tongue protruding from between her pretty lips, holding it away from her, doing it again, and finally when she was satisfied handing it to Tatiana, who had been watching her closely.

She smiled at Lizzie, obviously pleased at what she saw.

'Well, Elizabeth,' she said slowly, 'you show promise—especially since you have had no formal training. But we would see to that. I have a small workroom at the back where we design and make some of our clothes under my name. Some things we buy from Paris, I have quite a few very fussy clients who demand nothing but the best. You would have a spell in the salon, and I am afraid be nothing but a general dogsbody for the first couple of years—how do you feel about that?'

Lizzie felt she was dreaming—so much was coming her way, almost too much at once, yet here she was, and she had proved what she could do. Of course, the money was important. Perhaps she would have to pay for the privilege of working here?

Tatiana read her thoughts.

'Your wages would be minimal,' she said, 'enough for oddments, things like that, until I felt you should earn more, but I understand from Miss Lister than you may be staying with her so that should help.'

Oh, Lizzie thought, so Miss Lister had told her.

'Well, you have a position here, Elizabeth, if you want it. How do you feel about it?'

There was no doubting the sheer pleasure in Lizzie's eyes. 'Oh, thank you, Mrs Tetbury!'

'So what about Monday morning—will that suit you?'

'Oh, yes, Mrs Tetbury!'

'Nine o'clock then, Elizabeth, and don't be late.' Tatiana watched her disappear through the glass door. What a little beauty! She would be a real asset. That's if she didn't get carried off by some man and get married. Yet somehow, she had the feeling that Elizabeth Bartholomew was a determined young woman and not likely to get swept off her feet too easily.

Not like me, she thought ruefully. I hadn't the brains I was born with.

Lizzie couldn't wait to get back to Hyde Park Square to tell Miss Lister how she had got on. Isabel could see by her dancing eyes and smiling face that Tatiana was as good as her word and had decided to take her on.

'Oh, it was lovely, Miss Lister!' Lizzie cried. 'Mrs Tetbury gave me some material and asked me how I would use it, and I drew a design, and she seemed pleased with it, and asked lots of questions—and I can start next Monday!' It was all she could do not to fling her arms about Isabel's neck.

'Well, then!' Isabel said triumphantly. 'You see, I knew it was worth trying! Now come in and sit down and I must tell you what I have in mind.'

In the small study on the ground floor, Isabel sat behind her desk and asked Lizzie to sit down too.

'The only thing is, Miss Lister,' she began hesitantly, 'Mrs Tetbury didn't mention how much—I mean, the wages I would be getting. She said they would be minimal, and I wondered...'

Isabel looked down at her desk. 'Yes, well, I expect she means a pound or two a week—something like that. I am sure it would be as much as you received from Lady Devenoke. The point is if you stayed here, there would be no need to pay rent so you would save that.' She saw Lizzie's expression.

'I mean,' she said hurriedly, 'there would be no rent for you to pay. You could help me instead in lots of ways—as you did Lady Devenoke. That would count as rent. And your living here is hardly going to cost a fortune, is it? You would be a companion to me. Does that make you feel better?'

She smiled brightly, appealing to Lizzie, who was lost for words. Trying to sum it up, she thought, So here I am, board and lodging free—there must be a catch somewhere. Miss Lister is far too generous, commonsense reasoned, while her heart told her Miss Lister was a kind lady who only wished to help.

'Look, Elizabeth,' Isabel said, 'let's give it a try, shall we? As soon as you leave Lady Devenoke, come here with your luggage—whatever you have—and we'll make you as comfortable as we can. I'm sure you will be happy here, and it's not far to Brook Street. Now come upstairs and I'll show you the room I think you would like.'

She followed Isabel up the stairs to the second floor where she was shown into a cosy single room with flowered curtains and bedspread, a dressing table and wardrobe and another table, presumably for her to work at.

Isabel looked at her anxiously until Lizzie turned, her eyes brilliant.

'It's lovely,' she breathed, going over to the window and seeing all the roof tops and the plane trees in the square.

'And there is a bathroom at the end of the hall. For all the bedrooms, really, but there's no one else on this floor. So you see I have lots of room and no one to use it.'

Lizzie was beginning to see the justification for it all.

'You are very kind,' she said, feeling a bit choked, so long had it been since anyone had really thought about her enough to do something for her. 'Thank you. I'm going to love it, I know I am, and you won't worry about the sound of my sewing machine. It's really quite small and doesn't make much noise.'

'Bless you, of course not,' Miss Lister said. She hadn't felt so happy for a long time. At last she was going to have a family again.

Lizzie had to wait until the next morning to say her farewells, which seeing that her ladyship did not rise until well past eleven was rather late—Lizzie having been ready to leave before eight o'clock.

'Goodbye, milady, and thank you.'

'Goodbye, Lizzie,' Sarah said coldly, and that was that.

Lizzie couldn't have been happier than

when she presented herself at Miss Lister's house later that day. Armed with her luggage and small sewing machine, let in by Mrs Baines, she was shown to the little room on the second floor, the most comfortable room she had ever had.

She put her machine on the table, swept off her hat, shook her curls and began to unpack. This felt like home.

On Monday morning, it was pouring with rain. Not just pouring but sheeting down, while a gale raged at the same time.

Lizzie arrived at the shop, battling against the wind, her umbrella almost blown inside out, her raincoat drenched, falling inside the door like a bedraggled cat.

'Good morning, Elizabeth!' Tatiana said brightly. 'Not the brightest day in the world to start a new job—but take off your wet clothes, we'll have them dry in no time.' She showed Lizzie the small cloakroom which was warm. 'Come in to me when you're ready.'

'Thank you, Mrs Tetbury.'

Tatiana was in her small private office, sitting at her desk looking as immaculate as ever, her golden hair shining, perfect make up, the bright blue eyes glancing over Lizzie and not missing a thing.

'About your wages, I've had a little

think,' she began, which really meant that she had had a telephone call with Isabel, 'and I suggest that twenty-five shillings a week is fair. What do you say?'

'Oh, yes, Mrs Tetbury,' Lizzie said, having wondered whether she might get anything at all since she remembered meeting a girl in the park who worked for an exclusive gown shop and told her that she received half a crown a week. 'Pin money,' she said. 'At one time one had to pay for apprenticeship.' Now, Lizzie was delighted. It meant she could offer Isabel something for her keep.

'Well, come with me,' Tatiana continued, 'let's see what you can do.' And she showed Lizzie the sewing room where there were two other girl employees.

'This is my machinist, Ada Grimshaw —and this is Grace Taylor. Our new girl, Elizabeth Bartholomew.'

Both girls looked up and smiled at her, looking at each other after the door closed, each thinking the same thing—that lovely face, the dark curls and smiling green eyes.

'Some girls have all the luck,' Grace said, but didn't mean it unkindly.

'This way,' Tatiana said, leading the way to the fitting room which looked more like a boudoir with cheval mirrors and a dressing table elegantly fitted out with scent bottles and powder boxes and long-handled swansdown puffs.

'Now to the salon, where of course you have met Sophie, my vendeuse.'

Perhaps Sophie was naturally grand, Lizzie thought. At all events, she wasn't going to unbend—at least not for Lizzie.

'Good morning, Miss Bartholomew,' she said.

The air of disdain seemed quite natural to her, those arched thinly plucked eyebrows giving her an air of perpetual surprise, her round brown eyes looking through you, or so it seemed. She was lovely though, thought Lizzie, with those high cheekbones and beautiful sculptured mouth. She wore her black hair in a chignon at the back of her neck, and in her black satin dress which fitted her slim figure perfectly she looked like an artist's model.

Lizzie was soon in her element. Surrounded by luxury silks and satins and the new fashions, seeing the elegant clients coming into the salon leaving different perfumes behind them. There wasn't a dull moment, and when she emerged from the shop at five-thirty the sun was shining and the pavements dry. She hurried home to tell Isabel all about it.

She was as excited as if she had been there herself, and sat engrossed in the tale of Lizzie's day.

'So you see, Miss Lister, with twenty-five shillings a week, I can afford to give you something towards my keep.'

Isabel waved her offer aside.

'No, my dear, I won't hear of it. You will need every penny of that yourself. You may help me in other ways perhaps. Alter my clothes and press them, certainly advise me on what to wear. I am afraid I have been somewhat out of touch all these years.'

Then she brightened. 'Well, off you go, and come down when you are ready—but remember, your time is your own. You must do just as you please, feel this is your home.'

So Lizzie's new life fell into a pattern. Her work at the salon with never a dull moment, and settling in to Hyde Park Square. Isabel made no demands on her, but she liked to hear what had gone on in Lizzie's day. She took to going out herself occasionally, in order that she might have something to talk about to Lizzie when she came home, and found that she quite enjoyed her little forays.

Lizzie had found her niche. She was particularly good at fitting, and most days found her on her knees, a pincushion pad on her wrist, dealing with letting out, taking in, shortening or lengthening. She was an asset to the shop, Tatiana recognised even

176

after a few days. For one thing she looked so right, slim and youthful, her dark hair always beautifully brushed, the make up on that fine skin enhancing her beauty. She kept her eyebrows finely plucked as was the fashion, and below them the thick-fringed lashes and green eyes were shown to advantage. She looked her most stunning in figure-hugging black, something which Tatiana knew a lot of her best clients envied.

'Not everyone can wear black,' she reassured them, but most of them longed to. The young ones because it made them look older and more sophisticated, and the more mature clients hoping that it added an air of mystery to their already elegant appearances.

Tatiana, observing Lizzie closely, realised that she had found quite a treasure in this girl. She was talented, and showed a marked flair for design and anticipating fashion. She was going to be more useful than she had imagined. At the back of her mind was a plan to give Elizabeth a chance to test her strength, see what she was really capable of. After all, she was like a breath of fresh air.

The autumn faded into winter. One evening in October Isabel pulled the drawing-room curtains then sat by the fire, waiting for Elizabeth to join her.

She never failed to admire the girl's appearance: the way she walked with a new air of confidence, the stylish dress which she had designed and made herself.

'You look lovely,' she said admiringly when Lizzie came in.

'Thank you. Yes, I am very pleased with it,' Lizzie said. 'This material just lent itself to the pattern. It's new, elephant skin crêpe—and it feels like it.'

'Is that what it's called?'

'Yes, it's fashionable at the moment.'

'Elizabeth, I thought it was time we went out one evening.'

Lizzie looked up.

'I thought we might have dinner somewhere.' Isabel didn't add that it was her birthday soon, her forty-third birthday, and it was time she celebrated it.

'What a lovely idea,' said Lizzie. 'But—'

'I know what you are going to say but I would love to do it. It's a long time since I went out in the evening.'

She got up and went over to the fire and put on another log.

'My father used to take us to the Hyde Park Hotel—they have a very nice restaurant there. Would you like that?'

'Sounds wonderful,' Lizzie said, and it did. In the last six weeks she had been nowhere except to the park and wandering round the shops after she had finished at the salon.

'Then I'll book it,' Isabel said happily. 'Friday evening. And,' she added, 'I am going to buy a new dress from Tatiana.'

'Oh, that's wonderful!' Lizzie cried. 'When will you be coming in?'

'Tomorrow,' said Isabel.

'And I know exactly the dress that will be right for you.'

Isabel didn't say she was meeting Tatiana for lunch. Some things one had to keep to oneself.

While Isabel was getting ready for their special evening out, putting on the newly acquired dress of royal blue which was the season's new colour, she studied herself in the long mirror. Really, she wasn't bad for her age, having acquired a new lease of life with Elizabeth's coming. The dress was fitted, and the sleeves had the added interest of white touches at the wrist, godets which fell attractively over the wrist. Altogether it was a fashionable dress, and miles away from her usual tweeds and twinsets.

In her bedroom on the next floor Lizzie also was getting ready. She slipped into the green panne velvet dress which exactly matched her eyes. Fitting her slim figure like a glove, it flared out to mid-calf length, while her satin shoes had been dyed to match. She brushed her hair until it shone, and put on the pearl stud earrings she had bought at lunchtime. Her eyes sparkled back at her as she dabbed at her nose with a swansdown puff, and put a touch of rose lipstick on her soft curvy mouth.

Now for the final touch.

From her drawer she brought out the precious box, and withdrew from it the ornate silver chain with its locket. Opening it, she kissed the picture inside, then closed it, and put it around her neck.

It looked exactly right. She adjusted it, and with a last spray of perfume, picked up her black moire evening bag and sailed down to the drawing room.

Isabel was waiting for her with some excitement, and when she came in, she looked so beautiful she almost took Isabel's breath away. She saw Lizzie's green eyes smiling at her, and her own filled with tears for no accountable reason when she saw the necklace. Yet surely she had seen it before...

She glanced up at Lizzie.

'My dear, you look lovely—and what a pretty necklace.'

'Thank you. My mother gave it to me. It belonged to her—'

Isabel swallowed.

'And is there a picture inside?' she asked, her voice quavering slightly as she felt the

180

blood draining away from her cheeks. 'Sit down, my dear.'

Lizzie sat down beside her. 'Yes, of my father.'

Isabel took a deep breath.

'And may I see it?'

'Of course.' And Lizzie snapped the back of the locket open, and showed Isabel the photograph.

She was looking at a photograph of her brother, Edmund.

CHAPTER 11

So that was it—she had no more doubts. Her brother Edmund was the father of this young and lovely girl. Her thoughts in a tumult, Isabel had no idea what to say. Nothing that made sense—or would to Elizabeth.

One could hardly say: 'Oh, that's my brother, Edmund' or indeed anything at this stage. With shaking fingers she gently held the locket then looked up at the girl who was still staring at the picture with a fond, loving expression—it was probably her most prized possession.

Isabel wanted to weep—and yet she had known all along. How, then, she asked herself, to tell Elizabeth—or should she?

She let go the locket, and Lizzie closed it with a tiny snap, then took a deep breath and looked around her.

It was going to be difficult to explain to Elizabeth—it meant telling her that her mother had been in love with someone else before she married. Edmund Lister to be precise. It was he who had given her the locket, and why else unless they had been truly in love? Also, that her father was not Bartholomew—but then again, he could be. Oh, what a mess. How would she ever know, ever be sure?

Isabel was saved from further speculation by the arrival of the taxi which was to take them to dinner. Once inside, she sat back, her thoughts still on the locket.

If only she could say to her, 'Elizabeth, I am really your Aunt Isabel, and your father was...' But perhaps the girl would not wish to know that her mother had become pregnant before she was married by a man not her father. And was dismissed by the Listers—what an awful thought! Surely, Mama wouldn't have...

But then, Mama did. It was common during those war years. Girls became pregnant, especially in domestic service, and more often than not the girl's employer would dismiss her, for the added burden of a girl with a baby was not to be thought of. And Mama might have had some idea that Mary and Edmund... Oh, dear!

Later they went into dinner, an attractive couple, Isabel in her fashionable blue and the girl in the green dress, observed by more than one diner in the elegant dining room. Lizzie's eyes were brilliant this evening, and the dinner was superb, Isabel having chosen carefully and spared no expense to make it a memorable evening with wine and champagne.

She looked positively attractive these days, Lizzie thought, her little face animated, her eyes brighter, such nice hazel eyes beneath a smooth shining cap of fair hair which had a touch of auburn in it. She had even had her eyebrows shaped, not to the thin fashionable line but thinned out, and it made all the difference to her appearance—made her look younger.

'Are you sure we are not celebrating something special?' Lizzie asked, her smiling eyes meeting Isabel's across the table.

Isabel, enjoying herself enormously, smiled back.

'Well, as a matter of fact, it is my birthday,' she said. 'I'm forty three today.'

'Oh, that's wonderful!' Lizzie cried. 'Happy birthday! And many happy returns of the day—you should have told me,' she said reproachfully.

'I didn't want to make a fuss over it.'

'But you should—' Lizzie said, and meant it. Tomorrow she would send her flowers. Isabel had been so generous to her.

Later that night, as she lay in bed, Isabel mulled over the situation. The girl wore Edmund's photograph around her neck, but then she had no idea who it was. Her father, she had said. How would she know what her father looked like, never having seen him, nor he her?

She felt she couldn't have more solid proof, and yet there would always be a doubt—but did she mind that? Wasn't Elizabeth the daughter she would have loved to have had? A lovely girl. And she had had such an unhappy start in life, in an orphanage. Isabel's mind wandered back to Mary. She had been so fond of her, they all had. With her delightful soft Irish brogue, her gentle ways—she hoped Edmund had not persuaded her to sleep with him against her will. He could be a very persuasive young man, and Mary had obviously had a soft spot for him.

Weary of the interminable thoughts going round in her head, Isabel finally decided to keep the knowledge to herself. There was no hurry. Least said, soonest mended. When the right time came, she would know...

When the huge bouquet of flowers arrived the next day, Isabel was quite overwhelmed. She could never recall having been sent flowers before. When Lizzie arrived home, she was waiting for her in the hall, beside the white and gold chrysanthemums, such a blaze of glory at this time of year.

'Elizabeth, my dear.' And Lizzie smiled at her. 'You shouldn't have.'

'You deserve them,' Lizzie said, and in an instant Isabel had her arms round the girl, giving her a hug.

'Thank you.' And she swiftly walked off into the study.

Lizzie watched her go. What a nice old thing she was, kindness itself. And to think she remembered Mary all those years ago. No wonder she'd had a special feeling about this house.

Meanwhile, she was enjoying life. Becoming used to Tatiana's special clients, she got to know them and their likes and dislikes, and it was after she had made Tatiana a sketch of an outfit that would suit Lady Bethroyd, one of her best clients, that Tatiana decided perhaps she should give the girl her head.

She looked hard at the sketch. Backless evening gowns were de rigueur, and this one was in black crêpe, floor-length, with a very slight train, backless except for two narrow shoulder straps of silver, and a décolleté neckline. Over it went a hip length tunic of transparent black silk. Tatiana watched Lizzie, fascinated at the speed with which she sketched the figure, the flat smooth head of hair, the mouth and eyes which bore an uncanny resemblance to Lady Bethroyd's.

'Do me another,' she commanded. 'For, say, Joanna Spark—an evening outfit.'

A very different kettle of fish, Joanna was a sportswoman of some renown, daughter of a wealthy industrialist and heiress to a large fortune. It took Lizzie no time to design a gown for her, something slimming which would take attention away from the fact that her waistline was indistinct and her figure by no means perfect.

The dress was again black, a two-piece, an underslip, full length, and over it a tight-fitting coat in black velvet with narrow tight sleeves and long emerald green revers reaching down to the waist. The effect was startling and slimming. As Joanna's round face took shape, Lizzie added a headdress of a tall egret feather and a brilliant centre stone.

'That's wonderful!' Tatiana cried. 'I can just see her in it.'

Lizzie was pleased. Her head was full of ideas like this, and she was only too grateful for the opportunity to display them.

'You know, if we could make them in the workroom, we could add a line to our stock,' said Tatiana, thoughtfully tapping her pencil. 'Elizabeth—each model distinctive, unlikely to be seen anywhere else. If there is one thing clients hate it is meeting the outfit they are wearing, but there are so many copyists—little back street sempstresses, the scourge of the fashion trade. But this way, all the gowns would be original.'

Lizzie's eyes were wide. 'You mean it?'

'I'm thinking about it,' Tatiana said warningly.

The upshot was that Lizzie accompanied her to the wholesalers in Bruton Street, and there they selected the newest material, a soft silk jersey, and Lizzie began to work on it.

Lady Bethroyd was entranced. Eyeing herself in the mirror, she turned this way and that, seeing the soft folds of the gown as they swirled out at the hem, the chic little tunic which went over the top.

Her dark eyes glinted. 'With my white fox furs,' she murmured.

'Heavenly,' Tatiana said softly.

'Well—I must have it,' her ladyship said, stepping out of it with the help of Angelina, Tatiana's personal assistant.

Lady Bethroyd looked at the label —Elizabeth embroidered in gold just inside.

'New designer?' she asked, one delicate eyebrow raised.

Tatiana nodded. 'We are fortunate enough to have captured her before she left for Paris, where I may say,' she confided, 'she was about to embark on a new career with a very famous designer who shall be nameless.' She looked over her shoulder as her voice sank to a whisper. 'I recognised the talent at once, and I knew you would be interested.'

Lady Bethroyd was powdering her small nose delicately, but she hadn't missed a word.

'You will let me see her new things before...'

'You shall be the first,' Tatiana promised.

And so began Lizzie's career with Tatiana, for from then on she was much in demand. Her creations were sought after by society women, and to Tatiana's delight and surprise, her business doubled in no time.

'You know,' she said one day, 'you are amazing. You've had no training as such. Was your mother—is it in your family?'

Lizzie shook her head. She could hardly believe it herself sometimes. She spent her days sketching beautiful models only to see them come to life in the workroom under the skilful fingers of Grace and Ada.

Soon it was Christmas, although over the festive season hung the shadow of the King's illness, which had followed a strenuous year for him. The extra duties imposed on him during the twenty-fifth year of his reign had taken toll of his health, so that the end of the old year found him at Sandringham for Christmas surrounded by his family who felt it might well be his last.

Lizzie and Isabel spent Christmas quietly together, going to church on Christmas morning, then to lunch at the Hyde Park Hotel. Several times over that period Isabel was on the brink of saying something to Lizzie, but when it came to it, she held back. Leave well alone, she told herself. And trust that Elizabeth didn't delve too deeply into why she was doing all this.

Isabel gave her a slim gold bracelet which had belonged to her mother, and Lizzie was quite shocked.

'I can't take this. You really mustn't do it. You have been so kind, and I can't keep taking from you.'

'My dear,' Isabel said, 'take it. I shall never wear it and there is no one else. It would make me very happy. You give me your company and help me, and you're not unhappy here, are you?' looking anxiously at Lizzie.

'Good Lord, no!' she said. 'Why should I be? I've got a home, and a new job. I wish, though, you'd let me do more for you.'

'Your being here is sufficient,' Isabel said quietly.

There were times when Lizzie wondered how long she could retain her freedom. She would be eternally grateful to Isabel but would there come a time when she wished she was not under an obligation to her? Isabel had said she was selfish and was getting more out of the arrangement than Lizzie herself, but she knew that there were many girls in her position who would have jumped at the chance.

In for a penny, she told herself, realising just how difficult it would be to return to her old life after all the things she had seen and done.

1936 dawned and with it came the news that King George V was gravely ill. When he died in January the country was plunged into mourning. Lizzie arrived at Tatiana's to find the window draped in black, as were most other shop windows as a mark of courtesy to the old king. He lay in state at Westminster Hall as a million people passed his coffin, and when he was buried, the new king, Edward VIII, scattered the coffin with earth from a silver bowl, and the country entered a new era.

What, the people wondered, about Mrs Simpson?

'Not the brightest time to start a new year,' Tatiana said brightly. 'Still, we shall be inundated with orders.' There were many alterations to be done, especially now when many of Tatiana's clients were in mourning and had brought out their beautiful black model clothes.

The Prince of Wales, as King Edward VIII, brought changes to a new court which were reflected throughout the rest of the country. He broke down some of the more rigid conventions and was not above walking in the street like any other man. As the economy slowly edged upwards there was a feeling abroad that things were on the mend, there was hope, after all. Unemployment was down, business was thriving, and all sorts of new gadgets and machinery were to be bought for those who had the money. Telephones became more common and Isabel had one installed. She was busy reading *Gone With The Wind,* the year's best seller from the USA. Rave reviews had appeared in newspapers.

As winter gave way to early spring, Lizzie was happier than she had ever been. She received a percentage of the sale price of the clothes she designed and sold, for now clients were asking for her by name, and word spread that a dress or ensemble designed by Elizabeth was highly desirable and sure to be a success.

One day in April, when they were exceptionally busy designing and taking orders for Ascot week, Sarah Devenoke swept into the salon, her tiny chihuahua under one arm, and wearing a magnificent chinchilla wrap.

'My dear,' Tatiana told Lizzie afterwards, 'she wanted something designed by Elizabeth. Isn't that a hoot? I told her you would be here tomorrow—I thought I had better prepare you—and she's coming in at ten.'

'Golly!' said Lizzie.

When Tatiana showed her into the fitting room, Sarah wore her most imperious look, but as soon as she caught sight of Lizzie, she stepped towards her and gave her a hug. 'Missed you, you silly girl,' she said gruffly.

'Oh, Miss Sarah!' Lizzie said, pleased as punch.

Sarah turned to Tatiana. 'She's clever, isn't she?'

'She is indeed,' Tatiana said, thinking that this was a side of Sarah Devenoke she hadn't known existed.

'I'll leave you to it then,' she said.

They talked the hind leg off a donkey, until Lizzie got down to work, sketching hard, knowing exactly the sort of thing that

Sarah liked to wear.

'You must be absolutely delighted,' Isabel said proudly. She had taken a back seat all this time, having had faith in the girl, knowing that she was different and talented. Now she wondered how she would ever be able to tell her of her innermost thoughts and suspicions, for the longer the charade went on, the more impossible it became to imagine she could ever confide in her.

Maybe it would be enough to sit back and bask in her glory.

Lizzie, busier than she had ever been in her young life, was glad when the season ended. Ascot and Henley were over, and she looked forward to a few days somewhere in the country with Isabel.

She was coming to the end of a trousseau designed for a young debutante, and was sketching the costumes and hats.

'Oh, veiling,' Isabel mused, looking over her shoulder one evening at the going away outfit, the small perky hat tilted over one eye, the little veil which came down a few inches over the brim.

'My mother used to wear hats with veils, and there's nothing more flattering. Of course, in those days the veils came right down over the face. I remember one in particular...'

'Really?' Lizzie was interested.

'Sometimes they were of fine net, black, brown, grey or navy, and sometimes had spots, or were embroidered with small flowers.'

'Didn't that look a bit odd? Could they see?'

Isabel laughed. 'Of course. They looked delightful, very fetching. We still have some somewhere—Mama used to buy it from Harrods—and of course, riding in the motor car it protected one's hair and kept one's hat on.'

Lizzie loved to listen to these stories. What a wonderful childhood Isabel must have had!

Isabel sat thinking. 'Upstairs on the top floor, in the little attic, you'll find a box, a large box. There are lots of treasures in there—ribbons, velvet, some lace, I think. I've never had any use for that sort of thing, but you might find it interesting. Top floor, on the right.'

Lizzie climbed the stairs. She never got tired of living in this lovely old house which was home to her now. After the third floor, the stair carpet changed to lino but the views from the landing were wonderful: rows and rows of London chimneys, slate roofs, and church spires. She would never tire of looking at it.

There was a key in the lock of the small narrow door, and she turned it and went in. Greeted by a musty, dry smell of old things stored for a long time, she soon found a large black tin box in the corner. There was a key in this too, and sinking to her knees Lizzie turned it and lifted the lid. Everything was wrapped in tissue paper and packed neatly, and she began to unwrap each parcel, soon finding the cards of veiling, navy blue with fine spots, black fish net, a silky grey which looked very elegant, then some bundles of assorted ribbons. She feared if she began to unwind them they would turn to dust, but testing them she found them quite strong. So many treasures! A bag of strange necklaces, wooden and carved, and a cloth bag containing feather hat ornaments that would be every bit as fashionable today as they were then. Would Isabel allow her to have them?

Then, tucked down the side of the box, a sepia photograph on cardboard, the picture of a young couple: the girl aged about eighteen or so, the young man with his arm around her shoulders.

Lizzie's heart stopped beating. It was a photograph of her father and Isabel.

It couldn't be. She took it to the window. It was Isabel all right, no question of that, smiling into the camera, looking youthfully pretty, but the young man—in Oxford bags, handsome, fair-haired, smiling—it was...

And now her heart began to beat so fast it almost choked her.

How could it be? Who was he? They were somewhat alike...it could almost be Isabel's brother, Edmund. How did Lizzie happen to have his picture in her locket? Her heart hammering, she hurriedly put everything back in the box, almost forgetting the cards of veiling in her haste, then stuffing the photograph inside her blouse, forgetting everything except the veiling, she closed the lid, left the room and locked the door after her. She must go to her room, and sometime later return the photograph to its rightful place.

Once inside her room, she swiftly took the locket out of the drawer and compared it with the photograph. Of course it was the same young man! True, it was the head and shoulders only in the locket, but there was no mistaking the fact that it was one and the same person.

She flopped into a chair, thinking hard. Was that why...did Isabel...was it a boyfriend or a friend of Isabel's whom her mother had later married? Was this man George Alfred Bartholomew? A footman? A manservant? He didn't look like a manservant with one arm casually around Isabel's shoulders. Or was it her brother Edmund? And if so, how was it his photograph was inside her mother's locket?

It was strange when she thought about it—there were no photographs about in the rooms she had been in, even Isabel's bedroom. Just two silver-framed pictures, one of Isabel in her presentation gown, and one of her parents. Nothing at all in the drawing room or library, which was unusual. Sarah had had dozens of silver-framed photographs about—though to be honest, mostly of herself.

It was half an hour before Lizzie went downstairs, composed as far as she could be, the photograph safely back in its place, holding the cards of veiling, her face smoothed and powdered, her lipstick renewed, smiling a little as she rejoined Isabel in the drawing room.

Isabel looked up. 'Ah, you found it then.'

'Yes, no trouble,' Lizzie said, staring at her as she sat down in her own chair. She began to unwind the veiling from the card.

'It's so pretty,' she said, wondering if her voice sounded as weak as she felt.

'Oh, yes, that's it!' Isabel cried, having obviously noticed nothing wrong. 'Oh, and the grey.'

'Could I have it?' Lizzie asked, her mind on anything but veiling.

'My dear, of course!' Isabel cried. 'And

197

anything else up there you might like.'

Lizzie smiled weakly. 'Thank you.'

She knew, though, what she was going to do. And as soon as possible.

CHAPTER 12

Two evenings later, after leaving the shop, Lizzie made her way to Seymour Street, an area which was strange to her although it was quite near home. Here the houses were small terraced homes with no hint of former glory, front doors open to the road and with children playing outside by the railings. It was obvious that this was a working-class area. Glimpses down the dark passages showed how grim life could be for some Londoners.

When Lizzie came to the number she wanted, she knocked at the door with the heavy black lion's head knocker and waited, her heart pounding.

A young woman came to answer her summons with a baby in her arms and a toddler at her skirt, looking suspiciously at Lizzie, who looked so out of place in her smart costume and chic little Tyrolean hat. She narrowed her eyes.

'I'm sorry to trouble you,' Lizzie began,

'but I am looking for someone by the name of Bartholomew. I am Lizzie Bartholomew.'

The woman frowned. 'Don't know anyone of that name,' she said.

'It was a long time ago—during the war.'

'Good Gawd!' the woman said.

'I know, it's a long time ago, but my father George used to live here—or lodge maybe. I wondered—'

She looked so genuine and so earnest, the young woman relented.

'No, I s'pect there's been a lot of families 'ere since then, duck,' she said. 'We're Williams, and before us there was the Atkinsons, and before them—'

'Never mind,' said Lizzie. After all, she hadn't really thought her journey would come to anything.

'Tell you what, though,' the young woman said. 'Next-door but one, that way, there's a family called Barton. They've been there for donkey's years. Your father, you say? Well, they've one or two sons'd be about that age. Try there, duck.'

'Thanks very much,' she said, realising now that she had calmed down more than somewhat, for the idea was quite ridiculous. Still, while she was here, she would try. Nothing ventured, nothing gained.

This door was closed, too, and when

Lizzie knocked a stout middle-aged woman answered and gave her a friendly smile.

'Mrs Barton?'

'I don't want nothing if you're selling, duck,' she said. True, this one didn't look as if she was selling but still you never knew—sometimes the ladies from the missions called, or people from the health department. This one, though, was a lady—real smart—

'The lady next-door but one told me that you have lived here for a very long time.'

'Thirty years, duck,' the woman said proudly.

Lizzie's hopes soared.

'Well, then, I'm looking for information about my father. He's dead now, killed in the war, but he used to live along here.'

'What was his name?'

'Bartholomew, George Bartholomew—and I am Lizzie Bartholomew.'

'Well, Miss Bartholomew...' said Mrs Barton, her hand to her face, as she concentrated.

Oh, please, Lizzie prayed, let her remember!

'Arthur and Leslie went to school with a George Bartholomew, now I come to think of it. It was in the war...'is mum and dad 'ad the basement flat. Course, they're dead now, poor things. Went back up north when he was killed. Arthur's married now, lives out Willesden way. Look, come in, won't you?'

And Lizzie took the plunge.

The long narrow passage led to a dark kitchen with a small window looking out on to a brick wall. There was a bright orange fire burning in the range, and the strong smell of cooking and washing, and there were clothes airing over the clothes horse. And Lizzie was reminded of her dark days in the orphanage laundry and gave an inward shudder.

'I'll put the kettle on and we'll have a cuppa tea,' said Mrs Barton. She moved the big black kettle from one side of the blackleaded range to the centre, and delving below the dresser cupboard, brought out an album, much thumbed and torn, and began to turn its pages.

A cup of tea later, and many many pages of browned photographs which meant nothing to Lizzie, they arrived at the war years, and there it was at last.

'They joined the army together,' Mrs Barton said proudly. 'George and Arthur —here they are.'

And side by side, laughing in front of a garden shed, were two young men, neither of whom Lizzie recognised.

'Which one is George?' she asked,

knowing either way it didn't matter. Neither of them was the young man in her locket.

'This one's George—oh, he was such a nice chap. In service, he was, in a big house in Hyde Park somewhere. My Arthur was a coalman. But they was such good pals.'

Lizzie was staring at George Bartholomew: good-looking, dark-haired, dark-eyed, an impressive moustache. There was no way he could possibly be the man in her locket.

'Do you know what happened to him?'

'Well, he was called up and went to France, and then he married—some young girl, Irish, I think she was, and they went away to live, and next thing I hear he's been killed. Oh, it was a terrible war.' Her bright face darkened at the memory. 'He was one of the unlucky ones. My Arthur was all right.' And then she looked at Lizzie.

'So you're his daughter? Yes, I can see the likeness,' she said, pouring Lizzie another cup of tea. 'And you coming after all this time—well, I never!'

'And this really is a picture of him?' Lizzie asked. She couldn't afford to take chances.

'Oh, yes, that's George Bartholomew —course you could have that, but I don't

202

know if Arthur would mind. You know, these days, I think they can take copies. Would you like me to? I can ask him.'

'No. No, thank you, really. I just wanted to see where he lived.'

She hated deceiving the woman who was anxious to help.

'You've been very kind. I'm so grateful.'

Fancy young George having a daughter like that, the woman thought as she escorted her to the door.

'He was a lovely young chap,' she said. 'We was all very fond of Georgie.'

Lizzie bit her lip 'Thank you,' she said, and long after she had disappeared round the corner, the woman stood at the door looking after her. Well I never, she thought. Wait till I tell the others... And going inside spent the rest of the afternoon reliving her memories with the aid of the album and many cups of tea.

Lizzie walked away from Seymour Street and into the park, she walked right across to Knightsbridge and back again before making for Hyde Park Square. Now, she thought, she knew the answer. Her real father must be the man in the locket, Edmund Lister. Although she didn't know the whole story she was sure she was right. Isabel must have suspected this, having known her mother. Why had she never said? Lizzie felt furious with her, yet as

203

things fell into place she realised that Isabel too could not have been sure. Could Edmund Lister have confided in his sister so that she did know? Oh, surely not. And yet... Perhaps they might never know? But Lizzie had one more thing to do.

Isabel awaited her anxiously, aware that for the past few days Elizabeth had been a trifle preoccupied. She'd put it down to pressure at the salon, she had been so busy with orders.

'Oh, there you are.'

No wonder, Lizzie thought, that she clucked over me like a mother hen. Did she see me as her brother's daughter—her very own niece?

She still had a part to play.

'Yes,' she said, peeling off her gloves. 'We have been awfully busy.'

'My dear, you look tired,' Isabel sympathised.

After dinner they sat in the drawing room before Lizzie went up to her room, which she usually did, while Isabel embroidered or read.

'I'm thinking of going down to Brighton for the weekend—would you mind, Isabel?'

Surprised, she looked up. 'Of course not.'

'I just had the feeling I would like a breath of sea air,' began Lizzie.

'We could go to Eastbourne.'

'No, that's sweet of you, but I felt I want to go down to see one or two old friends, the school, my mother's grave,' she said vaguely, hating herself for the lie.

'Of course you must,' Isabel said, hoping that perhaps the change might do her good.

'I'll go on Saturday and stay in a small hotel somewhere and come back after lunch on Sunday. You're sure you don't mind?'

She gave one of her special smiles to Isabel who was reassured.

'It will do you good,' she said. 'You can't live all your life attached to an old woman.'

'You're not old,' Lizzie said firmly. 'You're in the prime of life, and I enjoy living here enormously.' Which was the truth, she thought.

A fleeting suspicion crossed Isabel's mind that perhaps there was a man in it somewhere, but she discarded it. Not that Lizzie wasn't entitled to boy friends, at her time of life and as pretty as a picture, but there never seemed to be time to meet them.

'No, my dear, you go off and have a lovely weekend. Brighton air is so bracing. And stay somewhere nice and cosy. There are several small inns—'

'Yes, I will, Isabel.' Lizzie said, surprised how easily she had got over that hurdle, and found herself getting quite excited at the prospect of the trip.

In the train she sat back and went over what she already knew for a fact. That George Bartholomew was not the man whose photograph was in her locket, and that was all she could be sure of...

Perhaps, though, her mother had fallen in love with Edmund who was her secret hero, despite the difference in their status, someone she knew she could never marry. Perhaps someone whom she had allowed to—

Lizzie smelled the sea as soon as she stepped out of the train, and her eyes sparkled for it was nice to be down here again, especially since she was free and had no ties.

Walking along the sea front, she whipped off her hat, breathless as she battled against the strong breeze. Then she made her way to the old part of the town where she booked into a small hotel for the night, and having done that, went to the church and the cemetery where her mother was buried, after buying a huge spray of pink roses which she knew her mother had loved.

It was such a plain green grassy mound, with a small name marker. No fine memorial stone, no marble edifice or gold lettering—a simple unadorned grave. As she knelt, with unshed tears, Lizzie bit her lip and knew that one day she would see to it that there was a stone. Perhaps one day her children would ask 'Where is grandmother buried? Where did she live? What was she like?' and she would tell them. 'There is a beautiful white marble grave in Brighton.'

Placing the pink roses gently on the grass, Lizzie got up and walked away.

After lunch she walked around the town, revisiting it all, and later that evening had dinner in a small, darkly lit dining room where more than one masculine eye roved towards her solitary figure.

In the morning, armed with a bouquet of fresh flowers, she hailed a taxi to take her to Kemp Town, not knowing if after all this time Mrs Ransome still lived at number fourteen Rodney Street, and there was no way of finding out since she would hardly be likely to have a telephone.

The street seemed so narrow, the houses much smaller than she remembered. Tiny dwellings, each with its well kept garden and lace curtains, here and there an aspidistra in the window, a relic of bygone days.

Taking a deep breath, Lizzie rang the bell and waited.

Mrs Ransome answered the door, not much changed, still as neat and self-confident as ever she was. Lizzie smiled and over Mrs Ransome's face came a look of disbelief.

'Lizzie! Lizzie Bartholomew! My God, girl, what are you doing here? Come in, come in.'

The house was incredibly small inside, hardly room for them to walk down the narrow passage and into the kitchen. How strange it all seemed now. Lizzie gave a fearful glance towards the stairs.

'Yes, I've still got tenants,' Mrs Ransome said. 'A nice young couple. Well, this is a surprise. Sit you down and tell me all about it. Oh, they're lovely, thank you.' And she took the flowers into the scullery to put into water.

The kettle went on the gas ring in the scullery, and pulling the bead curtain behind her, Mrs Ransome sat down opposite Lizzie, looking at her across the plush tablecloth.

'Well, you could have knocked me down with a feather!' she said. 'Fancy seeing you after all this time. What are you doing with yourself—'

And Lizzie told her everything that had happened, except for the events of the past week and her suspicions.

'My word!' Mrs Ransome said. 'A real

fairy godmother she turned out to be—and the same place where your mother worked? Well, it don't sound real.'

She busied herself making tea, and brought in the tray and cups.

'I came,' Lizzie began, 'because I was hoping you might be able to help me.'

Mrs Ransome suddenly looked very serious. 'And how might that be?'

'Well...' And Lizzie withdrew the locket from her neck and showed it to Mrs Ransome who looked away. 'The photograph?'

'Yes?'

'Is it my father?'

'Well, dear, I wouldn't rightly know about that. It's certainly the locket your mum always wore.'

'I know, but is it the man who was married to my mother—George Bartholomew? Is it a picture of him?'

The anguish in her eyes was obvious, and Mrs Ransome's shoulders slumped.

'Show me again,' she said, and when Lizzie snapped open the locket, stared hard at the photograph.

'No, my dear. I don't know who that is. I've never seen him before, although he's handsome all right. Your father was a lovely man, dark, good-looking, dark eyes. This man is fair, different.'

'Different class, you mean?'

'Well, he looks to be well born, shall we say, a gentleman. But so was your father.'

'I know,' Lizzie said, snapping the locket shut and letting it fall inside her blouse.

'Did you know anything about them before they came to you? Where they worked, that sort of thing.'

'Yes, your mother told me she worked in Hyde Park Square, I think it was, as a parlourmaid, and your dad, well, he was a footman before he went into the army. I think she said he worked in the same square.'

They both fell silent.

'I expect you've come to the same conclusion I did when you first opened that locket,' Mrs Ransome said at length, and met Lizzie's wide green eyes.

'Yes, I've put two and two together, and that's what I think—but we will never know, will we? I just wanted to ask you because, well, I felt Miss Lister had been so kind, and now I suspect she was trying to make amends.'

'From what you've told me, I think she's been a brick—after all she didn't have to do anything—and she still don't know for sure.'

'No,' Lizzie agreed. 'I'll have to live with it, but I feel better now that I've spoken to you. You can understand that, can't you?'

'Yes, lovey, I can. I've often wondered about it, that picture in the locket, but now you say it's a picture of Miss Lister's brother—well—you have to put two and two together.'

'And yet it doesn't have to be so, does it?'

She was lovely, Mrs Ransome thought, grown into a lovely young woman, and spoke so nicely—yet set about with anxiety and not knowing. Who could tell what she was thinking? It didn't always do for folk to be kind and generous like that Miss Lister. She had stirred up a hornet's nest. It might have been better if Lizzie had never known.

'Another thing,' she said, stirring her tea. 'This Miss Lister might guess at the truth and feel she shouldn't tell you in case you feel upset to think that your mother—well, had been with Mr Lister before she got married.'

'Yes, I did think of that—oh, there are so many things. But now I'm glad I started the search. Although I may never know, I just feel sorry for what my mother went through. It must have been terrible. Yet I can remember her when I was very small. She was pretty, always laughing and singing.'

Mrs Ransome smiled. 'Oh, yes, she was always singing, nice little voice she had.'

'Then there seems to be a gap between those days and when I went to live in the orphanage.'

'Yes, that should never 'ave been, duck,' Mrs Ransome said sadly. 'But there she was, a young woman racked with TB, and no one to look after you. I couldn't do it, I had my own youngsters.'

'I remember them—the boys,' Lizzie said slowly.

'Yes, they was a handful and no mistake. And my Bert—well, he was funny about it. Didn't see why I should take on the extra care of another child, and to tell the truth, he didn't much like your ma staying with us. But I put my foot down. "Where's she to go?" I said. Poor young thing—no family. Still, there you are, it was fate. When he was called up he was killed in France before I even 'ad a letter from 'im.'

She sniffed and blew her nose, while Lizzie's eyes darkened with sympathy.

'You've had your share of tragedy, too, Mrs Ransome.'

'Well, I've been spared. I've 'ad good 'ealth, and that's everything.'

'You've been very kind,' Lizzie said. 'I shall always appreciate it.'

'She was happy, though,' Mrs Ransome said. 'Really she was. And when you were born—well, she was that pleased there was no holding her. And I'll tell you this much, there's no doubt in this world who your mother was. You're the spitting image of her!'

Lizzie smiled through her tears as Mrs Ransome poured out a second cup of tea and handed it to her.

'Come to think of it, she did 'ave post at one time—before your father was killed. From France. Oh, he sent her lovely postcards, some of them silk-embroidered—I wonder she never kept them, they was so pretty. She had one or two letters from someone, nice writing—I used to leave them on the 'allstand for her. Not from your father, I got to know his writing.'

Lizzie felt excitement stir within her. 'Do you remember the postmark on them, Mrs Ransome? Was it Ireland?'

'No—she never had nothing from Ireland. I always used to wonder why, it seemed such a shame—after all, she must have had parents there. No, they was from London. The cream envelopes, lovely writing—she never mentioned them.'

Edmund Lister, Lizzie thought.

She stayed for an hour before leaving and catching the train back to London. Had it been worthwhile? Perhaps. She felt better and calmer about Isabel. When she turned up that time on the Listers' doorstep, what a shock Isabel must have had.

Lizzie planned to carry on as usual, glad to be going home after a pleasant week. She would bury the things she had found out in the dark recesses of her mind—no good would come of anything else—and carry on where she left off. After all, she was more independent now, she was earning and able to pay her way. In fact she had no good reason to stay with Isabel, but she knew she would. She was fond of her and loved being in the square. It was like home, the only roots she had.

Her resolutions were shattered the moment she put the key in the door, for on the other side of it stood Isabel, her blue eyes searching Lizzie's, the appeal in them more than she could bear. In a moment, they had their arms around each other.

'Isabel—'

'Oh, Elizabeth!' And Isabel wept.

Presently, together, they walked into the drawing room, Lizzie with an arm round Isabel's shoulders, and sat side by side on the sofa.

'How did you know?' Lizzie asked.

'I can't tell you exactly but I felt there was something, and I remembered that you had come down from upstairs somewhat preoccupied and it had started from there. So I went upstairs—and, Elizabeth, I wouldn't have had it happen for the world!'

'I know, but perhaps it was fate that it did. I'm glad I saw it, and I'm glad I did what I did. Shall I tell you how I got on?'

Afterwards, they sat silently for a long time.

'Well, we're both in the dark, but I feel strongly that you are Edmund's daughter. I have from the moment I saw you. You might say it was wishful thinking, perhaps it is, but there is a look of Mama about you, lots of small things. Besides...'

'Well, it doesn't make any difference to us, does it?' Lizzie asked. 'I'd like to go on as before.'

'There is one difference,' Isabel said seriously. 'I am sure you are a Lister and that means quite a lot to me.'

'If that's the case, I feel a bit sorry for George Bartholomew,' Lizzie said. 'I wonder if he knew?'

'Your mother would have told him—she was a good girl, and honest.'

'I'm glad,' Lizzie said, and Isabel saw that the anxious look had disappeared from her eyes. She looked more relaxed.

'I've always been glad that you were called Elizabeth,' Isabel said presently.

'Why?' Lizzie asked.

'It was my mother's name.'

CHAPTER 13

There was great excitement at the beginning of August in Tatiana's salon when an unexpected guest was announced and no one was in the slightest doubt as to who she was. Accompanied by a friend, Mrs Ernest Simpson arrived, her vivid blue eyes sparkling with curiosity. Immaculately dressed, her sleek black hair centre parted, she asked to see Tatiana herself. She would like, she explained, to look at some sketches of holiday wear, light, pretty dresses, simply cut and elegant, since she was about to embark on a cruise in the Aegean. She had heard of the new designer Elizabeth, who was enjoying such a success with her stylish models, perhaps she could see her?

Tatiana was over the moon. It was common knowledge that Mrs Simpson had filed a petition for divorce against her husband, from whom she had separated, and rumours were rife that the King had invited her to dinner at York House to meet Mr Baldwin, the Prime Minister. That the King must soon marry was not in doubt, but an American divorcee?

216

Tatiana was grateful for any publicity that might ensue from Mrs Simpson's visit, for if she chose anything from Elizabeth's collection, her future as a dress designer would be assured.

Elizabeth was cool and collected as Tatiana had known she would be. The girl seemed so self-assured that she was intimidated by no one. With the correct amount of respect and deference, Elizabeth dealt with her, overlooked by Tatiana, and by the time Wallis Simpson left, she had chosen four outfits.

She was perfect for clothes, Elizabeth decided. You could hang anything on that slim figure and it would look good, but there was a way of draping and hanging a dress to make it look even more attractive. Mrs Simpson listened politely, her head slightly to one side, but there was no chance of talking her into anything. She knew what she liked, and would be advised but not told. Which was as it should be, Elizabeth thought. When someone as elegant as this condescended to buy from you, you obviously tried to please her.

When Mrs Simpson left, settling into the back of the enormous Bentley, her companion beside her, Tatiana threw her arms around Elizabeth and hugged her.

'Golly!' she said. It was so unlike Tatiana to be demonstrative.

'Well, you are a clever little thing!' Tatiana cried. 'Now, let's see what she's decided on.' And together they pored over the swiftly drawn designs and the pile of clothes hanging over the chairs in the private changing room.

'Do you realise that one day she may be Queen?' Tatiana said, drawing her brows together. 'It doesn't seem possible, does it? I know she's stunning, but you wouldn't have thought with all the beauties there are, gorgeous girls, English girls who would be eminently suitable, he would choose an American. Still, who am I to complain? It's good for business.'

'But she is charming,' Elizabeth said, for want of a better word.

She couldn't wait to get home and tell Isabel, whom she knew would be as pleased as Punch, but Isabel had her own news. She had received a letter from the Far East.

'Do you recall my mentioning to you a Major Hetherington?'

'Yes, I do. Isn't he the son of a friend of your father's, lives in Malaya?'

'Yes, that's right. His father ran the rubber plantation. I've met him, but I don't know the son. Well, apparently he is over here, visiting an aged aunt who lives in Scotland, and says when he comes to London he would like to call on us.'

'Oh, Isabel, how nice!' Lizzie was pleased for her—she had so few friends.

'So now tell me your news.'

'You'll never guess who came into the salon today—shall I tell you? Mrs Simpson!'

'Not *the* Mrs Simpson, the King's...'

'Yes, none other. And she ordered four outfits, how about that?'

Isabel was delighted. 'Elizabeth, that's wonderful! You have arrived!'

'That's what Tatiana said.'

'You know, I always knew you had something there. I suppose it's a gift.'

'Must be.' And Elizabeth smiled.

'Oh, and another thing, this morning we received an invitation to Lady Devenoke's —to dinner.'

'No!' Elizabeth cried, her mouth open, eyes dancing at the thought.

'She obviously feels you've arrived—and this is before the advent of Mrs Wallis Simpson!'

'Well, she has bought a lot of my things at the salon.'

'For which Tatiana must be eternally grateful. I tell you, she must be awfully pleased I introduced you to her.'

Elizabeth didn't say that both Sarah and her mother had approached her privately and asked her to make outfits without reference to Tatiana.

219

'I'm sorry,' she had said sweetly. 'Can't be done. I work for Tatiana—all orders go through her.'

'But that's ridiculous!' Sarah said. 'You were making clothes for me long before you worked there!'

'Such a thing as loyalty. I work for Tatiana now.'

'You could make yourself a bit on the side,' Sarah suggested.

'I don't need to, I'm doing very nicely as I am.'

'Oh, come on, Lizzie,' Sarah pleaded, but a steely glint had come into Elizabeth's eye.

'Elizabeth, Sarah. That's my name.' And she'd decided that's what she would be from now on.

'Oh, sorry, Elizabeth, then,' Sarah said huffily, but soon the two of them were laughing. Their disagreements never lasted very long.

That evening, after dinner, Isabel turned to Elizabeth with a serious expression.

'When you have a moment, there's something I would like to talk to you about.'

'Is there something wrong?'

'No, my dear, of course not, but I must talk to you about my plans.'

'Your plans?'

'Yes, dear, I just want to get things

straight.' And that was all she would say.

'What about Friday evening after dinner?' Elizabeth suggested.

The leaves of the great trees had changed colour; where the sun had reached them they were red and gold, lending a splash of colour to the autumn evening as Isabel and Elizabeth sat in the drawing-room overlooking the square.

'How long have you lived here, Isabel?' Elizabeth asked.

'My dear, I was born here. In those days one always had one's babies at home, and Edmund and I were born here. In fact that's something I want to talk to you about.'

She settled herself in the deep armchair.

'I love this house—always have. I can't imagine ever living anywhere else, and that's something I wanted to discuss with you. We have it on a long lease, a hundred years to be exact, which expires in a few years' time. Of course, one would wish to renew it, since we have the option. What I am coming to is that I am making a new will.' She heard Elizabeth's intake of breath.

'I know you don't want me to talk about it but, my dear, I can't last forever, and I have to be sensible about this. Now, had my brother lived, he would have inherited the estate instead of me. But there, he didn't, so it came to me, and it is this I want to tell you. I am making an investment for you from which you will receive the interest annually until you are twenty-one, when you will inherit a lump sum.'

Elizabeth looked worried.

'I know you find this embarrassing, Elizabeth, but you will have to listen. I am doing this because I choose to believe you are Edmund's daughter, and would like you to inherit. There is no one else except distant relatives who don't count anyway, and apart from a few bequests to charities, the estate will be yours when I die. I hope you will keep the house on—if I am gone, that is. The Lister's have lived here for almost ninety years.'

Elizabeth was near to tears.

'I don't know what to say. I know you're doing this for me and because you think I am part of the family, but you don't know that I am, do you?'

'What's the difference?' Isabel asked. 'It's what I believe, what I choose to believe, and what more fitting than that you should be like a daughter to me? I don't want to hear another word about it.'

'But can you understand my feelings?' Elizabeth asked.

'You mean, you feel obliged in some way?'

222

Elizabeth frowned. 'Yes, sort of, in a way. It all came out of the blue—from nowhere. If I hadn't called that day you would never have known anything about me.'

'But you did, and I do,' Isabel said firmly. 'It was fate.'

'You will be advised by your solicitor, won't you?' Elizabeth suggested. 'He might not think it at all a good idea. And after all, I am earning money now, and making quite a success of my work.'

'And good luck to you, my dear.' Isabel said. 'No, my mind is made up, and unless you are utterly opposed to the idea, I shall consider you a Lister.' She saw the stubborn look come over Elizabeth's face.

'I don't want to change my name, Isabel.'

'I was afraid you'd say that. Well, that's for you to decide, but if ever...'

'No, I was born a Bartholomew, and until it's proved otherwise, I don't feel I could—or should—change it.'

'Then so be it.' Isabel smiled. 'Now—after all that—what do you think?'

Elizabeth was silent for a few seconds. 'I'm shattered at your generosity,' she said. 'After all, you don't really know me. You're taking me on face value.'

'And I like what I see,' Isabel said. 'So shall we leave it at that? You would make

223

me very happy if you would agree.'

Elizabeth kissed her swiftly. 'Then of course I shall,' she said. 'Goodness, why wouldn't I? It seems I am getting the best of the bargain.'

That night she lay awake thinking and going over the past two years, from the time she had called at Hyde Park Square to these latest events. Perhaps, as Isabel said, it was fate—and who was she to complain?

Except, of course, that she would not be entirely free, and this was difficult to take in when you had been used to looking after yourself from an early age and were still young with the whole world in front of you. She would always be beholden to Isabel for her actions, but then if ever she did feel inclined to throw her bonnet over the windmill and Isabel disapproved, she would be disinherited, so what did it matter?

All in all, she decided, she was a very lucky girl.

Arthur Hetherington came to dinner one evening in May and turned out to be a man in his late-fifties, tall and well dressed, with a military bearing. Isabel was very impressed and delighted to see him.

'How very nice of you to come!'

'It is a pleasure to meet you, Miss Lister.'

He gripped her hand firmly, which pleased her. She couldn't bear men with a weak handshake.

'And are you returned from Malaya for good, Major?' she asked leading the way to the drawing room.

'Yes, Miss Lister, I am now retired,' he said, smiling down at her. 'And delighted to be so. I have had a long sojourn out East, but times are changing, and not always for the better. Still, never mind. It is a joy to be back home.'

'And this is my niece, Elizabeth,' Isabel said with a swift conspiratorial look at her. Elizabeth could hardly believe Isabel had said it.

'How do you do, Major Hetherington?'

But Isabel was not going to meet her eye, and they went into the drawing room.

Over dinner, the Major kept them enthralled with tales of Malaysia, of his return to Eton to school in term time, and life on the rubber plantation when he left school. He had spent all his working life out East, except for brief visits home.

'I recall meeting your father—a fine man, held in great esteem,' he said, which pleased Isabel more than somewhat. She felt as though she had met an old friend.

Between them, she and Elizabeth had planned an excellent meal, on which they were complimented, and before leaving them alone to go to her room, Elizabeth joined them in the drawing room over coffee.

'I don't want to play gooseberry,' she whispered to Isabel, who blushed furiously and looked reproachfully at her.

'Elizabeth has been having a great success with her collection,' she said proudly.

The Major was very interested, and wanted to know more about it. On hearing that Mrs Simpson had been one of her customers, he was more than impressed.

'Oh, well done!' he cried. 'I know that she is very difficult to please. She has often visited a friend of mine who lives near Fort Belvedere, she and the King spend a lot of time there.'

'Have you ever met her?' Isabel asked, her eyes positively glowing with suppressed excitement, Elizabeth noted.

'Yes, I have,' he answered, 'she is most charming.'

He sat in her father's high-backed chair, and Isabel thought how well he fitted into the background. Straight-backed, his handsome face in the half light resembling her father's a little as a younger man, it was a long time since she had entertained anyone like him.

'Perhaps,' she suggested tentatively, 'you would care for a brandy?'

'How kind,' he said. 'Thank you.'

'Then you must help yourself.' Isabel pointed to the table on which sat the decanters, all of which had been filled earlier by Mrs Baines on her instructions.

He got up and walked over to the table, a tall, distinctive figure, and Elizabeth smiled across at Isabel. He looked very much at home.

'I was sorry to hear that your aunt had been so ill,' Isabel said.

'It is not surprising, since she is ninety-three years old and after all cannot go on forever. And she has an excellent nurse and housekeeper.'

'So you felt quite happy to leave her in such good hands?' Isabel asked.

'Yes, indeed.'

'Whereabouts in Scotland does she live?'

'Edinburgh.'

'One of my favourite places. At least it used to be,' said Isabel.

'Do you know it well?'

'I haven't been for some years but my mother came from Duntaig.'

'Oh, a delightful spot. I have been there many times.'

Isabel beamed. She hadn't enjoyed herself so much for ages.

'This is an excellent brandy,' the Major said.

'I expect it would be. My father put

down a good cellar, although of course these days it is not used much.'

They seemed to be getting on like a house on fire, Elizabeth thought, and excusing herself, went up to her room.

What, she wondered, would she wear to dinner at Sarah's house, which was in three days' time. She decided on the heavy cream satin-backed marocain.

Getting it out of the wardrobe, she slipped into it and was more than pleased at her reflection. Floor-length, it draped her slim figure, a slight cowl neckline in front which fell backless to the waist, where the material was gathered into a slight bustle and fell in folds. A huge green satin bow sat atop the bustle effect, and with it she wore her green emerald paste earrings and necklace, and green satin slippers.

She stood back from the mirror. Yes, it was just right. How strange it would be to enter that house again as a guest. She had come such a long way in a short time, it was almost unbelievable, from being a servant to an invited guest—and wondered how Isabel was getting on downstairs.

At ten-thirty she heard the front door being closed, and knew that the Major was on his way home.

She hoped Isabel had enjoyed herself. It would be nice if she could see him more often. That was what she needed, more company of her own age. Especially male, she grinned to herself. After all, Isabel was still young, not all that old to be left on the shelf.

When they arrived at the Devenoke house the butler ushered them in by name, and Sarah came forward to greet them, Josh staying in the background.

She looked stunning in floor-length black organza which showed off her fair skin to perfection, her thick fair hair upswept to disclose long diamond earrings. Isabel had a moment to notice how Joshua looked at her, his eyes devouring her as she graciously welcomed them.

'Elizabeth! Miss Lister—how nice to see you both. I am so glad you could come.' And then Joshua came forward to take Isabel's hand.

'I am so pleased to meet you, Miss Lister, after all this time. Surprising, is it not, that over the years we have never met?'

Isabel thought he was charming, and when he smiled into Elizabeth's green eyes, there was a glint of humour in his own.

'We meet again,' he said, 'and I believe congratulations are in order?'

'Thank you,' Elizabeth said softly, and moved on to join the other guests in the drawing room.

'Come and meet our guests,' Sarah said, every bit the perfect hostess. 'I'd like you to meet my brother Roger, and his fiancee Briony Cunningham. And this is her sister—Estelle.'

'Roger and Briony are getting married in the spring, and I thought a word or two in her ear about the wedding gown and trousseau,' she whispered in an aside to Elizabeth.

Elizabeth had a vision of the bride as she would like to see her—something that was happening to her more and more these days. She frequently re-dressed women mentally, now that she had learned what various materials did for certain women, and the cut of a dress for others. Colouring, she decided, was the most important thing, and this girl was lovely with dark hair and huge dark eyes.

Isabel was caught up with Lord Devenoke, where they sat in a corner chatting as if they had known each other for years.

'Look at them,' smiled Sarah. 'Just about the right age for each other! Hello, Daphne, so glad you could come.'

Sarah was naughty, Elizabeth thought, although she had to restrain a smile. Later, at dinner, she found herself next to Josh.

'And tell me, Elizabeth, what you have been doing since you left us?'

It wasn't difficult, he was a good listener,

and she found herself actually enjoying talking to him. He had an unexpected sense of wry humour, and she wondered if Sarah ever encountered that. He worshipped his wife so much, perhaps it never came into play? It seemed to her a sad marriage, although maybe he was happy to settle for what he had, a beautiful social butterfly whom most men found desirable according to the glossy magazines, for Sarah was never out of them, seldom with Josh, but always with a good-looking escort.

Sarah was in her element: on one side Richard Barrington a young handsome bachelor, and on the other Gervase Montel, a wealthy Argentinian who bred horses and who had a beautiful wife. Where was she this evening?

It was obvious that he was not missing her, and neither was Sarah. The looks that passed between them were eloquent and Elizabeth hoped that his lordship had not noticed, telling herself she knew Sarah so well that the slightest flicker of an eyelash would give her away.

'Tell me, Elizabeth,' Joshua asked with a smile, 'how long has your aunt lived in Hyde Park Square?'

She came back to earth.

'All her life,' I believe,' she answered, and looked up to find Richard Barrington's eyes on her. Then they smiled at each other, and the moment passed.

Catching the look between them, Josh offered, 'We were at school together, Richard and I. He's great fun. In the army, stationed in Knightsbridge. You must meet him later.'

And Elizabeth found herself quite looking forward to it.

Later, when the men rejoined them in the drawing room, Richard Barrington came straight over to Elizabeth.

Facing him, she found him taller than she expected, broad shouldered, fair, with amazing blue eyes which smiled into hers with open admiration. She was surprised to discover how much she was affected by his nearness.

'I have been waiting for this moment all evening,' he said. 'Miss Elizabeth Lister—am I right?'

She smiled back at him. 'And you are Richard—'

Barrington,' he finished for her.

He held out his hand and took hers, holding it a moment longer than was necessary.

'How do you do, Elizabeth? May I be so bold?'

'Of course.' She laughed.

He too her arm. 'Shall we—'

'It has—' Elizabeth began at the same time, and they both laughed.

'Let's find a corner,' he said, propelling her away from the group. 'I think we might discover lots to talk about.'

Elizabeth allowed herself to be led. Really, he had quite a commanding way with him—that came of being in the army, she supposed, a profession unknown to her. She could still feel the pressure of his arm on hers as he found a seat for her on a small banquette then took his place beside her.

'Tell me about you, Elizabeth,' he prompted, and she caught Sarah's eye across the room. Sarah lowered one eyelid slowly, and turned back to talk to her guests.

CHAPTER 14

When Arthur came to lunch on a Sunday, Elizabeth didn't mind for it left her free in the afternoon to work or to see Sarah, with whom she had struck up a second friendship. They sat in her boudoir one blustery October afternoon, gossiping and discussing Sarah's dinner party.

'You seem to have made a hit with Richard Barrington,' Sarah remarked. 'Josh said he couldn't stop talking about you.'

Elizabeth blushed. 'Really? I liked him too.'

'He's loaded—and there's a title there somewhere.'

'Sarah! Is that all you ever think about?'

'Well, it's important to make a good marriage.'

'Isn't that what you did?' Elizabeth asked gently, and saw Sarah flush.

'Well, you've got more sense than I had. Your feet are firmly on the ground.'

'That's true.'

'Did he ask to see you again?'

'Yes, he did. He's had to go to Germany, and says he'll give me a ring when he gets back.'

'Hmm.' Sarah looked impressed. 'He's not married.'

'I should hope not!' laughed Elizabeth.

Sarah studied her nails.

'What did you think of Gervase Montel?' she asked idly.

'I expect what's more to the point is what you think of him?' Elizabeth laughed. 'He's your type, that's for sure!'

'I know, he's gorgeous—he and his wife have an open marriage,' Sarah explained.

'I'm not surprised. He's such a good-looking man, and she's a beauty—I saw her the other day in Bond Street.'

'She's as tough as old boots,' Sarah sniped. 'He doesn't love her, you know.'

'I can't imagine why they stay together.'
'Convenience,' Sarah said laconically. 'When two people each have money they tend to stay together—it's a kind of protection, one for the other.'
Funny kind of marriage, Elizabeth thought, making her way home.

Major Hetherington became a regular visitor to Hyde Park Square, and when Armistice Day arrived in November, escorted Isabel and Elizabeth to the Cenotaph in Whitehall.
The special day had a particular poignancy this year. In October Mrs Simpson had obtained a decree nisi of divorce and rumours abounded that the King intended to marry her and give up the throne. It was a time of unease throughout the country, and all eyes were on him as he laid his wreath, a short, slight figure in naval uniform. They saw his mother Queen Mary receive his salute, and the same thoughts were going through everyone's mind. She stood stolidly, a regal figure in black, her small black toque worn tilted forward over her abundant grey hair.
What was going through her mind? they wondered. And his? Would he marry this woman, this divorced woman, could she be Queen—would she be allowed to be? If not, if he abdicated, the Duke and Duchess

of York would succeed, and he, poor man, not in the least anxious to take over the burden of state.

They stood for the two minutes silence, each with his own thoughts, Lizzie feeling more than she had ever done the sadness of those two young men, one of them her real father, dying out there on the battlefield in France.

On Monday morning she went round to Bond Street and made her way to Park Place where the wholesale premises were located. She always enjoyed her visits to the showroom; there was such a camaraderie between the staff and they were always so helpful.

'Good morning, Lily,' she said to the chief assistant, a woman of about forty whose dry humour she appreciated.

'Good morning, dear,' Lily said. Her smooth black hair was drawn back into a bun, her pale fair skin sprinkled with freckles. She always wore black satin which set off her colouring, and there was nothing she didn't know about materials. She had been a great help to Elizabeth on more than one occasion.

Elizabeth brought out her sketch pad, and small samples of silk.

'What do you think of this? I decided on it after all.'

'I knew you would—it's just right.'

Lily brought down a bolt of fine pink silk, embroidered with tiny white flowers. 'It's the prettiest thing,' she said, holding it against herself. 'Not for everyone, mind.'

'But just right for the client I have in mind. Ten yards will do.'

'Have a nice weekend?' Lily asked, spreading the counter with silk.

'Yes, and you?'

'I went for a walk in the park with Mr Battersby and the dog.' And she gave Elizabeth a wink from one of her pale grey eyes.

Mr Battersby, Elizabeth had learned earlier, was the name of Lily's boy friend, a man in his sixties who was, so he'd told her, happily married. Their friendship, or affair, had gone on for fifteen years to their mutual enjoyment and sometimes she appeared with a flower pinned to her bosom which usually meant he had taken her out the night before.

'Silly old codger,' she added affectionately, 'but I love him dearly.'

'That's that,' she said, carefully rolling the silk round a cardboard tube. 'What else?'

'This,' said Elizabeth, showing her the drawing of a three piece costume.

Lily studied it, seeing the mid-calf length straight skirt, edge to edge jacket with slightly raised collar, the tailored blouse beneath with the same collar line.

'Oh, that's lovely, dear! I love the waistline—and what did you have in mind?'

'A fine crêpe, dark green, with a boldly striped waistcoat effect blouse.'

Lily thought. 'The colour might be difficult but I know Paris is using green...wait a moment.'

She disappeared into the stockroom, and Elizabeth perched herself on a high stool and waited. At that moment, a tall young man walked through and smiled at her.

'Elizabeth, how are you?'

'Why, Louis.' And she held out her hand. 'We don't often see you here.'

Louis Vereker, the son of Adam Vereker who owned the wholesale business, greeted her warmly.

'I'm just back from China.'

'How wonderful!' Elizabeth said enviously. He looked down at her sketch.

'Very elegant. How are things going?'

She told him, and he was impressed.

'You've come on exceedingly well—it's not easy,' he said. 'Some of our customers went through a rough patch but things have picked up again.'

He smiled at her, showing excellent teeth.

'And how is your aunt?' He knew Isabel

238

from Elizabeth's taking her to the shop on one occasion.

'She's well—and your father?'

'Complaining mostly.' And he made a face. 'Looking forward to his retirement.'

'And then it will be your turn,' Elizabeth said. 'Do you mean to make any changes?'

'I don't think so—at the moment. I'm more interested than he has been in the new materials coming from the States. Synthetics, that sort of thing.'

Elizabeth frowned. 'Oh, but they're not at all like the real thing—how could they be?'

'Not perhaps for your clientele, but I am looking to the future, when maybe not everyone will be able to afford silks. And ladies like to dress up, so I may expand and go into the cheaper end of the market as well. After all, mulberry trees can't last forever.'

'You don't mean materials like rayon? That's horrible—'

'Well, it is improving all the time, and new fabrics are being invented.'

'I suppose I never thought about that side of it.'

'You'd have to if you ran this business.' He smiled. 'Ah, here's Lily. I hope to see you, Elizabeth, before I leave for the States in January.'

'Yes, that would be nice,' she agreed,

239

as Lily arrived with two bolts of fine wool crêpe, one olive green and one forest green.

'There!' she said, laying them down. 'I'm getting a bit long in the tooth to be carrying these things about.'

'You should get Harry to do it,' Louis said.

'Try finding him when you want him!'

Louis fingered the dark green cloth. 'Lovely,' he said. 'Fine, pure wool—and it's as soft as silk.'

Elizabeth's eyes were shining. The sight of colour and expensive materials always excited her.

'Well, I'll be on my way. Good day, Elizabeth.'

'Goodbye, Louis,' she said.

Lily watched his tall, elegant figure. 'I wish I was younger,' she said gloomily. 'I'd make a play for him. Smasher, that's what he is.' And unaccountably Elizabeth blushed.

'Louis? Yes, he's sweet,' she murmured. She wasn't going to admit that after she visited Vereker's she often found herself thinking about him.

Outside the world of fashion, things were hotting up, with the Bishop of Bradford making a speech at the beginning of December to the effect that the King must do his duty by the nation—the first implied criticism of the King's private life. It provoked a storm at last throughout the country.

Mrs Simpson had been sent to France, and now each day brought reports of what was going on between the King and Parliament, and conjecture as to what was to happen next. The people waited with bated breath.

They hadn't long to wait for on 10 December the King abdicated in favour of his brother Bertie, and the nation reeled with shock. They had a new King and Queen, King George VI and Queen Elizabeth.

Isabel thought it was the most romantic thing she had ever heard, while Arthur Hetherington was scathing.

'Silly young devil!' he said. 'Wants horsewhipping.'

Elizabeth had mixed feelings, remembering Mrs Simpson and her visits to the salon. How odd to think she had been the cause of rocking a nation and the abdication of a King.

As Christmas approached, she was inundated with orders for evening gowns and party dresses which kept her busy more than somewhat. When the telephone rang on Christmas Eve she was startled to hear Louis Vereker's voice.

'Elizabeth?'

'Yes.'

'I'm going to the States in January, as I think I told you, and I wondered if you would care to have dinner with me before I go?'

'Oh!' She was so surprised that she was lost for an answer.

'Would you, Elizabeth?' And she was suddenly quite excited at the thought. After all, when did she ever go out? Hardly ever, except on those few social occasions with Isabel.

'Yes, I'd like to.'

'Oh, good.' He sounded pleased. 'The first of January, does that suit you?'

She had no intention of consulting her diary. 'Yes, that's fine.'

'May I pick you up—say seven?'

'Yes. You know where I live?'

'Not far from me. I'll see you then. And, Elizabeth?'

'Yes?'

'Have a wonderful Christmas.'

'You too,' she said softly, and when she hung up the telephone, her green eyes were sparkling with pleasure.

'Who was that?' Isabel asked when she returned to the drawing room.

'Louis Vereker.'

'Who?' Isabel frowned.

'He's the son of the man from Vereker's.

You know—Bond Street, where I buy my materials.'

'Oh. What did he want?'

'He's asked me out to dinner on New Year's day,' Elizabeth said, smiling.

'Oh,' Isabel said, somewhat relieved. 'A business thing.'

'I'm not sure.' And Elizabeth made her way upstairs, leaving Isabel looking after her.

They spent Christmas at home quietly, and not by any small sign did Elizabeth betray the fact that she was waiting for Christmas to be over so that she could keep her January date. As the days went by, she grew more and more excited at the thought of seeing Louis again.

Isabel invited Arthur Hetherington for dinner on the last night of the Old Year, and he came bearing a sheaf of roses, such a wonderful sight at Christmas that Isabel was quite overcome with pleasure.

'Oh, Arthur, how lovely. You shouldn't have.'

'My dear Isabel, my pleasure.' And he looked down at her, the warmth of feeling in his eyes unmistakable.

'You go into the drawing room. I'll arrange them for you,' Elizabeth said, wondering not for the first time what the end result of this friendship would be. It had escalated by leaps and bounds. But it was nice for Isabel, who was obviously very fond of him. Perhaps he would ask her to marry him for he was a widower after all...

He stayed late, and they rang in the New Year, listening to the radio programmes coming to them from all over the world, and hearing the bells peal from nearby churches. At midnight, Elizabeth went up to bed, leaving them downstairs in the drawing room by the glowing fire.

Tomorrow, she thought, a few more hours, and I shall see Louis again.

He called for her at seven, looking terribly handsome in his dark suit, and Gertrude, the new maid, showed him into the drawing room where Isabel sat.

'Mr Vereker, miss.'

Isabel looked up and could quite see what Elizabeth found so attractive. He took her hand and bowed, French fashion.

'Please sit down,' she said, trying not to show how disconcerted she felt at the intrusion of this young man into Elizabeth's affections. Yet she told herself it was time the child had a life of her own.

'Thank you.'

'I think Elizabeth met you at your place of business? I accompanied her there once.'

244

'Yes, my father's business,' Louis said, not minding in the least that he was under interrogation and close scrutiny.

'In which you are actively involved?' Isabel asked.

'Yes, I take over soon when he retires—in March, as a matter of fact. Before that I am off to America on business.'

'I see,' Isabel said. Trade, she thought. This wouldn't do at all. Still, she must not read too much into it. It was just a pity that Elizabeth hadn't met any worthwhile young men. Perhaps she should do something about that...

'Hello.' And Elizabeth came into the room, a vision in midnight blue and vivid green.

There was no doubting the look in Louis' eyes as this vision of loveliness stood before him.

'Elizabeth, you look wonderful!'

'Thank you, I'm glad you approve. It's my latest design.'

'It might have come straight from Schiaparelli.'

'One day you'll know my name just as well!'

They made a handsome couple, Isabel thought, but surely Elizabeth realised she didn't have to fall in love with the first man who asked her out?

'Have a good evening,' she said as they

left, Elizabeth with a midnight blue velvet cape around her shoulders, Louis tall and handsome beside her.

Isabel resumed her embroidery. Well, it had to happen someday, but Elizabeth was worth more than a young man from a shop—whatever he was like. Arthur was coming round later. Perhaps she would have a word with him about it? She was coming to rely on him for so much these days, and he was such a dear.

Across the table in the restaurant, the young couple looked at each other, Elizabeth slightly flushed which made her green eyes look even more brilliant, her dark hair piled high. The green earrings sparkled in the light from the candle lamps.

She had always thought him handsome, now he appeared even more so with his slightly tanned skin, brown eyes and thick dark hair. He didn't look English, and she suspected French blood.

'You live with your aunt?' he asked.

'Yes, my parents are dead—although Isabel isn't really my aunt, only by adoption. But she's the only family I have.'

'I cannot imagine it—my family is so large. Not my immediate family, but my parents both have dozens of brothers and sisters, so the list of cousins is endless.'

'But you are an only child?'

'Yes.'

'Like me.'

'It has its advantages, though, don't you think?'

'Yes, possibly.'

The waiter came to take their order, and when he had gone, Louis studied her.

'You are a very gifted young woman,' he said. 'Do you know that?'

'I think I'm lucky in lots of ways.'

'You are beautiful, and gifted with your talent for designing.'

'Which I didn't discover until quite late.'

'And now you work for Tatiana. I know her well and like her very much.'

There was a slight pause. There was a serious side to him which belied his age, for she guessed he was no more than twenty-four or so.

'Tell me about your trip to the United States?'

Their talk continued throughout the meal; in fact the time flew by so quickly that by the time coffee was served, Elizabeth wished it would start all over again. And now he was off to America...

'How long will you be gone?' she asked him.

'A month or so. I'm going to the Du Pont factory to see what they are coming up with next, then on to Chicago.'

'I can't imagine you stocking some of these new materials,' Elizabeth teased. 'The House of Vereker is known for its fine silks.'

'Yes, but we have to look to the future. You see, silk is the most expensive material to produce. The mulberry tree, on which silkworms feed, will only grow in certain climates, and people have been experimenting since the last century to find an artificial silk which will be acceptable. Rayon was one, though I think it can be improved upon enormously.'

Elizabeth felt she could go on listening to him forever, watching that handsome face, the way he smiled, his eyes crinkling up at the corners.

By the time they were ready to leave, she had learned that he had been born in France of a French father and English mother, that he loved his involvement with the business and looked forward to taking it over.

In the taxi going home, he put an arm around her, and lifting her face to his, kissed her with such expertise that she knew he must have had a lot of practice. But it was easy to surrender herself to his kiss as he held her to him and she never wanted him to let go—only wishing the journey could have been longer.

When he released her, her heart was thumping wildly and in the gloom of the taxicab she met his dark eyes and felt herself lost. He let go of her hand and got out, going round to open the door for her to alight, then paid the taxi driver, and with a hand under her arm, walked across to the entrance of the house.

Her lips felt warm despite the cold January air. As they stopped and she turned to face him, he kissed her lightly again, then took both her hands.

'Thank you for a lovely evening, Elizabeth,' he said. 'May we do this again when I return from the States?'

'I'd like that. Thank you too. Have a good trip.'

He waited until she was inside the house before turning on his heel and walking home. He was used to seeing young ladies home, it was all part of the fun of being a young man about town, but there was something about this one—she had moved him more than he liked to admit. He wasn't ready to fall in love, he had a lot to do yet, taking over the business, and there were so many beautiful young women in the world. Still, the way she'd looked at him from those extraordinary green eyes...he had felt he was almost drowning once or twice. A chap wouldn't want to play fast and loose with her—she was a nice girl. He liked her directness. And if he was honest, he thought she was just about the most attractive girl he had ever met.

He inserted the key to the front door of the house in Kingham Street.

He could almost wish he wasn't going to America.

CHAPTER 15

Isabel Lister drew the heavy curtains in the drawing room to shut out the winter evening which was bitterly cold. Sleet was falling and snow was forecast for sometime in the next few days.

'One forgets what it is like to be young,' she said to Arthur in his accustomed place by the fire. She sat down on the sofa, and settled herself into the cushions. 'Such a dreadful night to be out but Elizabeth hardly notices the weather. I hope she is wrapped up well.'

She smiled apologetically.

'I fuss over her like an old hen, I suppose.'

'I never quite understood,' he began.

250

'She is your niece, is she not?'

'I would like to think so, Arthur,' she said, in a confiding mood. It would be nice to be able to talk to him about it, and of her ambitions where Elizabeth was concerned: that she should have a big wedding and a happy marriage, something Isabel herself had never known.

'Tell me about it,' he suggested. 'Though not if you'd rather not.'

'I would like to tell you, you have been such a good friend to us.'

'Elizabeth's mother, Mary, was a maid with our family during the war. She left when she was pregnant. I suspect Mama sacked her. Be that as it may, she left. But not before she had fallen in love with my brother Edmund.'

'I see,' he said gravely. 'So Elizabeth is your brother's child?'

'I think so,' she said, facing facts, and told him how she had met up with Elizabeth and the girl's story about her father, George Bartholomew.

'I would dearly love to think she is Edmund's child. Having no children of my own. In fact, Arthur, I'm as sure as I can be.'

'We often believe what we want to believe,' he said gently. 'But there is no harm in that, my dear.'

'So you can understand, why, having

251

found her, I don't want to let her go too easily. She's doing so well at the shop, has a great future in front of her, and she seems very keen on this young man, Louis Vereker.'

'Who is not what you would have chosen for her?' he interposed.

'Yes, that's it exactly. Oh, he's nice enough, Arthur, well mannered, polite, good-looking—all the things to turn a girl's head. His father has a business, a textile business.'

'I see.' And Isabel knew that he knew exactly what she meant.

They were silent for a time, then he spoke.

'I have sometimes thought that the girl is not making the most of her talents—and by that I mean that she could do more. After all, Isabel, she is making a great deal of money for your friend Tatiana.'

'I am not sure what you mean.'

'Well,' he began seriously, 'for instance, if she had her own business—her own clients—there's nothing like working for oneself. Why should Tatiana get all the profits?'

Now Isabel was interested.

'If, for instance, she had her own salon...'

Isabel was wide-eyed.

'You mean—'

'Quite. She could have premises very like her current employer's and work from there, have her own workroom staff, a salon assistant—whatever these places require.'

'I see.'

'And why not? If one could find the right premises.'

'But that would take a deal of money to set up, wouldn't it? Be a gamble?'

'Everything in life is, Isabel. To get anywhere today, it behoves one to work for oneself and keep the profits.'

'But is she experienced enough to run an establishment of her own? She is very young.'

'My dear, there is obviously a market for her creations. She designs them, someone makes them up, women buy them. There is not much more to it than that, surely?'

Isabel was doubtful.

'And she has proved that she can look after herself.'

'That's true.'

'It is not as if she would be hurting Tatiana Tetbury that much—after all, she had a good business before Elizabeth joined her. She has simply increased it—five or six fold, I shouldn't wonder.'

'But wouldn't it be rather a dirty trick to leave Tatiana after she has given her a chance?'

'My dear Isabel.' He put out a hand and

covered hers. 'All is fair in business. She owes Tatiana nothing. It is not as if she has a contract, has she?'

'Oh, no, nothing like that,' Isabel said. 'She was not even apprenticed.'

'There you are then, my dear. Room for thought, eh?'

'We don't know whether Elizabeth would like the idea,' Isabel said tentatively.

'Of course not, and it would have to be given a lot more thought. The cost of floating such a business, for instance. But I think you will find that Elizabeth is quite ambitious when it comes to making a success of her life.'

She looked at him questioningly but his expression was bland.

'And—' he said softly '—it might take her mind off the young man in question.'

That, more than anything, endeared the project to Isabel.

'Yes,' she said, 'you're right.'

'And she would have you behind her, and myself in the background. Leave it with me for a few days, and I'll go into it. Say nothing to her at the moment until I have something definite to go on.'

'Thank you, Arthur. You are such a help—'

'My pleasure, my dear,' he said.

Long after he had gone, Isabel lay awake waiting for Elizabeth to come home.

Somehow she couldn't sleep until she heard Elizabeth's key in the lock. Tonight she had gone to a charity show with Sarah Devenoke.

When it did come, Isabel turned over and closed her eyes. Yes, it might be a good idea, something for the girl to get her teeth into.

When, ten days later, Arthur came to dinner, a special intimate smile and a little nod betraying that he had something to tell her, Isabel was delighted, so used to the idea had she become.

With Elizabeth upstairs in her room, and she and Arthur cosily ensconced in the drawing room beside the fire, he let unfold what he had discovered.

'There seem to be few problems with this sort of thing providing you have something to sell which the public want. And I think we are assured of that?'

'Yes, Arthur.'

'Now I have to tell you that I have no previous experience of the retail trade, for that's what it boils down to—I am a business man, plain and simple, so you must bear with me.'

Isabel gave him her close attention.

'I consulted a solicitor friend of mine, also a few of my friends and acquaintances —without mentioning names, of course, my dear—and if there is one thing I am fortunate in, it is that I have many contacts. Important ones, too, some of them.'

He could see by Isabel's eyes which were fastened on his face that she had never had any doubts about that.

'Now firstly...' And he brought forth from an inside pocket the details of a bow fronted shop in Bruton Street.

'These are the particulars of this small dress shop which has apparently closed down because the owner, a titled lady—so you would be in good company, Isabel—has had to give up because of age and bad health. The lease has nineteen years to run at a fixed annual rent.'

A little frown between her eyes, Isabel pored over the details.

'It looks very pretty, but what does it all mean?'

'Well.' He spoke carefully and slowly. 'If—and I say that advisedly, if—one took it over, there would be a lump sum to pay for the goodwill.'

'What's that?'

'What it says really. You pay for the established business that has been built up, though, of course, apart from that one would be free to do what one likes. Fortunately, it has already been an exclusive gown shop and I must say,

256

I popped round to see it on my way here, is quite charming, with great possibilities.'

Isabel felt a glimmer of excitement.

'You mean we could buy it?'

'Buy the lease,' he corrected her. 'We should have to go and inspect it, you and Elizabeth—and myself, of course, if you would like me to come with you?'

'Oh, I couldn't manage it all without you,' Isabel cried.

'Then of course.' He smiled. 'As my solicitor friend advised me, one would need a fair amount to "float" the business, as they say. Decor to the shop can be a quite considerable expense, depending on how exclusive one would wish to make it. Then there is the employment of staff. I suppose three would be sufficient to begin with though let us hope she increases that, eh?'

Isabel was carried away to the point of excitement.

'An announcement in *Vogue* or *Tatler*, that sort of thing.'

'Oh dear!'

'No matter. The thing is, are you interested enough to broach it to her?'

'Yes, I think so. Are there any snags that you can think of apart from the cost? I know nothing about the commercial world at all and I am a little wary of putting my toes in the water.'

'Well put,' Arthur said, and drew out a small notebook and referred to his notes.

'Now I don't know what you will think of this, but with advice from people who should know, I have come up with a few figures.'

Isabel folded her hands.

'I would guess—and it is a guess—an outside figure of seven thousand pounds.'

'Goodness,' she murmured.

'That should cover everything. The lease, the stock, the first year's wages to staff, the decor of the shop, and incidentals—but of course I am happy to be a part of it. I would like to invest a little money in her myself. I would be a sleeping partner, and it would be an interest for me.'

'Oh, no, Arthur!'

'But of course, my dear. Why else would I broach the subject? I am on to a good thing, believe me. That girl is going to do very well.'

'Give me a few days to think it over before I tell her what we have in mind.'

'My dear, take all the time you want. After all, it is only an idea and certainly not something to worry over.'

Isabel couldn't help wondering what Elizabeth would think of the idea.

She had a feeling that this wasn't the best time to mention it. Lately the girl had been a little preoccupied probably with

258

pressure of work—they were inundated with orders for the forthcoming coronation in May.

Meeting her in the hall when she returned late from the shop, Isabel waylaid her.

'Elizabeth—'

'Oh, I'm sorry, Isabel, I'm in a frightful hurry—got to get changed. I have a dinner engagement with Sarah's brother and his fiancee. Come up and tell me while I dress.'

'It's all right, dear. There's no hurry.'

Elizabeth hummed while she was getting ready—life had taken on such a rosy hue since she had been taken out by Louis Vereker. Although he was in America, she thought about him every spare moment and knew without any doubt that she had fallen in love with him.

Isabel, seeing her radiant face, realised without being told that life had opened up for Elizabeth, and that could only mean one thing. She was in love with this young man—no business success could bring that dreamy look into her eyes. Was this the best time to suggest that her life take a new turn? She was so young—too young to be tied to an ordinary young man like Louis Vereker. She would soon become just another housewife married to him,

259

her talents buried, what chance would she have to show what she was made of? For you could be certain that like most men he would want his wife to stay at home and run the house. Any chance of making a name for herself would be gone. Yet Isabel wanted her to be happy and the very idea of Elizabeth having to lead a life without the man she loved was cruel—no, she wouldn't want that.

But to give her a new interest, an exciting interest in her future, surely that would be worthwhile? And she had to acknowledge, deep down, that the reason for it all was that she didn't want to lose her.

They sat in the drawing room after dinner, Isabel trying to find the right words to open the conversation. Finally, she took the plunge.

'Elizabeth—'

With the little half smile which played around her mouth these days, Elizabeth looked up dreamily from the newspaper, her eyes luminous.

'Sorry, Isabel?'

'I've had an idea—I don't know whether you would be interested—I have to say—Arthur—well—how would you like your own shop?'

There, it was out, and she hadn't done it too well. Elizabeth frowned.

'My own shop?'

'Your own salon, like Tatiana's. Your very own.'

'I am not sure I understand what—'

'Well, I—we—have been talking it over, you see, Elizabeth. I think you have great talent. You have made such a success of yourself at Tatiana's that it seems to me—us—that you are worthy of something better.'

Elizabeth came down to earth. 'What did you have in mind?'

'There's a small shop, a darling little place in Bruton Street which is empty. The lease is for sale and I thought it would be a great idea if we took it over and set you up in business on your own.'

There was an element of adventure in this which did not fail to interest Elizabeth.

'But what about Tatiana? I could hardly leave her now, could I? With all the coronation orders she has. And I do owe her something.'

'No, you don't,' Isabel said sharply. 'You are under no contract—no obligation to her—and you are perfectly free to do so if you wish. You have been there almost eighteen months, and that is quite long enough. Now is the time to branch out on your own, and I would be happy to invest in you. If you like the idea, of course.'

She took a deep breath.

'You know, I've never done anything with my life, it has been quite useless and empty, and it seems to me that you deserve this—you have talent. And already after such a short time, you have proved yourself.'

'What exactly does it entail?' Elizabeth asked. After all, she thought, she was used to surprises. Since she had met Isabel her whole life had undergone a change in the most unexpected way.

'Now you don't still feel you owe me something? You have done so much.'

'No, of course not. I can explain to you what I had in mind.'

At the end of it all, Elizabeth had to admit that her curiosity was aroused.

'So you discussed it with Arthur—naturally —and he really thinks that should cover everything. It's an awful lot of money, Isabel, and I have nothing. At least, nothing like that amount.'

'You could say in a way it is your money,' Isabel said. 'After all, it will come to you when I die.'

'Oh, please don't talk like that!'

'But it's true—you'd be investing in yourself.'

'Yes, I see. Well, I won't say I am not interested, it sounds too good to be true, though I don't much like the idea of telling

Tatiana I'd be leaving. Still, let's deal with the first thing, shall we? Let's see the shop in Bruton Street?'

Isabel beamed.

'Yes, shall we? We could all go on Saturday morning—how would that be?'

'Yes, of course.' Elizabeth smiled. Dear Isabel, she was so enthusiastic, especially where anything to do with Elizabeth herself was concerned.

They met at Bruton Street premises together with the agent and Arthur.

As Isabel had said, it was delightful. Small and pretty. Already Elizabeth imagined the look of it when redecorated and she turned to the agent with smiling eyes.

'I think it's lovely.' Isabel met Arthur's glance across the room.

Back home, they sat through lunch and afterwards discussing it, and by now Elizabeth as keen on the idea as they were.

'But I should say nothing to anyone at this stage,' Arthur advised. 'The idea is still in embryo, so to speak.'

When she had gone, the conspirators got down to business.

'Oh, it is exciting!' Isabel cried.

'Yes, but there's much to be done yet,' Arthur said. 'There's the business of giving her notice, acquiring staff, signing the lease, and so on.'

'Of course.'

'I have worked it out, Isabel. I am happy to invest two thousand—I have a little money unexpectedly from some shares.'

'Oh, no.'

'Look, I would be a sleeping partner—after all, it was my idea—and would waive the interest until she was well and truly established. I think it would lessen your feeling of responsibility if I came in—you wouldn't feel so much out on a limb.'

'I hadn't counted on your putting any money in,' Isabel said. 'I would rather have the full responsibility.'

'No, my dear, let us do it as a business transaction, and I would like to have an interest—I've had shares in many things, but never in a dress shop.' And they both laughed.

'Well, if you insist.'

'Now, we must set this up without fail—we don't want to lose the premises, do we? I calculate your investment will be five thousand. Would you still like me to deal with it for you? Or would you rather...?'

'Oh, no, you do it, Arthur! Would you?'

'If you wish, my dear. Now my solicitors are Forethy and Dunne of Lincolns Inn. Here is their card. Of course there will be fees, but I will see to that.'

Isabel took a deep breath. 'Thank you, Arthur.'

'Now, you would like me to tell the agent that it's definite? We are buying the lease and goodwill, in other words, to set the whole thing in motion. You are sure, Isabel?'

'Quite sure, Arthur.'

Life had suddenly become exciting.

CHAPTER 16

'I just can't believe it!'

Her face flushed with anger, Tatiana faced Elizabeth across the desk.

'Are you telling me that after all I have done for you, you are going to leave me in the lurch and start up on your own?'

Elizabeth stood her ground.

'Yes, Tatiana, I am. I have had the opportunity given to me, and I would like to take it. I shall honour all my obligations to you about the coronation orders.'

'Thank you,' Tatiana said sarcastically. 'Leaving me high and dry for Ascot!'

'No, not at all. I shall wait until the end of the season—say July—and I'm giving you fair notice.'

'And I'm supposed to be grateful for that?'

'Oh, Tatiana, be fair! It's too good an opportunity to miss—and I won't let you down.'

'Well, all I can say is I'm surprised at you, Elizabeth. I can see now I had you all wrong.'

'You'd take the chance in my position,' Elizabeth pleaded with her. 'Now wouldn't you?'

'The circumstances are very different,' Tatiana said haughtily, very much on her dignity.

Which made Elizabeth feel more wretched than ever. She felt she had let her employer down. She had been as happy as a sandboy at Tatiana's, but the chance of a business of her own was too good to miss. Left to herself, she might not have gone along with it, but Isabel was so keen, and it was, at the end of the day, a great opportunity to show what she was made of.

The atmosphere was tense and strained for a few days, but they were so overwhelmed with orders for the coronation and Ascot week, followed by Henley, that they hardly had a chance to look up. The small workroom was awash with lengths of fine silks, brocades and satins, and an extra sempstress and two extra embroideresses had been taken on, while Elizabeth found herself working late every evening in order to catch up with orders.

Each night she arrived home exhausted, her eyes strained from working closely on designs and materials, but it was all so rewarding that it made her hard work worthwhile. Only occasionally did she give thought to the new premises in Bruton Street and to what it would mean, and could hardly wait for Louis to get home to tell him all about it. What would he think of the idea? This morning she was due to go to Vereker's to order some silk brocade for a rather splendid ball gown to be worn by a countess who had been referred to them by her daughter. Elizabeth often thought how lucky she was to be working at something she liked and being such a success at it. She loved designing and the feel of luxury fabrics; there was something sensual about them, which made falling in love with Louis a perfectly natural thing since that was his life, the selling of silks and satins and rich materials, and if she married him—but there she was again, running away with herself. It was a month now since he had gone. Surely he would be back soon.

On the way to Vereker's she studied the various shop windows in Bond Street, exclusive shops whose windows held the minimum of merchandise—but whatever it was, it was luxury of the highest order. Hand made gowns, intricately cut and sewn, displayed with understated carelessness, the accessories of the finest quality that Britain had to offer. It was the most exclusive street in London and just to watch the elegant women with their male escorts was a joy as they paraded in furs, hats from Paris, hand crafted shoes and leather handbags. London was full of visitors from abroad for the coronation, for this was a very special year, and women were going to make the most of it.

She turned the corner into a small side turning where Vereker's stood, and pushed open the heavy glass door. Once inside it was like Aladdin's cave, with its jewel colours, myriad silks and satins, shelf after shelf of delicate materials of every shade and hue. Harry, the general factotum, ushered her in, and Elizabeth went straight over to where she could see Lily, her slim figure in its usual black satin, her black hair pulled back into a chignon, as she checked and re-checked the stock.

'Good morning, Lily.'

Lily turned and faced her. 'Elizabeth! Good morning—how are we today?'

'Absolutley fine,' she said as she looked around. 'I can see you've been busy...' as Lily rolled her eyes heavenwards. 'I'm looking for something rather special—a ball

gown for the Countess of Newminster.'
And Lily whistled.

'Well, now we have arrived!' she said
admiringly, as Lizzie drew out the sketch
from her folder. 'Oh, but that's lovely—and
I can think of several possibilities.'

'She has auburn hair—a lovely shade—and
I thought something greenish-gold, rich-
looking.' Lizzie followed her, looking at
the samples, draping them, holding them,
feeling the weight, consulting the sketch,
Lily as interested in what she selected as
she herself was.

It was an hour before she finally chose
the material, and watched as Lily's expert
hands dealt with it, carefully measuring
every inch of the outrageously expensive
fabric.

'There!' she said. 'That's it.' She rolled
the remainder. 'Anything else?'

On the spur of the moment Lizzie
decided to tell Lily about the plan for
her shop.

'Now it's my turn to give you some
news,' she said. 'Mind, it's not definite
yet, but I am toying with the idea of going
into business on my own.'

Lily's grey eyes were wide. 'No!'

'It's a bit of a secret at the moment, but
as far as we know it's all going ahead. I
should know more next week.'

'Well!' Lily was impressed. She finished

wrapping the parcel before putting it into one of Vereker's exclusive bags, then looked up at Elizabeth with sheer admiration. 'I have to hand it to you,' she said. 'You will let me know how you get on?'

'Promise,' Elizabeth said and picked up her parcel, smiling broadly at her. 'I must go—so much to do. 'Bye, Lily.'

She found Isabel highly excited when she reached home.

'Oh, there you are! I was waiting for you—such good news, darling. But you look so tired—you're working much too hard.'

'No, really, I'm fine.' Elizabeth took off her hat and shook her dark curls.

'Look, run upstairs and change, and when you come down, we'll have a little celebration drink.'

'Celebrate what?' Elizabeth's thoughts turned from Louis to Isabel with difficulty.

'I'll tell you when you come down—there's no hurry.'

Isabel was sitting in the drawing room trying very hard to keep calm when Elizabeth entered, having changed out of her black dress into a sweater and skirt.

Isabel got up and went over to the small table where the decanters sat, and poured her a glass of sherry.

'We'll keep the champagne for completion

day,' she said, clinking her glass with Elizabeth's.

'Well, it's almost signed, sealed and delivered,' she said triumphantly. 'Now sit down, and I'll tell you.'

Despite herself, Elizabeth caught some of the excitement.

'The shop?'

'Yes, my dear, the shop. Arthur has seen the solicitor, who is drawing up the agreement—whatever they call it—for the lease and goodwill, and the business is also being registered under the Business Names Act in your name as proprietor. We're going to call it "Elizabeth".'

Lizzie felt a sudden surge of excitement and her eyes began to sparkle.

'Oh, Isabel, I never really believed it!'

'Neither did I,' Isabel confided. 'Arthur called round on his way to the solicitor this morning, and we settled everything. He's putting in two thousand, and I'm putting in five.'

Lizzie frowned. 'It's an awful lot of money, Isabel.'

'Yes, but it's your money—you are investing in yourself, think of it like that. I gave Arthur the cheque, and by the end of the week, it should all be signed, sealed and delivered. Then we can take over the shop, and do as we please. After all, you have a few weeks before you leave Tatiana,

271

and we must advertise, and do up the shop
and furnish it. It's going to be wonderful!
I'm so proud of you, you clever girl! You'll
be the toast of London!'

'What have I done? It seems to me
everything falls into my lap.'

Isabel looked at her fondly.

'You deserve it,' she said sincerely.

'I can't wait to tell Sarah—she will be
delighted. She and Tatiana don't see eye
to eye quite often, and she has promised
to see that I get the orders for Bryony's
wedding in June.'

'There you are then! You're on your
way.'

Lizzie jumped up and kissed her impulsively.

'Thank you, Isabel, you've been so good
to me.'

'Nonsense, child, you've given me a new
lease of life.' And Isabel, well pleased,
poured herself another sherry.

'Well!' Sarah said when she was told. 'I
just can't believe it. Talk about Cinderella!
What does she get out of it—Isabel?'

'Some pleasure, I hope, but mainly an
interest in life. After all, Sarah, imagine
what it must have been like, never
marrying, looking after her parents...'

'More fool her,' Sarah said shortly.
'Which reminds me.' She looked at

Elizabeth, whose green eyes seemed to be focused on something elsewhere. 'How are you getting on with that boyfriend of yours? Is he back from the States yet?'

To her annoyance, Elizabeth flushed.

'He is not my boyfriend,' she said.

'Oh, sorry,' Sarah said, realising that she was not to be drawn. 'Anyway, I'm delighted you're leaving old Mother Tatiana—she's a pain in the neck.'

'Sarah, you're quite wrong, she's a poppet really and she's been awfully good to me.'

'Which is why you're leaving her?' Sarah said drily.

'No, not at all. I'm sorry to be leaving her, but this is a chance I don't want to miss.'

' 'Course not, sweetie.' Sarah put an arm round her. 'Let's go upstairs, we'll have a little chat.'

It was always cosy and warm in Sarah's room—the familiar things about, the scent that she always wore. It was like old times. Where Josh was on these occasions, Elizabeth never knew. He and Sarah seemed to live separate lives.

'So what have you been doing?' she asked, eyeing the black taffeta gown hanging on its hanger, the velvet shoes at its feet, the black velvet cape embroidered with silver beads, the huge pink cabbage

273

rose, which she knew would have been sprayed with Sarah's favourite perfume. It was not all that long since she had been doing this job, preparing Lady Sarah for an evening out.

'This and that,' said Sarah, eyeing her nails closely. 'Going to a dinner this evening at the Guildhall—ugh, so utterly boring, but needs must. And it pleases his lordship who likes to show off his beautiful wife every so often.'

'Sarah, you are horrible to him! And he is such a sweetie!'

'And such a bore!' Sarah cried, her real feelings showing through for a moment as her blue eyes flashed. 'He never wants to do anything exciting. Lizzie, you can't know—how could you? It's bad enough having Mummy at my heels every moment of the day, without you taking sides.'

'Sarah, I'm not, it just seems to me that you do quite well out of life.' And Elizabeth shook her head wonderingly.

'Is that what you think? You know, Elizabeth, you may have been brought up in an orphanage and cast out into the world at an early age, but believe me, I sometimes think you're positively nurtured, shielded...'

Lizzie turned puzzled green eyes to her, eyes that looked guilty, too.

'Does it seem like that to you?'

'Sometimes.' Sarah got up and walked over to the window. 'All they think about is when am I going to have a baby? Between them, Josh and Mummy, they don't give me a moment's peace—and it's not my fault. At least, I don't think it is, unless—'

'What?'

'Well, I do sometimes wonder if having that—you know—abortion, did something that prevented me from conceiving? And anyway, Josh may not be able to father a child.' It was clear she was feeling guilty. 'I mean, one minute my mother is arranging an abortion for me, the next she's asking why I don't have a baby! I'm sick of it!'

'Oh, Sarah, don't be upset,' Lizzie cried. She was genuinely fond of Sarah, felt closer to her than a sister might, despite their different backgrounds.

Then suddenly Sarah smiled. 'Of course, the hoot would be if I became pregnant and it wasn't his—Josh's—you know what I mean.'

'Sarah, you wouldn't!'

' 'Course not, don't be silly. Anyway, my latest has gone back home—whether he got fed up with me or his wife, I don't know.'

'Who? The Argentinian, what's his name?'

'Yes.' She went over to a drawer. 'What

275

do you think of these?' And opened a box to show a pair of ruby earrings which flashed brilliantly.

'Oh, Sarah, they're beautiful!'

'Yes. I'm not awfully keen on rubies but still, when I'm old and grey, if I get that far...'

She put the box away, and grinned at Lizzie. 'Now tell me more about your shop. Where is it, when do you open, what did Tatiana say?'

They talked for an hour, at the end of which Elizabeth got up to leave.

'You know,' Sarah said slowly, 'I think you should realise that the more Isabel does for you, the more obligated to her you become.'

'Yes, I know, I have thought of that, but honestly, Sarah, wouldn't you take the chances she's given me?'

She thought for a bit. 'In your place, probably. I'd rather have my freedom, but then I was born with a silver spoon in my mouth, or so they tell me—I've never known what it is to want. Until now.' And she turned away and bit her lip.

Elizabeth had seen this mood coming before. 'Well, got to go,' she said, picking up her coat. 'By the way, don't put the rose at your waist—pin it in your velvet choker or your hair.'

'Really?'

Sarah placed the rose at her neck, and looked at herself in the mirror. 'Oh, very fetching!' she said. 'I see what you mean.' The brief mood of self-pity had gone, and she was already thinking about the evening to come.

'Let me know how it goes, I'll be in touch.'

'I'll see myself out,' Elizabeth said, and hurried down the stairs.

London was ablaze with flowers which spilled from window boxes all along the coronation route; lamp posts were adorned with baskets of trailing flowers, stands were being erected in all the conspicuous viewing areas, and a festive air of excitement hung over everything. Once or twice Elizabeth and Isabel took an evening stroll to admire the flags and decorations, and to have yet another peek at the small shop in Bruton Street. The days sped by. The beds were in full bloom in the parks, cherry trees and budding lilac and laburnum blossomed side by side. It was a lovely time of the year.

'Once it's signed, the shop will be ours. Then we can take over,' Isabel said.

'Doesn't it take a time!' Lizzie said, impatient now to get going.

'Arthur said it would—legal matters always do. I remember when Father died...'

277

Late that evening the telephone rang and Isabel answered it with her usual friendly voice, then turned to Lizzie and said shortly, 'It's for you.' Lizzie's heart leapt, and she hurried to take over the receiver.

'Hallo?'

And the voice which could send the blood coursing through her veins, asked: 'Elizabeth?'

'Louis!'

'How are you?'

'I'm well. How was the trip?'

'Just fine. I missed you.'

Just to hear those wonderful words.

'May I see you?'

'When?'

'Tomorrow?'

'Yes.'

'Seven-thirty. I'll meet you outside Tatiana's.'

'See you then.'

She put the phone down, her green eyes sparkling—there was no doubt in Isabel's mind how much this young man meant to her.

Lizzie returned to her chair. 'It was Louis—Louis Vereker,' she said, realising only now that she had been careful to mind her words as though she recognised that Isabel would not approve.

'Oh, he's back then?' And Isabel dropped her eyes and went on with her embroidery.

'Yes, I'm seeing him tomorrow,' Elizabeth said. Isabel would have to realise that nothing would stop her from seeing Louis, even if she didn't approve—and there was no doubt that she didn't.

Her heart leapt as she saw him standing there, a tall shadowy figure the other side of the door. When she opened it and looked up into his eyes, it was all he could do not to sweep her into his arms in full view of everyone.

He took her arm and together they walked in silence, just happy to be together, feeling the close proximity of each other. Then they both spoke.

'Did you—'

'How shall—' and burst out laughing.

'Oh, Elizabeth!' He stood stock still and looked down into her eyes, which were radiant with joy at seeing him again. He gripped her arm. 'Come on.'

They crossed into the park, and it could have been empty for all they knew, for they only saw each other.

'I've so much to tell you,' Lizzie cried.

'And I you,' Louis said, looking down at her. 'Do you know you wrecked my visit to the States?'

Lizzie stopped in her tracks. 'I did? Why?'

'Because I couldn't get you out of my

mind. I couldn't concentrate.' And it was true, he thought. She had intruded at every point—whatever he was doing, he saw her face, thought of her. He had never felt like this before about any woman. He looked into her eyes and saw there what he wanted to see. Their lips seemed to meet of their own volition as they stood there in full view. Just like any other lovers in a London park.

Presently they pulled apart and walked on. On air as far as Lizzie was concerned. She had almost forgotten the shop project, Isabel, everything—just to be with Louis was all that mattered.

When they reached the other side of the park, he stopped.

'I thought we'd have dinner somewhere quiet then you can tell me all your news—'

In the small French restaurant, Lizzie told him about the shop, growing more and more excited as the story unfolded.

'Do you think it's a good idea?' she said at length.

'Yes, I do,' he said warmly. 'I think it's just the sort of thing you could make a success of—you have lots of drive and determination and, if I may say so, enormous talent.'

'It's important to me that you would think so,' Elizabeth said seriously. 'With your experience.'

'If there is anything I can do,' he said, taking her hand in his.

'That's kind of you. They're dealing with the legal side at the moment. After that I shall be glad of all the advice I can get.'

'Next week,' he said, 'I have to go to Paris and Lyons. After that I shall be free.'

'That means I shan't see you for a while. You'll miss the coronation.'

'Yes, I'm sorry about that but it can't be helped. It won't be long, and you will be glad of a break after all that work.'

She took a deep breath. 'Oh, Louis...' She couldn't believe it was all happening.

As coronation day drew nearer, and the last stitch was put into garments, collections and deliveries made, Tatiana, Elizabeth and the staff sank back with relief.

'I didn't honestly think we would ever be ready,' Tatiana said in a satisfied voice. 'I'm grateful to all of you—especially you, Elizabeth. You've worked like a Trojan.' And Elizabeth felt she had been vindicated in some small way. 'Well, let's hope it all goes well.'

Tatiana had a special seat for the coronation provided by a man friend, but Elizabeth and Isabel decided to take pot luck and join the thousands somewhere along the royal route.

'Arthur was hoping to obtain seats for

us, but I expect he had no luck,' Isabel said.

'Never mind, we will enjoy it anyway,' Elizabeth said. 'Is he coming round?'

Isabel beamed.

'Yes, early in the morning,' she said. 'Are you seeing—er—that young man tomorrow?'

'No,' Elizabeth said. 'He won't be back from Paris until the day after tomorrow so he will miss the coronation.'

Isabel couldn't shake off the slight feeling of relief.

'Well, my dear, you are welcome to join Arthur and me for lunch.'

'Bless you, but no thank you. I have lots to do.'

'An early night would do you no harm, dear.'

'Yes, you're right, Isabel.'

She had suddenly realised how tired she was.

CHAPTER 17

When coronation day dawned on a morning in May, Isabel and Elizabeth were up early. The whole nation was on holiday, and there was much excitement in the air. The radio was on all the time so that they wouldn't miss any small part of this momentous day and as Elizabeth put on her outdoor clothes and prepared to leave, Isabel waited back for Arthur's arrival.

'Now you are sure you wouldn't like me to wait with you—there really is no hurry. I thought I would pop out and see what's doing.'

'No, dear, you go ahead. He'll be here any minute now.'

Elizabeth closed the door behind her and walked down the steps. It would have been nice if Louis could have been there with her, but he would be back the following day. Arriving at the Bayswater Road, she was astonished to see just how many people there were for the roads were packed with them, children with flags, whole families out for the day intent upon enjoying themselves. The Marble Arch was a seething mass of people, and as far as she could see down Park Lane. Heaven knows what it must be like outside Buckingham Palace, she thought, where the carriages would leave with the King and Queen to drive towards Admiralty Arch and out towards Westminster Abbey. The day was dull but there was a feeling of excitement in the air, and she suddenly remembered that she had forgotten to bring her small Brownie camera, a recent acquisition. Today was history in the making, and it would be a pity not to get some photographs of such a momentous event.

She retraced her steps for the short walk home and let herself in. She found Isabel in the kitchen making coffee in preparation for Arthur's arrival, Gertrude and Mrs Baines having been given the day off.

'Do have a cup, Elizabeth, what's it like outside?'

'Incredible!' she laughed. 'Absolutely crowded, people everywhere...'

'Oh, dear,' Isabel said. 'I really don't like crowds.'

'Well, we don't have to get into the middle of it all, just to get outside is fun—it's really quite exciting.'

Isabel glanced at her watch.

'I think I'll give Arthur a ring. I'm surprised he isn't here by now.'

'Probably couldn't get a taxi,' Elizabeth said.

Sipping her coffee, she watched Isabel as she dialled his number and waited. Presently, Isabel hung up the receiver. 'I expect he's on his way. There's no reply.'

'Look,' Elizabeth said, sensing Isabel's disappointment, 'I really don't want to go without you. Why don't we wait for

Arthur and listen to the wireless. It's just as interesting, without all the pushing and shoving.

Isabel seemed pleased.

'Well, if you don't mind?'

'Not at all,' Elizabeth said stoutly. She did feel herself that it wasn't much fun on one's own.

They sat listening to the commentary which was riveting, and as the service was relayed from the Abbey were engrossed as the music swelled and filled their hearts with pride. Only as it died down and the trumpets blared did Isabel glance at her watch, and Elizabeth saw her bite her lip.

Presently she jumped up, squeezing her hankie.

'Elizabeth, you don't think anything has happened to him?'

'Of course not! What do you mean?'

'An accident. There are so many people about, dangerous drivers.'

'Oh, no, Isabel. I'm sure there is a perfectly logical explanation.'

But the joy of the day had gone. They made lunch and sat quietly all through the afternoon, until when evening came it was almost more than Elizabeth could bear to see the disappointment on Isabel's face.

She telephoned him once or twice, but when by nine o'clock there was no sign of Arthur, she became rather concerned herself. It wasn't at all like him, he was usually so punctual.

At the end of an exhausting day, but not in the way they had imagined it to be, they both went to bed where Isabel lay awake for most of the night fretting about what might have happened to Arthur.

In the morning she was up early, long before Elizabeth was preparing to go to the shop.

'Now what are you going to do today?' Elizabeth asked when she came down. 'I hope you are not going to worry about Arthur. I'm sure he's all right.'

'I shall telephone him and then go round to his flat. I can't bear not knowing.' And Isabel's eyes filled with tears.

That she had grown very fond of him, Elizabeth knew, but she hadn't known quite how much.

'Now I have to go, Isabel, but I want you to promise me that you will telephone the shop if you need me. Tatiana will understand.'

'No, dear, I know you have lots of orders to see to. Don't you worry, I shall be quite all right.'

Elizabeth wondered when Louis would be back, and if he would contact her, but she must come home at once tonight to see Isabel as soon as she had finished.

Elizabeth couldn't bear to see her so troubled.

'Oh, wasn't it beautiful!' Tatiana sighed when Lizzie arrived at work. 'Did you see it?'

'No, but we heard it. And it was lovely.'

They were all talking about it, there was no other topic but the majesty and splendour of the coronation, the robes, the music, the pomp and circumstance of it all.

Quietly, Elizabeth telephoned Arthur's flat, but as before, there was no reply, and she rang the operator to check the number.

'No reply, sorry,' the voice said, and Elizabeth got down to the designing of five more dresses for Ascot—last-minute orders.

'Phew!' Tatiana said. 'Oh, I'll be glad when it's out of the way—it's worse this year than ever!'

'But a super lot of orders,' Elizabeth said, eyes twinkling.

'By the way, that ghastly Tina Freshman wants the exact copy of Lady Dowson's Gold Cup day dress. In blue, she says.'

'I hope you told her where to get off?'

'Indeed I did, and she said she would take her order elsewhere.'

'Good. We can do without her sort of client.'

'You speak for yourself,' Tatiana said, and they laughed. Tatiana had quickly adapted to the idea of Elizabeth's leaving. She could never bear umbrage for long.

The day rushed by, with clients coming in for fittings until at the end of the day, tired but pleased with her efforts, Elizabeth made her way home. As she neared the square, the events of the day before came back to her and her heart began to beat faster as she wondered what news Isabel had for her.

She hadn't long to wait.

Isabel stood in the hall, eyes wide, looking as angry as Elizabeth had ever seen her. She took off her hat and put down her handbag.

'What's happened?'

'He's not there—checked out—with no forwarding address,' Isabel said, and at the relief of telling someone, burst into tears.

'Oh, Isabel! There must be some mistake.'

'No, unfortunately, there isn't.' Isabel dried her eyes. 'I telephoned all morning, then this afternoon I got a taxi to Earl's Court and found the apartment block, and—well, to cut a long story short he had checked out, and they had no idea where he had gone. I just can't believe it.'

Elizabeth went into the drawing room and poured a small sherry for both of them. Poor Isabel.

'Drink this,' she said. 'I'll have one too. But I am sure there must be some logical explanation.'

'I am afraid I think I have the right one,' Isabel said grimly. 'Aren't you forgetting he has my cheque for five thousand pounds?'

'Now, Isabel, you're jumping to conclusions.'

'Not really, dear. I have been trying since four o'clock to get his solicitors.' And she handed Elizabeth the card.

'Unfortunately the number is unobtainable. I checked.'

Elizabeth bit her lip. 'Oh, dear.'

'Tomorrow I shall go to the address on the card and also round to the agents. This must be cleared up as soon as possible.'

'Isabel, you don't think you're judging him too hastily? He might be lying injured somewhere in hospital.'

Isabel twisted her lip. 'I don't think so, since he checked out with no forwarding address. Oh, Elizabeth, how could I have been so foolish!'

She was devastated.

At nine o'clock the telephone rang and Elizabeth hastened to answer it, hoping it would be Louis, but Isabel forestalled her.

'Whoever it is, don't say a word. Not just yet. Don't tell a soul.'

'I won't,' Elizabth said, feeling enormous sympathy for her.

'Hello.'

'Elizabeth?'

'Yes—oh, Louis!' And her heart soared.

'How are you?'

'Just fine. Did you have a good trip?'

'Yes, in a way. Can I see you soon?'

She thought hastily. 'Yes, when?'

'Tomorrow evening?'

'May I say yes now, and I'll give you a ring if I have to cancel, but as far as I know—'

'Could it be later, around eight?'

'That's fine,' Elizabeth said. Oh, how wonderful to hear his voice again. Suddenly everything was all right now that Louis was back.

She turned to find Isabel staring pale-faced out of the window, and felt sudden compassion for her. What an awful thing to have happened—in more ways than one, if it were true, and it certainly seemed like it. Isabel had obviously grown fond of the man, and it came much harder with an older person. I have the rest of my life to look forward to, she thought, whereas Isabel... She had no right to leave her alone and go off with Louis just when she was needed. She made up her mind to ring him in the morning—she would see him perhaps when she went to Vereker's for more materials.

When she went to bed, the light was still on underneath Isabel's door. Half inclined to knock, Elizabeth decided against it and went on into her room.

In the morning when she came down, Isabel was already up and dressed to go out.

'Good morning, Isabel. Where are you going so early in the day?'

Isabel poured herself another cup of pale china tea.

'I have things to do,' she said coolly, 'and there's no time like the present.'

'Isabel?'

'Yes?' Isabel raised eyes with slightly swollen lids—she looked years older, Elizabeth thought, and felt like killing Arthur Hetherington.

'Don't do anything today. Why not wait until I can come with you? I don't like you tackling this alone.'

'Then you don't understand my strength,' Isabel said firmly. 'I don't know when I have felt so angry. Just because I have never been put to the test, doesn't mean I can't fight when I have to.'

Impulsively Elizabeth ran over to her and hugged her.

'Oh, bless you, that's the spirit!' she

291

cried. 'I don't blame you a bit.'

'Well, then,' Isabel said, somewhat mollified.

It's easy for me, I have a job to do which takes up all my time, thought Elizabeth, but Isabel has to live with this on her own. She must be allowed to do what she wants.

'Are you seeing that young man this evening?' Isabel asked, rolling up her napkin and putting it in its ring.

'Louis?' Elizabeth stressed. 'Yes, I did say I would but in the circumstances, I think—'

'Oh, don't put him off on my account,' Isabel said stiffly.

Elizabeth knew she would have to play this very carefully. She didn't want to cause Isabel unnecessary distress.

'No, I changed my mind. I have quite a few things to do,' she said. 'Anyway, I must fly.'

'Oh, Elizabeth,' Isabel called after her. 'Not a word to Tatiana—not yet anyway. I couldn't bear it.'

'Of course not.' Elizabeth came back and kissed her lightly.

'Be careful—and take care of yourself,' she said. She had really grown fond of Isabel. It had been easy to imagine she was family.

At the shop, apart from a tantrum

from the Honourable Lavinia Partridge who didn't like the set of the sleeve in her dress, and whose mother insisted that the decolleté neckline was far too low, the morning passed as usual, with one client after another coming in for a fitting.

Tatiana seemed in a very good mood these past few days, nothing seemed to upset her, and when Elizabeth thought how well she had adjusted to the idea of her leaving, she was more than pleased. She liked Tatiana and had no wish to fall out with her. Especially now, she thought ruefully. What on earth would Tatiana say when she was told that the idea of the shop had fallen through?

In the afternoon, in a quiet spell, she made her way to Vereker's, and after chatting to Lily, who asked her how the plans were going for the shop, had to avoid committing herself by saying these things seemed to take an awfully long time. She spent half an hour selecting her various requirements, was as vague as she could be and was relieved when she saw Louis come through from the back of the store, his eyes lighting up as he saw her. Watching her, Lily thought, Well, what have we here? Those green eyes sparkling, and if I'm not mistaken quite a pretty flush in her cheeks. Oh, if I could only look like that. Mind you, not for Mr Louis...'

'I thought it was you,' he said, holding out his hand to take hers. 'How are you?'

'I'm well,' Elizabeth said, the touch of his hand like an electric shock. 'How did you get on in Paris?'

'Very well. And by the way I have come back with the most fabulous new designs and materials—the colours are wonderful, aren't they, Lily?'

'You'll love them,' Lily stressed. 'Excuse me.' And she walked away to deal with another customer.

'Of course.' Elizabeth smiled up at Louis. 'Would you mind awfully if I didn't see you this evening?'

His face showed his disappointment.

'You see, Isabel—'

'She's not ill?'

'Er, no, but something has come up which is worrying her, and I would like to be with her this evening. Could we make it tomorrow, perhaps? I'm awfully sorry.'

He looked at her intently.

'You're sure there is nothing wrong?' he asked.

'Well, nothing that I can explain now,' she prevaricated.

'Don't worry about it,' he said, trying hard to hide his disappointment.

'Shall we just check these?' she asked Lily.

'I'll say goodbye then,' Louis said, with

a last lingering look at Elizabeth. 'Seven tomorrow.'

'Yes, thank you,' Elizabeth said, watching his broad-shouldered figure walk towards the back of the shop.

Lily's pale grey eyes sparkled.

'Was I supposed not to hear that or see the look on both your faces?' she asked.

'Oh, Lily!'

'Well, if anyone has to get him, I'd rather it was you.'

'Oh, come on,' Elizabeth laughed. 'Get on with the list.' And after checking it through, Lily promised the orders would be delivered the next morning.

That evening, before the shop closed, a well-dressed man came into the shop, an elderly gentleman on his own with a gold-topped cane and bowler hat which he removed as soon as he closed the door. Elizabeth was standing talking to Tatiana and saw the smile which she gave him, her cornflower blue eyes twinkling as she hurried forward and kissed his cheek.

'Darling, how nice,' she said as he looked down at her with positive adoration, not in the least put out at being in a lady's gown shop.

'Excuse me.' And Elizabeth made to disappear into the back room.

'Wait, Elizabeth,' Tatiana said, taking her arm. 'Teddy, I'd like you to meet my

friend Elizabeth—Elizabeth Bartholomew.
Elizabeth—Lord Daccrington.'

His fine grey eyes looked into Elizabeth's.
'How do you do, my dear?' he said,
taking her hand. 'So this is Elizabeth.'

'You see, I told him about you,' Tatiana
said.

She looked so happy, Elizabeth felt
instinctively that this was the man who
had taken her to the coronation, who was
responsible for that newly acquired relaxed
attitude towards everything, that sparkle in
the blue eyes.

'How do you do?' she said, returning
his smile.

'Teddy and I are going to be married,'
Tatiana said, taking his arm, 'and I'd like
you to be the first to know.'

'Oh!' gasped Elizabeth, surprised. Somehow she hadn't expected that.

Lord Daccrington smiled down at Tatiana.

'Congratulations,' Elizabeth said to him,
and kissed Tatiana. 'I am so happy for
you.'

And she was. What a surprise. She
had been so busy thinking about her
own affairs, she had quite overlooked the
fact that these days Tatiana was walking
on air.

Mmmm, she thought, walking home.
What difference will that make to the
shop? Would his lordship want his wife

to carry on with Tatiana as a business?

In the meantime, she must hurry home. Find out how Isabel had got on, feeling a little apprehensive as she neared the house.

She was overcome with sympathy for Isabel. How could anyone behave so badly towards her? Things might have worked out so differently. How could Arthur be such a swine? It wasn't the money so much but the let down just when Isabel might have imagined...

She sighed deeply, and let herself into the house.

CHAPTER 18

Isabel was sitting in the drawing room, embroidering as usual, when Elizabeth came in. She looked up, and the first thing Elizabeth noticed was the resigned expression on her face. So whatever she had found out, it was not good news.

Elizabeth took a deep breath, and sat down opposite her.

'Well, no need to ask how you got on, Isabel. Your worst fears confirmed.'

'Yes, I'm afraid so,' Isabel said, folding up her work and putting it in the basket at her side.

It was strange to see her looking so cold, her face empty of all expression. It had been a dreadful shock to her, Elizabeth realised. Worse than she'd thought.

'First of all,' Isabel said, 'the solicitors do not exist.'

'But—'

'He must have had the false cards printed. My solicitor checked, and no firm of that name exists in the records. Secondly, I went to the estate agents to discover they had had no word from Arthur since that day we all went round to see the premises.' Her voice faltered. 'And now the shop is let.'

'Oh, Isabel!' And Elizabeth bit her lip.

'He was a nice young man,' Isabel went on. 'He said he assumed on not hearing any more from us that we were not interested.' She took out her hankie. 'And of course the cheque was cashed—the same day.'

Elizabeth went over to her, and put an arm around her shoulders.

'You couldn't have known,' she said. 'How could you? You were not to know.'

Isabel buried her face in her hands. 'I feel such a fool! That's the worst part! How could I have been so trusting—so simple? My father would turn in his grave! I am so stupid, thinking I could possibly—giving him a cheque without—oh, well.' And she sniffed, put her hankie away, and turned tear-drenched eyes to Elizabeth.

'I feel sorry for you, putting you through all this, but all is not lost.'

She stood up, and put on a brave false smile. 'Let's go and have dinner, and we'll talk about it afterwards.'

They were sitting in the drawing room over coffee when Isabel made her pronouncement.

'I intend to go ahead,' she said decisively.

The coffee cup half way to her mouth, Elizabeth stared at her.

'Go ahead?'

'Yes, why not? We shouldn't let a little thing like a man's dishonesty stop us. You'd like a shop of your own and a business, wouldn't you? You haven't changed your mind?'

'No, of course not—'

'Well, then, I am going round to the estate agents to see what else they can offer, and then I shall put the whole thing in the hands of my solicitors, and let them work it out.'

'But the money—you've lost a great deal.'

'I can stand it, fortunately, but that doesn't mean that we have to sit back and do nothing about it. No, I shall do it all again. That way, there's a chance that we may even recoup the money, although that's not the point at issue—but we certainly won't if we sit back and do nothing. After all, we were expecting it to be a profitable business, were we not?'

'Yes, but—'

'It will take time, I know.' And Isabel smiled reassuringly. 'I am not going to push you into anything you don't want to do. Oh, well, except for one thing.'

'And what's that?' Elizabeth asked curiously.

'There is a proviso to this—a condition, I'm afraid I must insist upon.'

'What is it?'

'I would like you to change your name to Lister.' And Isabel waited for it to sink in.

Elizabeth was quite shocked. She'd had no idea that Isabel felt so strongly about it.

'Oh.'

'You see, it would make everything so much easier in every way—the two Miss Listers opening a shop, the deeds to this house, so many things. Even when you get married—Miss Elizabeth Lister, niece of Miss Isabel Lister.'

Elizabeth laughed. 'Oh, wait, wait—I haven't even met the man yet.' And Isabel wondered if she had been barking up the wrong tree about Louis Vereker.

'You see,' she went on, 'it's so much

more convenient in every way, and it makes sense—you may call me your aunt, if you'd rather. It is so much nicer when introducing and saves the odd question.'

'That means you have accepted me as your niece.'

'Yes, I have,' Isabel said seriously. 'I'm never quite sure of your thoughts on the matter, but that's how I see it, and how I would like to see it in future. What do you say?'

Elizabeth thought hard, unwilling to jump too quickly into something when she had had no time to think about it. But Isabel was right. What did it matter in the long run?

Elizabeth Lister sounded rather good...

'Very well, Aunt.'

'Oh, that's wonderful!' Isabel cried, and there were tears in her eyes. 'You've made me very happy.'

'And now I have some rather surprising news for you,' Elizabeth said. 'Tatiana is going to be married!'

'No!' Isabel's eyes were wide.

'To Lord Daccrington, no less.' Elizabeth smiled and they both stared at each other for what seemed like a long time as the same thoughts raced round their heads.

'You don't think—' Isabel began.

'She will give up the shop?' Elizabeth

finished for her. 'Well, it's a possibility.'

'Oh, wouldn't that be wonderful!' Isabel cried. 'The best solution ever.'

'I expect we're rushing our fences a bit,' Elizabeth said. 'After all, she didn't tell me until this evening.'

'It's not a secret, is it?'

'No, she just said I was the first to know.'

'Well, I shall wait a little, then telephone her and ask her to lunch and tell her what has happened. After all, she has to know sometime.'

Things were looking up, Elizabeth thought. Perhaps now Isabel wouldn't mind if she explained it all to Louis.

'I am seeing Louis tomorrow evening, and I would like to tell him that I am not having the shop in Bruton Street.'

Isabel frowned. 'Well, he doesn't need to know the reason for its falling through—just that it is no longer available. Although what business it is of his...' She seemed quite disgruntled again, but Elizabeth knew that this was to do with the fact that Isabel didn't like to think that her friendship with Louis was too close.

'After all, I had told them at Vereker's and it seems only fair—they are our biggest suppliers and they will be interested to know what's happening.'

'Yes, as a business thing, that's true.

Well, simply say that the shop has been let to someone else. There's no reason for them to know what a fool I've been.'

'Very well, Isabel. It did occur to me to wonder if you should go to the police.'

'Absolutely not!' she said, her cheeks flushing. 'That's the last thing I would do.'

'It might prevent other people being led up the garden path,' Elizabeth said gently.

'Well, I can't help that,' Isabel said, as annoyed as Elizabeth had ever seen her.

'I shall also tell Sarah,' Elizabeth said slowly. 'About my change of name.' And Isabel brightened. 'I should explain it to her, the whys and wherefores, don't you think?'

'Of course, dear!' Isabel said. 'I shall be able to show you off to the whole world as my niece—and nothing will please me more.'

Sometimes she thought she was in another world, Elizabeth reflected. Out of obscurity into this affluent life, her own business, living in a prestigious town house. Who would have thought it possible?

When she arrived at Tatiana's the next morning, it was to find Tatiana still in her outdoor clothes.

'Now, darling, I am going to leave you to hold the fort today—you don't need me. Teddy is taking me to lunch after—need I tell you?—we have bought the engagement ring!'

Her joy was infectious.

'It's in *The Times* this morning,' she said. 'Look, I'll show you.'

Elizabeth read the impressive announcement. So Tatiana herself was the daughter of an earl.

'This will be my third marriage,' she said, 'but for the first time I am truly head over heels in love—at my age. Isn't it wonderful?'

She looked radiant. 'Daddy would have been so pleased, it's a pity he's not here to see us. However...

'Enough about me. I haven't asked you, how is it all coming along? Your business plan? You see, at the end of it all it really didn't matter. And I was so upset! Nothing matters at the end of the day, does it?'

Elizabeth shook her head. 'Well, I have to tell you, Tatiana, that it's not coming off—we've lost the shop to someone else.'

'Oh, my dear, how ghastly. What happened?'

'Well, it's a long story but the net result is, due to some mix up or other, the shop has now been let to someone else.'

'Oh, Elizabeth, how disappointing for you.' But already Elizabeth could see that the news had meant more than a little to her. 'Er—well—so now you will not be leaving me?' she said thoughtfully.

'If that's all right with you?' Elizabeth laughed. 'I was going to tell you today.'

'Yes—well—look, I'm meeting Teddy at ten this morning so I haven't a moment now, but tomorrow we'll talk about it, all right?'

Elizabeth's hopes soared. Perhaps after all everything would work out right?

'Have a wonderful day,' she said, 'and don't worry about a thing.'

Tatiana swept out, her bracelets jangling, just in time to avoid Mrs Dalrymple-Oxted, who was one of her best clients—and one of the most difficult to please.

'Good morning.' Elizabeth smiled. 'Isn't it a beautiful day? Will you come this way, Mrs Dalrymple-Oxted?' Oh, who could be miserable on such a day, when things were looking up? And she was seeing Louis this evening.

Mrs Dalrymple-Oxted beamed. A woman in her sixties, she spent a small fortune every year at Tatiana's establishment, and always looked splendidly got up, like a ship in full sail. She was a very large woman but held herself very tall and had a beautiful fair skin. She knew what suited her and kept to the same style, but in different materials. With finely turned ankles, developing into muscular calves, her body was straight down with no figure to speak of, but she had a fine head of snow white hair carried well on what had to be admitted kindly was a sturdy neck.

'Now, my dear, what have you to show me?' she asked Elizabeth, of whom she was very fond. Just what she would have liked a daughter to be, had she had one. A great disappointment to her after four sons.

'Just come and look at some of the new materials from Paris,' Elizabeth enthused. She spread the swatches over the French table, mauves and greens and deep fuchsia. Mrs D as they called her, hardly ever changed her colours—varying shades of lavender down to purple, from pale green to olive, and the whole gamut of magenta to rose.

'My dear, this is beautiful!' She held the material between carefully manicured fingers, soft white hands with long almond shaped nails. It was quite the newest shade, a soft parma violet which would go very well with her colouring.

'This dark shade of purple for facing—the godets in the skirt, just showing a glimpse. Look, I'll show you.' And Elizabeth sketched the design, a slight departure from Mrs D's usual tailored suit, her deft fingers catching the design in an instant.

Mrs D was fascinated. 'Oh, that's lovely. But...' and she looked doubtful. 'Is it me?

Those godets in the skirt. A bit fussy. You know I always wear a straight skirt.'

'Be a little daring.' Elizabeth smiled, showing her lovely teeth, her green eyes sparkling with mischief. She didn't add that the godets would draw attention to her fine ankles as they moved, and would diminish the size of her calves.

'Really?'

'And it is the very latest from Paris,' Elizabeth said. 'But if you don't like the idea...'

'Oh, but I do!' Mrs D said, by now feeling quite adventurous and ready for a change of style. If it was successful, there was no end to the things she could have for the trip to Washington in September. After all, she owed it to Nicholas. They were ambassadors for Great Britain and it was time she had a change.

Slightly flushed with the effort of changing her style, she sank into a chair. 'Show me what else you have,' she said.

Altogether it was a successful morning, with orders from Mrs D for five outfits, to include the new design in parma violet. Elizabeth became quite excited at the thought of it. She loved anything new.

That evening she and Louis walked through the park, hand in hand, past rose beds in full bloom and beautifully mown grass which had a scent all its own, towards Kensington Gardens, bereft now of nannies and their charges in London and Milsom prams who were being bathed and tucked down in nurseries on many a top floor in a London house, while parents prepared themselves once more for a night out at the theatre or concert.

They sat down on a seat by the shrubbery where the birds sang their heads off on this lovely spring evening.

'First of all, tell me how the shop is progressing,' Louis said, taking her hand, and Elizabeth took a deep breath.

'It isn't,' she said. 'That is to say—it's all off.'

'Elizabeth! Why? What happened?'

Remembering Isabel's request, she skirted round it.

'I really don't know. There was a muddle of some sort, and the shop was let to someone else.'

Louis looked annoyed. 'That's disgraceful,' he said. 'Most unbusinesslike. Who was the agent?' But Elizabeth placated him.

'Louis, it doesn't matter. It was just one of those things.'

'But you were all geared up for taking it on. How did Miss Lister's friend manage to bungle it?'

'Well, there was a mix-up—one day, I'll explain it to you, but not now. Tell me about Paris.' And she looked up at him, seeing the dark eyes, the black hair, the way it grew on his forehead, the firm strongly shaped mouth. He was a man to depend on, she thought, and held his hand tightly.

He saw only green eyes in which he seemed to drown when he looked at her, the curve of her pale cheek, the slight freckling on the nose, the way her hair curled...and hated more than ever what he had to tell her.

'Did I ever explain to you about Paris?' he asked.

'No, what do you mean?'

'Well we've been having a bit of trouble over there and they need me so I've got to spend some time seeing to things. Probably the next three months.'

'Oh, Louis! Not all the time?'

'Well, a lot of the time.'

She looked so miserable, he put his arm round her.

'Let me explain. First of all, you know my father is French and Vereker's in Paris was the first venture? My grandfather started it—he came from Lyons.'

Elizabeth nodded. 'Silk,' she said.

'That's right. It did well. It's the most famous textile shop in Paris, in the Rue

Faubourg St Honoré.'

'I know it!' Elizabeth exclaimed. 'I've been there.'

He looked at her in astonishment. 'You have. When?'

'Oh, a long time ago, when I worked for Sarah—I'll tell you about it some time. We were there for three days buying her trousseau.'

'Well, then, I needn't tell you what a nice business it is, right in the heart of Paris.'

She could imagine it, elegant, full of delightful materials, expensive silks, luxury crêpes...

'Well, when my father met my English mother, and married her, for a time they lived in Paris. He fought all through the war in the French army, but when it was over my mother decided she didn't want to stay in France, so he came to England, opened a second Vereker's, and put the other one under management. My grandfather was alive then. It was always hoped I would take it over, but I happen to like living in England too. Especially now.'

And he kissed her on the top of her ear.

'So?' Elizabeth said. The touch of his lips was delightful.

'My father used to go over about once

a month at one time, but now he's determined to retire. But at a very inconvenient moment in the order of things. The chap who runs the Paris branch has decided to go to America and—well, I'm needed there.'

'Oh, Louis!'

'It won't be for long—just until we can find someone with the expertise needed. In the meantime I shall have to keep it going. Added to that, Papa needs me here, but as I told him, I can't be in two places at once, and he decided Paris it is. It's his favourite shop—after all, he is French—so he's going to defer retirement until everything is settled.'

All the laughter had gone out of her eyes; she couldn't bear to think that having found him, she might lose him. Once in Paris, there would be French girls—and Elizabeth knew for the first time in her life a stab of jealousy.

'But you would be coming back here every so often?'

'Of course,' he said. 'I can't say exactly when, not on a regular basis, but I hope to get the whole thing cleared up in three months at the outside.'

'Three months!' she wailed.

'But I shall see you in between times,' he consoled her. 'It's not what I want either.'

She took his arm.

'Of course not, and of course you must go—you really have no choice, do you? You know, I never really realised before that you are French—I mean French French.'

He laughed.

'I have dual nationality.'

'Well!' she said. 'As long as you haven't a dual personality! Shall we go? It's a bit chilly.'

'Yes, I thought we'd walk to the other side and back again before it gets dark. Do you have to be home early?'

She smiled. 'I don't want to be too late. Isabel has been a bit bothered by the shop business.'

'So that's why you wanted to cancel last night? Is your aunt very upset about it? By the way, she is your aunt, isn't she?'

Elizabeth laughed. 'Well again, that's another story, but I think I must tell you—it's quite romantic in a way, and something I never can quite believe.'

He listened, from the beginning, and looked more and more incredulous as she came towards the end of the tale.

'Romantic!' he said. 'It's more than that—it's unbelievable! And you are quite prepared now to adopt the name of Lister?'

'Yes, if it makes her happy. What difference does it make to me?'

'And—' he said slowly '—one day you will change it, eh?'

He held her arm tightly as she looked up at him with a smile. Oh, she hoped so! There was nothing she wanted more.

'You know, you and I would make a good combination,' he said presently. 'You with your own business—I still think you should go ahead. You can always find another shop.'

'Yes, I expect so, there's plenty of time.'

Before he left her, he put his arms around her and held her close.

'Elizabeth, now that I've found you, I don't want to let you go.'

She raised her face to his, her flower-like mouth inches from his as he bent his head to kiss her. When her lips met his, it was as if the world stood still, and nothing else mattered, as if they were the only two people in the world.

When he finally released her they stood in the darkness, still shaken by the impact of the kiss.

'I have to go,' Elizabeth whispered.

'I wish you didn't have to.'

'So do I.' And then she was gone, running up the steps then inserting the key in the lock before turning to wave, unaware that Isabel had seen them from the upstairs window.

She had gone to it to draw back the curtains before retiring, and had seen the closely entwined figures in the shadow of a nearby lamp post.

She frowned. Oh, what a pity Elizabeth had had to become involved with the Vereker man! He wasn't right for her at all. More than ever she was determined to find a business for Elizabeth. Not only did she deserve it, but it would take her mind off this young man...

'Ah, there you are!' she said as the girl came up the stairs. 'I was just off to bed. I thought I heard you. Did you have a nice evening?'

'Yes, thank you,' Elizabeth said, hating to come back to earth so soon.

'Good,' Isabel said briskly. 'Well, I'll say goodnight, dear.'

'Goodnight, Isabel.'

CHAPTER 19

When Elizabeth explained her change of name and the circumstances that had led up to it, Sarah opened her eyes wide in astonishment. 'I don't believe it!' she cried, yet within a very short time had accepted it. 'Didn't I say it was strange the way

314

she sort of adopted you, right from the beginning? You know, it's terribly romantic in a way. Just imagine...'

But Elizabeth was disinclined to dwell on the subject. She had said all she was prepared to say on the matter, Isabel had got her way, and that was enough. For herself, she could see the advantages of being a Lister. It was, after all, a well known and established family—not like the Bartholomews, she thought, never having lost the affection she had had for George, the warm memories of a father she had never known, and wondered what her mother would have had to say about it had she been alive.

Elizabeth decided to adapt to her new status as quickly as possible and get on with her life. Goodness knows, she was busy enough. The orders never stopped coming in.

A few days after Tatiana's engagement was announced, Isabel telephoned her, congratulating her on the news and asking her to lunch. Tatiana was pleased to accept for there was a lot to talk about with an eye to Elizabeth's future.

They lunched in Fortnum's and Isabel couldn't help observing how well Tatiana looked, like the cat who'd got the cream.

'Oh, this is nice, Isabel,' Tatiana cried, her eyes incredibly blue, and Isabel felt a pang of envy. But she swiftly put it to one side. After all, she had been fortunate too. She had acquired a new member of the family at a time when she might have imagined she was almost alone in the world, and if Arthur Hetherington was an example of what could happen between a man and a woman, then she was glad she had missed it.

'You must be so pleased with Elizabeth,' Tatiana said. 'What a lucky day it was for all of us when you suggested that she come to work for me.'

She speared her salad delicately, her long scarlet nails striking a bold contrast against the green of the lettuce. 'You know, you are a cagey old thing,' she went on. 'You never explained why you took her under your wing?'

'I was coming to that,' Isabel said. 'There is an explanation, as I am sure you've guessed, and in the last two days I have been putting it to rights legally. Only two or three people know the background, after all, we don't want everyone to know, but I think you are entitled to know the truth.' And she proceeded to tell Tatiana the story of the romance between her brother Edmund and the maid Mary Daly.

'Well!' Tatiana said, sitting back in her chair. 'Well, no wonder you wanted to help her.'

She put her hand out and patted Isabel's. 'I am so glad for you, really. You've acquired a daughter, something I would like to have had. Still, I mustn't complain, must I?'

She smiled brightly at Isabel.

'I expect you have come to talk about Tatiana's,' she said.

'Not just that,' Isabel said. 'The truth is, Tat, I made an awful fool of myself. I still can't believe that I did it, even now.'

Tatiana was astonished. 'What on earth do you mean?'

'I don't know whether Elizabeth mentioned Major Hetherington to you?'

'Yes, she did tell me that he had suggested that she have a business of her own.'

'Yes, and I agreed with him, I have to say. The rest of the story is not so pleasant. He was kind enough to work it out for us—the costs, the legal fees, the goodwill, etc. I became quite knowledgeable, Tat, about business.' And her lip twisted.

Tatiana, more worldly wise, thought she guessed what was coming.

'The short story is that I gave him a cheque for five thousand pounds—he was to put in two thousand and become a "sleeping partner". And we haven't seen him from that day to this!'

'Oh, Isabel. I am so sorry.' Tatiana was

317

genuinely upset for her.

'I was a fool,' Isabel said tersely. 'I fell for it, hook, line and sinker.'

'Did you get on to the police?'

Isabel shook her head.

'You should have done,' Tatiana reproached her. 'Men like him need to be stopped. Playing on women...it's quite criminal.' And wondered just how involved Isabel had become emotionally.

'I know, but I couldn't bring myself to admit it to anyone—much less the police. Imagine having it blazoned across the pages of a newspaper.'

'Hmm. I know what you mean.'

'Fortunately it was no great loss financially, just a blow to my self-esteem, and an enormous disappointment to Elizabeth. So what I wanted to ask you was—is there a possibility you might think of selling the business as you are getting married?'

Tatiana smiled.

'No, Isabel, I wouldn't sell it outright. But I might be interested in coming to an arrangement—say Elizabeth taking over, a sort of partnership, with me as a sleeping partner. A genuine one, Isabel, not like the Major.'

Isabel began to get excited. 'Really? Would you, Tat?'

'Yes, I had almost decided to do it, you see, Teddy is not all that keen on my

318

keeping it on. He says we're getting older, which means he is and he would like me not to be tied down to the business. He's quite right, of course, I've had a long run. It's exciting, too, with the new business that Elizabeth has brought in—she's a great girl, you know, Isabel. You should be very proud of her. She's talented. Does she get that from your family, do you think?'

'Well, who can say?' Isabel answered modestly. 'Mama was quite a good water colourist and loved clothes, but I am afraid none of that rubbed off on to me.'

'Well, whatever, Elizabeth is going a long way, take it from me.'

Lunch finished, she withdrew a long amber holder from her large crocodile handbag, and took out a cigarette.

'Do you mind?'

Isabel shook her head.

When the coffee came, Tatiana got down to her plans.

'I shall be getting married in September, and as I see it, if Elizabeth can carry on, as she is well able to do—we shall get someone else in to replace me—we shall tick over just as before. I shall call in from time to time. Now, this has to be sorted out legally—partnerships are not easy and in my experience don't always work out well. But, Isabel, tell your solicitor what we have in mind and he will get together with mine and work something out. How does that sound?'

Isabel was so pleased she could hardly contain herself.

'You have saved my day,' she told Tatiana. 'I was feeling so low, thinking that I had let the girl down as it were. Not that she complained, she was quite happy to go on as she was, but it occurred to me that marrying Teddy Daccrington...'

'Do you remember him?' Tatiana asked.

'Yes, from the old days. He was a poppet.'

'Still is, Isabel. He married Florence Sainsbury, you remember her? She died three years ago, and the poor lamb has been on his own ever since. So that's the background, Iz, and let's face it, I could do with a break—I've been at this business a long time, a lot longer than all those people imagined who said I'd go broke in three months. Look at me, owner of one of the best gown shops in Mayfair!'

'We were all jealous of you when we left school,' Isabel said.

'Really! How wonderful! I wish I'd known.' Tatiana picked up her handbag. 'I must fly. Thanks for the lunch, Isabel. It was lovely to see you. We must meet again. I'll be in touch as soon as I have seen my solicitors.'

'Goodbye, Tatiana.'

Isabel watched her leave the restaurant, an attractive slim figure in blue, her lovely legs skimming over the floor, her high heels flashing, and wondered whether she might indulge in a pair of those high-heeled patent court shoes. After all, she and Tatiana were the same age. But the very thought brought a grin to her face. She would be better to stay in her sensible sturdy brogues. It was too late now for the leopard to change its spots.

When Elizabeth heard the news, she hugged Isabel in her excitement. 'It's the very best thing that could have happened!' she cried. 'So everything works out for the best in the long run, see, Isabel? If we had taken the little shop in Bruton Street I might have missed the chance of getting Tatiana's—and I would have been upset at that. After all, I have put roots down there. I know all the clients. Oh, it's wildly exciting!'

Isabel felt she was getting back to normal. 'I'm so glad you're pleased. As you say, it's all turned out for the best.'

Then Elizabeth came back to earth. 'Isabel, I hope it isn't going to cost you an awful lot. Tatiana may want quite a lot of money for such an established business.'

'Yes, possibly, but I shan't know that until both sets of solicitors have got down to it. I'm not going to worry, Elizabeth, it will work out right, I am sure. After all, you are a designer in your own right now, and able to speak for yourself.'

Elizabeth was thoughtful. So she was. She felt she had enough confidence now to manage her own life without outside help, but nevertheless, to have backers, people who had faith in you, was a wonderful thing.

'Well, I must go,' she said, on her way upstairs. 'I'm meeting Louis this evening. We're going to the cinema.'

'Very well, dear.' And Isabel made her way back to the drawing room. Really, it was a pity. Elizabeth seemed to be getting more and more involved with that young man. He had come into her life at the wrong stage, in Isabel's opinion, and she had hoped that his spending so much time in France would have made a difference. But not so far.

She spent the evening embroidering, and thinking over the business deal with Tatiana. It was fairly obvious that she would not like to let the business go now that Elizabeth had joined it. She was, after all, a dedicated career woman otherwise she would not have stayed in it so long. Successful, too. She had proved her point. But Elizabeth's designs were now model gowns and cost a lot of money, she was becoming well known at home and abroad, and she was well able to sustain a business of her own.

On the other hand, she had become well known through Tatiana who had given her her first chance; not only that but Tatiana's was a well established business, and it was a good idea to take advantage of it. Yes, all in all, it was an excellent prospect.

When Elizabeth came in just before ten, Isabel put down her embroidery and looked up.

'You're early, dear.'

'Yes, Louis had to get back. He's taking the early ferry to Calais. Some business there, I think.'

'Oh. How did you get on at work today?'

'Tatiana and I had a chat about the future which looks exceedingly bright, I must say... Oh, and we have a new client—the daughter of an American diplomat. It seems her cousin bought one of my models at Christmas which she wore to a New Year's Ball in New York, and ever since then this one, Miss Marilyn Chatterton, has been determined that when she came to London, she would look me up and order a gown for herself. Isn't that wonderful?'

Isabel smiled triumphantly. 'There! You see, world wide acclaim.'

Elizabeth laughed. 'I don't know about

that, but it does mean that I have a foothold in the States.'

'Well done, dear.'

Two evenings later, Elizabeth had a call from Richard Barrington.

'Elizabeth, I've just arrived back from Germany—how are you?'

'Well, thank you. How are you?'

'Delighted to be back, I can tell you.' His voice sounded grim then suddenly lightened. 'Look, I have four seats for the theatre on Friday evening. Josh and Sarah can come—can you make it?'

Her eyes began to sparkle. Busy as she was she liked the idea of an evening out at the theatre.

'At the Haymarket,' he went on. 'Are you free?'

'Yes, I'd love to, Richard,' she said, already looking forward to the outing.

'I'll pick you up around seven-thirty, OK?'

'Yes, that's fine, I'll look forward to that,' Elizabeth said, and realised how few social engagements she had. No wonder she was excited. When she met Louis, they usually walked and talked of business most of the time, which she enjoyed, there was nothing more wonderful than seeing Louis, but to get away from business would be a change.

'That was Richard Barrington,' she said

after she had hung up the receiver.

Isabel made no effort to hide her pleasure.

'He has invited me to the theatre on Friday, with Josh and Sarah.'

'How nice, dear,' Isabel said. Now that was just what the girl needed. A break away from business—and Louis Vereker, of course.

'What will you wear?' she asked.

A little smile played around Elizabeth's mouth. 'I have just the thing upstairs—I haven't worn it yet. It's just sitting there, waiting to be worn.'

On Friday morning, Isabel took her usual walk in the park. It was high summer and the flower beds were full of roses. Children on their summer holidays were skipping or playing ball. Mothers sat on the grass, picnic baskets beside them, and the trees were in their full glory. Nowhere, she thought, were the trees more beautiful than Hyde Park. She sat down for a while to rest, observing everything about her—she loved this park, had known it all her life. When she was small, a nanny had pushed her in the pram to Kensington Gardens. Later when they were older, she and Edmund had sailed their boats on the Round Pond, stared up at the statue of Peter Pan, and chased each other round the shrubbery. Sometimes Father had walked with them; only on Sundays had Mama come, dressed in her lovely hats and elegant dresses. She had been so beautiful, fair-haired with blue eyes. They had said Isabel took after Mama, but only in colouring. She had none of Mama's magic, that something that had lifted her out of the crowd of ordinary women. When she entered a room, it was as if everyone stopped talking to look at her.

When I come into a room no one even sees me, Isabel thought with chagrin. Mouselike, her father had said. He could be so cruel. I mustn't think ill of the dead, she thought, getting up and walking on.

That evening Elizabeth came downstairs dressed in the outfit she was going to wear to the theatre on Friday evening—a dinner suit, the latest style for evening wear.

Isabel was spellbound. Never had Elizabeth looked so lovely. The black skirt was long and narrow, and over it was a fitted green velvet jacket, thigh-length, with high mandarin collar, buttoned all the way down with gilt buttons, Chinese embroidery worked in gold thread down the front and down the sleeves. She had pulled her dark lustrous hair up with combs, and beneath it the green eyes shone, her heart-shaped face with its pale skin so like her dead mother's that Isabel's heart almost stopped in her throat.

'Elizabeth, you look lovely!'

'Thank you. What do you think of the suit?'

'Words fail me. Another of your wonderful designs. I should think it would take on without doubt, so suitable. Dressy yet practical with that lovely jacket.'

'Well, I went to town on that.'

Elizabeth looked at herself in the large mirror.

'Yes, I'm pleased with it.'

'You have no idea how much like your mother you are,' Isabel said. 'At this age—well, she was a little younger than you are now when I last saw her—'

Elizabeth took off the jacket and put it over a chair. Underneath the jacket was a simple black top with a cut out neckline.

'Tell me about her, please, Isabel,' she said, sitting down on a chair opposite.

'Well, I think I've told you all I can remember, dear. It was wartime. She was here when I came back from Austria that summer—and she was so pretty and so sweet, with a lovely soft Irish voice, and an Irish face, heart-shaped, with greeny blue eyes and thick dark hair.'

'And your brother?' Elizabeth asked gently.

'Your father? Oh, he was wonderful. I adored him. He was two years older than I, and so like Mama. Good-looking with fair curls and blue eyes. He was a handsome little boy and grew up into a very handsome man. It broke my heart when he went away to war.'

She sat lost in the past, remembering.

'Edmund was at Eton, and when Father went away to Malaysia for five years, Edmund and I used to go out there every year for the summer holidays. The sea journeys were wonderful, we had such a time—everyone spoiled us.'

Elizabeth tried to imagine these two small children on board a huge passenger ship. 'Did you travel alone?'

'Oh, no!' Isabel said, shocked. 'We had a governess, a Miss Lethbridge, who was very kind to us. Mama hated it out East, she was always ill, couldn't wait to return home, but Edmund and I had a fine time.'

'What did your father do out there?'

'We had rubber plantations. My grandfather owned them, and my father had to do his part in the running of them. Of course there were overseers, men who were used to the climate, plantation managers who have always worked out East. My father was quite old when he married my mother and had always worked out East as a young man. When he went back for five years, Mother had to go with him, much to

328

her disgust. Edmund, had he lived, would also have gone out to Malaysia. But there you are.'

Sadly, Isabel stared out of the window. 'Now, there are no Listers left, which is why I was so pleased when you came on the scene.'

'Where else did you go on holiday as a family when you were young?'

'Oh, Cornwall, almost always to Cornwall where we rented a house. Sometimes to Bexhill, which Mama liked. She thought it more civilised than Cornwall. But Edmund and I loved the seaside and the beach, making sand castles and hunting for sea urchins—Edmund always found things that I didn't see.'

It must have been wonderful, Elizabeth thought, to have a brother, a close friend. Being an only child she had missed that, and fell to thinking of the home where she had been for so long. It was another world. Violet...what was she doing now? Still plying her trade, perhaps married by now. And suddenly she thought of Nancy, poor, sweet little Nancy.

'Oh, I've made you sad, talking about him!' Isabel said.

'No—no, I suddenly thought of a girl at the home, who died,' Elizabeth said, but Isabel didn't want her to remember that part of her life.

'You must put all that behind you,' she said sharply. 'It's gone—past and gone.'

'But it's still part of me. I can't change that, can I?'

'No, perhaps not, but you will forget it, in time.'

And hopefully, she thought, I shall lose some of the guilt I feel that she was there in the first place.

CHAPTER 20

Elizabeth had been in the salon only an hour on Friday morning when she was called to the telephone.

'Captain Barrington,' Tatiana told her.

'Thank you, Tatiana. Hallo, Richard?'

'Elizabeth, I'm sorry to bother you at this hour of the day—'

'That's all right.'

'Look, I wonder if you would mind not going to the theatre this evening?' And Elizabeth felt a pang of disappointment. She had been so looking forward to it.

'Of course not.'

'I can't explain now but would you come out to dinner with me instead?'

'Oh! Well—'

'Something has cropped up—I can't

explain—but will you? Please, Elizabeth. I'm going to Scotland tomorrow and I would really like to see you before I go.'

'Yes, that would be nice,' she said. 'Are Sarah and Josh coming?'

'No, but I'll pick you up at the same time—seven-thirty, is that all right?'

'That's fine,' Elizabeth said. 'See you then.'

Oh, well, to go out to dinner would be a change, too. Pity she couldn't wear the special dinner suit. It was perhaps a little overdone. It would depend where they went.

'Oh, what a pity!' Isabel cried when she told her. 'But you must wear the dinner suit. I am sure Richard will take you somewhere nice.'

Elizabeth arrived downstairs just before seven-thirty carrying the jacket, the simple black dress relieved by a three-strand pearl necklace. Isabel stared at her. 'Just wait until he sees you,' she said. 'That dress is lovely.'

When Richard arrived, Mrs Baines showed him in.

'Captain Barrington, miss.'

'Good evening, Miss Lister,' he said, taking Isabel's hand, and as before, she thought what a handsome and upright man he was.

'Good evening, Captain,' she was saying

331

with a smile as Elizabeth came in.

He went over to her. 'My dear, you look simply wonderful!' he said. 'What a stunning dress.'

'Isn't it?' Isabel beamed.

'Thank you,' said Elizabeth, picking up the jacket. Richard held it while she slipped into it, admiration in his blue eyes.

'Splendid,' he said. 'One of your own creations, I expect?'

'Yes.'

There was no doubt that he was proud to be taking her out for the evening, and Isabel prayed that it would be the first of many occasions.

Richard instructed the taxi driver to take them to the Hyde Park Hotel, and Elizabeth was pleased that she had worn the new suit. Once in the taxi, he became more serious.

'I'm sorry about the theatre,' he said. 'I'll explain when we get to the hotel.'

They were there in no time, and walking up the marble steps towards the restaurant.

'I thought we'd have a drink in the bar,' he said, taking her arm. 'Is that all right with you?'

She smiled as he led her over to a corner seat.

Having settled himself, he turned to her, and she saw by his expression that something was wrong. 'Elizabeth—'

'What is it?' she asked. 'I can see you have something to tell me.'

'I'm afraid I have,' he said slowly. 'I do apologise about the theatre.' And he wondered the best way to put what he had to say.

'The fact is that Sarah has left Josh.' There was no point, he thought, in beating about the bush.

'Oh!' Elizabeth covered her mouth with her hand. 'Oh, no!'

'Yes, she left the house yesterday morning as usual, Josh said, ostensibly to keep a hairdressing appointment. But when she hadn't come back by the evening, he went into her room and found the note.'

'Oh...poor Josh,' Elizabeth whispered. She felt like weeping. Oh, Sarah, Sarah! she thought. I never really thought you would. Although she had threatened to leave many times.

'How is Josh?' she asked. 'How has he taken it?'

'Badly,' Richard said. 'He's due to go to Scotland tomorrow—I was to go with him, and have persuaded him to stick to his plans. It will make no difference whether he goes or not, but I imagine he'll be better up there. No point in hanging about for Sarah to change her mind.'

No, Elizabeth thought. Once Sarah had decided, that was that. And she wondered

333

who the man was this time.

'Did she give no reason?' Elizabeth asked.

'No. I saw the note, very brief, to the effect that there was no point in his trying to find her, she had gone abroad.'

'No mention of going with someone?'

'No, although I am sure there was.'

'Hmmm,' Elizabeth said as the waiter came up with the cocktails.

She leaned back against the velvet seat. 'Oh, Richard. How could she? Josh was so kind to her.'

'Well,' he said slowly, 'there's always two sides to every question, but for my part, I felt he gave in to her too easily.'

'One never knows what goes on in a marriage,' Elizabeth remarked. 'I think they were temperamentally unsuited, but sometimes that works.'

'Not in this case,' Richard said grimly, then suddenly smiled. 'Well, let's try to forget about it. Here's to a good evening, and I'm sorry that I had to be the one to break the news to you but I thought, well, at least we can make something of the evening. The theatre didn't seem right somehow.'

Elizabeth sipped her Martini, the dryness burning her throat but glad of the warmth as it tingled through her. 'So you are off tomorrow with Josh?'

'Yes. I'm glad now I said I'd go with him. I was in half a mind—'

He didn't add that he had not been too keen because he wanted to see more of her. She had occupied a lot of his thoughts, this green-eyed slip of a girl, the sort he had never had much to do with before. Not at all the kind of girl he had been brought up with or had been going around with since he went into the army.

'We mustn't let this spoil our evening,' he said.

But it had a dampening effect, just the same. Over dinner they talked about each other. Elizabeth learned that his family lived in Northampton, that he had two brothers, one older and one younger than himself, that his father was an army man, too.

Elizabeth wondered if Sarah had said anything to him about her own background, and decided that she herself would say nothing. What was the point? He would have to take her as he found her. Isabel's adopted niece, that would have to do. In any case, it wasn't as if he were a potential suitor—just a friend. Nice though he was. And as the evening wore on she warmed to him more and more. He had a nice sense of humour, although at the back of both their minds was Sarah's disappearance.

'Sarah said you were stationed in

Knightsbridge?' she said over coffee.

'Yes, on and off,' he said. 'I'm with intelligence which means that I get sent here and there and everywhere—sometimes. At other times, there can be a complete lull.'

She found herself wishing more than once that it was Louis who sat there—Louis with his dark eyes looking into hers instead of the twinkling blue-grey eyes of the Captain.

'I understand that you are about to open a salon of your own? How are the plans coming along?'

'Oh, I'm afraid that came to nothing for various reasons, but I'm going into partnership with my present employer Tatiana Tetbury. She's getting married in September and giving up full-time work in the salon, so she offered me a partnership and I was more than pleased about that.'

'Well, I wish you luck,' Richard said. 'It's good to have something purposeful to do. Not,' he went on,' that you will be working in a salon for long. A young lady like yourself will soon be married, I daresay.'

Which observation Elizabeth did not take as the compliment he intended.

'Are you one of those men who think that the only life a girl can look forward to is sharing it with a man?' she asked, a twinkle in her eye.

'Good Lord, no!' he said, while realising that deep down he did. He hadn't realised she might be one of the new breed of young women who genuinely believed that a woman has some other purpose in life than being a wife and mother.

He thought about Jane, and Fiona, Catherine and Anne, all girls in his social circle, none of whom had ever had the slightest intention of doing anything but get married. This girl was different. His parents would say she came from another world—a different background. Well, perhaps she did, but there was nothing wrong with that. It surprised him the train of thought his mind was taking...

'I'd like you to come up to Brampton Priory sometime,' he said. 'I think you'd enjoy it.'

Elizabeth put down her coffee cup. 'Thank you, I'd like that.'

'By the way,' he said anxiously, 'you're not engaged or anything, are you?'

She laughed. 'No, I'm not engaged.' There seemed no point in telling him about Louis Vereker. That she was falling in love with a man whom she thought felt the same way about her. It was early days yet after all. She must take time to get the business off the ground and settle down in her own salon. But he was nice, Richard Barrington. Amusing. She liked him. When they parted, he promised to ring her on his return from Scotland at the end of a fortnight.

Isabel was upset about Sarah's disappearance, although she said more than once that she wasn't surprised. Elizabeth knew that Sarah wasn't one of her favourite people. Isabel thought her scatterbrained and selfish. 'That poor young man,' she said. 'He's better off without her. He needs a wife who will settle down and give him a family.'

Elizabeth's eyes darkened. Poor Sarah. She had paid a high price for her freedom. And Elizabeth's mind harked back to the carefree days when Sarah had crept back into the finishing school through the tiny window, her lovely cheeks flushed, eyes bright...and the dress Elizabeth had altered for her, her very first effort.

Now she was more concerned about seeing Louis when he returned from France at the weekend. She had so much to tell him about the opportunity of going into partnership with Tatiana. She knew he would approve of that.

Louis was waiting for her when she left the salon, his eyes lighting up at the sight of her. How handsome he was, so tall, his clear-cut features and dark hair, the brown eyes warm at seeing her.

Her heart was bounding with sheer excitement and pleasure at seeing him.

He took her hand and kissed it.

'Oh,' she laughed. 'You've been in Paris too long.' But she was delighted just the same.

He took her hand and tucked it into his arm. 'You look prettier than ever.'

'And you grow more handsome every time I see you.'

'Well,' he smiled, 'That sets off the right tone for the evening, wouldn't you say?'

They began to walk, her small strides struggling to keep up with his.

'I thought we'd walk through the park towards Bayswater to a nice little French restaurant where the food is superb,' he said, kissing his fingertips.

'Oh, Louis, sometimes you are so —French,' she laughed. 'Anyway, how's it going over there? Are you pleased?'

'Yes, things are going very well. Our new man is a distant cousin of mine—I told you we were a large family. He used to run the store in Nice, and is settling in nicely. He is what I suppose you would call charming, and of course that is a very desirable quality to have when you are dealing with women. He needs to get to know the stock more—after all, the Paris branch is four times as big as the Nice one—but he will. As soon as he is established I shall be home more. My father has put off retiring until everything is settled, did I tell you?'

'Yes, you did mention it.'

'Anyway, that aside we've just had a delivery of the most wonderful fabrics, I went down to Lyons whilst I was there.'

'I can't wait to see them!'

'You shall be the first. But enough of me. How are you? Got over your disappointment about not getting the shop?'

'Ah, well, I have some news for you.'

'Don't tell me he turned up again—your aunt's friend, the Major. How is Miss Lister?'

'Very well. But wait till we eat, and I'll tell you over dinner.'

As they walked through the park, Elizabeth was observing the clothes that women wore. It always took time for new fashions to get through to the masses but the evidence was there already. Slightly longer skirts and perky little hats, furs slung over the shoulder, high-heeled shoes and pointed heels, lots of tweeds, suits, open necked blouses, and lots of make up. Scarlet lipsticks and nails to match, plucked eyebrows and eye make up. Layer upon layer of curls but flat on top or arranged carelessly round the shoulders. Untidy, she thought, with tailored suits.

'So how are the orders going?' asked Louis. 'Let's sit down for a moment, shall we?'

They sat down and looked into each other's eyes.

'Oh, Elizabeth,' he said, 'you really are something. Those eyes—they bewitch a man.'

She sighed. It was nice to receive compliments, a girl could never have enough.

'I wonder if you know how I feel about you?' he asked. 'I think of you when I am in Paris and long to be back.'

'And I can't wait to see you again,' she said. 'Thank goodness I'm busy. Otherwise...'

'When I think of the talent in that pretty little head,' he said. 'You know, you're going a long way—and sometimes I think in all fairness we're both so busy we have no time to fall in love.'

'That's what makes it so wonderful,' she said. 'Despite all the pressures, we long to be with each other.'

'But I'd like to be with you every moment of every day, instead of seeing you at the odd times I can fit in.'

'And I,' she said, 'am about to embark—'

'On what?'

'—a partnership with Tatiana!' she said triumphantly. 'Now what do you think about that?'

'My dear Elizabeth! Really? But that's even better than a shop of your own. You're halfway there. Why, is Tatiana retiring?'

'Getting married,' she said. 'Her husband to be thinks she should spend more time with him so she has offered me a partnership, which as you say is even better. I'm used to the salon, my clients are already there—oh, I'm so excited, Louis!'

'You deserve to succeed,' he said, looking down at her, at the lovely face flushed with excitement.

'Come on,' he said, getting up and dragging her behind him. 'Let's eat, and you can tell me more about it over dinner.'

In the small intimate restaurant, she filled him in with all the relevant details.

'When do you expect to take over?'

'Probably by October. Tatiana is getting married in September, but by then it should be cut and dried.'

'But she is getting someone to replace her, isn't she?' he asked pouring red wine into her wineglass. 'She can't expect you to do everything.'

'Of course she is—especially since Sophie, our vendeuse, is also leaving to be married at the end of the year.'

'Just make sure you're not taking too much on,' he warned. 'You think you're the lucky one, but I can tell you that Tatiana is on to a good thing. She will be a partner in a thriving business, where she might have just had to get rid of it if not for you. Who is she marrying?'

'Lord Daccrington.'

'Well, then, there's no way he would have allowed her to carry on so she's lucky to have found you. This way she has an interest and stands to make some money.'

'Oh, Louis, you make it sound so hard. She's not like that.'

'Dear Elizabeth, you have a lot to learn about business, believe me. It's a cut and thrust world and you will have to learn to be tough. Up to now you have had none of the responsibility—Tatiana has.'

'I think I understand the pitfalls—I'm not exactly a spoiled little girl playing at running a dress shop!' she said crossly.

He took her hand. 'I just want you to realise what you are getting into when you go it alone. I'm sure Tatiana will be there for you, and if she isn't, I shall be.'

She relaxed. 'You are not trying to frighten me off it, are you?'

He laughed. 'No, just giving you advice. You have to grow an outer skin in business.'

'Well, Louis, I haven't exactly led a charmed life—not up to these last two or three years,' she said. 'I can be quite tough when I want to be. I've had to be! But I've also been lucky, I realise, finding Isabel.'

'How can anyone as beautiful as you be tough?' he asked, putting out a gentle finger and caressing her cheek. 'I would like to carry you off to my lair and look after you for the rest of your life.'

'Sounds wonderful,' she said dreamily, until she realised that, nice as it sounded, she really wouldn't like that—not all the time, anyway. Idleness didn't suit her.

CHAPTER 21

September came, and with it Tatiana's wedding day. It was a private affair with a few family guests, but Elizabeth was there with Isabel. Tatiana looked lovely in her long blue crêpe dress, its jacket edged with silver fox. Her new husband looked down at her and held her arm tightly, delighted with the elegant figure at his side.

Afterwards they left for a honeymoon in the south of France.

'Well, Elizabeth,' Isabel said, 'it won't be long now before everything is legal, and your name goes up over the door.'

Elizabeth was thinking about Catherine, the new girl. A distant relative of Lord Daccrington, she had had very little experience of the dress trade, or indeed of anything at all, but Tatiana had felt herself obliged to take her on to please her husband.

'You'll train her, darling,' she had said to Elizabeth. 'Look how quickly you caught on. And I shall be coming in one day a week.'

But it wasn't quite the same thing, Elizabeth thought. The girl was doing it as a hobby, for something to do. She had no interest in the business as such.

Elizabeth was due to spend the following weekend in Hertfordshire where one of her important clients was also getting married. She had insisted that Elizabeth be there for the wedding in order to dress her and see to the bridesmaids. Nothing, she insisted, must go wrong. *Tatler* magazine would be there, and she wanted everything to be just right.

It was like working again for Sarah, Elizabeth thought as she arrived at the Hall, a dark, imposing brick-built mansion standing in acres of Hertfordshire countryside. Sarah...she thought about her often.

She had seen Josh once or twice, but he had been very reserved and not anxious in the least to talk about his erring wife.

As for Sarah—not a word. The weeks went by, leaving a gap in Elizabeth's life, and she would have given anything at times to know where Sarah was, and if she was all right. Abroad, she had said in her note. Well, she had been swallowed up, wherever it was, for no one seemed to have news of her.

On this lovely Saturday in late-October, Elizabeth fitted the ivory silk gown on the bride, the Hon Lavinia Pembroke. The dress had a long train, heavily embroidered with pearls, which the six bridesmaids were to carry, all of them siblings of the bride or groom. They were wearing long dresses of ruby velvet, and although they were of differing ages and colourings, the dresses suited everyone. The bride carried a round cushion of dark red roses and stephanotis while the bridesmaids carried posies of ivory-coloured rosebuds. On her hair, the bride wore the traditional bridal coronet of orange blossom and a fine veil which covered her face then dropped down the back to cover the train.

It was one of the most successful weddings Elizabeth had ever done and she was complimented afterwards by so many people. The glossy magazines were there in force to take pictures, all of which would appear later and do nothing but good for the business.

She stayed for the wedding reception which was held in a marquee on the lawn, the weather being kind, and afterwards left on the train for London.

It had been a most successful day, and one of the most satisfying. She had also been assured by the bride's mother that she would be paying a visit to Tatiana on her next trip to London.

She watched the scenery passing, the countryside at its best after a dry summer. The trees were turning, everywhere, in this part of the country they were yellow and bronze, the fields gold with mown hay. It was a lovely time of year. Elizabeth was reminded forcibly of the train journey she had taken to London from Brighton. Such a different journey—how far she had come since then! Then, it had been for little Nancy's funeral—it seemed light years away in view of what had happened in her life since then. Elizabeth Lister...even her name had been changed, and she lived in a world that she could only have dared imagine five years ago.

Louis had not come home this weekend, which had worked out very well, but she had thought about him. Wondered what it would be like had she been standing there at his side in a wedding gown as his bride, Louis standing tall beside her, and who would give her away?

Her mind raced on, and she smiled to herself. Wishful thinking. But one day—who knew? When things had settled down, perhaps it would come to pass.

Isabel wanted to know every bit of news about the wedding from start to finish. There was nothing she enjoyed hearing about more. Most of the time, in her imagination, she substituted Elizabeth for the bride, with herself almost as the mother of the bride, and although the groom up to now was faceless, she sometimes hoped that it might be Richard Barrington. After all, it was not beyond the bounds of possibility, and Elizabeth had to marry sometime.

On Monday, Elizabeth arrived at the salon to find a furore. The four women in the workroom were very irate at the behaviour of the new girl, Catherine Beaufort.

'On Saturday when Mrs Anstruther-Browne came in Catherine was rude to her—I heard her,' Ada said. 'She sits there doing her nails, doesn't even get up to see what they want. Mrs Tetbury would never stand for that.'

But Tatiana wasn't here now, Elizabeth thought, making a mental note to have a word with the girl.

She could foresee problems. Tatiana had always been on hand to greet clients. She'd bowed them in, and quite literally bowed them out. Selling an expensive gown came naturally to her. In her reserved way she was firm but honest, knowing when to pressurise and when to let well alone. The clients knew her, they respected her—and they expected to see her.

Well, Elizabeth decided, I will have to do the best I can. This new girl is not the answer, and I can't be everywhere, but I shall manage somehow.

She watched from the small changing room when the next client came in, and Catherine, an elegant willowy blonde, got up from reading her books without the glimmer of a welcome, her perpetually raised eyebrows moving a fraction of an inch higher.

'Good morning,' the client said first, Elizabeth noted.

'Good morning,' Catherine answered.

'I would like to see Mrs Tetbury.'

'She is not here,' Catherine said. 'She's left.'

Elizabeth decided this was the moment to move in.

'All right, Catherine, you may go.' She smiled a welcome.

'Good morning, madam. May I help?'

The client was already looking a little frosty.

'I had hoped to find Mrs Tetbury here.'

'She's away at the moment.'

'Oh, I see. I usually see her when I come up to town. I am Mrs Robert Frost.'

An out of town customer, to be wooed and won.

'Do take a seat, Mrs Frost. Mrs Tetbury was married recently, I don't know if you knew, and we are having to manage without her for the present. However, if I can show you anything...'

'Mrs Tetbury knows my taste in clothes. I like tailored frocks. Perhaps you could show me some materials and styles?'

'Of course.' Elizabeth gave her a warm smile. 'It's quite early—would you like coffee?'

The woman smiled back at her. 'How very kind.'

'Then you can take your time. Here are some of our newest designs, and the very latest materials lend themselves very well to these.'

By the time she left, Elizabeth had received an order for two day dresses from Mrs Frost who had departed in a much better frame of mind than when she came in. By the end of the morning, Elizabeth had supervised orders from three clients, all of whom wanted their outfits at once, they stressed, had a word with the workroom girls, and it was lunch time before she got around to Catherine.

'Sit down,' she said. 'I would just like to clear up one or two points. Perhaps Mrs Tetbury hadn't time to go into this side of things before she left? She will, by the way, be coming in once a week, on Fridays, and I am sure she will wish to know how you are getting on.'

With a sweet smile at the girl, she saw a slight trace of apprehension on her face.

'First of all, Catherine, do you like working here?'

'Oh, yes, Miss Lister.'

'Good. Well, there are rules, Catherine. One is that the client comes first—with everything. Have you heard the old saying that the customer is always right?'

The girl nodded. 'Well, that applies to all aspects of selling, from the corner shop to an exclusive salon like Tatiana.'

The girl looked at her a little sullenly.

'The first thing to remember is that the client, whoever she is, has come in presumably to buy, and it is our business to sell to her. But a satisfied customer is the only one we want. So you greet her—good morning, good afternoon—whichever applies. Offer her a chair, make her comfortable. After all, don't you expect service when you go shopping?'

'Yes, Miss Lister.'

'Then having found out what she wants, find the appropriate person to deal with her. Usually me from now on. If I am not here, one of the workroom hands—Stella is the best, she knows what it is all about. In other words, Catherine, wait on her—hand and foot if necessary. You would be surprised how much pleasure you can get out of an ordinary job if you throw yourself into it.'

The girl looked down, her lower lip protruding.

'What do you think about the job, Catherine?'

'It's a bit boring.'

'Yes, I know what you mean, it can be. But try and get involved, try to help, and if after a time you find you are not suited to it, then let me know.'

'Thank you, Miss Lister.'

'You may go.'

Either you have it there or you haven't, Elizabeth thought. The girl was only marking time until she got married, what possible interest could she have in the salon? She'd be better off in a toy shop or behind a perfume counter.

As November came in and the run up to December and Christmas, Elizabeth was as busy as she had ever been. Mercifully Tatiana returned, and it was fairly obvious that she was going to like her new life as Lady Daccrington.

'It's wonderful to have so much leisure,' she said. 'Time to do things, have one's hair done, that sort of thing.' But even on Fridays, Lord Daccrington came to pick her up for lunch, and she often didn't return.

So that's the way it's going to be, Elizabeth thought. I shall have to get used to it.

She rushed around trying to get orders completed for Christmas, hurrying round to the wholesalers for the new materials for the demand was great. There had been a surprising interest in the new synthetic fabrics which were such a success in America, lending themselves to the latest styles. The new fabrics had more body, and the wholesalers were trying to stock the creaseless materials which would make such a difference to women's lives.

The stockists had been slow to catch on though. 'No ironing?' they'd said. It was a joke. They couldn't be much good. Could you imagine a fabric which would hang well and look expensive that was creaseless? Typical of the Americans.

But the interest was there, just the same.

Elizabeth had seen Louis once or twice in the meantime but he was always either just going to France or had just got back, and since she was busy herself, their meetings were brief.

The last time he had looked tired, and her heart went out to him.

'You're working too hard,' she said as they sat over coffee in the small French restaurant.

'Well, soon be over,' he said. 'I shall be home for Christmas and then, thank God, no more back and forth to France. I shall have to go to the States sometime in January—I went last year if you remember, to the Du Pont Factory—but that's way ahead.'

That night, outside the house when he said goodnight, he held her tightly as though he wouldn't let her go. He kissed her passionately, and for a moment, she forgot where she was—they were locked in a world where nothing else mattered. For the first time in her life, she was aroused to the point where had they been alone, she would have wanted him to go on. Her blood seemed on fire, her senses aware as they had never been before, emotions to the fore as she relaxed completely in his arms.

When he let her go she felt exhausted, drained of passion. She looked up and saw his eyes almost black in the darkness, glinting with unassuaged desire.

He went to kiss her again, but she eased herself away.

'I must go in. It's late.'

He kissed her hair, and her eyes, and finally her lips, softly, sweetly.

'Goodnight, little Elizabeth.'

She turned at the top of the steps, eyes misty as she watched him walk away in the darkness.

Later, lying in bed, she thought of the kiss and the effect it had had on her. She hadn't known it could be like that. The very thought of him sent her pulses racing. Was this what Sarah had been looking for with her lovers? Was that where Josh failed her? It was as if Louis had lit a spark in her that set her alight, and she had wanted him to make love to her with no inhibitions, had wished they were somewhere alone together where she could have abandoned herself to him totally. Her body was still tingling at the memory of it...at the thought of seeing him again in the morning when she went to Vereker's for new materials. Had Louis felt as she did? He must have done. Or was it different for a man? She felt her world had been turned upside down. Was it the same for him?

She finally slept, her mind in a whirl,

and when she woke her first thought was of Louis.

I'm in love, she thought happily as she looked at herself in the mirror, seeing the bright eyes and flushed cheeks. Would Isabel realise that the young girl she had taken out of her own world and made into something else had changed again? Into someone whose heart would belong to Louis Vereker, whether Isabel liked it or not.

But Isabel's thoughts were taken up with something quite different. She hardly had time to see Elizabeth's radiant face, for she had the newspaper open and her eyes were glued to the page that held an item she found riveting.

'Good morning, Isabel,' Elizabeth said pouring herself coffee from the silver jug in front of her.

'Oh, Elizabeth, good morning.'

Isabel put down the paper and stared into space, and Elizabeth saw that her face was ashen.

'Isabel, what is it?'

Wordlessly, she passed the paper over to her.

It was the picture that caught Elizabeth's eye. A small square photograph of a familiar face—the face of Major Hetherington. Major Arthur Hetherington, alias William Hayter, alias John Buchanan, was sentenced to five years imprisonment for embezzlement: defrauding lonely spinsters out of their money. In one of the worst cases he had ever heard, according to the judge, Hetherington, a man with a good background, an army officer who had been invalided out, had become a con man of the worst kind. He preyed on lonely women and persuaded them to part with their money, often when they could ill afford it.

Elizabeth read it silently and looked across at Isabel who looked shattered. What was going through her mind? Grief? Fury? It was hard to tell.

'Isabel—'

'Don't say anything, Elizabeth, please.' And getting up, she walked from the room. Presently Elizabeth heard her door closing upstairs.

'Will you want anything else, miss?' asked Mrs Baines, coming into the room.

Elizabeth wondered if she had seen the report.

'No, thank you, Mrs Baines. Just toast.'

Poor Isabel—Elizabeth's heart ached for her. But she was best left alone until she felt like talking about it—if she ever did. Until then, Elizabeth would say nothing. It was a closed book.

She was somewhat subdued as she made her way to Vereker's, the newspaper report leaving an unpleasant taste in her mouth, but she brightened when she opened the door, and found herself in the familiar world of lovely textiles and silken fabrics, the glorious colours which lit up the deep shelves as far as the lofty ceiling.

Even Lily, with her slightly eccentric appearance, this morning looked particularly attractive with her black silky hair drawn back into a chignon, her satin-backed black dress with its royal blue revers, her light grey eyes and pale skin.

'Good morning, Elizabeth.'

'Good morning, Lily. The showroom looks most appealing this morning.'

'You must have noticed the jars of poppies—our one concession to Christmas decorations.'

On either side of the door stood two enormous Chinese vases filled with scarlet oriental poppies.

'Mr Louis' idea—he brought them back from China last year.'

'They look wonderful!'

'Yes, they do,' Lily said, contemplating them with such a serious face that Elizabeth laughed.

'It takes a lot for you to show what you're thinking, Lily, doesn't it?'

'I suppose it does. I learned long ago not to wear my heart on my sleeve.'

'You know, it occurs to me, you always

wear something blue with black—a blue collar, blue cuffs, a blue flower.'

'It's to bring out my eyes, duckie,' Lily said. 'Fancy you noticing. An ex-boss of mine told me: Always wear something blue, Lily, otherwise your eyes look too pale.'

'You have lovely eyes,' Elizabeth said. 'Unusual.'

'Yes—kinda washed out,' Lily said, and Elizabeth laughed and laid out her sketch book on the counter.

'I am looking for this new silk taffeta —Louis said you had had some delivered from Paris?'

'Yes, it's super. Red and green tartan. I'll get it for you.'

They pored over the design. A full-length ball gown with nipped in waist and full skirt, off the shoulder neckline and a wide belt.

'That's lovely,' Lily said. 'I can just see it in this silk taffeta.'

The material with the sheen of silk was darkest red and forest green.

'The dress looks Scottish—a bit Flora Macdonald,' Lily said as she handled the material. 'You see, it will stand out. The material is stiff, and I like the way you have banded the skirt with green braid.'

'I'm delighted with it, now I've seen it,' Elizabeth said. As usual she couldn't wait to get back and work on the design.

At the end of an hour, all her orders given, she prepared to leave.

'Before you go, I've something to ask you,' Lily said, closing the order book.

Elizabeth pulled on her gloves.

'Now that you've settled in at Tatiana's,' Lily said, 'would there be anything there for me?'

Open mouthed Elizabeth stared at her.

'For you? In what way, Lily?'

'Well, I think I told you before that I worked for Harrods for five years in the gown department until I got bored with it and came here. This was different, interesting. It still is but I need a change, and the work is heavy, as you know.'

Elizabeth could think of nothing better than taking on Lily Cheshire—but Louis! What on earth would his reaction be?

'Lily, much as I'd like to, Mr Louis is not going to like it, is he?'

'What's it to do with him?' Lily asked. 'What are you trying to say, that he would suggest you had poached me?'

Elizabeth was serious. 'Well, it's a thought. He would miss you terribly, Lily.'

'You bet,' she said. 'He'll be lost without me.'

'Well, then—'

'It's not the money, Elizabeth. I want a

change, and I hoped—'

'I'm not saying we couldn't do with you. And, anyway, it would depend what Tatiana said. But even so...'

'Well, if you're worrying about Mr Louis' reaction I can tell you, I am leaving anyway. Whatever you say. So it's up to you. If you wish to acquire my services...'

Her dead pan face looked at Elizabeth, who was never quite sure when Lily was joking or being serious.

'You are serious?'

'Yes, I've made up my mind. Start the new year with a new job. Another thing is, my boy friend—well, it's finished so I need a break.'

A fleeting suspicion passed through Elizabeth's mind as to whether Lily's man friend was really Andre Vereker—Louis' father—but she swiftly dismissed it. What did it matter? The difficulty was that Lily was an institution at Vereker's. For herself, Elizabeth would be delighted to have her in the salon—she was just right with all the necessary qualifications and experience. She was good with clients, and she looked right. But Louis...she had the feeling that he could be very annoyed about something like this.

'And you are serious that you are leaving anyway?'

'Yes, m'dear. No doubt about it.'

'Leave it with me, Lily. I'll think about it.'

'The offer won't last long!' Lily called after her as she left the shop.

CHAPTER 22

When the Christmas card came Elizabeth recognised the writing, even though the postmark was Paris, France. She tore it open swiftly. It was from Sarah...

Happy Christmas, Elizabeth! In case you wondered where I had got to, here I am in Paris! Hope all goes well with you—I shall be in London on 14 January—could we have lunch? I'm longing to see you again. Please write to Madame Bouvier (that's me!) care of the above address. Love, S.

Elizabeth sat back and read it again.

'Who writes to you from France?' Isabel asked pleasantly.

Elizabeth handed her the card which Isabel scanned briefly and handed back.

'Well! And what is that young lady up to now, I wonder? I should keep well away from that quarter, Elizabeth.'

Elizabeth smiled. Nothing would keep

her from getting in touch with Sarah. She was too fond of her for that.

Upstairs in her own room she wrote off to Sarah straight away, telling her that lunch that day would be fine. She so looked forward to seeing her again.

The shops were ablaze with decorations and Christmas gifts and bright lights and enticing clothes, for it was dark around three thirty to four in the afternoon, and when the lights came on, Oxford Street looked like fairyland.

Wrapped up well in her thick winter coat with the enormous lynx collar and matching fur hat, Elizabeth made her way down Bond Street on this damp Friday morning, her umbrella held tightly to combat the wind and rain. Despite the weather, there was an element of excitement in her step, since she knew Tatiana would be in today and had to tell her about Lily's proposition. Even now, she could hardly believe their luck, and wondered what Tatiana would say.

Tatiana, lovely as ever, her blonde hair like a golden halo around her face, eyelashes thickened with mascara, lipstick perfectly applied, was already sitting at her desk in the small ante-room.

'Elizabeth! You look wonderful. I love the coat.'

'Thank you,' she said, peeling off her

gloves and standing her umbrella in the corner. She whipped off her fur hat and shook her curls.

'What an awful morning—it's good to be under cover!'

'Yes. I had half a mind not to come in this morning but my conscience pricked me, and here I am.'

'I'm so glad you did, I have something to tell you.'

'Oh, not bad news, I hope!' Tatiana said.

'No, if anything, good.'

Elizabeth sat down on the other side of the desk, and changed her small shiny bootees for high-heeled shoes, stretching out an elegant leg.

'Well, carry on then,' Tatiana said.

'I went to Vereker's early this week —incidentally, remind me to show you the newest thing—and Lily—'

'Lily Cheshire?'

'Yes. She says she is leaving Vereker's and wants to know if we have a vacancy here.'

Tatiana's cornflower eyes lit up. 'Did she? Wonderful! Of course we have.'

'Oh, but wait—'

'What's the problem?'

'Well—' Elizabeth began slowly. 'I don't imagine they would be too pleased.'

'Who? The Verekers?'

'Of course. She's their right hand man, as it were.'

'Why is she leaving?'

'Said she wants a change.'

Tatiana stared straight ahead. 'The number of times I have asked that girl to come and work for me—but no, she always refused for one reason or another.'

'Did you? Perhaps that's where she got the idea.'

'Well, it hardly matters, does it? As long as she's free.'

'Well, she says she's going to leave anyway, and will give in her notice when she gets a job.'

'Hmm. I wonder if it's anything to do with the old man retiring?'

Elizabeth stared at her.

'Didn't you know?' Tatiana asked. 'Well, no, you wouldn't—she's been Andre Vereker's girlfriend for years, and now the old boy is going down to the coast.'

'I had no idea,' Elizabeth said slowly.

'Yes, she left Harrods to work in Vereker's because of Andre.'

'Does Louis know?'

'Oh, I shouldn't think so. They kept it pretty dark, only saw each other once a week. Pathetic really. She wasted her life when you think what she might have done.'

Elizabeth was thoughtful.

'Ask her to come round and see us.'

Elizabeth bit her lip.

'The thing is, I think Louis would be absolutely furious at her leaving to come to us.'

'Can't be helped.' Tatiana said, matter-of-factly.

'Yes, but...'

Tatiana looked at her. 'Oh, of course, I forgot. You two have become quite friendly, haven't you?'

Elizabeth reddened. 'Well, sort of. I've been out with him once or twice.'

'I can't see the problem,' Tatiana insisted. 'The woman is free to do as she wants, isn't she? We'd be lucky to get her. It's business, Elizabeth. It has nothing to do with personal feelings. No, I shouldn't worry. Ask Lily to come and see me. No wait, I'll give her a ring.'

She picked up the telephone immediately.

Elizabeth had the awful feeling that she had burned her boats.

Three days later it was signed and sealed. Lily had come to see them after shop hours, and the whole thing was soon settled. Lily and Tatiana got on like a house on fire, and there was no doubt in Elizabeth's mind that Lily would be an asset to the business.

'That's that, then,' said Lily cheerfully on leaving. 'I shall give in my notice at the end of the week.'

'We look forward to seeing you on January the first.' Tatiana said, beaming. 'Happy Christmas, Lily.'

'And to you both,' Lily said, pulling on her gloves.

Elizabeth kept her fingers crossed.

That evening she had a surprise call from Louis, much to Isabel's irritation, who handed the telephone to her with a frown. 'That man from the wholesalers.'

'Louis?' Her heart racing, Elizabeth took the receiver. He hadn't waited long. But to her surprise, he sounded happy and excited.

'Are you doing anything this evening?'

'No. I thought you were still in France?'

'I was, I got back this morning. Look, may I come round? It won't take long.'

'When—now?'

'Yes, in about fifteen minutes.'

'Yes, all right, I'll be ready.'

'	'Bye.'

'You're not going out in this weather?' Isabel said. 'It's gone seven, and it's raining.'

'Yes, Isabel, I don't suppose I shall be long. Obviously something has cropped up.'

When the doorbell rang she went to answer it, and saw Louis standing there, grinning, while parked outside by the kerb stood a car. He looked back at it then turned to her proudly.

'Well—what do you think? It's my newest acquisition.'

'Louis! How wonderful!' She heaved a sigh of relief. So he didn't know yet. Well, it wasn't her business to tell him.

'Coming for a spin?'

'Yes, of course, just a moment.' She went back inside and called out.

' 'Bye, Isabel. Won't be long.'

She could imagine how cross Isabel would be. She made no secret of her feelings about Louis. But that was too bad.

He opened the door for her and Elizabeth got inside, sinking down into the deep leather seats.

'What is it? What make?'

'A Citroën,' he said proudly. 'A DS19 if you're any the wiser. She does sixty-five miles an hour. But don't worry, I won't go fast.'

He drove slowly round the square, and out into the Bayswater Road.

'I didn't know you could drive, Louis,' Elizabeth said, watching his competent hands on the wheel.

'Oh, yes, the old man taught me—but on his car. I've never had one of my own. Isn't this great?' He was like a schoolboy.

Forgetting all the problems, Elizabeth

gave herself up to the sheer pleasure of sitting beside him, watching the road disappear beneath them.

'We won't go far this evening. I just wanted you to see it. It'll be useful driving down to the coast to catch the car ferry to France, and also to see Mother and Dad when they've moved.'

'When are they actually going?'

'Sometime in the New Year when I come back from the States. Oh, Elizabeth, isn't this great?'

He drove for some time, and stopped about fifteen miles out of London by a roadside pub.

'Let's go in and celebrate, shall we?'

It was cosy inside, men were playing shove ha'penny, and darts, and they went through to the private bar with its red velvet high-backed benches and low yellowed ceiling.

'This place is quite old, I should think,' Louis remarked. 'What will you have?'

Elizabeth was not used to drinking.

'Try a dry Martini with me,' he suggested.

They sat in the warm cosy glow, and as the drink warmed her, Elizabeth began to relax. After all, what was the point of worrying? Losing Lily was not the end of the world for him, was it?

Louis wanted to talk about the car more

than anything and Elizabeth sat back and listened.

He saw that she was tucked up with a blanket on the way home. 'Are you warm enough?'

She assured him she was. 'We shall be able to go for long drives in the summer,' he said.

With Louis beside her, Elizabeth felt she could bear anything.

When he stopped the car outside the house, he turned to face her, and put his arm around her.

'This is better, isn't it?' he said, and she smiled up at him and nestled into his arms.

He felt her soft warm mouth open beneath his when he kissed her. Shivers of ecstasy flowed through her as his kiss become more passionate, but much as she wanted to surrender, to give herself totally, a tiny warning insinuated itself as his hand found her breast inside the fur collar of her coat. It was almost more than she could bear and she broke away, flushed, her mind in a turmoil, so intense were her feelings.

'Louis—'

He looked at her mouth, soft and seductive where he had kissed her, and made to kiss her again. She was irresistible, unlike any other girl he had met.

He kissed her lightly on the nose. 'I got carried away,' he said. 'It's time you went in.'

She was left with a feeling of disappointment, yet knew that he was right. She had to go in. This wasn't the time, not like this.

He got out and came round to open the door for her, taking her in his arms and holding her close, seeing those wonderful eyes and those lips just aching to be kissed.

It wouldn't do to rush her—she was precious.

He kissed her lightly. 'Goodnight, Elizabeth. I'll give you a ring in the morning.'

'Goodnight, Louis. And thank you for the run—'

She closed the door behind her, and saw that the house was in darkness with just the hall light on. Switching it off, she made her way upstairs, and saw that the light was on beneath Isabel's door.

She tapped gently. 'Goodnight, Isabel.'

There was no reply. She couldn't have heard.

Elizabeth was so busy fitting and measuring clients during the morning that it was lunchtime before she realised that Louis had not telephoned. She spent the whole afternoon in the workroom, and when she heard Catherine lock the front door, realised that it must be closing time. Yawning, she put her things together and cleared away.

A quarter of an hour later she locked the door behind her, just in time to see Louis coming towards her. Her face broke into a welcome smile. It was wasted, however, for his face was as black as a thunder cloud.

He grabbed her hand.

'You and I have some talking to do!'

She frowned. 'Louis! You're hurting my arm.'

'Sorry,' he said gruffly, and walked on swiftly as she hurried after him to keep up. Once clear of traffic they crossed into the park where he made for the nearest seat and sat down.

'Louis—' Elizabeth began.

'Lily gave in her notice today.'

'Oh.'

'But you knew that, of course.'

'Yes.'

'In fact, you must have known last night—but you said nothing.'

'It wasn't for me to tell you, Louis.'

'Wasn't it? Not that she was coming to work for you? What did you offer her—a substantial increase in wages?'

She was furious. 'Louis! It had nothing to do with me.'

'Didn't it? I should have thought it did.'

'I was as shocked as you when Lily said she was leaving.'

He turned to her in disbelief.

'Oh, you mean it was all her idea?'

'Yes, Louis, I do mean that. It was. It was also Lily who asked if there might not be something for her at Tatiana's.'

His mouth twisted. 'Oh, come on, Elizabeth. I wasn't born yesterday.'

She turned on him furiously. 'Are you suggesting that I lured her away from you? That's ridiculous, Louis!'

'You know how much she means to us. She's been there seven years, knows the business backwards.'

'Louis, I know! I know! I didn't instigate this, honestly. When Lily approached me, I was shocked. But she seemed adamant.'

'And so at that point you thought—fine! Now we can get her.'

She looked straight ahead, face flaming. How dare he speak to her like that!

'There's no point in going on like this,' she said. 'I'm sorry.'

'You're sorry?' he said with a bitter laugh. 'I'm sure you are, Elizabeth Lister!'

'What is that supposed to mean?' she asked icily.

'Nothing. That's your name, isn't it? I wonder sometimes... I have the distinct feeling you would do anything to get on in this world. No quarter given. It doesn't matter to you that Vereker's are having a dicey time at the moment with staff. You decided to filch her anyway.'

'Louis, we didn't! Honestly. It wasn't like that.'

'But you didn't try to persuade her to stay on with us? You jumped right in and offered her—'

'I didn't! She assured me she was leaving anyway.'

'Why would she? Why would she want to do that?'

There was no answer to that. Perhaps he did not know about Lily and his father?

There was a long silence between them.

'I think we're wasting our time sitting here arguing,' Elizabeth said at length, now thoroughly on her mettle. She could understand his shock and had felt for him, but was devastated at his reaction. That he should attack her in such a way—there was no feeling there for her, no understanding. She had obviously been wrong about him. Her first reaction had been one of sympathy. Now she was not so sure. Perhaps Lily had good reason for leaving the Verekers after all...

Wearily, she got up. 'I'm sorry to leave you like this, but obviously you're not

374

going to believe me,' she said, and began to walk away.

He made no answer, just sat staring in front of him, while she was on the verge of tears. By the time she reached the house, however, she had made a resolution. The whole thing was a closed book. She had no desire to talk or think about it ever again. Mr Louis Vereker could go and jump in the lake!

Seeing her arrive, flushed and tired, Isabel was all sympathy.

'Oh, you've had an exhausting day,' she said. 'I'm sure you must miss Tatiana, but I suppose it would have been like this too if you'd started on your own. Do you think you have taken on too much, dear?'

'Me? Absolutely not,' Elizabeth said.

It would take more than this to get her down.

The pressure of work died down the week before Christmas, and there was no word from Louis. She had an order to complete in a hurry and sent Catherine round to collect it.

If Isabel had any idea that Louis was keeping out of the way, she said nothing. Elizabeth was a little quiet, she saw, but did not comment. Perhaps, she thought, the two were connected, and the least said soonest mended.

On Christmas Eve, the florist delivered

a huge spray of pale yellow orchids from Richard Barrington. The card accompanying it read: 'Happy Christmas, Elizabeth, from Richard.'

Isabel was delighted. 'Oh, how lovely—so exotic.'

Elizabeth was pleased. It gave her a nice warm feeling after the unpleasant business with Louis. She still couldn't believe that he had been so unforgiving. Like Isabel with the Major, she had been wrong.

On Christmas Day they lunched at the Hyde Park Hotel where the festivities were in full swing and the lunch was excellent. They drank wine and pulled crackers in the beautiful dining room which looked so Christmassy with its huge tree decorated with presents.

During the festivities, Isabel leaned towards Elizabeth.

'Lord Devenoke is dining today, in the corner with a party of six.'

Elizabeth could hardly look round. Poor Josh, she thought.

When he left he saw them and came over to shake hands and wish them the season's greetings.

'You must come and have a New Year drink with us.'

'Thank you,' said Isabel. 'What a nice man,' she commented, when he left. 'Those lovely brown eyes—like a spaniel we used to have. Oh, dear, life can be very sad sometimes.'

Elizabeth made up her mind on the spur of the moment. 'I shall take you to see a show in the New Year. Now don't argue—it will be my treat. We shall choose one when we get home.'

Isabel was delighted. It did rather seem to her that there had been no mention of that Louis man for quite a time. Long may it last, she thought.

The New Year dawned cold and wet, with unrest in Europe as a man called Hitler began casting acquisitive eyes on Austria. Isabel was horrified. She had a special affection for Austria.

'What are we doing that we allow him to get away with it?' she asked.

Politics had always been able to move her—perhaps because she had been through a war, Elizabeth thought. She felt passionately about peace, and was very knowledgeable about events in Europe.

Elizabeth was more concerned with events at the salon where Lily had started at the beginning of January. She had settled in as though she had always been a part of Tatiana.

'Love it,' she said to Elizabeth at the end of that first week. 'You can't imagine what a change it makes after Vereker's. You

377

didn't have any trouble with Mr Louis, did you?'

'Well, he wasn't best pleased.'

'Anyway, he went to the States,' Lily told her.

'Now where is that toile for Lady Ledsham?' Elizabeth asked, and the moment passed.

The subject was brought up again, however, when Friday came round and Tatiana arrived.

'Oh, here you are, Lily!' she cried. 'How is it going?'

'Very well.' And Lily smiled.

'You didn't have any nasty moments with the Verekers?' Tatiana asked.

'No. I don't know if Elizabeth did...'

'Well, welcome. Glad to see you here,' Tatiana said, and decided to say no more about it.

On her next visit to Vereker's, Elizabeth found a young man in Lily's place. He told her he had served his apprenticeship in a wholesale house before moving to Harvey Nichols where he had been for the past four years. He was pleasant and helpful, but the place felt strange without Lily. Elizabeth had a moment's compunction before deciding her sympathy was wasted.

She was looking forward to lunch with Sarah, and received a telephone call from her the day before.

'Where are you staying?'

'In a small hotel in Kensington, but I'll see you tomorrow for lunch. Could it be somewhere round here? There's a nice little restaurant nearby.'

'Of course, I'll take a taxi.'

Elizabeth was surprised by how much she was looking forward to it.

Sarah was waiting for her inside the small restaurant, and at first sight Elizabeth was shocked at her appearance. She was pale and heavy-eyed and had lost weight, although she was beautifully dressed in the latest Paris fashion.

'Sarah!' Elizabeth bent and kissed her and took a seat opposite her. Unexpectedly, Sarah's eyes filled with tears.

'Oh, you can't know how glad I am to see you! You look wonderful—even prettier than I remembered—and that outfit!'

Elizabeth wished she could say the same thing.

'I was so pleased to receive your card. You had us worried, Sarah. We wondered what on earth had happened to you.'

'Who's we?' Sarah asked. 'Not Isabel. I expect she always thought I'd do a bunk. And I don't suppose you've seen much of Josh, or have you?'

Elizabeth shook her head. 'No...but tell me what you've been doing. Did you go to Paris straight away?'

'Yes, I went with Archie—his revue opened in Paris—and, well, I just had to go with him.'

'Archie Toogood! Oh, Sarah!'

'I know, I know, but there it is. You know how dotty I've always been about him.'

She looked up as the waitress came for their orders.

'Oh, just salad for me, please. And Elizabeth?'

'The same.'

'And we'll have some wine,' Sarah said.

Elizabeth saw the dark circles under her eyes and remembered how she had looked before. Please God she wasn't pregnant...

Sarah had always been able to read her thoughts. 'No, I'm not pregnant, if that's what's worrying you,' she said with an attempt at a grin.

'I can't help feeling glad about that,' Elizabeth said, buttering her roll. 'Anyway, are you over here for something special?'

'Mmm, in a way. But tell me how you are, what you've been up to. Did you get your salon after all?'

'No, but I've gone into partnership with Tatiana. She got married, you know.'

'Yes, I read it in *The Times*. You have to hand it to her, she's angled for him for a long time.'

'Really? Well, in that case she pulled it

off,' Elizabeth said. She didn't know the truth of it, and didn't care much. She was glad that Tatiana was happy, and certainly his lordship seemed so whenever he came to the salon. But there had never been any love lost between Sarah and Elizabeth's partner, she remembered.

'You're a glutton for punishment. When are you going to get married? Have you seen any more of Richard Barrington—he was quite gone on you, you know.'

'He sent me flowers at Christmas.'

'Oh, that's nice. What about the fellow from the salon, what's his name—Louis?'

Elizabeth blushed scarlet.

'Oh, I've put my foot in it, have I?' laughed Sarah. 'Do tell.'

'There's nothing to tell,' Elizabeth said shortly, and saw Sarah, after idly eating a little salad, push her plate away.

'You're not hungry?'

'No. Oh, Elizabeth, I'm so unhappy!'

'Now where have I heard that before?'

'No, really, I mean it. You can't imagine—he's such a swine.'

'Who? Archie Toogood? I thought you loved him.'

'I did, but you can't imagine what I've been through... I thought it was all going to be wonderful.'

'Oh, Sarah, I think sometimes you live in a dream world, you're such a romantic—beside being a horror in lots of ways.'

'Thank you,' Sarah said, taking out a gold cigarette case and lighting a cigarette. 'Do you mind?'

Elizabeth shook her head. 'You have so much, yet you are never satisfied.'

'That's true.' She obviously still felt very sorry for herself.

'He's been such a pig with other women.'

'Oh, spare me the details,' Elizabeth wailed. 'Didn't you know that? You always said all the girls were after him.'

'Yes, but I didn't know he was chasing them too. I thought he loved me.' She looked up. 'Anyway, what do you know about it? You've never been in love, so you don't understand.'

Elizabeth kept her thoughts to herself.

'No, you're right,' she said. 'You've obviously had a rotten time.'

'The revue has moved on to Nice,' Sarah said, 'and I thought it was a good time to get out. I'm over it now, Elizabeth. I never want to see him again.'

'So what will you do?'

Sarah inhaled deeply on her cigarette and blew out smoke before answering.

'I want to go back to Josh.'

Elizabeth sat back in her chair. 'Sarah!'

'Why—don't you think he'd have me?'

she asked. Her blue eyes held a mischievous glint.

'Now how would I know? I've only seen him once since you left, and then only for a moment.'

'I wonder how the poor lamb is?' Sarah ruminated.

'You treated him very badly.'

'Yes, I did.' And she stubbed out her cigarette in the ashtray as the waitress brought the coffee.

'What I wondered was, would you put in a good word for me? Tell him you've seen me and—'

Elizabeth's green eyes were blazing. 'Do your own dirty work, Sarah!' she said. 'I don't run after you now!' She felt she had returned to her origins slightly, it was just what she might have said to someone at the orphanage, but she meant it.

'Very well,' Sarah said coolly. 'I will. I thought you were a friend of mine.'

Elizabeth simmered down. 'The trouble with you is, you miss being Lady Devenoke.'

'I *am* Lady Devenoke,' Sarah said loftily, and suddenly they looked at each other and burst out laughing.

'You are incredible!' Elizabeth said.

Sarah actually looked ashamed.

'I do miss it, Elizabeth. There's something rather nice about the high life. I missed it. And I did miss Josh—no, don't laugh, I did. I missed him in an odd sort of way.'

'I'm sure you did,' Elizabeth said lightly, but she had an idea Sarah meant it. She began to pull on her gloves. 'Well, I must fly, I've a lot to do.'

'Thanks for coming. Not a word to anyone.'

'As if I would!'

'I'll be in touch,' Sarah promised.

Outside the restaurant, Elizabeth took a deep breath of fresh air. Sarah's effrontery never ceased to amaze her, but she couldn't help hoping that something might be worked out with Josh.

A few days later, she had a telephone call from Richard Barrington.

CHAPTER 23

When his army transport plane touched down at Northolt, it had been Richard Barrington's first thought to ring Elizabeth. Involved in top level talks with certain high-ranking officials in Austria, he had been through a gruelling time, but in his off duty moments his thoughts had all been of a green-eyed girl in London whom he couldn't get out of his mind. A slip of a thing but beautiful, intelligent, and, he suspected, strong-minded—Elizabeth was all he could wish for. And she was not engaged, as he understood it, not seriously going with any other man. Just dedicated to her dress salon, which was admirable but not important.

The army car drove him to Whitehall to report his findings, which took several hours. Then he was free to go back to barracks.

London was cold, though not as cold as where he had been. In his heart he feared there was trouble ahead, but for the moment had learned all he could, thanks to some excellent work done by British agents. Richard was satisfied he had done everything possible to pave the way for further talks.

That Sunday morning, Isabel Lister greeted him warmly, glad he was back. 'Do come in, Richard. Elizabeth will be down in a moment.'

He followed her into the drawing room and sat down.

'Are you keeping well, Miss Lister?'

Isabel could not have been more impressed. She had, unknown to Elizabeth, looked the family up in *Who's Who,* and had liked what she saw. That he was impressed with Elizabeth enough to want to see her again and take her to lunch pleased her more than somewhat. It justified what she had done. The girl deserved a good marriage—with her Lister background. Yes, all in all Isabel was pleased.

'Ah, there you are,' she said as Elizabeth came in, dressed in a pale tweed suit with a long jacket, a small velours hat with a side feather, a silver fox fur slung over her shoulder.

Richard got up to greet her, the admiration showing in his eyes as he took her hand.

'Hallo, Richard.'

'Elizabeth.'

They looked into each other's eyes.

'Well, then,' said Richard, somewhat overcome for once in his life. 'The car is waiting outside. Nice to see you again, Miss Lister.'

Elizabeth swiftly kissed Isabel. 'See you later.'

'Enjoy yourselves.' Isabel looked fondly after them. Such a nice-looking couple. She went to the window to see Elizabeth get into the black car and Richard close the door, then they were away.

'I thought we'd drive down to the river at Marlow and have lunch at the Compleat Angler,' Richard said. 'Do you know it?'

'No, I've never been.'

'Ah, well, I think you'll like it. The

wrong time of year, of course, but no matter.'

He drove expertly, as she imagined he would do everything, out of the city towards the country. Now and again he glanced at her with a smile, but otherwise he was silent. He was obviously a driver who liked to be quiet. Elizabeth spent the time looking out at the varied scenery as the suburbs gave way to the country. Even the air seemed different as they approached the outskirts of Marlow, and the scenery was beautiful. There had been an early frost which had now practically gone, and the bare trees against the sky were an artist's dream.

The hotel was beside the river which sparkled in the sun. The seats outside were empty now but inside it was warm and cosy, with a great log fire and a welcome from mine host.

After a pre-lunch drink in front of the fire, Richard took Elizabeth's arm.

'I expect you're hungry,' he said. 'Shall we go in?'

They were shown to a small table by the window where there was a view of the Thames in all its glory, tranquil and slow-moving, two or three swans gracefully gliding by.

'It's beautiful, Richard.'

'I thought you would like it.'

After scanning the menu, he looked up at her.

'Shall I suggest or is there anything special you would like? They seem to have everything.'

'You choose,' she said, glad not to have to wade through what looked like an extensive menu.

He chose soup, followed by a fish soufflé, and roast lamb.

'Now,' he said, handing the menu back to the waiter, 'tell me what you have been doing while I have been away? Have you been busy?'

'I can't remember now if you knew but I didn't get the shop I was after, so I have gone into partnership with Tatiana instead.'

'Oh, yes, I know her—at least my family does. Just married, hasn't she?'

'Yes.'

'So that means no more business for her, eh?'

'No, not quite. She's coming in once a week.'

'Really? Oh, well.'

'And what about you, Richard? I understand you went abroad.'

'Yes, several places. I was away for about three weeks.'

'By the way, thank you for the flowers —they were lovely.'

'My pleasure.'

'As a matter of fact, they're still fresh.'

'Oh, good.'

Whatever he had been doing must be fairly secret, and she decided not to pry.

'Any news from Sarah?' he asked.

The question was so sudden she was slightly nonplussed but decided to hedge.

'I had a Christmas card from her.'

He looked interested. 'Oh—where from?'

There was no point in not telling him.

'France.'

He looked across at her, the lashes sweeping her pale silky cheeks, the beautifully shaped eyebrows, that lovely mouth —and decided that he would like to kiss her. She looked up and, catching his eyes on her, smiled.

Her smile, he thought, was ravishing. He took a deep breath.

'Actually, one of the reasons I wanted to see you was to ask you if you would come up to Brampton Priory, my home in Northamptonshire, for a weekend at the end of the month?'

Elizabeth was a little surprised that the invitation had come so soon.

'It's my younger brother's twenty-first, and my mother always likes to give a party. Well, she's a great party thrower for any excuse, and we're having a weekend do the last week of the month. Do you think you would be free?'

Elizabeth knew she would. Unless Louis ...but she put him to the back of her mind, as she often did nowadays.

'Yes, I'm sure I am, unless anything unexpected crops up.'

'Wonderful,' he said. 'Josh is coming. He knows my family well, as I think I've told you. Poor old Josh. You haven't seen him, I suppose?'

'Briefly.' Elizabeth dabbed at her mouth with her napkin. 'Isabel and I dined out on Christmas Day and he was there with a party.'

'Rotten luck,' he said. 'Still, there you are. Tell me some more about you. What do you like to do? Ride? Play tennis?'

'No, I don't ride, and I don't play tennis,' she said. 'I suppose I've never really had the time.'

'Oh, we must remedy that. I'll soon teach you.'

Lunch passed pleasantly enough, and afterwards they took a stroll along the river path where they saw the afternoon sun disappearing in a cold red sky.

'Come on,' said Richard, taking her arm. 'We must get back. I don't like to think of you catching cold.'

'Oh, I won't.' She laughed. 'I don't catch cold easily.'

I can believe it, he thought. Although

she's so beautiful, she's not fragile. He didn't like delicate, fragile girls—preferred them to have a bit of spunk. And Elizabeth, he thought, had just that. Had to have if she ran her own business. He frowned. Mmm...he might have a bit of a problem there.

They arrived back in London around five, and he deposited her at Hyde Park Square, refusing to come in when she asked him.

'No, thanks all the same, but I must be off—I've some writing up to do.'

'Thank you for the lunch, Richard. It was lovely.'

'Glad you enjoyed it,' he said, and leaned forward to kiss her lightly on the cheek. 'I'll give you a ring about the weekend,' he said. 'Pick you up on the Friday evening.'

Elizabeth closed the door after him, and stood for a moment before taking off her fur and hat and gloves, regarding herself in the huge mirror with its girondelles, the twin lamps alight on this dark afternoon.

He is so nice, she thought. Good company. But he isn't Louis... Oh, Louis, how could you? And wondered what he was doing now. Perhaps she should get in touch with him again? After all, she had been in the wrong... Oh had she? When he came back she would telephone him.

She missed him so much.

'Elizabeth, is that you?'

'Yes, Isabel, just coming.'

'Come in, my dear, and tell me all about it.'

Isabel was delighted to hear of Elizabeth's day. 'It's years since I have been to Marlow-on-Thames—such a pretty town.'

'Richard has asked me up to his home, Brampton Priory in Northamptonshire, for the last weekend this month.'

Isabel was wide-eyed. 'My dear!'

'Apparently it's his younger brother's twenty-first birthday and his mother is giving a house party.'

'Oh, that's wonderful!'

Elizabeth could see she was way ahead, with a proposal thrown in for good measure.

'We're just good friends, Isabel.'

Isabel threw her a conspiratorial look. 'Yes, dear,' she said meekly.

Elizabeth immersed herself in work in the salon, and on one of her visits to Vereker's learned that Louis was still in the States. Sometimes she tried to visualise what she would do if he suddenly appeared from the stock room and confronted her. How would he greet her? What would they say to each other? Would he look at her accusingly—or take her in his arms?

392

The idea was delightful to contemplate...

The weekend of Richard's house party soon came round and Elizabeth packed her case in preparation for her stay.

When Richard called for Elizabeth, there was no missing Isabel's pleasure as she watched them go down the steps together.

'Have a lovely weekend,' she cried, and closed the door behind them. She was going to concentrate this weekend on a plan she had in mind, of doing something with her life. Perhaps voluntary work, helping someone. Goodness knows there were enough people in the world who needed help. There were many voluntary organisations, and she would apply herself quietly to thinking about it.

She was browsing through leaflets she had obtained from the Red Cross and St Dunstan's which looked interesting. Working for peace organisations appealed to her. The telephone rang.

She got up to answer it.

'Miss Lister.'

'Good evening, this is Louis Vereker.' And her heart froze.

'Yes?'

'Is Elizabeth there? Could I have a word with her?'

What a cheek! she thought. How dare he? 'I'm sorry, she's gone away for the weekend.'

'Oh.'

She could hear the disappointment in his voice.

'Yes, with a friend. He called for her about an hour ago.'

'I see.' Louis' voice had gone cold.

'I rather think it's going to be a special weekend. Certainly it is a celebration of some sort.'

'I see. Thank you.'

'May I give her a message?'

'No, thank you, Miss Lister,' he said. 'Goodbye.' And hung up the receiver.

That should settle that, thought Isabel. Well, she was justified in doing what she had. It was for Elizabeth's own good. One had to do what one had to do sometimes, for the sake of the young.

White-faced, Louis stood still. So that was it. Probably an engagement party. She had gone away for the weekend with a man—another man. She didn't waste much time! So much for his agonising about how rude he had been to her, not trusting her, losing his temper. What had she cared?

He slung on his overcoat and went out into the cold London air, walking without realising where he was heading. Elizabeth...but it was over. So much for the plans he had made, he and Elizabeth together, plans for the future where she would have been as much help to him as he was to her. Their name in lights in London and Paris—and who knew? maybe New York...

He was almost at the end of Bond Street when he saw his cousin Sophie coming towards him.

'Hi, Sophie, where are you off to?' he asked her, turning where he stood and looking down at her. She was the prettiest of all his girl cousins, with her dark Italianate looks.

'Just coming to see you—or at least your parents,' she said.

He could hardly know that she had been in love with him ever since she could remember and took every opportunity to visit her uncle and aunt in order that she might see him.

He put his arm in hers.

He liked Sophie. She was a constant visitor to the house and his mother was always pleased to see her.

'Come on, I'll walk with you.'

'Weren't you going somewhere, Louis?'

'Me? No, nowhere special.'

Sophie tripped by his side in seventh heaven. She couldn't believe her luck.

Best forget Elizabeth, he told himself. She had made a fool of him once too often.

CHAPTER 24

Once out of London traffic, Richard took the road north.

'I thought we'd stop en route for a meal,' he said. 'That way, we shall have some time to ourselves. Once we get home all hell will be let loose—when mother puts on anything like this, she really goes to town.'

Elizabeth laughed.

'By the way, I have some news for you...I was going to save it until we arrived, but I can't keep it back. Josh is bringing Sarah.'

'Richard! How? When?'

'Don't ask me—I only know that they're back together and Josh is over the moon. Aren't you pleased for them?'

'Delighted,' said Elizabeth, and found that she was. What a sly minx Sarah was, she could get away with murder, but if there was anything certain in this world, it was that Josh would be happy about it. She only hoped Sarah would be—and stay that way.

It was late when they arrived, almost dark, and as they turned a corner in a long lane, and the tall chimneys of Brampton Priory came into view, Elizabeth gave an involuntary gasp. The Elizabethan chimneys silhouetted against the evening sky made an unforgettable sight. The roofs of different heights, the low façade of the house, the way it sat into the countryside, appealed to her sense of beauty.

'I know.' Richard smiled. 'I know just how you feel. It always does that to me no matter how many times I come across it. Approaching from the other side is just as nice, too.'

There were lights on everywhere, cars were parked along the drive and up near the house. It was obviously going to be a large house party. Elizabeth could see Josh's Bentley along with several others, and was glad she had brought her very best and most fashionable clothes.

The house itself was magnificent, its age apparent at every turn, from the stone-flagged floor in the hall to the linenfold panelling, the wide staircase which curved up to the first floor and beyond, the impressive portraits that lined the walls. A great fire in a huge brick fireplace welcomed them.

General Sir Arthur Barrington and his wife were in the hall when they arrived, and Richard went straight over to his mother who greeted him warmly.

'Elizabeth—my mother—Elizabeth Lister.'

She was aware of being looked over by this tall and gracious woman who betrayed nothing in her expression—either approval or disapproval.

'How do you do, Elizabeth? So pleased you could come.' But there were more arrivals to be introduced and Richard took her arm and moved over to his brothers.

She was introduced to Timothy and Marcus, and was really glad she had come. She wouldn't have missed it for worlds. This house was far grander than anything she had seen on her travels with Sarah. Wouldn't Isabel have loved it? she thought with a smile.

Upstairs she was shown to her room on the first floor, a spacious room with a half tester bed and a massive wardrobe and flounced dressing table. An adjoining bathroom, somewhat old fashioned, with a huge bath and long windows from which, presumably, when bathing in daylight you could admire the view.

'Will you be comfortable here?' Richard asked. 'Gladys will look after you.'

'I'm sure I will—it looks lovely.'

'Would you like a nightcap?'

'No, thank you, Richard.'

'Then I'll see you at breakfast. Anytime you like from eight onwards. Unless of course you'd rather have breakfast in bed?'

'No, thank you.' Elizabeth smiled. 'I'll see you in the morning then. Goodnight, Richard.'

'Goodnight, Elizabeth.' And she closed the door after him.

The bed had been turned down, and looked most inviting. The curtains were drawn and the room was so cosy that there was nothing she wanted to do more than to slip in between those snow white sheets...

She woke early at seven and, getting up, went over to the window where the view was of park land with a lake in the distance. She stood looking out for a long time before running her bath and stepping into the delicious water, noticeably soft after the hard water of London.

Richard had suggested that they might like to attend a local point to point since everyone was free to spend the day how they wished, golfing, shooting, whatever. Emerging from the bath, Elizabeth changed into a tweed suit and cashmere sweater.

When she arrived downstairs for breakfast Richard was there to greet her and the dining room was half full. Most certainly, she thought, Sarah wouldn't be down yet. The dishes on the sideboard were inviting. She and Richard sat together, on the other side the birthday boy, Timothy.

He studied her with obvious admiration, until Elizabeth spoke to him.

'So you are at university?' she said. 'Which one, and what are you reading?'

'Oxford,' he said. 'Reading economics and political history.'

'Oh, well done,' she murmured. 'I envy you. I wish I'd gone to university.'

'Do you? Most people say that.'

'Do they?'

'I suppose it's because they get a certain idea about it, what it's like, and imagine they must be missing something terribly important in their lives.'

'And aren't they?'

'Not necessarily,' he said seriously. 'I think it's very important for some people. For others it might well be a mistake. Time wasted.'

'Oh, surely not?'

'And what do you do?'

She told him, stressing the designing part. It didn't sound half as well to say you kept a shop.

He was very impressed. 'Where did you meet old Richard?'

'I met old Richard at Josh and Sarah Devenoke's.' And she smiled.

Timothy's face broke into a grin. 'Dear old Josh! He's a great favourite of the family—my mother adores him. He always used to spend the hols with us when he and Richard were at school. They're great pals.'

'Yes, so Richard said.'

Richard took her arm. 'When you've finished chatting up my guest,' he said to Timothy.

'Sorry!'

They were served with more coffee, Richard having had an enormous cooked breakfast while Elizabeth could only manage cornflakes and toast.

'I say, you're not slimming, are you?' Richard asked anxiously.

She laughed. 'No, I'm simply not a breakfast person. Sometimes I just need coffee.'

He looked quite puzzled. 'Well, as long as you're sure.'

After breakfast, he led the way to the car, and they set off for the point to point.

'I expect Josh will come later. I don't know about Sarah. She may not join us—she's not all that keen on horses.'

He swung out of the drive and into the countryside.

'So you've never been on a horse, Elizabeth?'

'No, I am afraid I am a townie by nature.'

'But you do love the country?'

'Of course I do,' she said, realising that it had been a leading question. 'My home was in Brighton.'

'Ah, then you'll know the Downs—a

lovely part of the world,' he said pleasantly.

It wouldn't do to tell him the only part of the Downs she knew was where Sarah's school was situated and where she herself had worked as a stillroom maid.

Presently he pulled into a field where there were horses and riders, a couple of marquees, and crowds of spectators.

Elizabeth looked around her curiously. So this was a point to point race meeting.

The wind was blowing fairly strongly and she put on a headscarf, tying it under her chin, pleased that she had the sort of face that could wear one. Her boots sank into the soggy grass, and she thanked her lucky stars she had had the sense to bring them.

She enjoyed herself watching the riders and the punters. It was a fairly brisk day, chilly, but there were lots of people there—not the sort to be intimidated by a spot of bad weather, she realised.

From time to time Richard sauntered off to put on a bet, and on one race asked her what she fancied. Reading down the list she picked a horse called Lady Luck.

'How much do you want on it?' Richard asked. 'A pound each way?'

She nodded and gave him the money, and after the race, when the horse won, he handed her thirty two pounds.

'You are my lucky talisman,' he said. 'I

backed an outsider for a place and picked up fifty-six pounds. We must come here more often.'

Elizabeth pondered. She hoped she hadn't done the wrong thing by coming on this weekend. If a permanent relationship was what was in Richard's mind, then perhaps she had not been fair. She hoped she hadn't misled him. Perhaps he often took girls home? Maybe his parents were used to it?

'Well,' he said, when the morning came to an end, 'let's go and have a spot of lunch, shall we?'

'That would be nice.'

'There's an awfully good little pub in the village—we can grab a sandwich and a glass there.'

Over the trestle table in the corner they sat and munched sandwiches. Elizabeth felt very free and easy with him. Once or twice he gave her a lingering sort of glance, but there was always a glint of humour in his eyes.

'I thought this afternoon I'd show you round the estate,' he said, without any show of affectation. 'It's quite large and I'm sure you would find it interesting.'

'I'd like that.'

'Would you like another sandwich?'

She shook her head.

'I know Mother has a wonderful supper

planned for this evening.'

Back at the house, he left her to go up to her room to freshen up.

She washed her face and combed her hair. Looking in the mirror, she saw bright eyes and rosy cheeks from all that fresh air. There was no doubt that country air was good for you. That was what had been nice about Brighton—the air was wonderful. She missed it, living in town, but that was all she missed.

She sat reading for a while, looking up every now and again towards the garden. What a view! Imagine waking up every day to see this. And she knew that if that was what she wanted, she could probably have it...

It was quiet when she went downstairs and met Richard who was waiting for her. 'Everyone seems to be resting,' he said. 'Come on.'

They began by walking round to the back of the house where the vista was so beautiful. The lawns sloped down to the lake, and there was an Italian garden with rosebeds, pergolas covered with wistaria, and further on, the herbaceous borders.

'My mother's pride and joy,' he said.

'It must take so many gardeners to keep it looking like this,' Elizabeth said.

'Three,' he said. 'There used to be six in my grand-parents' day—but of course it has changed now.'

It certainly was beautiful, as far as the eye could see.

'This was my mother's home,' Richard explained. 'She was brought up here as a girl, and she and my father came straight here after they married.' And Elizabeth remembered that Sarah had told her that Lady Barrington was the daughter of an earl.

Imagine, she thought, running round these gardens when you were small, knowing that they were all yours. It was difficult to imagine.

They walked then across the gardens and out to the stables where he showed her Hercules, his own horse, before going on to the fields and meadows, coming back past a row of cottages which belonged to the estate then through the orchards. The estate was vast.

When they returned to the gardens, Richard stopped by a seat under the gnarled old wistaria.

'This is a sight when it's in bloom. It's early yet—it should be out in May.'

So he must like gardening too, thought Elizabeth.

He took her hand in his, and looked straight into her eyes, serious for once.

'Elizabeth, I know we haven't known each other very long, but I think you know how I feel about you.'

'Richard—'

'I am not asking you to commit yourself now but do you think you could consider—well, think about—us—for the future?'

It wasn't going to be easy to tell him.

'Richard, it's such early days... As you say, we've known each other such a little while, and meeting you has come at a time when I am so involved in the salon, building it up.' She saw an impatient look come into his eyes.

He frowned. 'Elizabeth, you don't understand. What's the salon got to do with it? You won't need a salon if and when we get married.'

'But I love it,' she said. 'I don't want to give it up.'

'Not even when you marry?'

Her lips set stubbornly.

'No, not even when I marry. Why should I? Really, Richard, I mean that. What harm is there in a married woman having a business?'

He looked at her in disbelief.

'Aren't you overlooking what a husband might feel about that? No man likes to feel his wife has to work—he wants to look after her, keep her.'

'Oh, Richard, it's not a case of having to work,' she explained reasonably. 'It's

406

something I want to do. I *am* doing.'

She looked so delightful when she was angry that he laughed suddenly.

'Oh, Elizabeth darling, what are we quarrelling about? A silly little shop—it doesn't enter into it...' He took her hand. 'Do you like me?'

'Very much,' she answered quietly. Although a little less now than I did before, she thought.

'Could you learn to love me?' he asked. 'Please, Elizabeth.' And leaned forward as though to kiss her.

But she turned her face. 'Richard, please, it's all a little too soon. I feel I hardly know you at all, and you certainly don't know me.'

'I know that I love you. There, I've said it.' And she wanted to say there and then, 'It's no good, Richard, I am in love with someone else.' But she refrained. He might ask then why on earth she had come away with him for the weekend, and she had no answer to that.

'Dear Richard,' she said. 'I think it's far too soon for you to know that either. I expect you'll have lots of girlfriends before you marry.'

'I don't want lots of girlfriends—I want you,' he said. 'I'm twenty-seven, Elizabeth. How old are you?'

'Twenty-one,' she said. 'A good deal

younger. You need someone older, more sensible. I'm just finding my feet.'

He relented at that. 'Bless you. And when you have found them, I hope they come to rest beside mine!' And they both laughed at his poetic turn of phrase.

'Come on,' he said. 'Let's go and get some tea.'

In the drawing room they found several couples. Among them Elizabeth could see Josh, and at his side Sarah. Perhaps she sensed her arrival for she turned, her bright blue eyes smiling.

'There you are!' she said. 'I've been looking all over for you.' As the men got into earnest conversation she pulled Elizabeth down beside her. 'Well, didn't I tell you?'

Elizabeth couldn't help laughing. Already Sarah looked happy and mischievous, and there was no doubting Josh's joy. He was talking animatedly to Richard.

'I'll talk to you later,' Sarah whispered.

'Well—where have you been?' she asked loudly.

'To a point to point, and then Richard took me over the estate.'

'O-oh,' Sarah said meaningly. 'I see.'

'No, you don't,' Elizabeth whispered. 'You've got it all wrong.'

'I have? I thought you liked him?'

'I do.'

'Then—'

'Sarah, I'm not looking to tie myself down at this point in time. I like to think there's a future for me designing, making a success of myself.'

'But what about a man?' Sarah whispered.

'Don't be so impatient,' Elizabeth said softly.

'You've got your priorities wrong.' There was no way Sarah would ever understand Elizabeth.

Later that day, Gladys, the chambermaid, came into Elizabeth's room.

'Which dress would you like me to put out for you, miss?'

'The green velvet,' Elizabeth decided. She always felt at her best in green.

'Shall I run your bath, miss?'

'Yes, please.'

What fun it was to be in the mistress's position!

Elizabeth lay luxuriating in her bath, taking her time, something she had little chance for nowadays, and reflecting on her conversation with Richard and what Isabel would make of it all. Perhaps she shouldn't blame Isabel for wanting the best for her. After all, if it were not for Isabel...

Presently, she stood in front of the cheval mirror, pleased with her reflection. The floor-length gown of soft dark green velvet was cut on the bias and hugged her figure. She pinned a curled egret feather to a tiny pillbox hat, which was the very latest thing from Paris, and attached it to her hair, while round her neck she wore a rope of creamy pearls. Her shoes were satin dyed green, her stockings of cream silk.

'Oh, miss!' Gladys cried, coming in at that moment from the bathroom. 'You look lovely!'

'Thank you, Gladys,' Elizabeth said, knowing from a maid this was a compliment indeed.

She dabbed powder on her nose, sprayed perfume on her wrists and behind her ears, then picked up the tiny jewelled box which was an apology for a handbag, and sailed out on to the great landing. At the top of the staircase Richard stood waiting for her.

He came towards her... 'Elizabeth! You look simply wonderful.' And offering her his arm, he led the way down the stairs to the drawing room where drinks were being dispensed.

His parents were waiting at the door to greet them.

Lady Barrington took Elizabeth's hand. 'My dear, so pleased you could come—what a lovely gown.' While the General, a large handsome man, stood looking at her in open admiration.

How formal, was Elizabeth's first thought.

Almost like a royal gathering. She hadn't expected it to be like this. Farther on there were lots of people she didn't know who greeted Richard warmly, and each time he introduced her with pride. She was relieved when in the corner she caught sight of Sarah and Josh, talking to another couple.

Sarah gasped with delight when she saw Elizabeth, took her hands and looked down at her dress.

'My dear, fabulous,' she whispered.

But Elizabeth's eyes were on the magnificent sapphire and diamond necklace which adorned Sarah's throat. She hadn't seen it before, and one look at Sarah's triumphant face told her everything.

'What do you think?'

'It's beautiful,' Elizabeth said. 'And you don't deserve it.'

Richard took her arm. 'This way.' And finding seats for them, sat down to enjoy the evening.

Elizabeth sat looking around her with interest. So many people, some of whom she knew from pictures in the press and magazines. She had not realised Richard came from such an exalted family. The gowns she was able to place easily. Seeing who had obtained what from whom was interesting. All these potential clients, she thought happily. With events like this going on everywhere, no wonder women were prepared to pay the earth for something different or outstanding.

From time to time she saw a dark-haired girl looking across at them, and realised that the object of her attention was Richard not herself. She smiled. Perhaps her arrival had put someone's nose out of joint.

There was much talk and hilarity during the buffet supper, where wine flowed and the food was excellent. There were toasts to Timothy on his birthday before they left the dining room and made their way to the drawing room, where a small orchestra now played dance music, and the carpets had been rolled back.

In Richard's arms, on the dance floor, Elizabeth felt as light as a feather. Who would have thought that he would be such a good dancer? Once or twice he held her closely and looked down into her eyes, but she gave herself up to the music and the joy of dancing. Goodness, she had had little enough of this in her life! She must make the most of it.

Afterwards, people sat around in little groups, in corners, on banquettes by the lovely windows, and Elizabeth watched Sarah dancing with Josh, who was looking down at her as though she was the most precious person in the world.

The dancing and small talk went on.

Presently, Richard's mother came and sat beside Elizabeth.

'How are you, my dear? Are you enjoying yourself?'

'Very much, I've had a wonderful time.'

'I am so glad,' Lady Barrington said. 'I hope you will come again.' And she got up and moved on.

Later, when they had danced and strolled out on to the terrace, Richard kissed her gently. I shouldn't have come, she thought. Louis, oh, Louis! It was all a misunderstanding.

They drove back on Sunday after lunch.

Elizabeth sat thoughtfully beside Richard. He was looking pleased, as though from his point of view it had all been a great success.

'Mother liked you,' he said.

'I'm glad. I liked her, too. It was a wonderful weekend.'

'I'm happy you enjoyed it,' he said.

Still driving, he put an arm around her, holding her close, and presently kissed her.

'Elizabeth, you will think about what I said, won't you? Promise?'

'Promise,' she said.

He saw her safely out of the car, then kissed her again at the top of the steps. 'Goodnight, Elizabeth.'

'Goodnight, Richard.'

Isabel was waiting for her, anxious to hear everything that had gone on.

'Well—' Elizabeth began, peeling off her gloves. Oh, it was so nice to be home!

'It was lovely.' She sighed. 'I feel I have been away for ages.'

She turned bright eyes to Isabel.

'Were there any messages?'

Isabel looked down at her sewing.

'No. No messages, darling.'

That night, Elizabeth went over the events of the weekend in her mind. She would be a fool not to see how much Richard liked her and what he was leading up to. She had enjoyed it enormously—it had been wonderful—yet much as she liked him, she knew she could never marry him. Looking back over her past, she realised just how far she had come. Her own salon, a country house weekend as a guest. It had been wonderful, and yet...

She tried to imagine Lady Barrington's life as a young woman, mistress of that enormous house, with servants to wait on her hand and foot, nursemaids for the children. Elizabeth had seen it all from the other side, and it didn't appeal. Some of it, of course. But there would be afternoon bridge, and charity dos, riding to hounds and point to points, tennis perhaps, even golf which so many women were taking up these days—she would be like all the women who came into her salon. Like Sarah Devenoke, not enough to do...

Couldn't Richard see that she just wasn't right for him?

CHAPTER 25

'I don't like the sound of this at all,' Isabel said at breakfast on a bleak cold day in February, and Elizabeth knew she must be referring to the situation in Europe. It was the one subject that Isabel could be relied on to discuss. She read the newspapers avidly, and absorbed every bit of news of the continuing antics of Hitler.

'Now, if you please, the Austrian Chancellor has visited him at Berchtesgarten —that's Hitler's secret abode—and the route was lined with Germany's 120,000-strong Austrian Legion. At the end of it, the Chancellor had to agree to take Austrian Nazis into his cabinet! Can you believe it?'

Isabel threw down the paper in disgust, her usually placid expression giving way to one of anger.

'No one seems to have the power to stop him, but mark my words there's going to be trouble. Don't they understand what's going on behind Hitler's machinations?'

Elizabeth, whose interest in the goings on in Europe were minimal, listened sympathetically. She supposed it was because Isabel had been through one world war that she was horrified that there might or could be another.

'Anyway,' Isabel said, cooling down, 'it has made up my mind for me. I am going to work for the Peace Movement.'

'Who are they?' Elizabeth asked. She was sceptical of some of these organisations which sometimes hid other less worthy causes.

'Don't worry, it's a national organisation for the preservation of peace,' Isabel said. 'Their premises are in the Brompton Road, and I shall go along there this morning to find out more about it.'

'Good idea,' Elizabeth said. She was all in favour of Isabel finding something to keep her occupied. 'Do wrap up well. It's awfully cold this morning.'

There was a heavy frost outside, and the pavements glittered like silver.

'Oh, don't worry about me,' Isabel said. 'I never feel the cold.'

Elizabeth walked briskly to the salon. There was always a feeling of expectancy when the week started. A new client, new orders—you never knew who might come in. As it was, she was due to go to

Mortimer Street to the wholesalers there to look at two gowns she had ordered from Paris. It would depend how busy she was. She might leave it until the afternoon.

When she arrived at the salon, the sun was shining and the pavements damp beneath her feet. Lily was already there. One thing about Lily, she was always early. A huge bowl of daffodils filled the front window, and Elizabeth eyed it with pleasure. Spring must be around the corner...

'Good morning, Elizabeth.'

'Good morning, Lily. The flowers look lovely—like a ray of spring sunshine.'

'That's what I thought, in that blue bowl.'

'Well done. Well, what have we on this morning?'

She hung up her coat and hat in the small cubicle and rubbed her cold hands together.

Lily referred to the appointments book. 'Mrs Jamieson at ten, the Lenham girls at eleven.' And she made a face.

The two pretty Lenham girls were the bane of the salon. They giggled and joked their way through every fitting, much to Lily's disgust.

'At eleven-thirty Lady Devenoke is coming in. Is it true that she is back with him? I heard a rumour.'

'Yes, Lily,' Elizabeth said, and Lily knew by her tone that there would be no more said on that subject.

'Well, perhaps I'll leave Mortimer Street until this afternoon.'

'It might be better,' Lily said. 'How's Miss Lister?'

'Oh, she's very well,' Elizabeth said, wondering if Isabel would do as she said, and go along to the organisation for peace.

Isabel had in fact done just that, and having called in at the address in Brompton Road, which turned out to be above a jeweller's shop, had ascertained from the two women there just what it was all about. It seemed authentic enough. They were women like herself, of about the same age or perhaps older, who believed passionately that peace must be maintained at all costs. They explained about their special speakers on public platforms, mentioning several famous people, and that distributing leaflets was one of their main functions—there were money raising activities in order to fund the association. All in all, it sounded the sort of thing that she would like to be a part of.

Armed with her leaflets and explanatory literature, and well pleased with her morning, Isabel decided to have lunch in Fortnums, and do a little shopping in Woollands.

It was most enjoyable. She should get out more, meet people—she had lived such a dull life. It had only really perked up when her father died and Elizabeth came on to the scene. Perhaps she spent too much time worrying about Elizabeth? And a frown crossed her face as she recalled the telephone call from Louis Vereker. She blushed. She had experienced quite a few pangs of guilt when she remembered that telephone call, which only went away when she assured herself that it was all for the best. Really, she must forget about it. What was done, was done.

Coming out of Woollands, she decided that it was far too nice now to take a cab, she would walk through the park. After her lunch, it would do her good. It was a lovely day, cold but bright, and across the road she could see the trees, still bare, but somehow there was a promise of spring in the air.

She didn't see the bus bearing down on her. After the cars and taxis, she had thought the road clear. It was all over in a second, the driver in his cab horrified as the small woman walked straight out in front of him—there was nothing he could do. People gathered round the lady in her fur coat, lying in a heap in front of the bus. She was still, inert—her face grey, legs twisted under her like a rag doll, blood seeping from her head...

When the ambulance came and cleared the small crowd, she was carried gently inside while a policeman took notes.

'I never saw 'er,' the driver said, visibly shaken. 'One minute I was driving along—the next minute she was there, right under me.'

Several onlookers verified his statement.

It was clear that she was dead, that she must have died instantly. Inside her handbag were letters and cheque books and a diary.

It was Mrs Baines who gave the news to Elizabeth, who at first could hardly believe it.

'Isabel? Dead? What do you mean?'

There seemed to be no doubt about it. Hurriedly giving orders to the staff and for Lily to telephone Tatiana she made her way by taxi to St Mary's Hospital, Paddington, and was taken to where Isabel lay, on a narrow bed under a white sheet. In deep shock Elizabeth identified her, and felt sick, without strength to stand, until a kindly nurse led her away to an ante-room and gave her a cup of tea.

Much later, with questions answered and evidence read to her from witnesses, she faced the fact that Isabel was dead. That she would never see her again—that was the worst part of all. It didn't seem possible. She prayed that she would wake up later and find it all a dream.

It was Mrs Baines who comforted her when she arrived home, and unknown to Elizabeth, telephoned Sarah who came round in the evening to see her.

She was almost as upset as Elizabeth, but her just being there helped.

'You're going to have an awful lot to do,' she said, 'and Josh and I will help you all we can.'

Elizabeth, still stunned, could only nod. 'Thank you, Sarah.'

'Look, you're coming in to us for a meal.'

Elizabeth shook her head. 'I'm not hungry.'

'You have to eat,' Sarah said, sensible for once in her life. 'Come on.'

Elizabeth was reminded of the time when her mother died, when dear Mrs Ransome had taken over and done everything. Somehow this was different. Her mother's death had been inevitable, she had always been ill—but Isabel, in the prime of life, an accident. How could it have happened?

'Look,' Sarah said, 'don't dwell on it. You'll never know why. Just accept it.'

It turned out to be sensible advice. Elizabeth got down to the task of attending the inquest and organising the funeral, after which came the reading of Isabel's will.

It was as she had expected. After a small legacy to Mrs Baines, Isabel had left the whole of her estate to Elizabeth.

Going upstairs to her room afterwards, she lay on her bed and for the first time wept, giving way to her grief.

Back in the salon, Tatiana, exquisitely dressed in black from top to toe which only enhanced her fair beauty, eased off her long fine gloves, her blue eyes sad for once.

'You know, Lily, it's hard on that girl. Isabel took her away from her natural environment in a way, and I have to say, if it weren't for Sarah Devenoke she would be almost without friends—except business ones. She thought the world of Isabel.'

'Yes, it's sad,' Lily agreed.

'What about that fella she's been seeing—Captain something or other? She went to his place for the weekend, didn't she?'

'Yes, he's a friend of Lady Devenoke's, but you can't tell me he means that much to her. No, it was Mr Louis she was keen on.'

'Louis Vereker? Really?' Now Lily had captured Tatiana's attention. 'I didn't know it was serious?'

'Oh, it was,' Lily said. 'We all knew at Vereker's... I think she was in love with him and he certainly was mad about her.'

'Well? What happened?' Tatiana demanded.

Lily looked embarrassed for once. 'Well, it was my coming here. I think he blamed her.'

Tatiana sat down. 'I'm beginning to see daylight.'

'Well, it seemed to me to be after that—he was in a rotten temper until I left. I don't know, I just put two and two together.'

'He had no right to take it out on Elizabeth,' Tatiana said, annoyed.

'Well, you know what men are like. I wouldn't put it past him.'

He's a chip off the old block, she wanted to say, but refrained from doing so.

'You do surprise me. I had no idea she was so keen on him.'

'Don't quote me but I think I'm right. Oh, good afternoon, Lady Delamere.'

Smiles were the order of the day again.

'Now,' Sarah said that evening, 'you are going to have to go through all Isabel's things. Would you like some help? There will be so much to sort out, I imagine it will be quite a harrowing business.'

'Thanks, Sarah, but I'll get round to it.'

'You will ask me, won't you? Josh tried to get in touch with Richard. He'll want to know, Elizabeth.'

'Yes, I understand that. But really, Sarah, it doesn't matter.'

'Perhaps this isn't the best time, but I have to know—did he ask you to marry him?'

'Yes, as a matter of fact he did.' And Sarah's blue eyes lit up.

'Oh, that's wonderful! You didn't tell me.'

'Because I didn't say yes,' Elizabeth said. 'Sarah, he's not for me. He's awfully nice, I like him, but in any case I have no intention of getting married yet awhile. For one thing I'm too busy, and for another—'

'Yes?'

'I don't love him.'

Which was all Sarah could get out of her.

That weekend, Elizabeth made up her mind to tackle the task of going through Isabel's possessions.

'Would you like me to give you a hand, Miss?' Mrs Baines offered.

'No—perhaps next week after I have made a start. I'd just like to feel my way this weekend. You go home. I'm sure your sister will be glad to see you, and don't worry about me—I can manage.'

Mrs Baines sighed, sorry for the girl who had such a sad task to do. It was a big house, as she well knew.

'You will leave the keys in the doors, won't you, Mrs Baines?' Some of the rooms upstairs she had never been inside.

Elizabeth began by going to the top of the house where there were three rooms, one large and two small. The two small ones contained a single bed and everything was covered with dustsheets. One of the rooms had originally been Mrs Baines', but after Isabel's father had died, Isabel had turned what was the breakfast room into a bedroom for her so that she wouldn't have the stairs to climb.

The large room was full of storage boxes, large suitcases, tin trunks, crates of china—Elizabeth had been up here before, the day she discovered the picture of Edmund Lister and Isabel that had started off the whole revelation... She closed the door. Another day, she thought. It can wait.

Downstairs on the next floor was the large front room which had presumably belonged to Isabel's parents. It still looked as it must have done when they were alive. A huge double bed, matching wardrobe and dressing table, linen chest, heavy curtains. She must ask Mrs Baines about this.

Along the hall were her own room and Isabel's, and what must presumably have been Edmund Lister's room. She turned the key in the lock and went inside. Her father's room, she thought wonderingly. In a huge corner cupboard were suits of men's clothes covered with wrappers, smelling strongly of camphor, hats on the shelf, boots stacked neatly, books on another shelf, and several boxes and a small tin trunk. Kept just as it was, she thought, all that time ago.

She left all the doors open and went on downstairs to the drawing room and dining room, where in the corner was the fitment that held the dumb waiter that carried the meals up from the kitchen.

She wandered downstairs to Mrs Baines' domain—they had long ago dispensed with Gertrude, the daily maid. She made herself a pot of tea, which she sat drinking at the scrubbed table. Afterwards, feeling somewhat fortified, she made her way up the stairs. It was her father's room which fascinated her.

Elizabeth dragged the tin trunk out on to the carpet, curiosity getting the better of her. There might be something there about her mother. Had anyone ever looked inside it?

It smelled musty as she prised open the iron fastener and inside were packets of letters and old shoe boxes filled with photographs, yellowing with age.

She sat back on her heels and drew out a packet of letters which felt crackly and crisp with age. Then there were photographs in large envelopes, sepia snapshots of Isabel and her brother when they were small. They seemed to have been the best of friends right up until they were adults, frequently photographed with their arms around each other, both fair and good-looking. She put them in a pile and took another batch of photographs.

These were taken later and showed Edmund with a friend, a fair-haired youth, also very good-looking, taken according to the writing on the back at Oxford before the war. The two seemed inseparable for they were together in every photograph: by a lake, swimming together; in plus fours playing golf dated Hythe 1914; and on the back of each photograph was written 'Edmund and Giles'. There were others of them cycling together, in a study in Oxford surrounded by books, lazing by the Thames.

Elizabeth laid them down carefully and opened a packet of letters—addressed to Edmund Lister in familiar writing... Her heart seemed to stop beating. Letters from her mother to Edmund!

She opened one carefully.

Dear Edmund

I do miss you and our little chats—you have been so kind to me, and now that you have gone away I miss you very much and the house is very quiet, but at least I have George but he will have to go in the army soon and it will break my heart. Look after yourself.

Mary Daly

With fast-beating heart, she opened the next one and looked at the signature: Mary Bartholomew. It was from her mother to Edmund and dated December 1914.

Dear Edmund

Thank you for the lovely Christmas present. The locket is beautiful, but you shouldn't have done it. I shall wear it for best and remember you always.

Your friend, Mary Bartholomew

Elizabeth picked up the next one dated February 1915.

Dear Edmund

Thank you for your letter. I wish you and Giles could have been together, real friends are hard to find. You mustn't blame your mama, she did it for the best, and I couldn't have gone on working with a baby anyway and George is very good to me. Take care of yourself.

Your friend, Mary Bartholomew

The postmark on the next one was March 1915.

Dear Edmund

I hope you are well. We have a nice flat in Brighton with a kind landlady, so I am being well looked after. I worry about you now you have no one to talk to. Couldn't you have gone to the same place as your friend? I don't see why you have to fight if you don't want to. Wars are wicked. Look after yourself.

The next one was dated 30 April 1915

Dear Edmund

I am writing to let you know I have a baby daughter, and she is beautiful, the image of George with his dark hair and long lashes. I wish you could see her, and I know George will be over the moon. Must close now and hope that the war will be over soon so that you can all come home.

Elizabeth picked up one of the photographs of the two young men.

So that was it. She felt stunned and sat staring into space. She wasn't a Lister at all—she was George Bartholomew's daughter. She had no right to any of this.

Oh, poor Isabel, for she would have had no idea—twenty years ago such things as acceptance of a man or boy loving his own sex was unheard of. In fact, it wasn't until she began working at Tatiana's that Lily had enlightened Elizabeth—and she had been shocked at first. It surely wasn't possible? Then several things fell into place. But Isabel wouldn't have known, she would have had no idea, it wouldn't have occurred to her... She simply wanted to believe with all her heart that Edmund had a daughter, and romanced herself into believing that Mary Daly and Edmund were lovers.

Her own mother must have seen Edmund and his friend as young men who liked each other, who were friends, but not surely in any other way? Her face flushed as she thought of the explanations Lily had given her. Truth to tell, she hadn't believed it at first, but it did explain lots of things. If you didn't know, you wouldn't have seen it, but once you knew—oh, how awful! There must be some way of proving this, but could she? In her own mind she was sure. It explained everything—and she might never have known if Isabel had not died when she did.

She clamped her hand to her mouth

involuntarily. Edmund's father, Gordon Lister—had he known? Suspected?

She went into the vast bedroom and opened the corner cupboard where there was a large black box on the floor. It was locked, and going to the linen chest and searching, she found a bunch of small keys. It took some time to find the right one, but at last she did. Opening it, she found it full of papers—most of them concerning Edmund. His school reports from Eton, his letters, and at the bottom a stiff brown official-looking envelope, with a red seal and War office stamp. It had never been opened.

Frowning, she slit it, withdrawing a package of documents and a letter from the War Office to the effect that the enclosed items belonged to Lieut Edmund Lister—his last effects, which they were returning.

Apart from the obvious official papers, there was a bundle of letters, all addressed to Edmund, and as she opened them one after another, all written by Giles in beautiful handwriting, her face flooded with colour. Hating herself for daring to read them, she stuffed them back in the envelope, near to tears. These things were private. There were several more photographs, all of Giles, who had one of the most beautiful faces she had

431

ever seen. Weeping, she picked them all up and gathered them together. No one had any right to see these, least of all herself...and Edmund's father had never even opened the envelope.

How he must have felt. His son, his only son...

Elizabeth carried them downstairs to the kitchen boiler and stuffed them in, watching them burn. The letters from her mother, all Edmund's private correspondence—she was not going to have anyone finding them in the future. She owed him that at least. And Isabel, who in her own dear way could never have understood but had only hoped, indeed prayed, that Elizabeth was Edmund's daughter.

So she was a Bartholomew...she was entitled to none of this. She wasn't a Lister after all.

Much, much later, she dragged herself up the stairs to bed, and slept, exhausted.

She woke in the morning, and somehow it was as if a weight had been lifted off her mind. She was a Bartholomew and proud of it. Last night she had thought she would not accept Isabel's inheritance, but now she knew that she would. It would be madness not to, for it was Isabel's wish that she should have the estate and enjoy it. That she would do.

From now on, she would take her time sorting things out—there was no hurry. The house was hers until the lease ran out. And who knew what would have happened by then?

One thing she knew she had to do. That was to make a telephone call to Brighton.

On Monday she found Tatiana already ensconced in the salon.

'Oh, that's better, my dear, you look more rested.'

'Yes, I feel it,' Elizabeth said. 'I didn't expect you in today, Tatiana.'

'Well, I thought I'd just better see if you were in. Now that you are, I'll be on my way. I'll see you on Friday.'

'Yes, I'll see you then. As a matter of fact, I'm going away for the weekend to Brighton—'

'Oh, Elizabeth, I'm so glad, the sea air will do you a power of good.'

'Yes, that's what I thought—a change of air. I shall stay at The Ship. I've always wanted to stay there, ever since I was small.'

'Good for you,' Tatiana said. 'Have you told Lily?'

'Not yet. I'm just going to.'

Lily looked at her, at those green Irish eyes that seemed to have been washed by rain. Golly, but she was a pretty thing. She'd been through a lot, losing her mother, then the loss of Miss Lister—and of Mr Louis. She deserved a break, she worked hard enough.

'Now don't hurry back,' Lily said. 'We can manage.'

'I'll make up for it when I get back.'

Right now, she felt exhausted. But she was lucky with Mrs Baines to hold the fort at home, and Lily and Tatiana at the salon. Elizabeth couldn't wait to breathe that wonderful Brighton air again.

CHAPTER 26

'Well, I'll be off now,' Tatiana said, pulling on her gloves. 'Unless you need me?'

'No, we can manage,' Lily assured her.

'Anything I can do before Friday?'

'No. I have to collect some georgette from Vereker's, but I'll do it on Thursday morning on my way to work.'

'Well, if you're sure?'

'Yes, there's only one appointment.'

'Right then. See you Friday, Lily.'

On Thursday morning, Lily got off the bus from Fulham and made her way to Bond Street and Vereker's. She had something to do, and hoped she would find Mr Louis in. Certainly he was back from the States, she had heard it on the grapevine.

The new assistant was there, and gave her a broad smile.

'Hallo, Lily. You're early.'

'How is everything going?'

'Very well,' he said. 'Come to collect your order?'

'Please,' she said. 'Is Mr Louis in?'

'Yes, in the back there.'

'May I go through?'

'Er—yes, I suppose so.'

She walked or rather marched over the old familiar ground and tapped on the door. Louis looked up, smiling. It changed to a scowl as he saw who it was.

'There's no need to look like that,' said Lily. 'I don't work here now. And I've a bone to pick with you!'

He sat still, looking at her. Handsome devil, she thought.

'What is it?'

'You've treated poor Elizabeth shamefully,' she said, and saw the flush gradually stain his cheeks. 'Yes, I mean it, poor little thing...'

'I can't discuss it,' he said very much on his dignity.

'Well, I'm going to,' she insisted. 'I want to clear up the whole rotten mess. I asked Elizabeth for a job at Tatiana's. In fact, I

435

begged her to take me on.'

'Really?' he said. 'Was it so bad here?'

'It wasn't that,' she said. 'I had made up my mind to leave. It was as simple as that. I talked her into it, poor girl, she had no choice, and then you come along and blame her—'

'Did she tell you that?' he asked dangerously.

'Of course not. But I could see how she was after you'd finished with her. You're a bully, just like your father.'

'Miss Cheshire!'

'Don't you Miss Cheshire me!' she said. 'Well, I've said what I had to say and now I'll go, but I still think you behaved abominably,' she nearly tripped over the last word, 'and you should apologise. As if she hasn't had enough to put up with, losing her only relative and all.'

'What's that?' he said. 'Miss Lister?'

'Didn't you know? She was killed, fell under a bus. Imagine what Elizabeth has had to do—and without anyone to help her.' She turned to go, and out of the corner of her eye saw his expression change.

'Is she at the salon?'

'Yes, but she's going off this evening to Brighton for the weekend.'

'Hmm,' he said, 'probably with her boyfriend?'

'What boyfriend? You must be joking. What time does she have for a boyfriend?'

He coughed. 'Er—where is she staying there, do you know? I'll drop her a line.'

Lily smiled to herself. He'll do more than that, she thought.

'The Ship, I think,' she said. 'Well, I'll be on my way.'

'Good morning, Miss Cheshire.'

Pompous young devil, she thought, going on her way, but Elizabeth could handle him. She was sure of it.

Louis was well away from the London traffic on Friday and on his way to the coast, going over in his mind all the things he would say to her. If she was with someone—well, then he would know once and for all. But he had to find out. It was a cold day. He would make straight for the hotel. No point in hanging about.

He drove straight to The Ship, parked and made enquiries at the desk. After a short conversation with the desk clerk, he drove just out of Brighton along the shore towards Rottingdean. Outside a pretty church he stopped the car and walked up through the lych gate to the small churchyard. His heart leapt as he saw the slim figure in black standing by a new headstone.

He went up behind her and stood quietly

until she turned, and all the colour drained away from her face.

She had never looked more beautiful.

'Louis!'

'Elizabeth.' And he folded her in his arms. 'Oh, Elizabeth...'

Tear-drenched green eyes looked up at him. 'Oh, I don't believe it! How did you know I was here?'

'They told me at the hotel.'

'But how did you know...'

'Shh.' He sealed her lips with a kiss.

It seemed a long time afterwards that she broke away and looked down at the new headstone.

'They've just finished it,' she said. 'Don't you think it's beautiful?'

The stone was of white marble. The inscription read:

In loving memory of
Mary Grace Bartholomew
who died on the 29 April 1930
Also of her husband
George Alfred Bartholomew
Killed in action in France 1915

'My father,' she said proudly. 'Oh, Louis, I have so much to tell you.'

He gripped her hand firmly as they slowly walked away.

Other MAGNA General Fiction Titles In Large Print

FRANCES ANNE BOND
Return Of The Swallow

JUDY GARDINER
All On A Summer's Day

IRIS GOWER
The Sins Of Eden

HELENE MANSFIELD
Some Women Dream

ELISABETH McNEILL
The Shanghai Emerald

ELIZABETH MURPHY
To Give And To Take

JUDITH SAXTON
This Royal Breed

Other MAGNA General Fiction Titles In Large Print

Other MAGNA General Fiction Titles In Large Print

DENISE ROBERTSON
The Stars Burn On

ANGELA THIRKELL
Pomfret Towers

PATRICIA CAVENDISH
Always And Forever

MARY JANE STAPLES
Rising Summer

IRIS GOWER
The Shoemaker's Daughter

NICHOLAS RHEA
Constable By The Stream

JANET EDMONDS
Rivers Of Gold